LAURELL K. HAMILTON

"Faeries, fornication and forensics fuse for yet another darkly fantastic frolic for Hamilton fans."

—*Publishers Weekly* on *A Stroke of Midnight*

"[Hamilton is] writing to entertain. . . . and entertain she does. Sex, violence, mystery, pain, pleasure—Hamilton blends all the elements of several genres together, from romance and high fantasy to detective story."

—*St. Louis Post-Dispatch* on
Seduced by Moonlight

"Hamilton weaves the modern and magical seamlessly in [this] compelling tale."

—*Booklist* on *A Caress of Twilight*

By Laurell K. Hamilton
Published by The Random House Publishing Group

A KISS OF SHADOWS
A CARESS OF TWILIGHT
SEDUCED BY MOONLIGHT

A STROKE OF MIDNIGHT

a novel

LAURELL K. HAMILTON

BALLANTINE BOOKS • NEW YORK

2006 Ballantine Books International Edition

Published in the United States by Ballantine Books, an imprint of The Random House Publishing Group, a division of Random House, Inc., New York.

BALLANTINE and colophon are registered trademarks of Random House, Inc.

Originally published in hardcover in the United States by Ballantine Books, an imprint of The Random House Publishing Group, a division of Random House, Inc., in 2005.

ISBN 0-345-49249-8

Cover design: David Stevenson
Cover illustration: Judy York

Printed in the United States of America

www.ballantinebooks.com

OPM 9 8 7 6 5 4 3 2 1

To J.,
who holds my hand and my heart;
who helps me play in the darkness
but not to live there

ACKNOWLEDGMENTS

To all my friends, both writers and nonwriters, who love me still, even though most phone conversations have begun lately with “Hello, Stranger.” Hope to see more of everyone this next bit.

A STROKE
OF MIDNIGHT

Chapter 1

I HATE PRESS CONFERENCES. BUT I ESPECIALLY HATE THEM when I've been ordered to hide large portions of the truth. The order had come from the Queen of Air and Darkness, ruler of the dark court of faerie. The Unseelie are not a power to be crossed, even if I was their very own faerie princess. I was Queen Andais's niece, but the family connection had never bought me much. I smiled at the nearly solid wall of reporters, fighting to keep my thoughts from showing on my face.

The queen had never allowed this much of the human media inside the Unseelie's hollow hill, our sithen. It was our refuge, and you don't let the press into your refuge. But yesterday's assassination attempt had made allowing the press into our home the lesser evil. The theory was that inside the sithen our magic would protect me much better than it had in the airport yesterday, where I'd nearly been shot.

Our court publicist, Madeline Phelps, pointed to the first reporter, and the questions began.

"Princess Meredith, you had blood on your face yesterday, but today the only sign of injury is your arm in a sling. What were your injuries yesterday?"

My left arm was in a green cloth sling that matched my suit jacket near perfectly. I was dressed in Christmas, Yule, red and green. Cheerful, and it was that time of year. My hair was a deeper red than my blouse. My hair is the most Unseelie part of me, sidhe scarlet hair for someone who looks good in black. Not the gold or orangey red of human hair. The jacket brought out the green in two out of the three circles of color in my iris. The gold circle would flash in the camera light sometimes as if it truly was metallic. The eyes were pure Seelie sidhe, the only part of me that showed that my mother had been of the golden court. Well, at least half.

I didn't recognize the reporter who had asked the question. He was a new face to me, maybe new since yesterday. Since yesterday's assassination attempt had happened in front of the media, on camera, well, we'd had to turn away some of the reporters, because the big room wouldn't hold more. I'd been doing press conferences since I was a child. This was the biggest one I'd had, including the one after my father was assassinated. I'd been taught to use names for reporters when I knew them, but to this one I could only smile and say, "My arm is only sprained. I was very lucky yesterday."

Actually, my arm hadn't been injured in the assassination attempt that got on film. No, my arm had been hurt on the second, or was that the third, attempt on my life yesterday. But those attempts had happened inside the sithen, where I was supposed to be safe. The only reason the queen and my bodyguards thought I was safer here than outside in the human world was that we had arrested or killed the traitors behind the attempts on me, and the attempt on the queen. We'd damned near had a palace coup yesterday, and the media didn't have a hint of it. One of the old names for the fey is the hidden people. We've earned the name.

"Princess Meredith, was it your blood on your face, yesterday?" A woman this time, and I did know her name.

"No," I said.

I smiled for real, as I watched her face fall when she realized she might be getting just a one-word answer. "No, Sheila, it wasn't mine."

She smiled at me, all blond and taller than I would ever be. "May I add to my question, Princess?"

"Now, now," Madeline said, "one question per."

"It's okay, Madeline," I said.

Our publicist turned to look at me, flipping off the switch at her waist so her microphone would not pick up. I took the cue and covered mine with my hand and moved to one side of it.

Madeline leaned in over the table. Her skirt was long enough that she was in no danger of flashing the reporters down below the dais. Her hem length was the absolute latest of the moment, as was the color. Part of her job was paying attention to what was in and what was out. She was our human representative, much more than any ambassador that Washington had ever sent.

"If Sheila gets to add to her question, then they will all do it. That will make everything harder, for you and for me."

She was right, but... "Tell them that this is an exception. Then move on."

She raised perfectly plucked eyebrows at me, then said, "Okay." She hit the switch on her mike as she turned and smiled at them. "The princess will let Sheila ask another question, but after that you'll have to keep it to the original rule. One question per." She pointed to Sheila and gave a nod.

"Thank you for letting me add on to my question, Princess Meredith."

"You're welcome."

"If it wasn't your blood yesterday, then whose was it?"

"My guard Frost's."

The cameras flashed to life so that I was blinded, but the attention of everyone had moved behind me. My guards were lined up along the wall, spilling down the edges of the dais, to curl on either side of the table and floor. They were dressed in everything from designer suits to full-plate body armor to Goth club wear. The only thing that all the outfits had in common was weaponry. Yesterday we'd tried to be discreet about the weapons. A bulge that ruined the line of the jacket, but nothing overt. Today there were guns under jackets or cloaks, but there were also guns in plain sight, and swords, and knives, and axes, and shields. We'd also more than doubled the number of guards around me.

I glanced back at Frost. The queen had ordered me not to play favorites among the guard. She'd gone so far as to tell me not to give any long lingering glances to one guard over another. I'd thought it was an odd demand, but she was queen, and you argued with her at your peril. But I glanced back; after all, he'd saved my life. Didn't that earn him a glance? I could always justify it to the queen, my aunt, that the press would think it strange if I hadn't acknowledged him. It was the truth, but I looked because I wanted to look.

His hair was the silver of Christmas-tree tinsel, shiny and metallic. It fell to his ankles like decoration, but I knew that it was soft and alive, and felt oh so warm across my body. He'd put the upper layer of his hair back from his face with a barrette carved from bone. The hair glittered and moved around his charcoal-grey Armani suit that had been tailored over his broad shoulders and the athletic cut of the rest of him. The suit had also been tailored to hide a gun in a shoulder holster and a knife or two. It had not been designed to hide a gun under each arm, or a short sword at his hip, with a leather scabbard strapped tight to his thigh. The hilt of a second sword rode over his shoulder, peeking through all that shining hair. He bristled with knives, and Frost always had other weapons that you couldn't see. No suit was designed to cover that much armament and hold its shape. His jacket couldn't be buttoned at all, and the guns and sword and one knife glinted in the camera's flash.

Cries of "Frost, Frost" filled the room, while Madeline picked a question. The man was another one I didn't know. Nothing like an assassination attempt to attract the media.

"Frost, how badly were you hurt?"

Frost is a little over six feet, and since I was sitting down, and the microphone was adjusted to my height, he had to lean down, way down. With a weapon of any kind he was graceful. But bending low over that mike he was awkward. I had a moment to wonder if he'd ever been on mike before, then his deep voice was answering the question.

"I am not hurt." He stood back up, and I could see the relief on his face. He turned away from the cameras, as if he thought he'd get off that easily. I knew better.

"But wasn't it your blood on the princess?"

His hand was gripping the pommel of his short sword. Touching his weapons unnecessarily was a sign of nerves. He leaned over the mike again, and this time he bumped my bad shoulder with his body. I doubted the press saw such a small movement, but it was too clumsy for words, for Frost. He braced a hand flat against the table, steadying himself. He turned eyes the grey of a winter sky to me. The look asked silently, "Did I hurt you?"

I mouthed, no.

He let out a sigh and leaned back to the microphone. "Yes, it was my blood." He actually stood back up, as if that would satisfy them. He should have known better. He had been decorative muscle for the queen at enough of these over the years to know that he was being a little too concise. At least he didn't try to go back to his spot behind me this time.

A reporter I did know, Simon McCracken, was next. He'd covered the faerie courts for years. "Frost, if you are not hurt, then where did your blood come from and how did it get on the princess?" He knew how to word the question just right, so we couldn't tap-dance around it. The sidhe don't lie. We'll paint the truth red, purple, and green, and convince you that black is white, but we won't actually lie.

Frost leaned over the mike again, his hand pressed to the table. He'd moved minutely closer to me, close enough that his pants leg touched my skirt. His sword was almost trapped between our bodies. That would be bad if he had to draw the weapon. I looked at his hand, so big and strong on the table, and realized his fingertips were mottled. He was gripping the table the way you grip a podium when you're nervous.

"I was shot." He had to clear his throat sharply to continue. I turned my head just enough to see that perfect profile, and realized it was more than nerves. Frost, the queen's Killing Frost, was afraid. Afraid of public speaking. Oh, my. "I have healed. My blood covered the princess when I shielded her from harm."

He started to stand back up, but I touched his arm. I covered the mike with my hand, and leaned in against him, so I could whisper against the curve of his ear. I took in a deep breath of the scent of his skin, and said, "Kneel or sit."

His breath went out so deep that his shoulders moved with

it. But he knelt on one knee beside me. I moved the microphone a little closer to him.

I slid my hand under the back of his jacket, so that I could lay my hand against the curve of his back, just below the side sweep of the big sword sheath. When fey are nervous, any fey, we take comfort from touching one another. Even the mighty sidhe feel better with a little contact, though not all of us will admit it for fear of blurring the line between royalty and commoner. I had too much lesser fey blood in my veins to worry about it. I could feel the sweat that was beginning to trickle down his spine.

Madeline started to come closer to us. I shook my head. She gave me a questioning look but didn't argue. She picked another question from the throng.

"So you took a bullet to protect Princess Meredith?"

I leaned into the mike, putting my face very close to Frost's, touching carefully, so I didn't get makeup on him. The cameras exploded in bursts of white light. Frost jumped, and I knew that was going to be visible to the cameras. Oh, well. We were blinded, vision blurred in bursts of white and blue spots. His muscles tightened, but I wouldn't have known it if I hadn't been touching him.

"Hi, Sarah, and yes, he took a bullet for me," I said.

I think Sarah said "Hi, Princess" back, but I couldn't be sure, since I still couldn't see well enough, and the noise of so many voices was too confusing. I'd learned to use names when I knew them. It made everyone feel more friendly. And you need all the friendly you can get at a press conference.

"Frost, were you afraid?"

He relaxed minutely against me, into the touch of my hand and my face. "Yes," he said.

"Afraid to die," someone yelled out without being called on.

Frost answered the question anyway. "No."

Madeline called on someone, who asked, "Then what were you afraid of?"

"I was afraid Meredith would be harmed." He licked his lips, and tensed again. I realized he'd used my name without my title. A faux pas for a bodyguard, but of course, he was more than that. Every guard was technically in the running to be prince to my princess. But we were sidhe, and we don't marry until we're pregnant. A nonfertile couple is not allowed to wed, so the guards were doing more than just "guarding" my body.

"Frost, would you give your life for the princess?"

He answered without hesitation. "Of course." His tone said clearly that that had been a silly question.

A reporter in back who had a television camera next to him asked the next question. "Frost, how did you heal a gunshot wound in less than twenty-four hours?"

Frost gave another deep, shoulder-moving sigh. "I am a warrior of the sidhe." The reporters waited for him to add more, but I knew he wouldn't. To Frost, the fact that he was sidhe was all the answer he needed. It had been only a through and through bullet wound from a handgun and no special ammunition. It would take a great deal more than that to stop a warrior of the sidhe.

I hid my smile and started to lean into the mike, to help explain that to the press, when the sweat along his spine suddenly stopped being wet and warm. It was as if a line of cold air swept down his back. Cold enough that I moved my hand away, startled.

I glanced down at his big hand on the table and saw what I'd feared. A white rime of frost was drifting out from his hand. I thanked Goddess that the cloth on the table was white. Only that was saving us from someone noticing. They might notice later when they went back over the camera footage, but that I could not help. I had enough to worry about without thinking that far ahead. In a way this was my fault. I'd accidentally brought Frost into a level of power that he'd never known. It was a blessing of the Goddess, but with new power comes new responsibilities, and new temptations.

I moved my hand from under his jacket to cover his hand with mine, as I spoke into the reporters' puzzled murmur. I was braced for his hand to be as icy as that slide of power down his back, but surprisingly, his hand wasn't nearly that cold.

"The sidhe heal almost any injury," I said.

The frost was spreading out. The edge of it caught the microphone and began to climb it. The mike crackled with static, and I squeezed Frost's hand. He saw it then, what his fear was doing. I'd known it wasn't on purpose. He balled his hand into a fist, but with my hand on top of his, my fingers entwined with his. I did not want anyone to notice the frost before it melted.

I turned my face toward his, and he faced me. There was a snow falling in his iris, like a tiny grey snow globe set in his eyes. I leaned in and kissed him. It surprised him, because he'd heard the queen's admonition about not showing favoritism, but Andais would forgive me, if she gave me time to explain. She'd have done the same, or more, to distract the press from unwanted magic.

It was a chaste press of lips because Frost was that uncomfortable in front of all these strangers. Plus, I was wearing a red lipstick that would smear like clown makeup if we did a tonsil-cleaning kiss. I saw the explosion of the cameras like an orange press against my closed eyelids.

I drew back from the kiss first. Frost's eyes were still closed, his lips relaxed, almost open. His eyes blinked open. He looked startled, maybe from the lights, or maybe from the kiss. Though Goddess knows I'd kissed him before, and with a great deal more body English. Did a kiss from me still mean that much to him, when we'd kissed so many times I couldn't count them all?

The look in his eyes said yes more clearly than any words.

Photographers were kneeling as close to the front of the table as the other guards would let them get. They were taking pictures of his face and mine. The frost had melted while we kissed, leaving only a light wetness around our hands. It barely darkened the white cloth. We'd hidden the magic, but we'd exposed Frost's face to the world. What do you do when a man lets the whole world see just how much your kiss affects him? Why, kiss him again, of course. Which I did, and this time I didn't worry about clown makeup, or the queen's orders. I simply wanted, always, to see that look on his face when we kissed. Always and forever.

Chapter 2

WE HAD RED LIPSTICK SMEARED OVER BOTH OUR FACES, BUT WE were sidhe, and one of the lesser powers we possessed was glamour. A little concentration, and I simply made my lipstick look perfect, though I could feel it smeared around my mouth. I spilled the small magic across Frost's face, so that he looked as he had before, and not like he'd laid his face into a pot of red paint and rubbed back and forth.

It was illegal to use magic on the press. The Supreme Court had declared that it infringed on the First Amendment, freedom of the press and all that. But we were allowed to use small magic on ourselves for cosmetic purposes. After all, there was no difference between that and regular makeup or plastic surgery for celebrities. The court wisely didn't try to open that particular can of movie-star worms.

I could have worn glamour instead of makeup in the first place, but it took concentration, and I'd wanted all my concentration for the questions. Besides, if there was another assassination attempt, the glamour would go, and the queen was just vain enough that she'd ordered me into makeup, just in case. I guess so that if the worst happened, I'd look good dead. Or maybe I was just being cynical. Maybe she simply didn't trust my abilities at glamour. Maybe.

I told Frost that he'd answered enough questions for one day, and it was a feeding frenzy of "Frost, Frost." There were even a few rude enough to shout out questions like "Is she good in bed... ? How many times a week do you get to fuck her?" Gotta love the tabloids, especially some of the European ones. They make our American tabloids look downright friendly.

We all ignored such rude questions. Frost took his post behind me against the wall. I could feel the small magic around him. If he walked too far from me, the glamour would break, but this close I could hold it. Not forever, but long enough to get us through this mess.

Madeline chose one of the mainstream newspapers, the *Chicago Tribune*, but his question made me wonder if we'd have been better off answering the tabloids. "I have a two-part question... Meredith, if I may?" He was so courteous, I should have known he was leading up to something that wouldn't be pleasant.

Madeline looked at me, and I nodded. He asked, "If the sidhe can heal almost any wound, then why is your arm not healed?"

"I'm not full-blooded sidhe, so I heal slower, more like a human."

"Yes, you're part human and part brownie, as well as sidhe. But isn't it true that some of the noble sidhe of the Unseelie Court are concerned that you are not sidhe enough to rule them? That even if you gain the throne, they will not acknowledge you as queen?"

I smiled into the flash of lights and thought furiously. Someone had talked to him. Someone who should have known better. Some of the sidhe did fear my mortality, my mixed blood, and thought that if I sat on the throne I would destroy them. That my mortal blood would take their immortality. It had been the reason behind at least one, maybe both, of the extra attacks yesterday. We had an entire noble house, and the head of another, imprisoned now, awaiting sentencing. No one had briefed me on what to say if the question arose, because no one had dreamt that any sidhe, or lesser fey, would have dared talk to the press, not even to hint.

I tried for half-truth. "There are some among the nobility that see my human and lesser fey blood as inferior. But there are always racists, Mr...."

"O'Connel," he said.

"Mr. O'Connel," I said.

"Do you believe that it is racism then?"

Madeline tried to stop me, but I answered because I wanted to know how much he knew. "If not racism then what, Mr. O'Connel? They don't want some mongrel half-breed on their throne." Now if he pushed it, he'd look like a racist. Reporters from the *Chicago Tribune* don't want to look like racists.

"That's an ugly accusation," he said.

"Yes," I said, "it is."

Madeline stepped in. "We need to move on. Next question." She pointed to someone else, a little too eagerly, but that was all right. We needed to change topics. Of course, there were other topics that were almost as bad.

"Is it true that a magic spell made the policeman shoot at you, Princess Meredith?" This from a man in the front row who looked vaguely familiar in the way that on-air personalities often do.

The sidhe do not lie. We make a sort of national sport out of almost lying. We can lie. But if we do, then we are foresworn. Once upon a time you were kicked out of faerie for that. The answer to the question was yes, but I didn't want to answer it. So I tried not to. "Let's drop the 'princess,' guys. I've been working as a detective in L.A. for three years. I'm not used to the title anymore."

I wanted to avoid having anyone ask who had done the spell. It had been part of the attempted palace coup. We were so not sharing that a sidhe noble had caused one of the police helping to guard me to try to kill me.

Madeline picked up her cue perfectly, calling on a new reporter with a new question. "This is quite a display of sidhe muscle, Prince—Meredith." The woman smiled when she left off the "princess." I was hoping they would like that. And I didn't need the title to know who I was. "Is the extra muscle because you fear for your safety?"

"Yes," I replied, and Madeline moved us on.

It was a different reporter, but he repeated the dreaded question. "Was it a spell that caused the policeman to shoot at you, Meredith?"

I drew breath, not even sure what I was going to say, when

I felt Doyle move up beside me. He leaned over the microphone like a black statue carved all of one piece—black designer suit, black high-collared dress shirt, shoes, even his tie, of the same unrelieved blackness. "May I take this question, Princess Meredith?" The silver earrings that traced the curve of his ear all the way up to its point flashed in the lights. Contrary to all the faerie wannabes with their cartilage implants, the pointy ears marked him as not pure high court, as something less, something mixed like me. His black hair was ankle-length, and he could have hidden his "deformity," but he almost never did. His hair was pulled back in its usual braid. The diamond stud in his earlobe glittered next to my face.

Most of his weapons were as monochrome as the rest of him, so it was hard to spot the knives and guns, darkness on darkness. He had been the Queen's Darkness, her assassin, for more than a thousand years. Now he was mine.

I fought to keep my face as blank as his, and not let the relief show. "Be my guest," I said.

He leaned down to the microphone in front of me. "The attempt on the princess's life yesterday is still under investigation. My apologies, but some details are not ready to be discussed publicly." His deep voice resonated over the mike. I saw some of the female reporters shiver, and it wasn't fear. I'd never realized he had a good voice for a microphone. I think he, like Frost, had never been on mike before, but unlike Frost, it didn't bother him. Very little did. He was Darkness, and the dark isn't afraid of us; we're afraid of it.

"What can you tell us about the assassination attempt?" another reporter asked.

I wasn't sure if the question was directed at Doyle or me. I couldn't see his eyes through his wraparound black-on-black sunglasses, but I swear I felt him look at me. I leaned into the mike. "Not much, I'm afraid. As Doyle says, it's an ongoing investigation."

"Do you know who was behind it?"

Doyle leaned into the mike again. "I am sorry, ladies and gentlemen, but if you insist on asking questions that we are not free to answer for fear of hindering our internal investigation, then this press conference is over."

On one hand, it was neatly done; on the other hand, he'd said a bad word—internal.

"So it was sidhe magic that bespelled the policeman," a woman yelled.

Shit, I thought.

Doyle had caused it; he tried to clean it up. "By 'internal' I meant that it involves Princess Meredith, the potential heir to Queen Andais's throne. It does not get much more internal than that. Especially not for those of us who belong to the princess." He was deliberately trying to distract them into asking about my sex life with my guard. A much safer subject.

Madeline cooperated by picking one of the tabloid reporters for the next question. If anyone would fall for sex over internal politics, it was the tabloids.

They swallowed the bait. "What do you mean, you belong to the princess?"

Doyle leaned in closer to the mike, close enough that his shoulder brushed against mine. It was very subtle and very deliberate. It would probably have been more eye-catching if Frost and I hadn't played kissy-face first, but Doyle knew how to play to the press. You had to start slow and give yourself someplace to go. He'd only started playing to the media in the last few weeks, but as with everything, he learned quickly and did it very well. "We would give our life for her."

"The Secret Service are sworn to give their life for the president but they don't belong to the president." The reporter emphasized the word *belong.*

Doyle leaned closer to the mike, forcing him to put one arm against the back of my chair, so I was framed in the curve of his body. The cameras exploded so that I was blind again. I allowed myself to lean in against Doyle, partly for the picture, and partly because I liked it.

"Perhaps I misspoke," Doyle said, with all my Christmas brightness framed against his blackness.

"Are you having sex with the princess?" a female reporter asked.

"Yes," he said simply.

They actually almost sighed as a group in eagerness. Another woman said, "Frost, are you sleeping with the princess?"

Doyle stepped back and let Frost come up to the mike again, though I would have preferred keeping him away from it. He was brave and he came and bent over the mike, bent over me. But Frost wouldn't play for the cameras. His face was arrogant, and perfect, and showed nothing, even though his grey eyes were bare to the camera's glare. He always said he thought it was beneath us to play to the media. But I knew now that it wasn't arrogance that made him not play, it was fear. A phobia, if you will, of cameras and reporters and crowds. He leaned over stiffly, and said, "Yes."

This shouldn't have been news to any of them. Publicly I'd returned to faerie to seek a husband. The sidhe don't breed much, so the royals get to marry only if they get pregnant first. The queen and I had explained this at another press conference, when I first visited home. But she'd kept the guards away from the mikes, and there was something about the guards admitting it, on mike, that excited the media. Almost as if it was dirtier because they were saying it.

"Are the two of you having sex with the princess at the same time?"

"No." Frost fought not to frown. We were lucky the reporter hadn't asked if they slept together with me. Because that we did. The fey sleep in big puppy piles. It's not always about sex; sometimes it's about safety and comfort.

Frost stepped back to the wall, stiff and unhappy. The reporters were yelling even more sexual questions at him. Madeline helped us out. "I think our Killing Frost is a little shy at the mike, boys and girls. Let's pick on someone else."

So they did.

They yelled out names and questions to the men. One or two of the guards onstage had never been paraded in front of the media at all. I wasn't certain that Adair or Hawthorne had ever seen a television or a movie. They were in full-plate mail, though Adair's looked like it was formed of gold and copper, and Hawthorne's was a rich crimson, a color no metal had ever been. Adair's was metal; Hawthorne's just looked like metal, though I couldn't say what it was made of. Something magical. They had both chosen to keep their helmets on. Adair, I believe, because the queen had shorn his hair as a punishment for trying to refuse my bed. Hawthorne's hair still fell in thick black-green waves to his ankles. I had no idea why he kept his helmet on. They must have been roasting in front of this many electric lights, but having decided to wear the helmets, they'd wear them until they fainted. Well, Adair would. I didn't know even that much about Hawthorne. They knew what a camera was because the queen was fond of her Polaroid, but beyond that and indoor plumbing, technology was a stranger to them. I wondered how they felt about being thrown to the lions. Their faces would show nothing. They were the Queen's Ravens; they knew how to hide what they felt.

Thankfully, no one yelled their names, probably because no one knew who they were.

Madeline finally picked a question, and a victim for them. "Brad, you had a question for Rhys."

The reporter stood up a little taller, and most of the others sat down like disappointed flowers. "Rhys, how was it being a real detective in Los Angeles?"

Rhys was on the far end near the edge of the dais. He was the shortest of the purebred sidhe, only five and a half feet tall. His white curls fell to his waist, capped with a cream-colored fedora with a slightly darker band. The trench coat he wore over his suit matched the hat. He looked like a cross between an old-time detective with better fashion sense, a male stripper, and a pirate. The stripper came from the pale blue silk T-shirt that clung to his muscular chest and washboard abs. The pirate came from the fact that he wore a patch over one eye. It wasn't affectation, but to save the press from seeing what was left after a goblin had torn out his eye, laid scars down a boyishly handsome face. The remaining eye was three rings of blue. He could have used glamour to hide the scars, but when he realized the scars didn't bother me, he'd stopped bothering. He thought the scars gave him character, and they did.

Rhys had always been a huge film noir fan, and the reporter clearly remembered that. I liked her better for it.

He put one hand flat on the table and the other across my shoulders as he moved into the mike, similar to what Doyle had done. But Rhys knew how to play to the camera better because he'd been doing it longer. He took off the fedora and shook his hair out, so it fell around his shoulders in thick white curls.

"I loved being a detective in L.A."

"Was it like in the movies?" someone asked.

"Sometimes, but not very much. I ended up doing more bodyguard work than actual detective work."

The next question was interesting. "There were rumors that some of the stars you and the other guards protected wanted more body than guarding?"

That was a hard one, because a lot of the clients had asked or indicated a willingness for sex. The men had either ignored the invitation or said no. So technically the answer was yes, but if he said yes, then all the semi-famous, or even famous, for whom Rhys had bodyguarded would be in the tabloids tomorrow, and it would be our fault. Our former boss, Jeremy Grey, deserved better than that from us. So did our clients. And the right kind of clients would stay away from Grey Detective Agency, and the wrong kind would come and be disappointed.

I leaned into the microphone, and said suggestively, "I'm afraid that Rhys was too busy bodyguarding me to bodyguard anyone else."

That got me laughter and distracted them all. We were back to sex questions about us, and those we could answer.

"Is Rhys good in bed?"

"Yes," I said.

"Is the princess good in bed?"

"Very."

See, easy questions.

"Rhys, have you ever shared a bed with the princess and one of the other guards?"

"Yes."

Then the reporters started working together. The first reporter tried to ask who with, but Madeline said he'd had his question. The next reporter she picked asked, "Rhys, who did you share the princess with?"

He could have tap-danced around that one, but he chose truth, because why not?

"Nicca."

The cameras and attention turned to Nicca like lions spotting a newly wounded gazelle. This particular gazelle was six feet tall with deep brown skin and rich chestnut hair that fell to his ankles, thick and straight, held back only by a thin copper diadem. He was naked from the waist up except for the rich gold silk suspenders that graced his chest and caught the faint yellow pattern in the brown of his suit pants. He had two 9mm guns in the front of his pants, because no one could figure out how to get him in a shoulder holster, or how to strap on his armor, or his swords, without damaging his wings.

They towered above his shoulders and a little above his head. They swept out and down to his calves, so that the edges of them almost brushed the floor. They were huge moth wings, as if a half-dozen different kinds of giant silk moths had had sex one dark night with a faerie. Only two days ago the wings had been a birthmark on the back of his body, but during sex the wings had suddenly burst forth from his skin and become real. The back of his body was now one smooth brown piece.

He moved to join us while the cameras made us go blind again. Rhys stayed with me, as Nicca stood beside us, towering over us both. He looked out at the crowd, his face puzzled. He wasn't accustomed to being front and center for the queen, or me.

"Nicca, do you really sleep with the princess and Rhys?"

He bent over toward the mike, so he was on one side of me

and Rhys was on the other. The wings fanned out above my head. "Yes," he said, then stood back up.

The cameras clicked and reporters shouted questions until Madeline picked someone. "How did you get wings?"

Good question. Unfortunately, we didn't have a good answer. "You want the truth?" I asked. "We're not sure."

"Nicca, what were you doing when the wings appeared?"

When Nicca knelt back over, the wings flexed so that for a moment I was backdropped against one of them. I couldn't see anything but flashes. "Having sex with Meredith."

The reporters did everything but giggle like junior high school kids. The American reporters, and some of the European, had never quite gotten used to the fact that the fey, as a whole, don't see sex as bad. So admitting to sex with someone, unless it makes your lover uncomfortable, isn't bad, or scandalous.

"Was Rhys with you?"

"Yes." Technically, Rhys had been beside the bed, not in it, but Nicca didn't see a reason to quibble.

"Was anyone else in the bed with you and the princess when it happened?"

"Yes." That was Nicca, and very sidhe. You either distracted with a story that had nothing to do with what was asked, or you answered exactly what was asked, and absolutely nothing else. Nicca wasn't good at stories, so he stuck to truth.

"Who?" someone yelled.

Nicca glanced at me, and he shouldn't have. The glance was enough to let the reporters know that he wasn't sure I wanted him to tell the name. Shit. Most sidhe women do not like admitting that they've fucked a lesser fey, but I wasn't ashamed. The reporters would make more of that one glance than there was to make. Damn.

The trouble was that Sage wasn't on the stage. He wasn't sidhe, and his own queen had demanded him at her side. Besides, our queen didn't want him onstage with me. In Andais's own words, "Oral sex, fine, but he doesn't get to fuck you. No demi-fey, no matter how tall, is sitting on my throne as anyone's king." So Sage got to stay out of sight. Which made this moment even more interesting.

"The other third, or would that be fourth," I said with a smile, "isn't onstage today. He's not certain he wants the media attention."

"Is he going to be one of your lovers, and potential kings?"

"No." Which was the truth.

"Why not?" someone else shouted out. I wouldn't have answered it, but Nicca did. "He's not sidhe."

Oh, hell. That started another frenzy of shouted questions. I leaned into Nicca and asked him to go back to his piece of wall on the dais. Rhys went back to his section on the edge where he could watch the crowd. He was trying not to laugh. I guess it might as well be funny. But Nicca had to stay away from the mike from now on. I wasn't ashamed of what I'd done with Sage, but I wasn't sure how much of it my aunt wanted me to explain to the media. She did seem embarrassed about it.

Madeline finally found a question that she thought I would be able and willing to answer. She was wrong. "Which of them is the best in bed, Meredith?"

I fought not to glance at Madeline. What was she doing taking that question? She knew better. "Look at them all. How could anyone choose just one?"

Laughter, but they didn't let it go. "You seemed to have a preference for Frost earlier, Princess."

It wasn't a question so I didn't answer it. Another reporter asked, "Fair enough, Princess, but if not just one, who are your multiple favorites?"

That was trickier. "Everyone that I've had sex with is special to me in their own way." Truth.

"How many have you had sex with?"

I leaned into the mike. "Gentlemen, if you would just take a step or two forward."

Rhys, Nicca, Doyle, and Frost moved forward. Only three extra men stepped away from the wall. Galen's skin was almost as white as my own, but in the right light there was an undercast of green to that paleness. His curls were green in any light, except in the dark, where they looked blond. He had cut his own hair just above his shoulders, leaving only one thin braid to remind me that once it fell to his ankles. Of the men of faerie, only the sidhe were allowed to grow their hair long. Galen had cut his hair voluntarily, unlike Adair. Or Amatheon, who stood next to him. Amatheon's rich red hair had been French-braided so that the reporters would have a harder time realizing that his hair only touched his shoulders now. He'd given in to the queen's order sooner than Adair had. The fact that cutting the men's hair had been a punishment, a humiliation that persuaded them to do as the queen bid, said how very odd it was that Galen had done it on his own. He was the youngest of the Queen's Ravens, only seventy-five years older than me. Among the sidhe it was almost like being raised together. I'd thought that open, handsome face was the perfect face since I was fourteen, or maybe younger. It was Galen that I wanted my father to let me be engaged to, but he had chosen another. That engagement had lasted seven years, but there had been no children, and in the end, he had told me I was too human for him. Not sidhe enough. It had made me wonder even more why my father wouldn't let me have Galen in the first place.

He turned lovely green eyes to me and smiled, and I smiled back. He was as armed as any of them with blade and guns, but there was a softness to him that most of the others had lost centuries before either he or I had been born. He'd give his life for me, and would have when I was a child, unlike the rest of them. But as a politician he was something of a disaster, and that could be fatal in the high courts of faerie.

Someone touched my shoulder. I jumped, and found Madeline with her hand over my mike. She leaned in and whispered, "You're staring at him. Let's not repeat the Frost incident, shall we?" She stepped back with a smile ready for the press, hitting the switch at her waist.

I had to keep my face turned away from the crowd because I was blushing. I didn't blush much, and by human standards it wasn't too dark. Sidhe skin just doesn't flush the way human skin tones do. Of course, keeping my face away from the cameras meant that Galen could see me. Some days it's only a choice of embarrassments, not an escape from them.

Madeline was saying, "Princess Meredith is getting a little tired. We may have to cut this short, guys, sorry."

There was a general outcry, and a renewed flash of cameras, which was bad, because Galen came to me. He knelt in front of me, beside my chair, and was tall enough that, from the shoulders up, he was still clearly visible to them. He touched my chin, so gently, with just the tips of his fingers. It made me look at him. It made me forget that we were both in profile to the cameras. He leaned his face closer to me, making me forget that we were onstage. I leaned in toward him, and his hand cupped the side of my face. That made me forget everything else. I have no explanation for it. We'd shared a bed for months. He was a disaster politically, and showing him this much favor in front of everyone could endanger him, but I wasn't thinking that when we kissed. I wasn't thinking anything, and all I could see was the pleased look on his face, the look in his eyes. He'd loved me since I was seventeen, and that was, in his eyes, as if nothing had changed and no time had passed.

The queen had ordered me not to show favoritism. She was going to be angry with me, with him, with us, but after Frost's little incident, as Madeline called it, what was one more? It was bad, and still I kissed him. Still I wanted to kiss him. Still, for just a moment, the world narrowed down to Galen's face, his hand against my skin, and his mouth on mine.

It was a soft, chaste kiss, I think because he knew if he kissed me too hard, I'd lose my hold on the glamour that kept Frost and me from looking like lipstick casualties. Galen drew back, and his eyes held that soft surprise that they did sometimes, as if he still couldn't believe he was allowed to kiss me, allowed to touch me. I'd caught the same look on my face in the bedroom mirror a time or two.

"Do we all get a kiss?" The voice was deep and held the rough sloughing of the sea. Barinthus moved toward us in a swirl of his hair, the color of oceans. The turquoise of the Mediterranean; the deeper medium blue of the Pacific; a grey-blue like the ocean before a storm, sliding into a blue that was nearly black, where the water runs deep and thick like the blood of sleeping giants. The colors moved and flowed into one another so that the actual where and what his hair looked like was ever-changing, like the ocean itself. He'd once been a god of the sea. I'd only recently discovered that he had been Manannan Mac Lir, but that was a secret. Now he was Barinthus, a fallen god of the sea. He moved gracefully across the stage, all near seven feet of him. His eyes were blue but with a slit pupil like a cat or a deep-sea animal. He had a second clear membrane that could close over his eye when he was underwater, and would often flicker when he was nervous. It flickered just a touch now.

I wondered if anyone in the crowd of reporters knew how much it cost this very private man to have suggested a kiss, and make himself the target of all these cameras?

Galen had realized he'd misbehaved because he showed me with his eyes that he was sorry. Unfortunately, his face wasn't that hard for anyone to read, including the reporters. The queen had said no favorites. Our behavior was going to force me to try to prove I had none. After what Galen and I had just done, that was going to be difficult.

A lot of the men standing with me would have played for the cameras, and it would have cost them, or me, nothing. Barinthus was not one of them. He'd been my father's friend, and by American standards we hadn't had sex. Not even by Bill Clinton's standards. If I'd been him, I would have stayed against the wall, but he held to a higher standard of truth even than most of the sidhe.

I looked up at Barinthus, and with me sitting and him standing, it took a while to get all the way to his face. "If you like." I kept my voice light and my face pleasant. Barinthus and I had never kissed, and the first kiss should not be on film.

It was Rhys who saved the day. "If Barinthus gets a kiss, then so do I."

Doyle said, "To be fair, we all should."

Barinthus gave a slight smile. "I would bow to the larger need, and take my kiss in private."

"Galen and Frost have already had theirs," Rhys said, and as Galen went back to his place in line, Rhys pretended to box his ears.

Barinthus did a very graceful bow and tried to slink back to his place. But that wasn't happening. A reporter asked, "Lord Barinthus, have you decided to go from being king-maker to being king?" No sidhe would have called him king-maker to his face, or queenmaker either. But the media, well, he couldn't box their ears.

He knelt beside me, rather than lean into the mike. Kneeling down, his head was about even with mine. "I doubt I will stay with the princess as a permanent member of her guard."

"Why not?"

"I am needed elsewhere."

Truth was that before Queen Andais had accepted him into the Unseelie Court after the Seelie Court kicked him out, Barinthus had to promise that he would never accept the throne here, not even if it was offered. He'd been Manannan Mac Lir, and the queen and her nobles all feared his power. So he'd given his most solemn oath that he would never, personally, sit on our throne.

He bowed to the room in general and simply went back against the wall. He made it clear that he was done with questions for the day. Kitto, the half-goblin sidhe, had already moved back to his place. He was only four feet tall, and that made a lot of the media try to portray him as childlike. He was old enough to remember what the world was like before Christianity was a religion. But his appearance made the media uncomfortable. His short black curls, pale skin, and sunglasses made him look ordinary in his jeans and T-shirt. The queen didn't have a designer suit to fit someone so short. There hadn't been time even for the queen's seamstress to make those kind of alterations. He got away with hugging his section of the wall.

"Princess Meredith, how will you choose your husband from among all these gorgeous men?" a reporter was asking.

"The one who gets me pregnant wins the prize," I said, smiling.

"What if you are in love with someone else? What if you don't love the one who gets you pregnant?"

I sighed, and didn't fight the smile slipping away. "I am a princess, and heir to a throne. Love has never been a prerequisite for royal marriages."

"Isn't it traditional to sleep with one fiancé at a time, until you either get pregnant or don't get pregnant?"

"Yes," I said, and cursed that anyone knew our customs that well.

"Then why the marathon of men?"

"If you had the chance, wouldn't you?" I asked, and that got them laughing. But it didn't distract them.

"Would you marry a man you didn't like just because he was the father of your child?"

"Our laws are clear," I said. "I will marry the father of my child."

"No matter who it is?" another reporter asked.

"That is our law."

"What if your cousin Prince Cel gets one of his female guards pregnant first?"

"Then, according to Queen Andais, he will be king."

"So it's a race to get pregnant?"

"Yes."

"Where is Prince Cel? No one has seen him in nearly three months."

"I'm not my cousin's keeper." In fact, he was in prison for trying to kill me one too many times, and for other crimes that the queen didn't want even the court to know. He should have been executed for some of them, but she'd bargained for her only child's life. He was to be locked away for six months, tortured with the very magic he had used against sidhe-ancestored humans. Branwyn's Tears, one of our most guarded ointments. It was an aphrodisiac that worked even against someone's will. But more than that, it made your body crave to be touched, to be brought. He was chained and covered in Branwyn's Tears. There were bets around the court that what little sanity he'd been born with would not survive it. The queen had given in to one of his guards only yesterday, to let the woman slack Cel's need, save his sanity. And suddenly I had not one, but two, no, three attempts on my life, and one on the queen's. It was more than a coincidence, but the queen loved her son.

Madeline was back in front of me, looking at me. "Are you all right, Princess?"

"Sorry, I'm getting a little tired. Did I miss a question?"

She smiled and nodded. "I'm afraid so."

They repeated it, and I wished I'd missed it again. "Do you know where your cousin the prince is?"

"He's here in the sithen, but I don't know what he's doing this exact moment. Sorry."

I needed off this subject, off this stage. I signaled to Madeline, and she closed it down with a promise of a photo op in a day or two, when the princess was fully healed.

A tiny faerie with butterfly wings fluttered into camera range. This was a demi-fey. Sage, whom I'd "slept with," could make himself human tall, but most of the demi-fey were permanently about the size of Barbie dolls, or smaller. The queen would not be happy about the little faerie fluttering in front of the cameras. When there was press in the sithen, the less-human-looking stayed away from them, and especially away from cameras, or faced the queen's wrath.

The figure was a pale blue-pink with iridescent blue wings. She fluttered through a barrage of flashbulbs, shielding her eyes with a tiny hand. I thought she'd land on me, or maybe Doyle, but she flew the length of the stage to land on Rhys's shoulder.

She hid herself in his long white curls. She whispered something in his ear, using his hair and hat as a shield. Rhys stood up and came to us smiling.

Doyle was standing beside me, but even that close I couldn't hear what Rhys whispered to him.

Doyle gave a small nod, and Rhys left the room ahead of us with the tiny fey still tangled in his hair. I wanted to ask what could be important enough for Rhys to leave early in front of the press.

Someone shouted, "Rhys, why are you leaving?"

Rhys left the room with a wave and a smile.

Doyle helped me stand, then the rest of the guards closed around me like a multicolored wall, but the reporters weren't finished.

"Doyle, Princess, what's happened?"

"What did the little one say?"

The press conference was over; we got to ignore them. It might have been wise to give them an excuse, but Doyle either didn't think we needed to bother or he didn't know what to say. There was a tension in his arm where he touched me that indicated that whatever Rhys had said had shaken him. What does the Darkness fear?

My wall of bright-colored muscle marched me down the steps and out. When we were in the hallway, clear of the media, I still whispered. Modern technology was a wonderful thing, and we didn't need some sensitive microphone picking us up. "What's happened?"

"There are two dead bodies in one of the hallways near the kitchen."

"Fey?" I asked.

"One, yes," he said.

I stumbled in my high heels because I tried to stop, but his arm on mine kept us all moving. "What about the other?"

He nodded. "Yes, exactly."

"Is it one of the reporters? Did one of them go wandering?"

Frost leaned in from the line of men. "It cannot be. We had spells that would make them unable to leave the safe path inside the sithen."

Doyle glanced at him. "Then explain a dead human in our sithen with a camera beside his hand."

Frost opened his mouth, then closed it. "I cannot."

Doyle shook his head. "Nor can I."

"Well, isn't this going to be a disaster," Galen said.

We had a dead reporter in the Unseelie sithen, and a mass of live reporters still on the premises. Disaster didn't even begin to cover it.

Chapter 3

I'D SEEN MORE VIOLENCE IN THE COURTS THAN IN ALL MY years as a private detective in Los Angeles, but I'd seen more death in L.A. Not because I was included in murder cases—private dicks don't do murder cases, at least not fresh ones—but because most of the things that live in faerie land are immortal. By definition, the immortal don't die very often. I could count on one hand how many fresh crime scenes the police had called us in on and still have fingers left over. Even those cases were because the Grey Detective Agency could boast some of the best magic workers on the West Coast. Magic is like everything else; if you can do good with it, some people will find a way to do bad with it. Our agency specialized in *Supernatural problems, Magical solutions.* It was on the business cards and everything.

I'd also learned that all bodies are an it, not he, not she—it. Because if you think of the dead body as a he or a she, they begin to be real for you. They begin to be people, and they aren't people, not anymore. They're dead, and outside of very special circumstances they are just inert matter. You can have sympathy for the victim later, but at the crime scene, especially in the first moments, you serve the victim better by not sympathizing. Sympathy steals your ability to think. Empathy will cripple you. Detachment and logic, those are your salvation at a fresh murder. Anything else leads to hysterics, and I was not only the most experienced detective in the hallway, I was also Princess Meredith NicEssus, wielder of the hands of flesh and blood, Besaba's Bane. Besaba was my mother, and my conception had forced her to wed my father and live, for a time, at the Unseelie Court. I was a princess and I might one day be queen. Future queens do not have hysterics. Future queens who are also trained detectives aren't allowed hysterics.

The problem was that I knew one of these bodies. I'd known her alive and walking around. I knew that she liked classical literature. When she was cast out of the Seelie Court and had to come to the Unseelie Court, she'd changed her name, as many did, even among the Seelie. They changed their names so they wouldn't be reminded daily of who and what they had once been, and how far they had fallen. She called herself Beatrice, after the love interest in Dante's *Divine Comedy*. Dante's *Inferno*. She said, "I'm in hell, I might as well have a name to match." I'd taken world literature as one of my forced electives in college. When I finished the class, I gave most of my books to Beatrice, because she would read them and I wouldn't. I could always buy extra copies of the handful of books that I actually enjoyed. Beatrice couldn't. She couldn't pass for human, and she didn't like being stared at.

I stared at her now, but she wouldn't mind. She wouldn't mind anything ever again. Beatrice looked like a delicate human-size version of the tiny demi-fey that still clung to Rhys's hair. Once Beatrice had been able to be that small, but something happened at the Seelie Court, something she would never talk about, and she lost the ability to change sizes. She'd been trapped at around four foot two, and the delicate dragonfly wings on her back had been useless. The demi-fey do not levitate, they fly, and in the larger size, their wings can't lift them.

Blood had formed a wide, dark pool around her body. Someone had come up behind her and slit her throat. To get that close to her, it had to have been someone she trusted, or someone with enough magic to sneak up on her. Of course, they had also needed enough magic to negate her immortality. There weren't that many things in faerie that could do both.

"What happened, Beatrice?" I said softly. "Who did this to you?"

Galen came up beside me. "Merry."

I looked up at him.

"Are you all right?"

I shook my head, and looked down the hallway to our second body. Out loud I said, "I'll be fine."

"Liar," he said softly, and he tried to bend over me, tried to hold me. I didn't push him away, but I moved back. Now wasn't the time to cling to someone. According to our culture, I should have been touching someone. But the handful of guards that had come to L.A. with me had only worked at the Grey Detective Agency for a few months. I'd been there a few years. You didn't huddle at crime scenes. You didn't comfort yourself. You did your job.

Galen's face fell a little, as if I'd hurt his feelings. I didn't want to hurt him, but we had a crisis here. Surely he could see that. So why, as so often happened, was I having to waste energy worrying about Galen's feelings when I should have been doing nothing but concentrating on the job? There were moments, no matter how dear he was to me, that I understood all too well why my father had not chosen Galen for my fiancé.

I walked toward the second body. The man lay just short of the hallway's intersection with another, larger hallway. He was on his stomach, arms outspread. There was a large stain of blood on his back, and more of it curling down along the side of his body.

Rhys was squatting by the corpse. He looked up as I approached. The demi-fey peeked out at me through Rhys's thick white hair, then hid her tiny face, as if she were afraid. The demi-fey usually went around in large groups like flocks of birds or butterflies. Some of them were shy when on their own.

"Do we know what killed him yet?" I asked.

Rhys pointed to the narrow hole in the man's back. "Knife, I think."

I nodded. "But they took the blade with them. Why?"

"Because there was something special about the knife that might give them away."

"Or they simply did not want to lose a good blade," Frost said. He took the two steps that moved him from the big corridor to the smaller one. He'd been coordinating the guards who were keeping everyone away from the crime scene. I had enough guards with me to close off both ends of the hallway, and I'd done it.

When we'd arrived, the hallway had been protected by floating pots and pans, courtesy of Maggie May, the chief cook for the Unseelie Court. Brownies can levitate objects, but not themselves for some reason. She'd gone with Doyle to see if she could get any more sense out of the scullery maid who had found the bodies. The fey was having hysterics, and Maggie couldn't decide whether the woman had seen something that frightened her, or was simply upset over the deaths. Doyle was going to try to find out. He was hoping the woman would react to him as if he were still the Queen's Darkness, her assassin, and tell him the truth out of fear and habit. If she were just scared, he would probably frighten her into having a fit, but I let him try. I could play good cop after he'd played bad.

I'd sent Barinthus to tell the queen what had happened, because of all of the men, he had the best chance of not being punished for being a bearer of such terrible news. The queen did have a tendency to blame the messenger.

"Possibly," Rhys said, "just habit. You use the blade, you retrieve, clean it, and put it back in its sheath." He pointed to a smear on the man's jacket.

"He wiped the blade off," I said.

Rhys looked at me. "Why 'he'?"

I shrugged. "You're right, it could be a she."

I didn't hear Doyle come down the hallway, but I knew he was there a second before he spoke. "He was running when they threw the blade."

I actually agreed, but I wanted his reasoning. Truthfully, I wanted not to be in charge of this mess, but I had the most experience. That made it my baby. "What makes you say he was running?"

He started to touch the man's coat, and I said, "Don't touch him."

He gave me a look, but said, "You can see where his coat is raised on this side, that the wound in his shirt does not line up with the coat as it lies. I believe he was running, then, when they retrieved the knife, they went through his pockets, moved his coat around."

"I'll bet they didn't wear gloves."

"Most would not think about fingerprints and DNA. Most here will be more worried that magic will find them than science."

I nodded. "Exactly."

"He saw something that scared him," Rhys said, standing up. "He took off down this way to try and outrun it. But what did he see? What made him run?"

"There are many frightening things loose in the corridors of our sithen," Frost said.

"Yes," I said, "but he was a reporter. He came looking for something odd or frightening."

"Perhaps he saw the lesser fey's death," Frost said.

"You mean he witnessed Beatrice's murder," I said.

Frost nodded.

"Okay, say he witnessed it. He ran, they threw a blade, killed him." I shook my head. "Almost everyone carries a knife. Most of them can pin a fly to the wall with one. It doesn't limit our suspect pool much."

"But Beatrice's death limits it." Rhys gave me a look that was eloquent. Should this be discussed where the new guards, whom we didn't entirely trust, could hear us?

"There's no reason to hide it, Rhys. You can't kill the immortal with a knife, but she's dead. It needed a spell, a powerful spell, and only a sidhe, or some few members of the sluagh could have done it."

"The queen forbid the sluagh to be out this night. Simply to be seen while the reporters are in our sithen would raise suspicion."

The sluagh were the least human of faerie. The nightmares that even the Unseelie fear. They are the only wild hunt that is left to us. The only frightening group that can hunt the fey, even the sidhe, until they are caught. Sometimes they kill, sometimes they only fetch you back for the queen. The sidhe fear the sluagh, and its threat was one of the reasons to fear the queen. I'd agreed to bed the King of the Sluagh to cement an alliance with them against my enemies. It was not widely known in the court that I had made the bargain. There were sidhe, even lesser fey, who would think it a perversion. I thought of it as a political necessity. Beyond that, I tried not to dwell too much on the mechanics. Sholto, their king, the Lord of That Which Passes Between, was half-sidhe, but the other half hadn't been even close to humanoid.

I shook my head. "I don't think a member of the sluagh could have hidden themselves enough to wander about the sithen tonight. Not with all the spells we had on the corridors to keep everyone boxed into that one tiny section."

"Just as the reporter should not have been able to leave the area," Frost said. He had a point.

"Let me say what we're all thinking, even the guards who don't want to think it. A sidhe killed Beatrice and the reporter."

"That still leaves us with several hundred suspects," Rhys said.

"The scullery maid is very frightened," Doyle said. "I cannot tell if she is afraid in general or about something specific."

"So you scared her," I said.

He gave a small shrug. "I did not do it on purpose."

I looked at him.

"I did not, Meredith, but Peasblossom took it ill that the Queen's Darkness had come. She seemed to think I'd come to kill her."

"Why would she think the queen wanted her dead?" Rhys asked.

I had an idea, an awful idea, because Queen Andais would hate it. I didn't say it out loud, because though the new guards knew as well as we did that a sidhe had done this, they probably wouldn't be thinking what I was thinking in that moment. Andais had saddled me with several men I did not know and a couple who I outright didn't trust. The awful thought was, What if it had been Prince Cel's people? What if the maid, Peasblossom, had seen one of Cel's people leaving the scene of a double homicide? She'd never believe that the queen would want her to tell anyone.

The trouble was that I couldn't see what Cel, or anyone serving his interests, would gain from killing Beatrice. The reporter seemed accidental, just in the wrong place at the wrong time.

"You've thought of something," Rhys said.

"Later," I said, and let my eyes flick to the backs of the men just a foot away from us.

"Yes," Doyle said, "yes, we do need some privacy."

"We should hide the body," said one of the men at our backs. Amatheon's hair, in its tight coppery red French braids, left his face bare, but nothing could leave it unadorned, for his eyes were layered petals of red, blue, yellow, and green, like some multicolored flower. It often made me a little dizzy to meet his gaze, as if my own eyes rebelled at the sight of him gazing out at the world with flower-petal eyes. His face was square-jawed but slender, so that he managed to be both strongly masculine and vaguely delicate at the same time. Almost as if his face, like his eyes, couldn't quite decide what it wanted to be.

"The reporter will be missed, Amatheon," I said. "We can't just hide his body and hope this will all go away."

"Why can we not? Why can we not simply say we don't know where he has gone? Or that one of the lesser fey saw him leave the sithen."

"Those are all lies," Rhys said. "The sidhe don't lie, or did you forget that in all those years you hung around with Cel?"

Amatheon's face clouded with the beginnings of anger, but he fought it off. "What I did, or did not do, with Prince Cel is not your business. But I know that the queen would want to hide this from the press. To have a human reporter killed in our court will ruin all the good publicity she has managed to acquire for us in the last few decades."

He was probably right on that last part. The queen would not want to admit what had happened. If she even suspected that I suspected that one of Cel's people was responsible, she'd want to hide it even deeper. She loved Cel too much, and always had.

The fact that Amatheon had suggested disposing of the body made me wonder even more if Cel's interests were somehow behind this. Amatheon had always been one of Cel's supporters. Cel was the last pure-blood sidhe of a house that had ruled this court for three thousand years. Amatheon was one of the sidhe who thought me a mongrel and a disgrace to the throne. So why was he here to compete to bed me and make me queen? Because Queen Andais had ordered it. When he refused the honor, she made certain that he got her point, her painful point, that she was ruler here, not Cel, and Amatheon would do as he was told or else. Part of the "or else" had been to cut his knee-length hair to his shoulders, still long by human standards, but a mark of great shame for him. She'd done other things to him, things more painful to his body than to his pride, but he hadn't shared details and I didn't really want to know.

"If Beatrice were the only one dead, then I might agree," I said. "But a human is dead in our land. We can't hide that."

"Yes," he said, "we can."

"You haven't dealt with the press as directly as I have, Amatheon. Was this reporter alone when he came here to the sithen? Or was he part of a group that will miss him right away? Even if he came alone, he will be known to other members of the press. If one of us had killed him out in the human world, we might be able to hide who did it, and let it be just another unsolved crime. But he was killed here on our land, and that we cannot hide."

"You sound as if you are going to tell the press of his death."

I looked away from his confusing eyes.

He reached out to touch my arm, but Frost simply moved in the way, and he never completed the gesture. "You will announce it to the press?" He sounded astonished.

"No, but we have to contact the police."

"Meredith," Doyle started to say.

I cut him off. "No, Doyle, he was stabbed with a knife. We'll never figure out whose blade did it. But a good forensics team might."

"There are spells for tracing a wound to the weapon that made it," Doyle said.

"Yes, and you tried those spells when you found my father's body in the meadow. You did your spells, yet you never found the weapons that killed him." I did my best to make those words empty, to have nothing in my head with them. My father's death, like the capital of Spain. Just a fact, nothing more.

Doyle drew a deep breath. "I failed Prince Essus that day, Princess Meredith, and you."

"You failed because it was sidhe that killed him. It was someone who had enough magic to thwart your spells. Don't you see, Doyle, whoever did this is as good at magic as we are. But they won't know modern forensics. They won't be able to protect themselves against science."

Onilwyn stepped away from the guards. He was blockier than any of the other sidhe, tall but stocky, and yet he always moved with grace, as if he'd borrowed his movements from someone more slender. His hair fell in a long wavy ponytail over the back of his black suit and white shirt. Black, the queen's color, and Prince Cel's color. A very popular color here at the Unseelie Court. His hair was a green so dark it had black highlights. His eyes were pale green with a starburst in the center around his pupil.

"You cannot mean to bring human warriors into our land?"

"If you mean human policeman, yes, that is exactly what I mean to do."

"You will open us up to that over the death of one human and the death of a cook?"

"Do you think the death of a human is less important than the death of a sidhe?" I looked him straight in the face and was happy to see that he realized his faux pas. I watched him remember that I was part human.

"What is one death, even two, over the damage it will do to our court in the eyes of the world?" He tried to recover, and it wasn't a bad job of it.

"Do you think the death of a cook is less important than the death of a nobleman?" I asked, ignoring his attempt to fix things.

He smiled then, and it was arrogant, and so very Onilwyn. "Of course, I believe that the life of a noble-born sidhe is worth more than the life of a servant, or a human. So would you if you were pure sidhe."

"Then I'm glad that I'm not pure sidhe," I said. I was angry now, and I fought not to have it translate to power, not to start to glow, and raise the stakes of this fight. "This servant, whose name happens to be Beatrice, showed me more kindness than most of the nobles of either faerie court. Beatrice was my friend, and if you have nothing more helpful to add than class prejudice, then I'm sure that Queen Andais can find a use for you back among her guards."

His skin went from pale whitish green to just white. I felt a swift burst of satisfaction at his fear. Andais had given him to me to bed, and if I didn't bed him, he would suffer. So would I, but in that moment, I wasn't sure I cared.

"How was I to know she meant anything to you, Princess Meredith?"

"Consider this my only warning to you, Onilwyn"—I raised my voice so that it carried down the hallway—"and for the rest of you who don't know me. Onilwyn assumed that the death of a servant meant nothing to me." Some of the men at the far end turned and looked at me. "I spent a great deal of time with the lesser fey while I was at court. Most of my friends here were not among the sidhe. You made it plain that I was not pure-blooded enough for most of you. You have only yourselves to blame, then, that my attitude is a little more democratic than usual for a noble. Think upon that before you say something as foolish to me as Onilwyn just did." I turned back to the guard in question, and let my voice go lower. "Bear all that in mind, Onilwyn, before you open your mouth again, and say something else equally stupid."

He actually dropped to one knee and bowed his head, though I think that was to hide the anger on his face. "As my princess bids, so I do."

"Get up, and go stand somewhere farther away from me."

Doyle told him to go to the other end of the hallway, and he went, without another word, though the starbursts in his eyes were glittering with his rage.

"I do not agree with Onilwyn," Amatheon said, "not completely, but are you truly going to bring in the human police?"

I nodded.

"The queen will not like it."

"No, she won't."

"Why would you risk her anger, Princess?" He seemed to be truly puzzled by that. "I would not risk her anger again for anything, or anyone. Not even my honor."

He had been one of the sidhe who had made my childhood hellish, but lately I'd seen another side to Amatheon. A side that was frightened, and vulnerable, and helpless. I always had trouble hating people who showed me they could feel pain, too. "Beatrice was my friend, but more than that she was one of my people. To rule a people is to protect them. I want whoever did this. I want them caught and I want them punished. I want to stop them from doing it to anyone else. The reporter was our guest, and to kill him like this is an insult to the honor of the court itself."

"You don't care about the honor of the court," he said, and I watched him struggle to understand me.

"No, not really."

He swallowed hard enough for me to hear it. "There is no one's death that I fear, not even my own, enough to bring the human policemen down into our home."

"Why do you fear the police?"

"I do not fear them. I fear the queen's anger at inviting them in."

"No one gets away with killing people I have sworn to protect, Amatheon, no one."

"You are not sworn, not yet. You have taken no oath for this court, you sit on no throne."

"If I do not do my utmost to solve these deaths, to protect everyone in this sithen, from greatest to least, then I do not deserve to sit on any throne."

"You are mad," he said, and his eyes were very wide. "The queen will kill you for this."

I glanced back at Beatrice's body, and I thought of another body so many years ago. The only reason she hadn't hidden my father's body from the press is that they found him first. Miles away from the faerie mounds, cut to pieces. They found him and took pictures of him. Not only were his bodyguards too late to save his life, they were too late to save his dignity, or my horror.

The police had done some investigating because he was killed off our lands, but no one had helped them. They had not been allowed inside any of the faerie mounds. They had been forbidden to question anyone. They had been stopped before they began because the queen was convinced we would find who had done this terrible thing, but we never did.

"I will remind my aunt what she said when my father, her brother, was murdered."

"What did she say?" he asked.

It was Doyle who answered, "That we would find who had killed Prince Essus, that the humans would only hinder us in our search."

I looked at him, and he met my gaze. "This time I will say to her that the humans have things the sidhe cannot hide from. That the only reason to keep the police out is if she does not want these murders solved."

"Merry," Rhys said, "I'd put it a different way, if I were telling her." He looked a little pale himself.

I shook my head. "But you aren't princess, Rhys, I am."

He smiled, still pale. "I don't know, I think I'd look cute in a tiara."

I laughed, I couldn't help it. I hugged him then. "You'd look adorable."

He hugged me back. "You will discuss this with the queen before telling the press or contacting the police, right?"

"Yes, and just the police. We're going to try to get the press out of here first."

He hugged me tighter. "Thank the Consort."

I drew back from the hug, and said, "I'm determined, Rhys, not suicidal."

"You're hoping she loved her brother enough to feel guilty," Amatheon said, and the fact that he'd grasped that made me think better of him.

"Something like that," I said.

"She cares for no one except Prince Cel," he said.

I thought about that. "You might be right, or you might be wrong."

"Will you wager your life on that?" he asked.

"Not wager, no, but I'll risk it."

"Are you so certain that you are right?"

"About the queen, no, but I am right about what we need to do to find our murderer. I am right about that, and I'm willing to tell the queen so."

He shuddered. "I would rather stay here and guard the hallway, if you do not mind."

"I don't want anyone with me who's more afraid of the queen than of doing what's right."

"Oh, hell, Merry, then none of us can come," Rhys said.

I looked at him.

He shrugged. "All of us fear her."

"But I will go with you," Frost said.

"And me," Galen said.

"Do you need to ask?" Doyle said.

It was Adair who finally spoke for most of them. "I think this is foolishness, though honorable foolishness, but it does not matter. You are our ameraudur, and that is a title that I have not let pass my lips for many years."

Ameraudur meant a war leader who was chosen for love, not bloodline. Ameraudur meant that the man who called you this would give his own life before he saw yours fail. It was the word that the Welsh had used for Arthur, yes, that Arthur. It was the term that some of my father's men had used for him.

I didn't know what to say because I hadn't done enough to deserve the title. Not yet. "I haven't earned such a title from you, Adair, or from anyone. Do not call me so."

"You offered yourself in our place last night, Princess. You took the might of the queen herself upon your mortal body. Seeing you draw magic against her was one of the bravest things ever I saw, my oath on that."

I didn't know whether to be embarrassed, or try to explain that it wasn't brave. That I'd been afraid the whole time.

"You are our ameraudur, and we will follow you wherever you may lead. To whatever end. I will die before I let another harm you."

"You can't mean that," Amatheon said.

I agreed with Amatheon. "Do not give your oath to keep me from harm, Adair, please. If you must, give your oath to save my life, but not all harm."

But it was as if I wasn't there for him, or for Amatheon in that moment. I was the object of the conversation but that was all.

"She saved us last night," Adair said. "She saved us all. She risked her life to save ours. How can you stand there and not give her your oath?"

"A man without honor has no oath to give," Amatheon said.

Adair put his mailed hand on the other's shoulder. "Then come with us to the queen, regain your honor, rediscover your oath."

"She took my courage with the rest. I am too afraid to go before her with such news." A single tear glittered down his cheek.

I looked at the despair in his eyes, and said the only thing I could think of. "I will try for guilt to allow this. Her guilt over never solving her own brother's murder. But if guilt won't work, then I will remind her that she owes me the life of her consort and her pet human."

"It is not always wise to remind the queen she owes you a debt," Doyle said.

"No, but I want her to say yes, Doyle. If she says no, then it's no, and I need it to be yes."

He touched my face. "I see in your eyes a haunting. I see in your eyes your father's death like a weight of injustice on your heart."

I closed my eyes and let my cheek rest against the warmth of his hand. His hand was worn from centuries of sword and knife practice. It made his hand seem more real, more solid, more able to protect. Some sidhe, those pure enough that they couldn't get calluses, thought it a sign of impurity. Racist bastards.

With Doyle touching me, I could let myself remember that awful day. It's funny how your mind protects you. I saw the bloody sheet and the stretcher. I held my father's hand, cold but not stiff, not yet. I had his blood on my hands from touching him, but it wasn't him. It was just cool flesh. That feeling of terrible emptiness when I touched him was like going into a house that you thought would be full of people you loved, only to find it empty, and even the furniture taken. You walk from room to room, hearing your footsteps echo on the naked floors. Your voice bounces back from the empty walls, where the lines of beloved photos still show like the line around a body at a crime scene. He was gone. My tall, handsome, amazing father. He was supposed to have been immortal, but there are spells to steal even the life of a god, a once-upon-a-time god.

If I poke at the memory of that day too hard, try to make myself remember too much, it isn't my father's body or blood that I remember. It is his sword. One of his guards laid it in my hands, the way you lay a flag at a military funeral. The hilt was gold inlaid, carved with a tree on either side. Cranes danced around the tree. And sometimes there were tiny carved bodies hanging from the branches of that tree, bleeding across the gold. Literally the little sacrificed people could bleed onto the sword hilt. The sword hilt was bare that day, cool to my hands. The branches of the trees empty of little sacrifices because the biggest of all had already been made.

The hilt was leather set with gold, and I spent much of that day with my face pressed to it. I breathed in the scent of good leather, the oil that he'd used to clean the sword, and over all that was the scent of him. He had carried that sheath next to his body for centuries, and the leather had absorbed the smell of his skin. I could touch the hilt and feel where even this magical metal had shaped to the constant use of his hand.

I had slept with that sword for days, huddled around it as if I could still feel his hand on it, his body near it. I swore on the hilt of my father's sword that I would avenge his death. I'd been seventeen.

You cannot die of grief, though it feels as if you can. A heart does not actually break, though sometimes your chest aches as if it is breaking. Grief dims with time. It is the way of things. There comes a day when you smile again, and you feel like a traitor. How dare I feel happy. How dare I be glad in a world where my father is no more. And then you cry fresh tears, because you do not miss him as much as you once did, and giving up your grief is another kind of death.

I was thirty-three now. Sixteen years had passed since I slept beside my dead father's sword. The sword had simply vanished about a month after his death. It had gone the way of so many of our great relics, as if without Essus his sword could find no hand fit to wield it. So the sword chose to fade and vanish into the mists. Perhaps the great relics do not choose to go. Perhaps Goddess calls them home when they have done their work. Or perhaps she calls them home until someone comes again that is fit, or suited, for them. I felt that small swell of warmth and comfort that was the voice of the Goddess. That tiny quiet voice that lets you know you've thought a smart thing, or asked the right question.

I would try to use guilt to get Andais to agree to allow me

to call in the police. I did not have much faith in her ability to be emotionally blackmailed, but she still did not know that one of the greatest relics of the faerie courts had returned. The chalice, the one that mankind's wishes had changed from a cauldron of plenty into a golden cup, had returned from wherever it had been. It had come to me in a dream, and when I woke it was real. The chalice had been one of the great treasures of the Seelie Court, and one reason to keep its reappearance a secret was that the Seelie might try to reclaim it. The chalice went where it would, and definitely had a mind of its own. I was almost certain that it would not stay at the Seelie Court even if we allowed them to take it back. And if it kept disappearing there and reappearing here, the Seelie would think we'd stolen it. Or at least accuse us of it, because if the chalice simply found them unworthy, that was not something that King Taranis would ever admit. No, my uncle would blame us, but never himself and his shining throng.

If guilt and family connections could not sway the queen, then perhaps the knowledge that the chalice had come to my hand would.

I still hoped, someday, to know who had killed my father, but the case was cold. Sixteen years cold. For Beatrice and the reporter, though, the case was literally still warm. The crime scene was fresh. The suspect list wasn't endless. Rhys said a few hundred as if that was a lot. I'd helped the police in a few cases where almost the entire population of Los Angeles had been suspects. What was a few hundred to that?

We could do this. If we brought in modern police work, we could get them. They wouldn't be expecting it, and they wouldn't know how to protect themselves against it. It would work. All right, I was 99.9 percent certain it would work. Only a fool is 100 percent certain, when it comes to murder. Either about committing one, or solving one. Both can be equally dangerous and hazardous to your health.

Chapter 4

THE QUEEN STOOD IN THE MIDDLE OF HER ROOM, WRAPPED only in a fur and her own long black hair. One bare slender shoulder and the curve of her neck showed white and perfect above the ruffled grey of the fur. I would have said the fur was wolf, but no wolf that walked the earth today was ever so huge. She made certain that we all had a good view before she turned her head and looked full at us. Charcoal, storm grey, and the pale whitish grey of a winter's sky were the colors of her eyes, in three perfect circles of color around her pupil. Those same colors spread through the fur, framed her face, and made her eyes look bigger than I knew they were, richer in color. It took me a moment of staring into those eyes to realize she had some eyeliner helping to emphasize all that grey and black and white elegance.

It occurred to me for the first time that I could do with glamour what she had to do with makeup. I had never seen the queen do small personal glamour. I wondered if she could. Or had she lost that power along with so many others? I kept my face very still, empty of my speculation. I was about to be in enough trouble without questioning her magical abilities. Oh, yes, that would have guaranteed some very special aunt and niece bonding time. Or should I say some very painful bondage time. I liked pain, but not nearly as much as Aunt Andais did.

"Well, Meredith, I see that you have brought more trouble upon us."

I opened my mouth to begin the speech I'd prepared in my head as we walked down the hallway. Now I swallowed the words because if she planned on blaming me for the deaths, even indirectly, I was sunk. Not only would I not be having the police to help me solve the crime, I would most likely be bleeding before I left this room. There is a saying in the Unseelie Court, "You visit the queen at your peril." What sense of misguided justice had made me forget that?

I dropped to one knee, and my guards followed my lead, dropping like graceful, dangerous flowers around me. Doyle and Frost were with me, but we'd left Rhys in charge of the scene. He would have come, but after me, he'd done the most actual detective work in Los Angeles. Adair had come, and Hawthorne in their colored armor. Galen, of course. He would never have let me walk into such danger without him. Usna had surprised me, and I think Doyle, by insisting that he come with us. It wasn't that we doubted his bravery—he often took foolish chances just to amuse himself. I think it had something to do with the fact that his mother had been transformed into a cat when she had him, and his father was, well, a cat. It gave Usna a very unique perspective. He was every inch a sidhe male, except that his long hair and pale body were decorated with large patches of red and black like a calico cat. I'd left Nicca behind, because his beautiful new wings looked so fragile. I could not bear to see her shred them as some punishment to me. The moment I realized that that was why I'd left him behind, I knew that I had half-expected her to find a way to be angry with me about all this. She had to be angry with someone, and I'd always been a favorite target when I was younger. But only when my father was not at court, never when he was close enough to interfere. After his death, things had been worse in so many ways.

"Answer me, Meredith," the queen said, but her voice didn't sound angry. She sounded tired.

"I am not certain how to answer you, Aunt Andais. I am not aware that I did anything to bring on the deaths of Beatrice and the reporter."

"Beatrice," she said, and she started walking toward me, toward us. Her pale feet were bare except for the silver-grey polish on her toes. Her legs were long and slender where they pulled free of the fur. She had no thighs to speak of. The sidhe women are the perfect models for this era; they have no curves, and it's not due to dieting. The sidhe do not have to diet, they are simply supernaturally thin.

Even for a sidhe woman, Andais is tall, six feet, as tall as most of her own guards. She stood with all that height over me, leaving one leg artfully bare, and bent so that the line from upper thigh to toe was graceful and framed by the charcoal grey of fur.

"Who is Beatrice?"

I would like to have thought she was toying with me, but she wasn't. She truly did not know the name of her own pastry chef. She knew her head cook, Maggie May, but beyond that, I doubted she knew any of the kitchen staff. She was queen, and there were layers of servants and lesser fey between her and someone like Beatrice.

If I had not been here to say her name, no one else would have known it. That made me angry. I fought to keep it from my voice as I answered, "The fey that was killed. Your pastry chef. Her name was Beatrice."

"My pastry chef. I have no pastry chef." Her voice was thick with scorn.

I sighed. "The Unseelie Court's pastry chef, then."

She turned and whirled the fur around her like a lightweight cloak. It would have been so heavy I would not have had the strength to move it like that. I was stronger than a human, but I was not as strong as pure-blooded sidhe. I wondered if she'd done that little movement to remind me of that or just because it looked pretty.

She spoke with her back to us. "But all that belongs to the Unseelie Court belongs to me, Meredith, or did you forget that?"

I realized that she was trying to pick a fight with me. She'd never done that before. She'd struck out in anger with someone else or with me. She'd tormented me because it pleased her. She argued with me if I disagreed with her, or argued first, but she had never tried to start a fight with me. I didn't know what to do.

"I have not forgotten that you, my aunt, are queen of the Unseelie Court."

"Yes, Meredith, remind me that I am your aunt. Remind me that I need your blood to keep my family on the throne."

I didn't like the way she worded that, but it hadn't been a question, so I didn't try to answer. I stayed kneeling and mute.

"If you had been strong enough to protect yourself yesterday there would not have been reporters in my sithen." There was the first warm edge of anger in her voice.

"It was my duty to keep the princess safe," Doyle said.

I reached out to him with my good arm before I could stop myself, but he was just out of reach. I shook my head. Do not bring her anger upon yourself, I tried to tell him with my eyes.

"Our duty," Frost said from the other side of me.

I looked at him and gave him exasperated eyes. If she was determined to be angry, I did not want that anger to fall upon them both. It wasn't just that I loved them, I needed them. If we had any hope of solving this mess, and keeping me alive despite some very determined enemies, I needed my captain of the guard and his lieutenant.

She was suddenly in front of me again, and I hadn't seen her move. Either she had clouded my mind, or she was simply that fast, even tugging along that much fur. She knelt in front of me in a pool of fur and glimpses of white flesh.

"You have stolen my Darkness from me, Meredith. You have thawed the heart of my Killing Frost. My two best warriors, taken away, as if by a thief in the night."

I licked suddenly dry lips and said, "I did not mean to take anything that you valued, Aunt Andais."

She touched my face gently. It made me wince, not because it hurt, but because I'd feared it would hurt. "Yes, Meredith, remind me that I neglected my Darkness and my Frost." She caressed my face with her fingers, and the back of her hand. "Neglected so many things that were mine."

Her hand cupped my chin, and began to squeeze. She could crush the bones of my body into splinters. "I can feel the glamour, girl, drop it. Let me see what you are hiding."

I dropped the glamour on me and on Frost, so that the lipstick smeared across our faces.

She raised me to my feet using my chin as a handle. It hurt, and it would probably bruise. She raised me faster than I could stand. Only her harsh grip kept me from falling.

The men stood with me.

"I did not bid you stand," she yelled at them.

They stayed on their feet. I could not look away from her to see exactly what they were doing, but this was about to go badly.

Barinthus's deep voice came from farther into the room. He must have been standing there the entire time, and I hadn't seen him. It takes a commanding presence to make you not see a seven-foot-tall, mostly blue demigod. Andais was that commanding presence. With her hand bruising my chin, forcing me to meet her grey gaze from inches away, she was more than commanding, she was frightening.

"Queen Andais, Meredith has done nothing but as you have bid her."

"Silence, Kingmaker!" She had glanced back at him when she yelled, and I realized that she must have made him kneel, because I could not see him in that part of the room.

She turned back to me, and her eyes shone as if there was light behind them. It was like watching the moon behind grey clouds, pushing light up through the colors of her eyes, but the eyes themselves did not truly glow. It was an effect I had never seen in any other sidhe's eyes.

"Then what is this smear of red on her mouth, and on the face of my Killing Frost?" She let the fur she'd wrapped herself in fall to the floor, as she put her thumb against my mouth and rubbed hard enough that I had to fight not to make a small pain sound. There was still enough lipstick left to stain her white thumb.

She stood there nude and pale and frightening. If she was beautiful I could not see it. Andais often stripped before she tortured people, so she wouldn't ruin her clothes. Her nudity did not bode well.

I finally realized that she intended to get angry about me

playing favorites in front of the media. She was going to throw a fit, and punish me for kissing Frost, instead of dealing with the murders. Displacement is a fine coping mechanism, but this was not sane.

No logic would save me. All the arguments that I had prepared were dust before her incomprehensible anger.

"Do you think that I give orders simply to be ignored?"

I spoke carefully around her grip on my chin. "I had to distract the cameras . . ."

She let me go so abruptly that I stumbled. Doyle caught my arm, then took me into the circle of his arm, putting me farther from her and closer to the middle of the men. I couldn't argue with the precaution. She was not acting like herself. Andais was temperamental and a sadist, but she never let either interfere this badly with the business of her court. We had a dead human reporter, and cameras still in the faerie mound. It was an emergency, and we needed to act swiftly to minimize the damage, no matter what choice we made. Even if the choice was to hide the bodies and act as if it hadn't happened, it needed to be done quickly. The more people who knew the secret the less chance of keeping it.

If the police were going to bring in forensics for the crime scene, every minute contaminated the crime scene. Every second might be losing us some clue.

"Madeline told me that our Frost had lost control in front of the cameras." She paced a tight circle, then turned back to look at Frost. It was as if any target, any problem, was better than addressing the murders. Did she think Cel's people had done this? Was that why she didn't want to decide on a course of action? Was she afraid to find the truth, afraid of where it would lead?

"Are the reporters gone then?" I asked softly.

"They were about to file out all nice and neat," she said, and her voice was rising as she spoke and paced, naked and dangerous, "until one group realized they were missing a photographer. A photographer!" She screamed the last word. "How did he break through the spells that were supposed to make it impossible for him to leave the guarded areas?" She didn't seem to be asking anyone in particular, so no one answered.

"Was there a camera found?" she asked, and her voice was almost normal.

"Yes, my queen," Doyle said.

"Would it have pictures of the crime?"

"Perhaps," Doyle said.

"We'll need to send the film out to be developed," I said.

"Have we no one of faerie who could do it for us?"

"No, my queen."

"What else did you find on this reporter?"

"We haven't searched the body thoroughly," I said.

"Why have you not searched the body thoroughly?" she asked, and the edge of near hysterical anger shadowed the last word.

I swallowed, and let my breath out slowly. It was now or never. Doyle's hand squeezed my arm, as if he was saying, "Don't." But if I were ever to be queen, Andais would have to step down for me. She was immortal, and I was not, so she would always be a presence in the court. I had to get some control between her and me now, or I would never truly be queen. Never truly be safe from her anger.

"There are clues on the body that a scientific team could find. The less we touch it, the better the science will work."

"What are you babbling about, Meredith?"

Doyle squeezed my arm tighter. "Do you remember what you said when my father was killed?"

She stopped her pacing and looked at me. Her eyes were wary. "I said many things when Essus died."

"You said we were not to allow the human police inside the faerie mounds. That no one was to talk to them or answer their questions, because we would find the assassins with magic."

She stood very still, and gave me unfriendly eyes, but she answered. "I remember those words."

"We failed with magic because the assassins were as good or better at magic than those who bespelled the wounds and the body."

She nodded. "I have long thought that among my smiling

court, my toadie nobles, the murderer of my brother sits. I know that, Meredith, and it is a small constant torment that that death went unpunished."

"As it is for me," I said. "I want to solve these murders, Aunt Andais. I want the person or persons responsible caught and punished. I want to show the media that there is justice in the Unseelie Court, and we are not afraid of new knowledge and new ways."

"You are babbling again," she said, crossing her arms under her tight firm breasts.

"I want to contact the police and bring in a forensic team."

"A what?"

"Scientists who specialize in helping the police solve crimes in the human world."

She was shaking her head. "I do not want the human police tramping through here."

"Nor do I, but a few policemen, and a few scientists. Just a few, just enough to gather evidence. All the sidhe are royal, titled; they all have diplomatic immunity, so technically we can dictate to an extent how much police involvement we allow."

"And you think this will catch whoever did this?"

"I do." I stepped a little away from Doyle, so I wasn't huddling against him. "Whoever did this is worried about magic tracking them down, but it will never occur to them that we would use forensic science inside the land of faerie. They will not have protected against it, and in fact, they can't protect against it, not completely."

"What do you mean by that?"

"We, even the sidhe, shed skin cells, hairs, saliva; all of it can be used to trace back to the person. Science can use a smaller piece than is needed for a spell. Not a lock of hair, but the root of a hair. Not a pound of flesh, but an invisible fleck of it."

"You are certain that it will work? Certain that if I allow this intrusion, this invasion of our privacy, human science will solve this crime?"

I licked my lips. "I am certain if there is evidence to find, they will find it."

"If," she said, and she started pacing the room again, but slowly, quietly this time. " 'If' means you are not certain. 'If' means, dear niece, that you may bring all this upon us and the murderer may go free. If we bring in the police and they do not solve the reporter's death, it will undo all the good publicity I have acquired for us in the last two decades."

"I think it will work, but either way the media will be impressed with your willingness to allow the modern police into your faerie mound. No one has ever done that, not even at the golden court."

She glanced back at me, but she was moving, slowly, toward Barinthus. He was indeed kneeling at the foot of her bed, on a black fur rug. "You think we will gain media points over Taranis and his shining people."

"I think this will show that we meant no harm to anyone, and that such things are not tolerated among the Unseelie, contrary to all those centuries of dark talk."

She stood in front of Barinthus now, but still spoke to me. "You truly believe that the media will forgive us allowing one of their own to be murdered simply because we invite in the police?"

"I think some of them would slaughter their own photographers on altars, with incense and prayers, to get a chance at covering this story."

"Clever, Meredith, very clever." She turned to Barinthus then. She stroked her hand down the side of his face, like you'd touch a lover, though I knew she had never taken him to her bed. "Why did you never try to make a king of my son?"

Unless Barinthus and the queen had been having a very different conversation, the question seemed out of nowhere.

"You do not want me to answer that question, Queen Andais," he said in his deep, sighing voice.

"Yes," she said, still stroking his face, "yes, I do."

"You will not like it."

"I have not liked many things of late. Answer the question, Kingmaker. I know that if my brother, Essus, had been willing, you would have had him kill me and put himself on the throne. But he would not slay his own sister. He would not have that sin on his heart. Still, you thought he would be a better king than I a queen, didn't you?"

Dangerous questions. Barinthus said again, "You do not want the truth, my queen."

"I know the truth of that question. I've known that for centuries, but I do not know why you never looked to Cel. He approached you after Essus died. He offered to help you slay me, if you would help put him on the throne early."

I think all of us across the room held our breaths in that moment. I had not known this. The looks on everyone's faces around me said that most of them had not either. Only Adair and Hawthorne behind their helmets were still hidden from their surprise.

"I warned you of his treachery," Barinthus said.

"Yes, and I had you tortured for it."

"I remember, my queen."

Her smile did not match her words, but then neither did the constant caressing of his face and shoulders. "When Meredith came of age, you turned to her. If she had had the magic she now possesses since her stay in the lands to the west, you would have offered her what you offered Essus, wouldn't you?"

"You know the answer, my queen."

"Yes," she said, "I do. But Cel always had the power to be king. Why did you not put him on the throne? Why did you foster a half-breed mongrel of a princess over my pure-sidhe son?"

"Do not ask me this," he said.

She slapped him twice, hard enough to stagger him even on his knees. Hard enough to have blood spill from his mouth. "I am your queen, damn you, and you will answer my question. Answer me!" The last was screamed into his face.

Barinthus answered her, blood flowing from his mouth. "You are a better queen than Cel will ever be a king."

"And what of Meredith? What of my brother's child?"

"She will be a good queen."

"A better queen than Cel a king?"

"Yes," he said, and that one word dropped into the silence of the room like a stone thrown down a great height. You know it will make a sound, but only after a very, very long fall.

The sound came with her words. "Meredith, you will do nothing with Barinthus that will chance you being pregnant by him. Nothing, is that clear?"

"Yes." My voice sounded strained and hoarse as if I'd been the one screaming.

"Contact the police. Do what you think best. I will announce to the court and the media that you are in charge of this little problem. Do not bother me with it again. Do not report to me unless I ask it. Now go, all of you, get out."

We went. All of us, even Barinthus. We went, and were grateful to go.

Chapter 5

I CALLED MAJOR WALTERS OF THE ST. LOUIS POLICE DEPARTMENT, who had been in charge of our security at the airport the day before. I called from the only landline phone in the Unseelie sithen. The phone was in the queen's office. Which always looked to me like a black and silver version of Louis the Fourteenth's office if he had liked going to Goth dance clubs for the dissipated rich. It was elegant, dark, expensive, and exciting in that chill-up-your-spine way; modern, but with a feel of the antique; nouveau riche done right. It was also a little claustrophobic to me. Too many shades of black and grey in too small a space, as if a Goth curtain salesman had persuaded them to cover every inch of the room with his wares.

The phone was white and always looked like bones on the secretary's black desk. Or maybe that's just me projecting. I did not understand the mood of the queen tonight. I'd asked Barinthus, as we walked to the office, if she'd given him any clues as to why she was behaving so oddly, and he'd said no. No clues.

Why was I calling the St. Louis police when the faerie lands are technically in Illinois? Because Major Walters was the current police liaison for the lands of faerie and the human police. Once upon a time, a few hundred years ago, there'd been an entire police unit assigned to us. Why? Because not everyone in America agreed with President Jefferson's decision to bring the fey to this country. The local people who were going to be close to us were especially upset. They didn't want monsters of the Unseelie Court coming to live in their state. At that time, St. Louis was the closest major city with a working police department. So even though we were technically located in Illinois, police problems had been sent to Missouri and St. Louis. They got the joyous duty of protecting us from the angry humans and also walking the perimeters of our lands so we couldn't sneak out and wreak havoc. If the courts of faerie hadn't come with a sizable bribe for several different branches of government, and certain powerful individuals, we might have never made it into this country. No one wanted to mess with either court after the last great human-fey war in Europe. We'd shown ourselves entirely too powerful for comfort.

What no one really understood about us—from Jefferson on down to the yelling mob—was that a line of human police wasn't really going to keep the fey, any fey, from leaving the area. What kept them inside and behaving themselves were threats and oaths to and from their respective kings and queens. But the police did keep the humans from harassing us.

Gradually, when nothing bad happened, the police presence was reduced, until they left altogether, and we only called on them when they were needed. As the local humans realized that we mostly wanted to be left alone, we had to call on our private police less and less. Soon, the police assigned to us had other jobs in other areas of the police force until they were needed for faerie duty, as it came to be called. Come up to present day and the unit had become a single detective or officer. The last time he'd been used was my father's death, but since that had been on government-owned farmland, the locals had been cut out twice. Once by the feds and once by us. All right, by the queen. I'd have taken a platoon of soldiers into the mounds if I thought they could have caught my father's killers.

After the liaison was so ineffective with my father's murder, I thought the post had been abandoned. But I'd been wrong.

Doyle had found out that Major Walters was still our liaison. The last remnants of a unit created by Thomas Jefferson himself. We'd also never had anyone as high a rank as major in the job. Major Walters had volunteered for the job, because the last person to have it had also done our security at press conferences, and that had landed Walter's predecessor a large salary as chief of a big corporation's security. Executives like to be guarded by someone who's guarded royalty. It adds a certain panache to the résumé. Doyle had even learned that Walters had a very well paying job lined up. I wondered how the big corporation felt about Walters after yesterday. It looks great on your résumé to guard royalty, but not so great to let them get injured on your watch. Nope, probably the executives would be a little nervous about being guarded by someone who let Princess Meredith get shot at by one of his own officers. Humans believed in magic, but not as an excuse for screwing up. No, they liked to blame someone, not something.

Walters would be needing to recoup. He'd need to redeem himself in the public eye. Though my guards and I knew that he'd had no chance to prevent what had happened, the humans wouldn't accept it. The major had been in charge. He'd take the fall. It was simply how they thought.

Christine, my aunt's secretary, was petite, well-endowed, and more plump than was the fashion. In her day she'd been perfect. Her blond hair curled over her shoulders, and her youthful face was eternally beautiful. One of our noblemen had lured her away centuries ago, but he'd grown tired of her. To stay in faerie she needed to be useful, so she learned shorthand and computer skills. She was probably one of the most technologically savvy people in either court.

She suggested that we call the Bureau of Human and Fey Affairs. Logical, I suppose, but they were more useful for social difficulties or diplomatic problems. If you want something done, don't call a politician or a bureaucrat. Call a cop.

I took a deep breath, said a little prayer to the Goddess, and dialed the number the secretary had given me.

He answered on the second ring. "Your Highness," he said.

He must have had caller ID "Not exactly," I said. "Princess Meredith, actually."

His first words had been professional, his next held the hint of suspicion. "Princess, to what do I owe this honor." In fact, he sounded positively hostile.

"You sound angry at me, Major Walters."

"The newspapers say you don't trust my men to keep you safe. That human cops aren't good enough for your guard detail."

I hadn't expected him to be so blunt. He was more cop than politician. "I can only say that I never even hinted to the media that I doubted your men."

"Then why were we barred from the second press conference?"

Hmm, that was a sticky wicket. "You and I both know that it was a spell that made your officer shoot at me, correct?"

"Yeah, our unit psychic found the magical remnants on him."

"I'm safer here in the sithen, but your officers won't be. Someone did a spell in a building of metal girders and beams, with technology all over the place. Put that same spell caster inside the sithen, inside faerie, with no damper of metal and technology on them, and your officers would be in even greater danger of being bespelled."

"What about the human reporters; aren't they in danger of being bespelled?"

"They aren't armed," I said. "They can't do that much damage."

"So we just aren't up to your standards, is that it?" He was angry, and I wasn't sure why.

The queen's secretary must have caught enough of the conversation to give me a hint. She flashed the headline of the *St. Louis Post Dispatch:* POLICE FAIL TO PROTECT THE PRINCESS. Oh.

"Major Walters, I've just been shown a newspaper. My apologies for not understanding the effect this situation was having on your life. I was a little too preoccupied with my own being in danger."

"I don't need your apologies, Princess. I need my men to be good enough to protect you at public events."

"How much crap are you getting about what happened? Are they trying to scapegoat you?"

"That's not your business," he said, which was almost as good as a yes.

"I think we can help each other, Major."

"How?"

"You sitting down?"

"Yeah," and that one word was not happy.

I told him the briefest version I knew about the reporter and Beatrice, and that the queen had given it to me to clean up.

There was utter silence on the other end of the phone for so long that I finally said, "Major, you still there?"

"I'm here," he said, in a hoarse voice.

"I'm sorry that being on faerie duty has just gotten so horribly complicated. I'm sorry that it is screwing with your plans."

"What do you know about my plans?"

"I know you want to be chief of security at a certain place of business when you retire early next year. I know you took the job as liaison to us for your résumé. I know that letting me get shot at probably didn't win you any points at your soon-to-be new job."

"You know a damn lot for a princess."

I let that go, not sure if it was compliment or insult. "But what if I show, plainly, that I have utter confidence in you, Major Walters?"

"What do you want from me?" The suspicion was thick enough to walk on.

"I want a Crime Scene Unit down here. I've got the crime scene itself isolated, but I need science, not magic, on this one."

"Didn't you just lecture me about my men being in danger from enchantments if we came into your place?"

"Yes, that's why I want only you, the CSU, and maybe one or two others, tops. My guards can protect you individually from magic if you are a small enough group."

"The entire department is being crucified in the press, especially the St. Louis press."

"I know that now. Let's show them that Princess Meredith and her guards don't believe all that bad press. I do have confidence in you, Major Walters. You and a good forensic unit. How about it, Major? Do you want to play, or do I leave you out of this? I can pretend I didn't call, and just start with the chief of police."

"Why didn't you start with him?" Walters asked.

"Because you're my police liaison. I respect that title. You're who I'm supposed to call. Besides, you're almost more motivated than I am to solve this case."

"What makes you say that?"

"Don't be naïve, Major Walters. The department is taking heat. They'll hang someone for it, and it will most likely be you. Let me show the department that you still have my trust and they'll back off. They'll be desperate to solve this second violent episode and have someone to punish. They'll fall all over themselves to give you anything I ask for."

"You seem to know how it works."

"Politics is politics, Major, and I was raised in the thick of it." I sat on the edge of the desk and tried to get my shoulder to loosen up. The injured muscles had tightened sometime during the interview with the queen. Funny that, but now my arm ached, and that wasn't funny, at all. Of all the things I missed with being part human, not healing instantly was one of the biggest envies I had. "I need a cop, Major Walters, not a politician. I need someone who understands that my crime scene is aging even as we speak. That valuable evidence may be getting contaminated right this minute. I need someone who will worry more about solving this mess than the political ramifications of it. I think you're that man, and now that your political star runs beside mine, you are doubly motivated."

"What makes you so sure of that? What makes you think I won't cut my losses and run for the hills?"

I thought about that, and said, "The look in your eyes yesterday at the airport when you were angry with having to share leadership with Barinthus. The fact that you showed anger to me now on the phone rather than trying to toadie to me. I wasn't sure with a rank as high as major, but you're more cop than politician, Walters. And if you knew how little I like politics, you'd know what a compliment that is."

"You seem pretty good at politicking for someone who doesn't like the game."

"I'm good at a lot of things that I don't enjoy, Major Walters. As I'm sure you are."

Silence again. "If we don't solve this, my ass is grass, and no amount of confidence shown in me, by you or anyone else, will save it."

"And if we solve it . . ." I said.

He laughed, a deep chuckle. "Then I'll be the department's shining star, and the executives will be climbing over themselves to give me an even bigger salary. Yeah."

"Are you my man, or do I pretend that I didn't make this call?"

"I'm your man."

I smiled. "Good. You start making calls, and get me some CSU out here as soon as possible."

"What do I tell the chief about why you're letting us into your precious faerie land?" he asked. Oh, yeah, he was definitely a better cop than politician.

"Explain that whoever did this has diplomatic immunity,

but we are allowing this investigation to happen out of our mutual desire for cooperation and justice."

"You want the bastard who did it, don't you?"

"Yes," I said.

"You probably don't remember me—I was just another uniform keeping the crowd back—but I saw you the day your father died. They gave you his sword."

If I'd had any doubts that I'd called the right person, that one sentence took them away. Out loud I said, "Yes, yes, they did."

"Catching this bad guy won't catch your father's killer."

"That is a very insightful remark for a man I've only met twice."

"Well, I've been the uniform on faerie duty off and on."

"My mistake, but it was still insightful, uncomfortably so."

"Sorry. Sometime after we've caught this guy, and if faerie princesses have drinks with lowly police majors, I'll tell you why I became a cop."

It was my turn to be insightful. "You lost someone, and they didn't catch the bastard who did it."

"You knew that already." He sounded accusatory.

"No, I swear I didn't."

"Then that was a hell of a guess."

"Let's just say that those of us who bear a particular wound recognize it in others."

He made a *humph* sound, then sort of growled, "Yeah, I guess we do. What will you be doing while I make phone calls and get everyone out there?"

"I'll be questioning witnesses."

"You know, it'd be nice if I were there for the questioning."

"Most of the fey who may have witnessed anything are ones who almost never travel outside of faerie. They're a little shy around humans, especially humans in uniforms. They all remember the last great human-fey war."

"That was almost four hundred years ago," he said.

"I'm aware of that."

"I'll never get used to it."

"What?"

"How you guys look so young, but you remember this country before my great-great-great-grandfather took a boat here."

"Not me, Major. I'm just a poor mortal girl."

"Poor my ass," he said.

"I'll let you know if we learn anything that's useful from the witnesses."

"I'd like to decide what's useful and what's not."

"Then hurry up, Major, but I do not promise that any fey will talk to you. I can't even promise that you'll be in the room when I question everyone. Some of them will simply not talk to the human police."

"Then why am I coming?"

"So that when the press follow us around we can stand shoulder to shoulder and show that you are helping solve this case. And bring the officer who shot at me with you."

"Why in the name of God?"

"Because his career is ruined unless he gets a chance at this, too."

"Won't he be a danger to you?"

"We'll give him a charm to help bolster his psychic shields. If I think he's too fragile for the duty, I'll let you know and we'll escort him out."

"Why do you care what happens to one young uniformed cop?"

"Because he could have gone his whole career and not ever had anything like this happen to him, if he'd only stayed away from the faeries. The least we can try and do is minimize the damage."

"I'll make calls now, but you puzzle me, Princess Meredith. You're almost too nice to be true." He hung up.

I put the phone back in its cradle. Too nice to be true. My father had taught me to be nice first, because you can always be mean later, but once you've been mean to someone, they won't believe the nice anymore. So be nice, be nice, until it's time to stop being nice, then destroy them. I wondered if he'd taken his own advice that summer's day, or if he'd hesitated because someone facing him had been his friend. I would have given a great deal to find the person in question, and ask him.

Chapter 6

THERE WAS ANOTHER PHONE CALL I WANTED TO MAKE. I looked at Christine's smiling, pleasant face, and said, "Can you wait outside for a moment, Christine?"

She blinked big blue eyes at me, but took a deep breath, stood up, rustled out her full skirts, and left without a word. I couldn't tell if I'd offended her, but then she was always hard to read. That she could smile and smile through everything the queen did in front of her always made me wonder about her. Did she enjoy the queen's little shows, or did she not know what else to do?

With Christine gone I was left with Doyle, Barinthus, and Usna. Frost, Galen, Hawthorne, and Adair were at the door to make sure we weren't interrupted. Besides, the office just wasn't large enough for all of us. Not comfortably anyway. I trusted everyone but Usna. I didn't know him well enough to trust him.

"Usna, wait out in the hall," I said.

He gave me a little smile, but he didn't argue. He just hesitated by the door. "Do you want me to send someone else to take my place?"

I thought about it, and said, "Galen."

He gave a little bow, then opened the door and told Galen to come in. Galen looked a question at me as he closed the door behind him.

"I'm going to call Gillett."

Galen was shaking his head. "I'm not sure that's a good idea."

"Who is Gillett?" Barinthus asked.

"He was one of the federal agents who investigated Prince Essus's murder," Doyle said.

"I don't know why I'm surprised that you remember that, but I am," I said.

Doyle looked at me, and his face was unreadable, dark and closed to me. "Gillett was the most persistent of all the human investigators."

I nodded. "Yes, he was."

"You've been in touch with him?" Doyle asked.

"More like he kept in touch with me, Doyle. I was seventeen, and he seemed to be the only one who wanted to solve my father's murder more than he wanted to obey the queen or his superiors."

Doyle took in a lot of air, and let it out slow. "And Galen knew of this?"

"Yes," Galen said.

"And it never occurred to you to tell your captain that the princess was keeping in touch with a federal officer?"

"It made Merry feel better, and just after Essus died, I'd have done anything to help her feel better."

"And after that?" Doyle asked.

"They exchanged cards twice a year, that was all."

Doyle turned his dark gaze to me. I shrugged, then wished I hadn't because it hurt. "He sent me a card every year around the anniversary of my father's death. I sent him a Yule card."

"How did no one notice this?" Doyle asked.

"The queen didn't care enough about me to pay attention, and you paid attention where the queen told you to. You all did."

He rubbed his eyes with thumb and forefinger. "How badly does your arm hurt?"

"It aches."

He took in air again, then let it out slow. "You need to rest, Princess."

"You're not mad at me or Galen," I said. "You're angry with yourself for not knowing this."

"Yes," he said with the tiniest edge of anger.

"When my father died, what other guard could I have trusted but Galen?"

"Did you not trust me?" Barinthus said.

I looked at him, my father's closest friend. "You were almost as distraught over his death as I was, Barinthus. I needed someone who was touched by grief but not consumed by it. Galen was that person for me." I reached out to Galen, and he took my hand, as if it were the most natural thing in the world.

"If you could marry where your heart lies," Doyle said, "I fear what it would do to the court."

I looked at him, trying to see behind his careful face. I squeezed Galen's hand and drew him in against me. Once, Doyle would have been correct. Once it was Galen in my heart and no other, but that was before I grew up enough to understand what it would mean to be at my side. It was a dangerous place to be, a treacherous place to be.

I hugged him not because he was the only name written across my heart now, but because he no longer was. A part of me was saddened by that, and another part of me was almost relieved. I understood what my father had known decades ago: for Galen the title of king would be a death sentence. I needed someone hard and dangerous by my side, not gentle and placating.

I looked into Doyle's face as I held Galen to me. Did Doyle not know that my heart's list had grown larger, and that his name was on that list? The way he was acting, he seemed jealous, or envious, or angry. He was hiding his emotions so well that I couldn't decide what emotion he was hiding, just that it was something strong that he didn't want to share. Even being able to see that much meant the Darkness's legendary control was slipping.

"I'm going to call Gillett." I turned back to the phone, and since I had only one good hand, I had to let go of Galen. He kept himself touching the back of my body, his body insinuated against me. He fit against me as he always had, as if he'd been born to be there. If all I'd ever wanted in my bed was gentle lovemaking, then Galen would have been wonderful, but we'd had months in bed to discover that his idea of passion and mine did not match. He did not understand my desire for roughness, or pain, or just simply being a little more forceful. Galen gave me pale, uncomprehending eyes when I asked certain things.

I dialed Gillett's number by heart, though his number had changed over the years. I'd always had to memorize it for fear of someone caring enough to look through any address book I might have. I could have saved my worry; Doyle's reaction had shown plainly that no one had been paying me that close attention. It was a little sad, and a little frustrating. So much wasted effort in hiding from people who weren't even looking.

I waited for Gillette's cell phone to ring. I'd promised him that if anyone else ever died in circumstances similar to my father's, I'd let him know. These weren't really that similar, but a promise is a promise. I felt half silly and half excited, as if somehow just being able to make this one call would change things. I was over thirty, but part of me was still seventeen and wanted justice. I should have known better by now.

He answered, "Gillett."

"Hey," I said.

"Merry?"

"Yes."

"Are you all right?"

Over the years he'd become protective of me. As if he felt some debt to my dead father to keep me well. If he only knew, but I hadn't shared all the attempts on my life. The endless duels that made me flee faerie for years and let everyone think I was gone for good.

This was the first time I had spoken to him since I'd resurfaced. "A little worse for wear, but I'm fine."

"I thought they'd killed you, too, three years ago. Why didn't you call?"

"Because if you'd spoken my real name near a darkened window the Queen of Air and Darkness would have known. The sound of our conversation would have traveled back to her. It would have endangered you. It would have endangered anyone."

He sighed over the phone. "And now you're 'princess' again, and looking for a husband. But you didn't call up just to chat, did you?"

"Have you heard something?"

"A rumor that the reporters left the faerie mound, but are now all gathered in the parking lot. The press conference is over, so why are that many national and international media types hanging around in the middle of a cornfield in Illinois?"

I told him the broad outline of the problem.

"I can be there with a team in less than..."

"No, no team. I've already got a few police coming with a forensic unit. You can come, but you can't bring dozens of agents with you. This happened inside the sithen, not on federal land this time."

"We could help you."

"Maybe, or maybe there would just be more humans to get injured. We've got a dead reporter, that's bad enough. We can't afford to have an FBI agent get killed by one of us."

"We've talked about this for years, Merry. Don't cut me out now."

"My father's murder is sixteen years old; it is secondary here, Raymond. The priority is the new deaths. Hearing your voice now, I'm not sure that would be the case for you."

"You don't trust me." He sounded hurt.

"I'm in line to the throne now, Raymond. The good of the court outweighs personal vengeance."

"And what would your father say to hear that from you, his daughter?"

"He'd say that I had grown wise. He'd agree with me." I was wishing I hadn't called him. I realized that Special Agent Raymond Gillett was part of a child's wish. I couldn't afford that kind of wishing, not anymore.

I was suddenly tired, and my arm ached from shoulder to wrist. I turned and leaned against the desk, half sitting on it. It forced Galen farther away from me, and that was fine. He kept his hand playing lightly on the edge of my thigh, moving the skirt back and forth as he petted me. It was comforting, and I needed the comfort.

Doyle was looking at me, and something in his eyes softened his face. I had to look away from the kindness I saw there. I wasn't sure why such a look from him made my throat grow tight.

"Don't come, Gillett. I'm sorry I called."

"Merry, don't do this, not after almost twenty years."

"When we've solved this one, if I'm still alive and still have the carte blanche in this area, I'll call you, and we can talk about you coming down. But only if it's about my father's death."

"You don't think the FBI might be helpful on a double homicide?"

"I don't know what we've got here, Gillett. If we need something fancier than the local lab can handle, I'll let you know."

"And maybe I'll answer the phone, and maybe I won't."

"As you like," I said, and I struggled not to let my voice show how tight my throat felt, how hot my eyes were. "But think on this, Gillett. Did you start all this with a seventeen-year-old child because you felt sorry for me, or because you were angry that the queen cut you out of the investigation? Was it pity that moved you, a desire for justice, or simply anger? You'd show her. You'd solve the case without the queen's help. You'd use Essus's daughter to help you."

"It wasn't like that."

"Then why are you angry with me now? I shouldn't have called you, but I gave you a promise. A child's promise to call you if ever a similar murder happened. It isn't similar in detail, but whoever did it has similar magic at their call. If we solve this, it may get us closer to finding my father's murderer. I thought you'd like to know."

"Merry, I'm sorry, it's . . ."

"That the murder has been eating at you all these years?" I said.

"Yes," he said.

"I'll call you if anything pertinent comes up."

"Call me if you need better forensics than the locals can give you. I can get you DNA results that they can only dream of."

I had to smile. "I'll be sure to let Major Walters know that the FBI has such confidence in the locals."

He gave a dry little laugh. "I'm sorry if I made this harder for you. I tend to get a little obsessed."

"Good-bye, Gillett."

"Bye, Merry."

I hung up and leaned heavier on the desk. Galen held me against him, careful of my hurt arm. "Why didn't you let Gillett come down?"

I raised my face and looked at him. I searched that open face for some hint that he understood what had just happened. His eyes were green and wide and innocent.

I wanted to cry, needed to cry. I'd called Gillett because the murders had raised ghosts for me. Not real ones, but those emotional pains that you think are gone for good until they just rise again to haunt you, no matter how deep you bury them.

Doyle came to me. "I watch you grow more worthy of being queen every day, Meredith, every minute." He touched my good arm lightly, as if not sure I wanted to be touched at that moment.

My breath came out in a sharp cry, and I threw myself against his body. He held me, his arms fierce and almost painful. He held me while I cried because he understood some of what it had cost me to let go of childish things.

Barinthus came up to us and put his arms around us both, hugging us to him. I glanced up, and found tears running down his face. "You are more your father's daughter in this moment than you have ever been."

Galen hugged us from the other side, so that we were warm and close. But I realized in that moment that Galen, like Gillett, was a child's wish. They held me, and I wept. Crying didn't cover it. I wept the last of my childhood away. I was thirty-three years old; it seemed a little late to be letting go of childish things, but some wounds cut us so deep that they stop us. Stop us from letting go, from growing up, from seeing the truth.

I let them all hold me while I cried, through Barinthus cried, too. I let them hold me, but part of me knew that Galen, and only Galen, didn't understand what was happening. He'd been my closest confidant among the guards. My friend, my first crush, but he'd asked, why didn't I let Gillett come?

I cried and let them hold me, but it wasn't just my father's loss I was mourning.

Chapter 7

I CLEANED OFF THE REMNANTS OF THE MAKEUP THAT I HADN'T cried away. Got the lipstick that still looked like clown makeup off, and even gave Frost a makeup cleansing cloth so he could do his own face. We were clean and neat and presentable when we started back to the crime scene. I felt hollow inside, as if a piece of me were missing. But it didn't matter. Walters would be here soon with the CSU team. We needed to have finished the questioning of the witnesses before then in case they said something that we didn't want the human police to know. I wanted justice, but I also didn't want to make the bad publicity worse by sharing some dark secret with the human world.

Doyle stopped so abruptly that I ran into him. He pushed me farther back into Galen and Usna's suddenly waiting arms, as if he'd given some signal that I had not seen. With Doyle and Adair in front and Galen and Usna suddenly very close on either side of me, I could not see what had frightened everyone. Barinthus, Hawthorne, and Frost were bringing up the rear. They had turned to face back down the hall as if they were worried about someone sneaking up behind us. What was happening? What now? I couldn't even manage a drop of fear. I'm not sure it was bravery so much as exhaustion. I was simply too tired emotionally and physically to waste the adrenaline on fear. In that second, if we'd been attacked, I'm not sure I would have cared.

I tried to shake it off, this feeling of desolation. I called, "Doyle, what is it?"

Barinthus answered, "The Queen's Ravens are in the hall, blocking our way." I guess being seven feet tall does give you a better view.

I realized then that my guard feared almost every sidhe right now. They were right. One of the sidhe had committed murder, and I was in charge of catching the killer. Wonderful. I'd just given someone else a reason to want me dead. But what was one more?

Adair moved to the center of the hallway to hide me behind his armored back, as Doyle moved down the hallway. Barinthus answered my question before I'd even thought it. "Doyle is conferring with Mistral."

Mistral was the master of winds, the bringer of storms, and the new captain of the Queen's Ravens. He'd taken Doyle's place when it became clear that Doyle wasn't coming back to his old job.

"What's happening?" Galen asked, and his voice held enough anxiety for both of us.

Usna bent over me, sniffing my hair. "You smell good."

"Keep your mind on business," Galen said, looking up the hallway toward where Doyle had gone. He had a gun out, held down along his leg. If I'd been choosing between sword and gun, I'd have made the same choice. When I first came back to faerie, guns were outlawed inside the mounds, but after the last few attempts, my aunt had decided that my guards and hers needed all the help they could get. So our men could carry guns, if they knew how to use them. Doyle and Mistral had been the judge of who was competent to carry and who wasn't. Some guards treated guns the way others treated the idea of carrying around a poisonous snake. It might be useful, but what if it bit you.

Usna had a short sword in either hand, pointed both directions up and down the hallway. His grey eyes, which were the most ordinary thing about him physically, were keeping watch, but his face was pressed against the top of my head. He put first one cheek, than the other against my hair. He was looking down each end of the hallway as he did it, but he was also almost scent marking me. Catlike and inappropriate for the situation, if he'd thought like a human. But it was Usna, and I knew that he was aware of everything in the hallway, even while trying to put the scent of his skin against my hair.

I found it oddly comforting. Galen did not. "Usna, stop it."

A soft sound somewhere between a purr and a growl sounded from the other man. "You worry too much, my little pixie."

"And you don't worry enough, my little kitten." But Galen grinned as he said it. We all felt a little better for Usna's teasing.

"Quiet, both of you," Frost said from behind us. They shut up, looking a little sheepish but happier. Usna stopped trying to rub his face against my hair. Which meant he'd done it almost more to tease Galen than to tease me.

Doyle was taking too long. If something had gone horribly wrong, Barinthus or Adair would have warned us. But it was taking too long. The unnatural calm was beginning to slip away from me on tiny cat paws of anxiety.

I had a license to carry a gun in California. I also had a diplomatic waiver that pretty much covered me anywhere, anytime, on the basis that my life was in danger often enough that being armed was a necessity. I had guns. But Andais wouldn't let me go into the press conference armed. I was a princess; princesses did not protect themselves, they had others to do that for them. I thought the idea archaic and short-sighted and downright ironic coming from a queen whose claim to fame had been as a goddess of battle. Standing there with Galen and Usna pressed against me, with the others like a wall of flesh around me, I vowed that the next time I left my room, I'd be armed.

Doyle returned, and Adair gave him room to pass, then moved back to the center of the hallway like some golden wall. I realized that Adair was being just that, a wall of flesh and metal to keep death from me. He'd said I was his ameraudur, another echo of my father's ghost, for he had been the last ameraudur among the royals of either court. To be called ameraudur held more honor than king, because the men chose you, and followed you through love, the kind of love men have shared with one another on battlefields as far back as time can see. Oaths bound a guard to risk his life for his charge, queen or princess, but ameraudur meant he did it willingly. It meant that coming back from a battle alive with his leader dead was worse than death. A shame that he would never live down. Two of my father's guards took their own lives for shame of letting their prince die. To lay your life down for your ameraudur was the highest honor.

Seeing Adair standing there so straight, so proud, so ready to die, made me think about my new title. Made me afraid of it. I did not want anyone dying for me. I had not earned it. I was not my father and never would be. I could never ride into battle with them and hope to survive. How could I be their ameraudur if I could not do that?

Doyle's dark face was empty for me. Whatever he thought about Adair's new pet name for me, he was keeping it to himself. His face was so empty now that the only thing I was certain of was that I wasn't in immediate danger. Other than that, he could have worn the same expression for anything. I wanted to yell at him to show me what he was feeling, but he spoke before I could lose that much control.

"The queen sent them to fetch you back when you are finished with your 'murder business,' as she worded it. Vague enough that they cannot fetch you immediately." Doyle gave a small wry smile, and shook his head. "In truth, Mistral is now in charge of the crime scene."

"What?" Galen and I asked together.

"Did the queen rescind her offer to Meredith?" Barinthus asked. "Are Mistral and the queen now in charge of this murder?"

"No," Doyle said. "Rhys thought of a different spell to search for our murderer. He wished to chase this new magical clue down, but needed someone to keep the crime scene safe. When Mistral and the others came, he put them to guard the hallway."

"That was rashly done," Frost said.

"Knowing Rhys, he got Mistral's oath," Usna said, "and once you have Mistral's oath, you have his honor. He would not break it, not for all the joys of the Summerlands."

Doyle gave one sharp nod. "I trust Mistral's honor as I do my own." He looked at me, and something passed over his impassive face, but I couldn't decipher it. Months in my bed, weeks in my body, and I could not read the look in his eyes. "He has requested an audience with you, Princess. He says that he has a message from the queen."

"We do not have time for this," Frost said.

I agreed, but I also knew that ignoring messages or messengers from the queen was not wise. "We left her less than an hour ago, what could she want?"

"You," said a deep voice behind them.

Doyle looked a question at me, and I gave a nod. At a gesture from Doyle, Adair and he parted like a curtain to reveal Mistral.

His hair was the grey of a sky that promised rain, held back from his face in a ponytail. I had only a glimpse of his storm cloud grey eyes before he dropped to one knee and gave me only the back of his head. It was the first time that another sidhe, any sidhe, had voluntarily showed me such . . . respect. I stared down at the broad sweep of his shoulders in their tight leather armor, and wondered why he'd done it.

"Get up, Mistral."

He shook his head, sending his grey hair like a fall of water down his back, barely held in check by the leather thong that held it at the nape of his neck. "I owe you this at the very least, Princess Meredith."

I had no idea what he meant by that.

I looked at Doyle. He gave a small raise of an eyebrow, a slight turn of the head, his version of a shrug.

"Why do you owe me such a bow?" I asked.

He raised his head just enough so he could roll his eyes at

me. "If I had dreamt that you would take one look from me so seriously, I would have been more careful of you, Princess. My oath on that."

I knew what he meant then, for it had been the look of contempt on Mistral's face the night before that had helped me be brave enough to confront Andais when she was in the grip of an evil spell. A spell that had made her slaughter her own men, and be a danger to anyone near her. It had been a very clever assassination ploy. Mistral had told me with his eyes alone that I was just another useless royal, and he hated us all. It wasn't the hatred, but the uselessness that had moved me to action. Because I agreed with him. In that moment I had decided that I would rather die than see them slaughtered.

"Are you so certain one glance from you was what moved me forward?" I meant it to be a joke, but I'd forgotten how long it had been for some of the Queen's Ravens since they'd had a woman joke with them.

He lowered his face quickly, his voice uncertain and uncomfortable. "I am sorry, Princess, I presumed too much."

My kidding had not only fallen flat but embarrassed him. I'd had no idea my words had such power over Mistral. I touched his bowed head, the queen's ring on my right hand. Mark of her rulership, her first gift to me, and an artifact of power.

My fingers brushed his face a breath before the metal of the ring did. He turned those storm-grey eyes up to me. His lips parted as if he meant to speak, but the metal touched his skin, and there was no time for words.

I knew that our bodies still stood and knelt in the hallway inside the Unseelie Court. I knew it, because I'd had this happen before when the magic of the chalice and the ring combined. But to Mistral and me, we were on the top of a hill that was crowned by a large dead tree. I had seen this hill, this tree in one form or another in dreams and visions. Mistral knelt before me with my hand cupping his cheek. He put his hand over mine, holding my touch against his face, as he gazed around at the plain that spread out as far as the eye could see. It was green and lovely, but strangely empty.

"What have you done, Princess?"

"Not me," I said.

He gazed up at me, and there was puzzlement in his eyes. "I don't understand."

"Look at the tree."

He turned, with his hand holding mine now, rather than pressing it to his face. The tree was a huge, blackened thing, its bark crumbling in the growing wind. The first time I'd seen the tree so dead it had had a large cleft in the center. This tree did not. It had taken me a while to understand that the tree wasn't real, or the hill. Neither were any place a map could get you. The tree represented the Goddess, and the power of faerie; the hill was The Hill. We stood at the center of the world, but the center of the world changed at the thought of the gods. In this moment, this was the center, and Mistral and I stood at that center. We stood hand in hand, while the wind blew across the sky.

The wind smelled of apple blossoms and roses—sweet and clean and good. I heard a voice on the flower-scented wind. Or perhaps it was merely a thought. Mistral did not seem to hear it, so perhaps the voice was only for me.

"Kiss him," the wind said, "kiss him. Let him taste the chalice." But the chalice is not here, I thought. The wind said, "You are the chalice." Oh, of course. It made perfect sense in that moment, though I knew that later it might not make any sense at all.

"Mistral," I said, and the wind grew stronger, sweeter, at the sound of his name.

He looked at me, and there was a hint of fear in his eyes. Had it really been that long since he was touched by the Goddess? Yes, the voice in my head said, it had.

"Kiss me, Mistral," I said.

His gaze searched my face. "Who are you?"

"I am Merry."

He shook his head, even as he let me draw him in against my body. I realized that my arm was not injured in this place of dream and vision. I slid my arms around the smooth strength of his back, over the leather of his armor. His hands slid around my waist, but he was still shaking his head.

"No, you are not the princess."

"I am, but I am more, that is true." My voice had taken on that echoing softness that I'd heard before, like listening to someone else's voice in your own ears.

"What are you?" he whispered.

"Drink of the chalice, Mistral." The flower-scented wind wrapped around us like invisible arms, binding us until our bodies were pressed as close together as we could manage with clothes on. He held me, but he was afraid, and fear is not a good aphrodisiac for most people. The queen has never understood that.

His face bent toward me, but his body was tense, and he tried not to bend closer. The wind pushed at him, forced his head downward. I understood in that moment that he was once the master of the winds, bringer of storms. Once he had controlled it all as a man controls a horse, but now Mistral was the horse, who was being ridden, and he didn't like it.

Mistral fought against the push of the sweet wind. He fought to move his body away from mine, but the wind was like chains, and the best he could do with all that strength was keep his mouth just above mine. Keep himself just out of reach.

"Why do you fight when this is what you want?" the voice said, using my lips.

"You cannot be the chalice. You cannot be the Goddess; she cast us out long ago."

"If I am not real, then you cannot kiss me."

"You cannot be real."

"You were always my doubting Thomas, Mistral. Kiss me, kiss me, and discover the truth. Whether your doubts are real, or whether I am real." The wind pressed so tightly that it was hard to breathe. "Kiss me!" The voice came from my mouth, and echoed through the wind, and the drowning scent of blossoms.

His mouth touched mine, and the moment it did, he stopped fighting. He gave himself to the kiss with his lips, his mouth, his arms, his body. The wind was only wind again, but Mistral did not notice. He picked me up in his strong arms, his hands pressing me against his body. One hand gripped my ass, an almost crushing grip that brought a small sound from my mouth. That sound seemed to urge him on. The kiss had been thorough before, but it had had a certain gentleness to it; now he kissed me as if he would climb into my body through the opening of my lips. He kissed and ate with teeth at my mouth, biting and holding my lower lip until I cried out for him.

The smell of flowers was gone, and the wind smelled like ozone. Every hair on my body raised in goose bumps. Mistral drove us to the ground with him on top. I wasn't certain if it was to protect me, or to press the swollen front of him against my body. But we were on the ground a second before a jagged white blast of lightning fell from the clear sky and struck the dead tree.

Bolt after bolt fell from the sky hammering the tree, and with each strike the dead bark fell, revealing fresh pale bark underneath.

Mistral covered my body with his, shielding me as the lightning furrowed the earth on either side of the tree, even as it shook the dead away. Until at last the tree stood naked and new and alive. The broken, snaggled branches began to grow longer, fuller, and buds formed on the end of those branches. Blossoms spilled out, white and pink, and the scent of apples was thick and sweet. Her voice came to us at the end of the vision. "Go now, my doubting Thomas, and shake the dead away from the quick."

We came back to the hallway with Mistral still kneeling before me, my hand on his face, my hurt arm in a sling.

There were more of Mistral's men on the other side of us, but Doyle and Barinthus were keeping them back. I doubted much time had passed, but I heard Barinthus say, "The princess brought me back into some of my power with only a touch. Would you take that chance away from your captain, simply because you do not understand what is happening?"

Mistral smiled up at me, a fierce baring of teeth. His eyes boiled black with storm clouds so that he looked blind. He was suddenly on his feet, my hand still gripped in his. He jerked me against his body so hard it jarred my arm and drove a small moan of pain from me.

A sound came from his throat and deep in his chest, a sound that started as almost a purring, but ended in the low bass growl of distant thunder.

He ran his fingers through my hair, pulling a fistful sudden and tight in his hand. It was a small sharp pain but it was just this side of being too tight, too much.

He stared down at me, his face filled with a raw, naked lust, something separate and primeval like darkness and light. That divine spark that thrust into the first dark and brought life. That power was in Mistral's hands, in the press of his body hard and eager even through the prison of his leather.

He felt so big, so thick, against the front of my body. The press of him, the strength of his hands made me shudder against him. He tightened his grip on my hair, forcing me to fight my body's reaction, or cause myself real pain. My body wanted to buck and fight against his grip, but he'd given me a choice. Control myself or hurt myself. He knew the game, did Mistral.

The feeling of being trapped, of being helpless against his strength, his lust, and what my body needed was almost overwhelming. My eyes shuttered closed at the effort of not struggling in his harsh grasp.

He whispered against my face, and I could not focus enough to see him. "Do you want to ride the storm?" His breath was hot against my skin.

His voice promised no gentleness, no compromise. I knew the kind of sex he was offering, and the thought of it tightened things low in my body, drew another small sound from my throat. "Yes," I whispered, "yes."

The roll of thunder echoed down the hallway, shuddering between the stone walls. The sound seemed to vibrate out of his body and into mine as if my body were a tuning fork struck against the rim of some great metal cup. His voice growled against my skin, with the taste of thunder in it. "Good," he said and forced me to my knees.

Chapter 8

MISTRAL HELD ME ON MY KNEES, MY HEAD IMMOBILE IN HIS grip, as his other hand undid the front of his pants. Just watching him do it made my body react so strongly that I might have fallen to all fours if he hadn't held me up. Most of my lovers wouldn't let me go down on them because that wouldn't get me pregnant. Oral sex wouldn't make one of them king to my queen, and they would not waste seed on any other part of my body. I'd offered it as a part of foreplay, but most had refused even that for fear that I would bring them, and a chance would be wasted. I was left begging for the touch of them in my mouth.

Mistral was not worried about being king or making me pregnant. In this moment, he simply wanted me with no plan, no agenda, only his own long-denied need. That he would think first of pleasure and second of politics made me love him, just a little.

My skin began to glow softly. That faint dance of magic underneath my skin traveled up his hand and into his body. A faint white radiance started underneath his skin, like light reflected around a corner. Not the full-out shine of my skin, but something fainter, less sure of itself. I wondered if his glow had always been so hesitant. His body spilled out of his pants. He forced my mouth down on the long, thick shaft and I sucked long and hard on him. It threw his head back, bowed his body, and light burst from his skin. Cool white fire, blazing inside him, so that for a moment my eyes were dazzled.

If I had not held him in my mouth, felt his hand like a comforting pain in my hair, I would have believed that he had become light and power and magic, and had no true substance at all. But he shoved that wide and very solid piece of himself so far down my throat that breathing became an issue. I liked my men large, but I liked breathing more. I began to fight against his hold, my body starting to struggle to breathe.

I pushed at his body, and his hand relaxed, drawing my mouth down his thickness until I could draw breath, around the tip of him. I expected him to draw the rest of the way out of my mouth, but he didn't. He kept the tip of himself just inside me. When I'd drawn enough air, I ran my tongue delicately underneath the rim of his foreskin where it stretched tight across the hardness of him. It made him shudder from the hand in my hair, to the flesh in my mouth, to his hips under the press of my hands.

His body emerged from the radiance in edges, an outline of solid lines melting out of the brightness. His hair had burst its leather ribbon, and fell around him like a fall of white light. It was as if the rest of his body thrummed with light and power, except the part I held in my mouth. Maybe I couldn't have held him inside me if it all glowed like something carved of power.

He shoved himself deeper into my mouth, but I was afraid that he would shove too far as he had before. I distracted him with just an edge of teeth. It made him hesitate, and let me pull myself to the end of him again. I edged my tongue gently but firmly farther underneath the skin than I had before, so that I could lick inside that taut skin and the top of the shaft at the same time. It made him shudder and writhe above me. He looked down at me and his eyes were wide and wild with the sensation of it.

Wind began to play down the hallway, and his white, shining hair flared in that wind, a nimbus to frame his body. The wind grew until it streamed down the hallway in both directions, and I realized it was Mistral.

My hands slid to his pants, and I pulled carefully on the leather fastenings, until I could touch the soft skin of his testicles. They were loose enough that I could tease the skin between them, and roll them in my hands like delicate balls of tender flesh.

I forgot my earlier fear, and drove myself down the shaft of him, struggling to hold the width of him in my mouth. He'd gotten harder, which was more difficult to swallow, but it was worth the effort. Worth it to rest my mouth against those tender bits of skin and flesh, until I could lay the circle of my lips against the solid vibrating warmth of his body. Touching even that much of myself to the shining center of him left my lips tingling, and as I drew myself back down the length of him, it was as if that shivering power followed me. As if the touch of my lips had somehow allowed it to flow down this last length of his body.

I gave a final flick of my tongue, and when I drew him out of my mouth, he did not fight me. He gazed down at me with those wild eyes, and light flashed through them. It took me a second to realize I was seeing lightning. Lightning flashed through Mistral's eyes. Then came the first distant breath of ozone, like a storm that hadn't quite reached us yet, but the scent of it rode the wind and promised great and terrible things.

He made a sound low in his throat, and thunder growled down the hallway in answer.

My skin shone as if the moon had climbed inside me and was trying to melt out through my skin. We painted shadows along the walls. He dragged me to my feet by hair that had bled to red light, and I knew that my eyes were a blaze of green and gold like Christmas lights caught behind snow.

He turned me sharply in against the wall so that only my hands against the stones kept me from hitting face-first.

He kept his hand in my hair, but the other hand slid under my skirt until his fingers found the edge of my panties. He balled his hand into the satin, and I had a breath to brace before he ripped them from my body. The violence of it staggered me, and only his hand in my hair kept me against the wall. I realized that I was using my hurt arm, and it didn't hurt anymore. My hands pressed into the cool stone of the wall, as Mistral pulled my hips against his body.

He moved between my legs but not inside me. The feel of him hard and solid sliding between my thighs made me cry out, but he was more than a foot taller than I. There was no way to have intercourse with me facing the wall, not unless someone brought a box for me to stand on.

He shoved himself against me, sliding all that hard length across the most intimate parts of me. The feel of the head of him gliding back and forth across the sweetest of spots started that heavy warmth building between my legs. It wasn't just the softness of his skin and the hardness of his erection, but the power. The power acted as a sort of vibration against my body. I realized that if he didn't stop soon he'd bring me. I both wanted him to and didn't. Would my orgasm bring his, before he'd shoved himself up inside my body? Did I want him to spill himself across the outside of my body, or deep within? I was still hesitating when Mistral made the choice for me.

He jerked me back from the wall by my hair, so hard that I stumbled. He steadied me with his other hand on my arm, as if he hadn't meant to be quite that rough. He put me on my knees, and released his grip on my hair. It made me fall to all fours.

"On your back," he said, his voice hoarse, and followed by an echo of thunder between the stone walls. "I want you on your back."

I started to roll over, but it wasn't fast enough for him. His hands found my hips and rolled me onto the stone floor. He put his hands beneath my buttocks and pulled me forward, my knees bent, with only my jacket-covered back touching the floor.

Lightning flashed in his eyes so bright that it flickered around us like a strobe of light. It left my eyes dazzled, and when I could see clearly again, he was pushing himself against the opening to my body. His skin, his hair, everything was white with light and power. The only color left to him was the storm sky color of his eyes between lightning strikes.

He pushed himself inside me, using his hands to hold my

body where he wanted it. The feel of him entering me fluttered my eyes closed, parted my lips, and made me raise my hips up to meet his body.

He shuddered inside me, and when I opened my eyes he still had half his length to go. His fingers had tightened painfully on my body. He held me immobile with just his hands on the cheeks of my ass. "Don't help me," he said in a voice that was almost lost to a growl of thunder. "If you help, I won't last, and I want to last. I want this," and he squeezed his fingers tight enough to make me cry out, "to last."

I nodded because I didn't trust my voice.

He tried to shove himself inside me in one last movement, but he hadn't made enough room. He had to fight for it, pushing hard and deep with his hips, to work his width up inside me. He seemed to fill up every inch of me, as if I couldn't have held another piece of him. He almost drew himself out of me, then again that slow, hard push inside. The feel of him filling me was too much. He brought me screaming, back arching, before he'd made me open enough for him to truly do what he wanted.

I thought it would bring him, but when my pleasure passed, he was still hard and firm between my legs. But the orgasm had done one thing, I was more open. He finally had room to truly thrust, and he knew what to do with the room.

He let me slip to the floor, but I kept my legs up, knees bent, and he stayed propped up on his arms, hands flat on either side of me. I watched him go in and out of my body, as the twin glows of our power grew bright and brighter. I'd always described my glow as moonlight, but this was more like sunshine. My hair and eyes reflected around us like burning blood and emeralds and gold that had gotten so hot they melted into light.

Mistral found his rhythm and it was hard and fast and deep. He did it as if he could have done it all night. I smelled ozone. The hairs on my body stood to attention, and the air squeezed tight around us. I felt that warm building of pressure between my legs, and just as it rolled over me, spread through my body, he thrust one last time inside me. I knew in that instant that he'd been gentle before, because it was deep enough that it drove me up off the floor screaming. I dug my nails into his arms, half in pleasure, and half in pain.

Lightning cracked down the hallway in both directions. It didn't exactly come out of Mistral's body, but it came from the glow of him. His body shuddered inside me, and the lightning crashed down the hallway, thunder beating against the stones as if the force of it all would bring the walls down around us. And I didn't care.

I was trapped under the force and power of his body, blinded, deafened, by the explosion of his magic. My body became light, became magic, became pleasure. I forgot that there was skin to hold me, bones to move me. I simply was the pleasure.

When I was aware of my body again, the weight of Mistral was collapsed on top of me. He was still inside me, but not as hard or solid. He had thrown those wide shoulders to the side, so I wasn't suffocated under the bulk of him. I could feel his heartbeat thudding through his body as he fought to regain his breath. His hair was its usual grey, and his skin back to its normal slightly off-white, not as pure a color as my own. The armor on the one arm I could see was torn, and blood showed through. I tried to raise my hand to touch the damage, but I couldn't make that much of my body move yet.

A movement in the hallway beyond us made me turn my gaze to where Doyle and the others had been standing. Doyle was kneeling beside the far wall, dazed. Most of the others were flat on the floor, some immobile. Frost got to all fours, as I watched, shaking his head as if to clear his senses.

Rhys came around the corner with Kitto in tow. He drew his gun, obviously thinking it had been an attack. I couldn't blame him.

"Sex," Doyle said in a hoarse voice, "sex and magic." He cleared his throat sharply and tried again. "The Goddess and Consort have blessed us all."

"Shit," Rhys said, "and we missed it."

Galen's voice came heavy with afterglow. He was flat on his back, and the front of his pants was stained dark. "It sort of hurt. I don't like my sex that rough."

I heard groans from the other side of the hallway, and I could turn my head now. Mistral's men were all flat on their backs. Some were struggling to sit up. Adair tried to climb to his feet against the wall, and fell over with a metallic clatter. There was a black burn mark across the front of his armor.

"Goddess save us," someone said in a voice hoarse with pleasure.

"She just did." Mistral moved slowly so he could raise up enough to gaze down at me. He smiled, and his eyes were the blue of spring skies with fluffy little clouds floating through. I'd never known there was a sky that peaceful inside his eyes.

Hawthorne sat up in his green plate mail, propping his back against the wall. He, too, had a black burn mark across his chest. "The next time you plan to call lightning, warn those of us wearing metal. Mother of Gods, that hurt."

"And felt good," another voice said.

Hawthorne dragged his helmet off, showing a pale face, and his dark green hair braided to fit under the helm. He nodded. "And felt good." He looked at me, and for just a moment in the triple colors of his eyes—pink, green, and red—I saw a tree. A tree on a hill, and that tree was white with blossoms. He blinked and it was just the colors of his iris again.

I remembered the vision and how the lightning had cleared away the dead from the tree. Had we cleared away the old wood here? Had we done more than give them pleasure and pain? Time would tell. For now, we had a double homicide to solve. The police were on their way, and we hadn't even started to question the witnesses.

I said a little prayer. "Goddess, can we slow down the magical revelations until after we solve the murders, or at least until we get presentable for the police?" I didn't get an answer, not even that warm pulse that lets me know she's listening, which I took for a no. It wasn't that I didn't understand that bringing the magic back to faerie was important, maybe more important than solving murders. But I did not want the human police to find us spread around the hallway like an orgy gone horribly wrong.

Someone moved at the far end of the hallway. The person who sat up was female, decidedly female even under the armor. She took off her helmet and gasped at the air. Her curly black hair was cut very short, which was different from last I'd seen her, but the face was still Biddy. She was one of Cel's guards, half-human and half–Unseelie sidhe, even though she'd never been a fan of Cel. She'd once belonged to my father's guard, and when Cel co-opted many of my father's guards, she was trapped in the turnover. What was she doing here?

A shadow formed over her face and flowed down the bright silver of her armor. The shadow held a figure, a tiny figure. A baby like some dark ghost coiled in front of her.

The ring on my finger was suddenly warm against my hand, as if someone had breathed across the metal.

I gazed down the hallway, still trapped under Mistral's body. Biddy sat at the turn of the hall that was farther than the hallway to the kitchen. I shouldn't have been able to see her this clearly from this angle. But she stood out to my gaze as if she was outlined in something more real than the rest of the figures in the hallway.

Mistral whispered above me, "Do you see it?"

I whispered back, "I was going to ask you the same thing."

"A child," he said.

"A baby," I said.

"Go to her quickly, for the vision will not last. Somewhere in this hallway is her match. The father of that shadow child."

"What is that in front of Biddy?" Galen asked. He'd raised up on his elbows.

Mistral raised himself off of me. "Go to her, Meredith, go to her before the magic of the ring fades." He pulled me to my feet with his pants still undone. "Hurry." The tone in his voice made me start down the hall, unsteady on my feet in the high heels. The sex had been too good for my legs to be steady. I stumbled and had to catch myself against the wall. Hands steadied me, and I looked down to find Hawthorne's hands on my hips. "Are you all right, Princess?"

I nodded. "Yes." I gazed down the hallway at that solid shadow in front of Biddy. I felt as if that phantom child was whispering to me. Whispering, "I'm here." Other hands touched me as I stumbled and hurried. A handful of the others could see the shadow child. Their hands seemed to push and hurry me as much as catch me. The ring was like a warm weight on my hand, heavy with pressure. The pressure of a spell building, building to a great conclusion. I had to be touching Biddy before the spell burst. I wasn't sure how I knew that, but I was absolutely certain that the ring needed to be against her skin before the spell finished. Something would be lost if I failed.

Biddy had struggled to her feet, though her tri-grey eyes were a little unfocused, and she leaned heavily against the wall. I found my legs could move as the pressure built in the ring, like some warm living thing against my skin. I was running full out, and Biddy's eyes were wide and frightened. She couldn't see the spell, but she knew something was wrong.

I reached for her hand, and she reached automatically out to me. Her hand wrapped around mine just as the spell burst over us. It was as if the world held its breath, as if time and magic stopped, and there was a moment where Biddy and I stood outside of all of it. There was no sound, not even the hush of my own pulse. She stared at me, eyes huge with fear, or something I couldn't feel. The spell wasn't for me. I was merely the vessel for it. I had no idea what was happening to Biddy. I knew it didn't hurt, and that it was good, but what she heard in that moment must have been for her ears alone. The Goddess spoke to her, and I held her hand, let the magic take her while I was in silence, because I simply didn't need to know.

Sound came back with an audible pop. The change in pressure was real enough that we staggered when the magic released us. Our hands convulsed around each other as if the touch of flesh was all that kept us from falling. Her eyes were wide, her skin pale with shock. Biddy was tall, broad-shouldered, and wearing the remnants of her armor. Her gauntlets and her helmet, and other pieces lay scattered around her, as if she'd begun to shed the outer covering long before I reached her. She was dressed in bits of armor and the padding that even the sidhe must wear under such things. Her short hair was in disarray from the helmet and the magic that had put her against the wall. She was still lovely—nothing could take that away from her—but I'd seen her look better. Still, the way the men in the hallway looked at her, you'd have thought no woman had ever been more desirable than Biddy was in that moment.

Their faces held a soft wonderment, as if they saw something I did not. Some vision of female loveliness that left them speechless and immobile, literally stunned by what they saw or felt. The magic was not for me because if I'd been as besotted with Biddy as they all seemed to be, I couldn't have looked down the long corridor until I came to the right man.

For a moment I thought it was Doyle, and the thought squeezed my heart tight, but it was simply that his face did not hold the stunned look of the rest. In fact, his face looked suspicious, as if he was trying to decipher what he was seeing, or smelling, for he scented the wind as I watched. Frost was immobile against the wall, but his face, too, did not hold the wonderment. He seemed angry, sullen; his usual self. Galen's face was as lost as any of the other men's. I realized that Mistral, too, was seeing whatever I was seeing, because he had started down the hall ahead of my gaze, as if he saw things, too. I wore the ring, but he had been part of the magic that had brought this to life.

He paused by Doyle and Frost, and looked back at me, as if to make certain I saw them. I wasn't certain why it was important to him, but he nodded as if satisfied when he saw me see them.

Rhys stood at the end of the hallway. His face was sad but not enthralled. I looked at each of the men in turn with that same hyper-focus that I had seen in Biddy earlier. The magic was looking for something.

Kitto crouched at Rhys's feet as if he had been struck down by the magic, but his face held the same wonderment that the other men's did. I thought I was looking for someone who wasn't affected, but it was Mistral who showed me that I was looking for the man who was most affected, not least.

Mistral stopped before the colored glow of Nicca's wings. He held his hand out to the still-kneeling man. Nicca took his hand, but his face, now that I could see it, looked blind to Mistral, to anything but what he saw in Biddy.

His face had never looked more beautiful than it did in that moment, a delicate, almost feminine beauty that was usually disguised behind broad shoulders and a six-foot warrior's frame. In his sleep he could be soft and as gentle as he truly was, but awake he always had to be more.

Mistral drew him to his feet, and Nicca was suddenly himself, awake and moving with the smooth strength of his bare chest, and the huge wings like a shining colored frame for all that gentle beauty.

I admit that, for a moment or two, I felt regret. Regret that I would lose him, that he would never again grace my bed. But that selfish impulse was drowned in a feeling of such warmth, such peace, that I couldn't regret it, not truly. What I saw on his face as Mistral led him toward us was what I'd felt in the bed with him. He was too gentle for my tastes, and far too gentle for the queen's. The only thing he would ever have done as king was die.

I looked at Biddy's face, and saw in her eyes what I saw in Nicca's. Each of them saw the whole world in the eyes of the other, and it was a nice, safe, beautiful world.

The four of us stood at the end of the hallway, women on one side, men on the other. I expected Biddy or Nicca to reach out to the other, but they were immobile. Mistral and I clasped their hands together. That shadow child that I had seen at first was back, but it wasn't a phantom now. I saw a smiling face with Nicca's warm brown eyes and Biddy's black curls. I saw their child laughing and real, as if I could have touched the round baby curve of his face. I pressed my hand, and the warmth of the ring, into their flesh, and Mistral's big hand covered mine. We bound their hands together with magic, and the tears that I shed. I saw their child, and knew that he was real, and all we had to do to make that vision flesh was let them be together.

It was as if Mistral read my mind. "If the queen will allow it."

I blinked up at him as we drew our hands away and let Nicca and Biddy embrace for the first time. They kissed, a melding of body and hands, and they drew back from that first kiss with laughter.

I frowned up at Mistral, the tears still not dry on my cheeks. "The ring is alive again. It's what she wished. Life is returning to the courts."

He shook his head, and he looked so sad. "She wants her bloodline to rule the courts more than she wants the courts to thrive. If that were not true she would have made different choices centuries ago."

Doyle's deep voice came to me as he walked to us. "Mistral is right."

I frowned at both of them. "She'll demand that Nicca stay in my bed, until what, I get pregnant?"

They exchanged glances, then both nodded. Their solemn expressions were too well matched for my comfort. "At the very least," Mistral said.

I looked at Nicca and Biddy, oblivious to our worries. They touched each other as if they'd never seen a man or woman before, with light wonderment, as if they couldn't believe that they were allowed to touch this person in just this way.

I sighed, and it was as if wind trailed down the hallway. The magic was still there, still heavy with promise just behind my heartbeat, just underneath my skin. I could feel it. But as strong as it was, it was also fragile. I realized that the ring, like the chalice, had chosen to leave, or chosen to fade. It had decided that we didn't deserve its magic anymore. If Queen Andais did not allow Biddy and Nicca to be together, the magic was quite capable of leaving again, for good. Of leaving us to die as a people, for the gods only give so many second chances before they search for some other people to bless. We had a second chance and I didn't want Andais to throw that chance away.

I spoke out loud without meaning to. "If I'd known we'd be this deep in metaphysical wonders, I might not have called in the police." I shook my head, and tried to think of a way around the queen's obsession with her bloodline and mine. Nothing came to mind.

"I have an idea," Rhys said. "I'm not sure you're going to like it, though."

"Gee, Rhys, with an opening like that, how can I resist? Tell me your idea."

"If you told the queen you wanted both Nicca and Biddy in your bed at the same time, she might let that go."

"Yes," Doyle said, "she might. She has done it often enough herself." He turned solemn black eyes on me. "It would make her think better of you."

I frowned. "Better of me, in what way?"

"More like her," he said. "She searches in you for signs of herself. Signs that you are truly blood of her blood."

Frost was nodding. "I do not like it, but it would amuse her. It may work."

"If Biddy agrees," I said, looking at the happy couple.

"To be together after the ring has bound you," Mistral said, "you would do anything. Anything to be with your true love."

The sorrow in his eyes was something visible, tangible. I did not have to ask to know that once the ring had found his true love, and somehow he had lost her.

"Fine then," I said, "that's settled."

Frost touched my shoulder, then dropped his hand as if he wasn't allowed to. I took his hand in mine, held that gesture against me. It earned me a sad smile. "I know you are not a lover of women. It is good of you to take Biddy into your bed night after night until they are with child."

I squeezed his hand. "One time together and they will be

with child. I am certain of that. Even the queen won't divide them if they're pregnant."

"Andais knows you are not a lover of women," Doyle said. "She may insist on watching."

I sighed, then shrugged. "So be it."

Doyle and Frost both gave me a look. "Meredith," Frost said, "will you truly be part of her entertainment?"

"I want them together, Frost, and if I have to include myself in it the first time, and let the queen watch, so be it."

"When will you make your offer to the queen?" Doyle asked.

"After we've questioned the witnesses, and gotten the police safely inside the sithen. And only if she objects to them being a couple on their own." I smoothed my short skirt down. I was going to need underwear. The police tend to discount your authority if you flash them.

"I think most of us need to freshen our clothing," Doyle said.

I couldn't help it, I glanced down at his groin. It was hard to tell in the dim light of the sithen.

He gave that masculine chuckle. "Black is a wonderfully concealing color."

Frost flashed his grey jacket open just enough to show a stain. "Grey is not."

I looked at them. "Are you saying the magic brought everyone in the hallway?"

"Everyone who was standing here," Rhys said. "We missed the fun by moments."

There were other voices up and down the hallway, agreeing or bemoaning the paler colors they had chosen to wear. "We cannot all go freshen our clothes at the same time," Doyle said. "Some of us must stay here and work. The human police are on their way, and this has taken much of our time."

I wasn't wearing a watch; no one was, because watches and clocks ran oddly inside faerie. So oddly that telling time by them was useless. How did anyone know where to be and when? They approximated, and we spent a lot of time being fashionably late.

"Fine, divide everybody into shifts for a change of clothes, and could someone get me fresh underwear?"

Mistral held up my ripped panties. "I don't suppose these would be very useful. I am sorry that I damaged them." He held them out to me.

"I'm not sorry," I said, and pressed his hand back around the satin.

A pleased look filled his eyes, replacing the sorrow. His hands convulsed around the bit of satin. I noticed that he'd found time in all the fuss to tuck himself back inside his pants. "May I keep it as a sign of my lady's favor?"

I nodded. "You may."

He raised his hand to his face in an old-fashioned salute, but the look in his eyes made me shiver. He turned with a smile to get his men on their feet and give them their duties.

Frost had turned away. I caught his arm. "What is wrong?"

"Nothing, I'm going to go change." But he wouldn't look at me. Frost had a tendency to be moody. If I'd had more time I would have asked more questions, but the humans were coming, and we were out of time. I promised myself that if he stayed sulky I'd find out what was wrong. I was hoping it was some momentary mood and nothing more.

Doyle said, "Let him go, he'll need a little time to adjust."

I frowned at him. "Adjust to what?"

Doyle gave a smile that was more sad than happy. "Later, if you still need to ask, I will explain, but now we have very little time to question our witnesses. You have called the police into the sithen, Princess, and we must prepare."

He was right, but I wanted to know what had I missed. It couldn't be just about sex with Mistral, they'd all seen me have sex with others. But if not that, then what? I shook my head, smoothed my short skirt, and put it from my mind. We had a crime to solve if the Goddess would give us enough free time to do it. I couldn't seem to control the wild magic that was returning to us, but I could at least pretend to control the murder investigation. Though the tight feeling in my stomach told me I didn't have much control over either.

Chapter 9

SOME OF THE MEN WENT TO CLEAN UP. OTHERS WENT TO AWAIT the police at the door to the sithen because they would never find their way in on their own. The door moved, and it didn't like strangers. Only magic could hold the door open for mortal step that had never crossed its threshold before. When we had divided everyone up, we found we were missing someone. Onilwyn hadn't been in the hallway. He hadn't gone with Rhys, so he hadn't returned with him. He was simply gone. He'd been Cel's creature for centuries. I did not like that he had gone missing just after such a major magical happening. It made me think he'd gone to tattle to his true master, or whoever was bearing tales to Cel in his prison cell.

We threaded our way between the two bodies that were still waiting for the police. When we were close to the large kitchen door, I heard shouting and barking. Maggie May's accent was thick because she was angry. "You are a bla'guard, tree man, that you are. Get out of my kitchen!" Her little terriers were doing their version of shouting right along with her.

"I'm trying," a man's voice yelled.

We got to the door in time to see a cast-iron skillet the size of a small shield smash into Onilwyn's back. It staggered him, and other pots and pans drove him to all fours. Pans of copper and stainless steel flashed their polished brightness as they hit his body, but it was the deep black cast-iron skillets in their various sizes that were beating him down. Cold iron has been proof against faeries for a very long time. The sidhe may rule faerie, but cold iron still hurts.

Maggie May stood in her kitchen, surrounded by a storm of pots, pans, ladles, spoons, forks, and knives, like an evil metal snow globe with her small brown figure as its centerpiece. The ladles joined the attacks of the pots and pans. Onilwyn was now flat to the floor, arms over his head for protection. Three faerie terriers were darting in and out to nip at him. The plumpest dog had sunk teeth into his boot top and was trying to shake it to death.

His sword lay on the floor by the large black stove. If you're going to attack a brownie never do it on their home turf.

"She's gone bogart," Galen said over the crashing of metal.

I looked harder at her face. All brownies have skull-like faces because they have no nose, just nostrils. But if their faces look like evil grinning skulls, then they have gone evil—bogart. Brownies can thresh a field of wheat in a single day, or build a barn overnight. Think of that much power turned destructive, insanely destructive. They still tell stories in a lonely part of Scotland border country of a laird who raped and murdered a local girl. He didn't realize her family had been adopted by a brownie. The laird and all his household were cut to pieces.

Maggie May was not quite a bogart, but she was working up to it.

"No," Doyle said, "not bogart, not yet, but we must find a way to distract her before the knives join the battle."

"Seems a shame," Rhys said.

I agreed, but true bogarts are part of the sluagh, the evil host, not true Unseelie Court anymore. Maggie deserved better, no matter how I felt about Onilwyn.

Rhys shouted, "Maggie May, it's Rhys! You sent for me, remember!"

The spoons swirled in to join the ladles, which left only the heavy iron forks, big enough to turn a side of beef, and the knives. We were running out of time.

I said the only thing I could think of that might shock her into listening. "Aunt Maggie, what happened to upset you?"

The pots began to slow like a swirl of heavy snowflakes brought to rest by a gentle wind. That wind laid them in neat lines on the heavy wooden table. "What d' ye say?" she asked, and her voice was thick with suspicion.

"I said, Aunt Maggie, what happened to upset you?"

She frowned at me. "I'm not Aunt Maggie to you, girl."

"You are my great-grandmother's sister on my mother's side. That makes you my great-aunt Maggie."

She still looked unhappy, but nodded slowly, and said, "Aye, that be true. But you are a princess of the sidhe, whatever your blood be or be not. The sidhe donna acknowledge us."

"Why not?" I asked.

She rubbed her hairy fingers across her noseless face and frowned harder. "Princess Meredith, ye needs be more careful of who you be talkin' in front of." She looked at Onilwyn, who was getting painfully to his feet. There was blood on his pale skin.

"Yes, he is Cel's creature. But Cel knows my bloodlines."

"The sidhe know only what they wish to know about the blood that runs through their veins." As she calmed her accent began to vanish. Her voice was cultured and midwest, nowhere like a news anchor. She'd cultivated that voice by talking on the phone to other faerie terrier fanciers across the country and the world. You couldn't get a new breed of terrier recognized by the American Kennel Club if no one could understand what you were saying to them.

"Denying my heritage won't change what I am," I said. "It won't make me one inch taller, or look one bit more royal sidhe."

"Mayhaps," Maggie said, smoothing her hands down her shapeless dress, "but it is not brownie blood that will put you on the throne."

I reached over to the big cast-iron skillet where it lay on the table. I wrapped my hand around its cool metal handle. It was inert under my hand, just metal to me. I lifted the heavy skillet, changing my grip until I had the balance of it. "But it's brownie blood that helps me do this."

Her eyes narrowed at me. "Aye, or human."

"Or human," I agreed.

Onilwyn swayed and collapsed back to his knees. If he'd been human, he would probably have been dead.

"What set you and your dogs on him?" I asked.

Two of her terriers had come to her feet, but the plump one still growled at Onilwyn. I realized the dog wasn't fat, she was pregnant. The bitch was so full of puppies that she waddled when she finally went back to Maggie's call.

"Dulcie went to sniff his foot," Maggie said. "She growled at him a bit. She would nae have bit him." Her thin strong hands balled into fists. She seemed to be controlling herself with effort. "He kicked her, and her full of puppies. He kicked ma dog."

My first memory was of being in a small dark cupboard with squirming puppies. One puppy was more than my lap could hold. A huge dog sat by the thin line of light of the curtains that covered the front of our hole. The silky fur of the faerie terrier puppies and that alert dog is still an utterly vivid memory. My father once told me what I, at around eighteen months, didn't remember. My father and Barinthus had both been called away, so my father had left me with Maggie May. The queen's steward had come unrepentantly to check on some dish for that night's banquet. If the queen knew my father hid me in the kitchens, it would no longer be a haven for me.

I'd crawled into the cupboard with the puppies and their mother, as I often did. I was very gentle with them even then, Maggie had told me once. When the steward came, she just closed the drapes hiding both me and the puppies. The steward didn't believe it hid just puppies, so he tried to peek and the mother dog bit him. She protected her puppies and me.

To this day the scent and feel of the terriers was a comforting thing to me. I don't know what I would have said or done to Onilwyn about his behavior because he decided for me.

Rhys and Galen both yelled, "Don't!"

I sensed Doyle and others moving, but I was next to the

kneeling Onilwyn as he raised his hand and called his magic, pointing it at Maggie May.

I didn't think, I just reacted. My hand was still wrapped around the iron skillet. I hit him full in the face with as much strength as I had in one arm. I'm not as strong as a full-blooded sidhe, or even brownie, but I can punch my way through a car door and not hurt myself. I did that once to discourage a would-be mugger.

Blood flew from around the skillet, a bright surprised scarlet spray. He collapsed to his side, moaning softly. His nose looked like a squashed tomato, and there was so much blood it was hard to tell what other damage I'd done to his face.

There was a thick silence in the room. I think I surprised everybody, including myself.

Rhys shook his head, squatting down by the fallen man. "You really don't like him, do you?"

"No," I said, and realized that the thought of letting Onilwyn touch me was repulsive. He'd been one of my main tormentors when I was a child. I still hated Cel and some of his cronies enough to feel nothing but a sense of utter satisfaction at the ruin of Onilwyn's face. It wasn't like he wouldn't heal.

The little terrier he had kicked came up to him growling. She sniffed his blood, then sneezed sharply as if he smelled bitter. She turned her back on him, and dug her feet into the floor, throwing blood into the air, a dominant, defiant gesture.

The dog went back to her mistress and the two other dogs so the three of them sat in a smiling, butt-wriggling row at Maggie's feet. Maggie May was grinning at me with strong yellow teeth showing. "Oh, ah, you be kin."

I nodded, and handed the bloodied skillet to her. "Yes, yes, I am." I smiled at her and she laughed, a great roar of laughter. She wrapped her arms around me, hugging me tight. It surprised me for a heartbeat, but then I hugged her back just as tight. Here was someone else who wasn't touching me to gain anything. She hugged me because, just because. Hugs for no reason, just because were nice, and lately I wasn't getting enough of them.

Chapter 10

A HIGH, RINGING SOUND CAME. WE ALL LOOKED AROUND THE room, but there was nothing to account for the sound. It came again. It was as if the finest crystal goblet were being struck with metal, so that it made that high, ringing, bell-like tone only the best crystal makes.

Rhys was unsheathing his short sword. "I left Crystall in charge outside with the police." He held the naked blade up before his face. "You rang?"

Crystall's face appeared dim and pale in the blade. "Rhys, I am unsure how to proceed."

"What's wrong?" Rhys asked.

"I think that we need someone here who is more conversant with modern police and modern politics."

Rhys shook his head. "I didn't ask what you needed. I asked what's wrong."

"As far as I can ascertain, the humans are arguing about who is in charge."

"In charge of what?"

"Everything," Crystall said. "They seem to have no clear hierarchy. It is like a game of too many princes."

Rhys sighed. "I'll be there as soon as I can, Crystall."

"I am sorry, Rhys, but none of us here spend much time outside the land of faerie."

"It's all right. I'll be there." Rhys wiped the blade clean with a movement of his hand. He looked at Doyle. "I didn't think we needed someone more modern with the police; I should have."

"Do not apologize," Doyle said. "Simply fix it."

Rhys gave a bow and went for the door. He walked past me, but it was something on the other side of the room that attracted my attention.

I saw something over Maggie May's shoulder. Movement. The curtain under the sink, where I'd hidden as a child, fluttered. Something was behind that piece of cloth, something bigger than a small dog.

Adrenaline rushed through me so hard and fast that my fingertips tingled with it. I had assumed that someone had searched the area for the killer. Had I assumed wrong?

I broke the hug with Maggie May with a squeeze, fighting to control my face and body. I wanted to alert Doyle and the others without alerting whoever was hiding.

Doyle was just beside me as if I'd given myself away, by some hesitation or movement. He opened his mouth, but I touched his lips with my fingers. He took the hint. He stood mute before me and did not ask what I'd feared, not out loud. With his dark eyes, he asked, What is wrong? But not out loud.

I glanced, using only my eyes, behind me. I tried for the angle I wanted but wasn't certain he'd understand.

He knelt by Onilwyn's moaning form and said, "Why did you leave us, Onilwyn? Why did you come ahead to the witnesses?"

The only answer was a soft, bubbling moan.

Doyle positioned himself so he could see the sink area while he questioned the fallen man.

I fought not to look behind me.

Doyle leaned in close to Onilwyn. "Are you saying a brownie and a half-human princess have struck you such a blow that you are brought low?"

He made no sign that I could see, but Galen called out, "Peasblossom, Mug, come out and talk to us." He walked around the table, and for a moment I thought the two little fey had been the ones hidden under the sink and I was simply too suspicious.

I turned to see him go to the open cabinets above the sink area. Mug, the pale blue fey that had come to fetch Rhys, and another tiny winged figure were peeking out from among the teacups. It was Mug's voice, high and twittering like the song of birds made human speech, that answered, "We feared Maggie'd forget us in her anger, Galen Green Knight."

He was by them now, gazing up at them. "So you hid among the teacups."

"Unless she was bogart for good, she'd not bust up the good china. No she wouldn't!" Mug walked carefully out from between the cups and flittered sky blue wings to flutter down to Galen's shoulder. I remembered Mug now; she'd been a pet once of one sidhe or another. But when her last master had grown tired of her, Maggie had invited her into the kitchen, so she could earn an honest living and not have to cater to the whim of one of the large ones. Large one was an insulting term used by the lesser fey for the sidhe. Mug had come to the kitchen about the time I left faerie. Peasblossom, on the other hand, her I knew.

I called to her, "Peasblossom, there's no need to hide."

Frost had moved up on the other side of the sink from Galen, who was chatting away with the tiny blue fairy on his shoulder. She'd cuddled close to his neck, hands as delicate as pale blue petals, stroking along the bareness of his ear. Mug had a real "thing" for sidhe men. I'd never asked, nor wanted to speculate, what pleasure she and her masters had gotten from each other. She was smaller than a Barbie doll and more delicate looking. I did not need the visuals. I was able to look at them and keep an eye on the curtain without staring at it. Galen gave us all a reason to look in that direction.

Frost said, "Come down, little one, so we may question you."

The tiny face scooted back among the good china, like a mouse ducking back into its hole. Her voice was like the sighing of the wind, a delicate spring breeze that warmed the skin and made you believe that the flowers merely slept under the snow. And were not dead. Her voice brought a smile to my face before I had time to think glamour.

"I don't remember your voice being so sweet, Peasblossom," Galen said.

"I'm frightened," she said, as if that explained it.

Maggie May translated, "When the demi-fey be scared, they use what defense they have."

"Their glamour," I said.

"Aye," she said. She was watching us all with narrowed eyes. She knew something was up.

"Come, little one," Frost called, and even extended a hand like you'd offer a perch to a bird.

"I fear you, Killing Frost, as I fear the Darkness," the voice said from among the cups.

"Do you fear me, Peasblossom?" I asked.

Quiet for a moment, or two, then, "No, no, I do not fear you."

"Then come to me," I said, and held my hand out to show I preferred a less intimate perch for her.

"You will protect me from the Darkness and the Killing Frost?" she asked.

I fought the urge to smile. It took concentration to fight off that pleasant sound. Touching would make it harder still, but I wanted her away from the sink area. She was a civilian, and if whatever was under the sink fought, I didn't want any civvies in the line of fire.

"Come, Peasblossom, I won't let them hurt you."

"You promise?"

Doyle interrupted, "She cannot promise, for we do not know you are innocent."

"Innocent," she said, her voice rising with her fear, the wind clanging among chimes. "Innocent of what, Darkness?"

He stayed kneeling by Onilwyn, who had not risen to bait or answered questions. He was either that hurt or feigning. "It is but a step from finding a body to pretending to find a body that you put there."

I frowned at him. No wonder he'd scared her.

He gave me a calm flick of his eyes, as if he saw nothing wrong with what he'd said.

Peasblossom was moaning in terror, hysterical. The illusionary wind was not warm now but cold with that icy threat of storm on its edge.

The teacups rattled with her frantic attempt to shove herself tighter against the back of the cabinet.

I had to raise my voice to be certain she could hear me. "I promise that neither Frost nor Doyle will harm you."

Doyle said, "Merry," as if I'd surprised him.

Silence from the teacups, then in a very neutral voice, "You promise?"

"Yes," I said. I didn't think she was guilty of anything, but just in case, I'd promised only that Frost and Doyle would not harm her. If she took that to imply that I'd promised her none of my guards would harm her, that wasn't my fault. I was sidhe enough and fey enough to split the difference with her and not feel guilty. Every fey from least to greatest knew the kind of games we all played. To lose meant you were careless. Your own damned fault. She eased around the china cup and came to the edge of the shelf. She was one of the rare demi-fey that had skin like a human's. Her hair was dark brown, falling in waves around her face. Only the delicate black lines of antennae ruined the perfect doll look. That and the wings she flicked across her back.

Her dress looked like it was formed of brown and purple leaves, though when she stepped off the shelf the "leaves" moved like cloth. She flew toward me, and a glance from Doyle made me move farther away from the table, farther away from the curtain.

One of the other guards called, "Maggie May, could you come here for a moment?" I think if she hadn't been suspicious, she'd have argued, but she let herself be called out of the line of danger.

Peasblossom adjusted her angle to follow me and put delicate feet on the palm of my hand. Her feet were not as baby soft as Sage's had been, but her weight was like his, heavier than it should have been, as if there was more to her than a doll-size body and butterfly wings.

Ivi and Hawthorne moved in front of me, so my view was blocked, but they were offering their very bodies as shields to keep me safe. I could not protest.

Ivi whispered, "I hope I get to fuck you before you get me

killed." Hawthorne smacked him in the chest with his mailed fist.

He made an *oof* sound, then I heard cloth rip and the shouting begin.

Peasblossom darted to my shoulder, hiding in my hair, screaming wordlessly and in terror.

Such a small creature to make so much noise: I heard the men yelling, but what they yelled was lost to Peasblossom's shrill screams. The broad bodies of the guard kept me safe, but also hid the action from me, so I was left unknowing, unseeing, and could only trust that nothing too bad was happening. I took it as a good sign that the guards were still merely standing in front of me and didn't feel the need to hide me between the floor and their bodies. Things weren't deadly, yet.

Peasblossom clung to my hair and jacket, shrieking right next to my ear. I fought the urge to grab her and stop the screams. I was afraid I'd crush her wings, and with Beatrice's death, I was no longer certain what would and would not heal on the lesser fey.

I put my hand between her and my ear but jerked it away, because something pricked me, like a thorn or pin.

She stopped screaming and started apologizing. Apparently I'd caught my fingers on her rose-thorn bracelet. My fingertip held a minute spot of blood.

Doyle's deep voice cut off Peasblossom's babbling apology. "Why were you hiding from us?"

A rough male voice said, "I wasn't hiding from you; I was hiding from him."

I tried to peer around Adair and Hawthorne, but when I tried to move around them they moved with me, blocking my view and keeping me safe.

I called, "Doyle, is it safe?"

"Hawthorne, Adair, let the princess see our prisoner."

"Prisoner?" the rough voice said. "Princess, there's no need for that." There was something vaguely familiar about the voice.

The two guards moved, and I was finally able to see the

hairy, smallish figure Frost and Galen held between them. He was a hob, a relative to the brownie.

Harry Hob, he'd worked in the kitchens off and on for years. Off when Maggie May caught him drunk on the job, on when he could control himself. He was only about three feet tall and covered in so much thick, dark hair that it took a minute to realize he was naked.

"Why are you afraid of Onilwyn?" Doyle asked.

"I thought he'd come to kill me, the way he killed my Bea."

I think we all took a breath and forgot to let it out.

"Did you see him do it?" Doyle asked. His deep voice fell into the silence like a stone thrown down a well. We waited for the stone to hit bottom.

But it was Onilwyn's voice that came first. "I did not." His voice was thick, not with emotion, but with blood and the broken mess of his nose. "I did not know her well enough to kill her." He struggled to his feet, and with no prompting from anyone, Adair and Amatheon took his arms, as if he were already a prisoner. In that moment I knew I wasn't the only one who disliked Onilwyn.

He kept protesting his innocence in that same thick voice that sounded like he had a very bad head cold, but I knew it was his own blood he was choking on.

"Silence!" Doyle said, not a yell, but his voice carried all the same.

Onilwyn was silent for a moment, until Harry Hob said, "I saw—"

Onilwyn cut him off. "He lies."

Harry made himself heard then, bellowing loud enough to shake the cups on their shelves. "I lie! I lie! It takes a sidhe to be a liar inside fairie."

Doyle stepped between them, motioning them both to silence. "Hob, did you see Onilwyn kill Beatrice?" He turned at a sound from Onilwyn. "If you interrupt again, I will have you dragged from this room."

Onilwyn made a sound, then spat blood on the kitchen floor.

Maggie May stalked toward him with a small iron pot in her hand.

"No, Maggie," Doyle said, "we'll have no more of your bogarting."

"Bogarting? Why, Darkness, if you think that was bogarting, you must never have seen a true bogart." There was something threatening in her golden eyes.

"Don't force me to have to ban you from your own kitchen, Maggie May."

"Yo' wouldna' dare!"

He just looked at her, and the look was enough. She backed off, muttering under her breath, but she put the pot down and went to the far corner. Her dogs boiled about her feet like a furry tide.

Doyle looked back to Harry Hob. "Now, once more, did you see Onilwyn kill Beatrice or the reporter?"

"If not to finish the job, then why did he come ahead of you all into the kitchen? Why not ask him that?"

Doyle's voice was low and almost evil sounding, with an edge of a growl. "I ask you one last time, Harry. If you do not answer me straight and simply, I will let Frost shake you until some answer falls out."

"Ah, now, Darkness, no need to threaten old Harry."

"Old Harry, is it?" Doyle smiled. "You can't claim age here, not among us. I remember you as a babe, Harry. I remember when you had a human family and farm to tend."

Harry scowled at him, a look as unfriendly as he'd given Onilwyn. "No need to bring up hard memories, Darkness." He sounded sullen.

"Then answer me straight, and no one here need know how you lost your place."

"You wouldna' tell," Harry said.

"Give me truth, Harry Hob, or I will give you truth you don't wish shared."

Harry scowled at the floor. He looked somehow diminished and more delicate than he should have, held between the two tall guards. Maybe he was playing for sympathy, but if so, he was playing to the wrong audience.

Doyle knelt in front of him, staying on the balls of his feet. "One last time, Harry; did you see Onilwyn kill Beatrice and/or the human reporter?"

The "and/or" had been a nice touch, because without it Harry would have room to wiggle: if he'd seen only one murder, but not both.

He answered, still staring at the floor, "No."

"No, what?" Doyle asked.

Harry looked up at that, his dark eyes glittering with anger. "No, I didna' see the tree lord slay my Beatrice or the human."

"Then why did you hide from him?"

"I did not know he was hid there," Maggie May said. "Mayhaps, Darkness, it was na' the tree lord he first hid from."

"Very good," Doyle said, acknowledging it with a nod of his head. He stood and asked Maggie's question: "Why did you hide yourself, Harry?"

"I saw him," and he used a nod, since his arms were still held, to point at Onilwyn, who was also still being held.

We waited for him to say more, but he seemed to think he'd said enough. Doyle prompted him, "And why should the mere sight of Onilwyn make you hide?"

"Thought he was her sidhe lover, didno' I."

I couldn't help it. I laughed. Harry gave me a dirty look.

"I'm sorry, Hob, but Onilwyn doesn't think even I am pure-blooded enough. I can't imagine him having a completely non-sidhe lover."

"Thank you, Princess," Onilwyn said in that still thick voice.

I gave him the look he deserved and said, "It wasn't a compliment."

"Just the same," he said, "I am grateful for the truth."

"Who but her sidhe lover would come here alone?" Harry asked.

"Good question," I said and looked at Doyle.

He gave a small nod and said, "Why did you abandon us, Onilwyn?"

"I had no interest in watching the princess perform with someone else. The queen cured me of voyeurism a very long time ago."

None argued with that, but Doyle asked, "So you came ahead to begin questioning the witnesses on your own, without either of your captains' or even your officers' permission?"

"You all seemed . . . busy." And even with the broken nose the sarcasm came through loud and clear.

"You didn't hit him hard enough, Merry," Galen said, and my gentle knight had a decidedly ungentle look on his face.

"Did you come ahead to seek answers, or to hide them?" Doyle asked.

"I was not the lover of anyone. And I would most certainly not risk the queen's mercy for anything less than a sidhe." The disdain in his voice was thick enough to walk on.

"Did any of the rest of you know that Beatrice had a sidhe lover?" Doyle asked.

Maggie May said, "No, I've told all mah' people that you leave the big ones alone. Only grief comes of it."

"So, if Beatrice had taken a sidhe," I said, "she'd have hidden it from you?"

"Ah, most like."

I looked to the dainty blue figure that was almost hidden behind Galen's neck. "Mug?"

Galen had to say, "The princess is asking you a question, Mug."

She'd been too busy playing in the curls at the back of his neck to pay attention to anything else. She wasn't stupid, but I'd seen her like this before, as if the touch of a sidhe was intoxicating to her.

She peered around his neck, her wings flicking nervously. "What?" she asked.

"Did Beatrice have a lover that you know of?"

She pointed to Harry. "Him."

"Did she have a sidhe lover?" I asked.

Mug's eyes went wide. "A sidhe for a lover? Beatrice . . ." She shook her head. "If I had known, I would have asked her to let me touch him."

"Beatrice would never have told Mug," Peasblossom said.

I looked for her and found her perched on the pots that hung from hooks on the near wall. "Did she tell you?"

"She did."

"Who was her sidhe lover?" Harry asked, voice eager.

None us said anything, because it was one of the things we all wanted to know.

"She wouldn't tell me, said he made her promise not to tell anyone or he would break off the relationship."

"Why would that end the relationship?" Doyle asked. "Unless . . ."

Frost said it. "Unless he was a royal guard."

"Who would risk death by torture for less than sidhe flesh?" Amatheon said.

I gave him an unfriendly look.

"I do not deserve that look, Princess; it is only truth."

I started to argue but hesitated. I had had lesser fey lovers in Los Angeles, and it had been wonderful, but . . . but I had craved other flesh. Once you have had the full attention of another sidhe, all else was truly lesser. I wanted to argue with Amatheon, but I could not, not and be truthful.

"I will not argue with you, Amatheon," I said.

"Because you cannot," he replied. He kept his grip on Onilwyn, but his attention seemed all for me.

I acknowledged the truth of it with a nod.

"But if not a guard," Galen asked, "then why would he care if others knew of his relationship with Beatrice?"

I looked at him, searching his face for any hint that he knew how naïve that question was, but there was nothing in his face that said he understood anything.

Mug cuddled in against his neck and spoke for most of us. "That is so sweet."

"What?" Galen asked.

"A fair few dabble among us lesser folk," Maggie May said, "but few wish to acknowledge us publicly."

Galen frowned. "Why not?"

Amatheon said, "Have you been living in the same court as the rest of us?"

Galen shrugged, almost unseating Mug. He helped her catch her balance by holding up his fingers so she could catch herself. "Love is too precious to be ashamed of."

If I hadn't already loved him, I would have in that moment.

"You are right, my friend," Doyle said, "but that is not always how our free brethren feel about such things."

"Arrogance, such arrogance, to be ashamed of that which the rest of us would give so much to have," Adair said.

"Who would admit to bedding something with wings?" Onilwyn said.

"Good enough to fuck, but not to love?" Maggie May asked.

Some of the men would not meet her gaze. Doyle had no trouble meeting those hard golden eyes. "Was Harry Hob her lover?"

She nodded. "Aye."

Mug and Peasblossom answered together, "Yes."

Doyle turned back to Harry. "It's not every hob who gets to share a mistress with a sidhe."

"Mistress, nay, I loved the girl."

"How did you feel about sharing the girl you loved with another?"

"Beatrice had broken up with Harry," Peasblossom said.

"But we was back together," Harry said.

Peasblossom acknowledged that was true.

"She had broken up with the sidhe," he said.

"Dumped a sidhe for you?" Mug said, and laughed, a high twittering sound.

"Don't you laugh at him, Mug," Maggie May said. "Sometimes love is more than a magic or grand power."

"Did you know that Beatrice had let Harry go?" I asked.

"Aye, and that she'd taken 'im back, too."

"If she'd broken with him," Doyle said, "why did Harry expect him down in the kitchens?"

"Beatrice said he wanted her to do awful things for him. She'd agreed at first, then changed her mind."

"What kind of awful things?" Doyle asked.

"She wouldna' tell me. Said it was so awful, no one would believe it of him."

We were Unseelie, not Seelie, which meant we were willing to admit most of what we wanted. What could be so terrible that it wouldn't be believed? What perversion that Beatrice had turned from it in fear?

"Her sidhe lord had demanded one last meeting, to try and persuade Beatrice to reconsider. I begged her not to meet with him."

"Why? Did you fear for her safety?" Doyle asked.

"No, not that. If I had ever dreamed such a thing, I would never have let her meet him alone," Harry replied.

"Then why didn't you want them to meet?"

"I was jealous, weren't I? I feared he'd win her back. Goddess help me, but all I could see was my jealousy."

Doyle must have given some signal, for Frost and Galen let go of Harry's arms. He stood there rubbing the arm that Frost had held.

"And you hid when you saw Onilwyn, because you thought he was her lover."

"We thought he'd come back to kill Harry," Peasblossom said. "If she'd have told anyone the secret it would have been Harry. I told him to hide."

"If you feared only Onilwyn, why didn't you come out when you knew we were all here?" Doyle asked.

"Would you want anyone to know that you hid, 'stead of fight the man you thought had killed the woman you loved? Did I want the Darkness or the Killing Frost to know I was such a coward?" Tears gleamed in his eyes. "I didna' know meself I was such a coward."

"Onilwyn," Doyle said, "the real reason you came ahead?"

He opened his mouth, had to clear his throat sharply before he said, "Truth then, I know the princess loathes me. With this many men at her beck and call, she could keep me from her bed for some time. I wanted to touch a woman again. I thought if I found some clue, helped solve this mess, it might help my cause."

I stared at his bloody face, those angry eyes. He met my gaze.

"Why don't I believe you?" I asked.

His eyes were angry and sullen in the bloody mask of his face. "Would I admit such weakness to you, if it were not true?"

I thought about that for a second or two. "You hate me, too," I said.

"I would do near anything to end this need, Princess. Whatever I felt once, the chance to slake this thirst outweighs whatever loyalty I thought I held."

We stared at each other, and I didn't know what I would have replied because suddenly Doyle said, "Do you smell that?"

Chapter 11

DOYLE SNIFFED THE AIR, AND A MOMENT LATER I SMELLED IT, too. Fresh blood. I moved toward him. "What do you smell, Darkness?" Maggie May asked.

He put his hand to his sword, and the other men were suddenly unsheathing weapons. I don't think any of them had smelled what we had, but they trusted Doyle's instincts.

"It's all right," he said, but he unsheathed his sword, and that didn't comfort anyone in the room. When he had the blade completely free of its sheath, blood welled on the naked blade, as if the sword were bleeding.

Harry stumbled back away from him and that dripping sword. I couldn't blame him. Peasblossom screamed, and Mug hid her face against Galen's neck.

"Goddess save us," Frost said. "What is it?"

"Cromm Cruach," Doyle said.

It took me a second to realize he was using Rhys's original name, when he'd been a deity. Cromm Cruach, red claw. As

I watched the blood drip on the scrubbed kitchen floor, I began to understand where the name may have come from.

Maggie May said, "Cromm Cruach, aye. Well, what does he say?"

The blood formed letters on the floor: DON'T YOU CARRY ANY NONMAGICAL WEAPONS?

"Oh," Doyle said, and I swear he looked almost embarrassed. "May I borrow a kitchen knife, Maggie May?"

She narrowed her eyes at him, but nodded. "Aye."

He took one of the long, wicked-looking chopping blades and laid a finger down the flat of the blade. The silver of the blade fogged instantly.

Rhys's face shone in the shiny surface. "Do you know how much blood I've had to waste trying to get you?"

"I did not think I was carrying only enchanted blades," and again, I had the rare treat of seeing Doyle shamefaced at not thinking of something.

"Whose blood did you use?" Galen called.

"Mine. I heal now, but it still hurts to do it, and it's totally freaked the cops out."

"How many additional men do you need?" Doyle asked.

"I'm not sure. It all depends on how many of the police Merry lets into the sithen."

I went to stand by Doyle, so Rhys could see me better. "How many police are there?"

"Counting the local cops or the feds?" Rhys asked.

"Feds?" I said. "You mean FBI?"

"Yep."

"I didn't call them into this."

"They say you called an Agent Gillett."

"I called him, but not to invite the FBI."

"Well, Agent Gillett called the local contingent of feds and invited them to the party. He told them, or implied, that you wanted federal help."

"Are you calling to ask if the feds get to come inside?"

"Not exactly, I'm calling because the area around the faerie lands is federal property, and the feds are trying to tell the locals they have no right to be here."

"Please, tell me you're exaggerating," I said.

His image blurred for a moment before I realized he'd moved his head. "I'm not exaggerating. We have a major mine's-bigger-than-yours contest starting out here."

"Can you put the head agent on?"

"No. Do you have any idea how many times I had to cut myself to get enough blood on the blade to write that message? None of them are going to come near this blade. If you want to talk to the humans you are going to have to pick a more mundane method of communication. Though I don't think a phone call will do it."

"What do you suggest?" Doyle asked.

"Get the princess out here because she's the one who made the calls. What little credibility I had with them vanished into the blood-soaked snow. They're afraid of me now." He sighed hard enough that it fogged the blade for a moment. "I'd forgotten that look in a human's eyes. It was a part of being Cromm Cruach that I didn't miss."

"Forgive me for making such measures necessary," Doyle said. "The princess and I will be there soon."

"See you then," and the blade went back to just brightly polished metal.

"Your Agent Gillett misunderstood you, I think."

I shook my head. "He didn't misunderstand. He hasn't seen me in person since I was eighteen or nineteen. He's reacting as if I'm still that person."

"He hopes to push his way into this investigation," Doyle said.

I nodded.

"You don't want to make the feds angry at us," Galen said. "There's a chance that the local police lab might need a little more help with something they find tonight." He began walking to me, forcing Mug to raise her face and adjust her balance.

It was a good point, a good clearheaded point. I smiled and went to him, and touched his face. I touched the cheek opposite the one Mug sat by. "Always looking to make peace."

He laid his hand over mine, pressing it against his cheek. "Just to keep as much of it as I can."

I went up on tiptoe, and he bent down so I could lay a gentle kiss upon his mouth. Mug made a sound, not a bad sound, almost a yummy sound like she liked being this close to both of us. "Give us room, Mug," I said. She pouted, but flew off. I let myself lean into him for a moment, let his strong arms wrap around me. If we lived in different times, gentler times, Galen would have been perfect—if peace was truly what we were after, but it wasn't, not exactly.

"What will you do about the FBI?" Doyle understood that I wasn't going to do exactly what Galen had suggested.

"I'll go introduce myself to the local agent, and give him a message to take back to Gillett."

"And what will that message be?" he asked.

"That I'm not a child anymore, and he can't manipulate me like one."

Frost frowned. "You invited human science into our sithen to help solve these murders. That is all well and good, but I know enough of their system to agree with Galen. We cannot afford to alienate them completely."

"Because we may need them later," I said.

Frost nodded. "Yes."

It was rare for Galen and Frost to agree so completely, which meant they were probably right. "I will do my best not to offend the FBI, but if we go out there and appear weak, they won't leave, and they will delay everything. We do not have time for everyone to play turf wars. And besides, this is our turf."

"Then let us go make that point to the authorities," Doyle said, "both local and federal." He actually offered me his arm, and I took it, feeling the solidness of muscle underneath the leather of his jacket. I realized, then, that my winter coat was still back at the airport, unless someone had thought to rescue it. I was going to need something to wear out into the December cold. I wondered whose coat I'd borrow.

We sent Onilwyn to find a healer. I still didn't know whether to believe what he had said. Had he come ahead of us to curry my favor, or had he something else in mind?

Something more sinister, or maybe I was just looking for an excuse not to have sex with him. Maybe, or maybe Onilwyn had earned my distrust.

Chapter 12

DOYLE AND FROST ESCORTED ME BACK TO MY ROOM FOR FRESH clothes. And warmer ones. I don't know whose cloak I borrowed, but it fit me, the hem barely brushing the floor of my room. The fur was cream and amber and a gold that was almost auburn. It was truly beautiful, but I felt about it the way I usually felt about fur coats; I thought the fur would have looked better on the animal it belonged to. I'd actually tried to argue that I wanted a leather coat, or something out of wool, but since it had been centuries since the sidhe had had domestic animals of their own, wool and leather were in short supply. Besides, Frost assured me that when it was killed, they had eaten it.

"What was it?" I asked. I'd never seen anything with fur quite this color.

"Troll," he said.

I stopped petting the fur. I'd never seen a troll, but I knew they were a type of fey, and though not the brightest, they still had culture, were still people. "That's not exactly an animal; that's more like cannibalism."

"He never said it was an animal," Doyle said, "you did. Shall we go? The police are waiting."

"If I have a problem wearing animal fur, didn't it occur to either of you that wearing something made out of what amounts to one of us would bother me even more?"

Frost sighed and settled back into a huge black chair, which unfortunately matched the new decor the queen had put in my room. It looked like a set for a gothic porn movie, or a funeral where the corpse was going to get a little too much attention.

"I killed the troll. The fur is a trophy. I don't understand your problem with wearing it." Frost looked ghost pale against the black leather chair, and strangely decadent in his fur coat. His ankle-length silver-fox coat had made it back from the airport. It made me think that the leather coats had gone missing because no one was certain who they belonged to, and the fur stayed because who else but one of my men would have a full-length fur coat that would fit over a set of shoulders that broad.

I turned to Doyle. "It would be like wearing a person's skin for a coat."

Doyle grabbed my arm. His grip was bruising, and his face held the anger that his hand pressed against my flesh. "You are a princess of the Unseelie Court. You will rule us someday. You cannot show this much weakness, not if you expect to survive!"

His black eyes held bits of brilliant color like psychedelic fireflies. There was an instant of vertigo, and then I was on solid ground in my snow boots, and I could look into his eyes and not be swayed. If he'd done it on purpose, it might not have been so easily cast aside, but it was his anger that brought his power, not his will. Anger is easier to avoid than force of will.

Frost had pushed to his feet. "Doyle, it is not such a large problem as all that." He sounded uncertain, and I knew why. This was Doyle, their captain, the immobile, unfeeling Darkness. He did not have fits of temper, ever.

Doyle jerked me close to his body, and I felt the creeping line of energy as his power began to unfold. He snarled into my face, "Won't wear the skins of our honored enemies. The police await us, our men stand in the cold, and you don't like your coat! Such delicate sensibilities for someone who just fucked a stranger on the floor in front of us all."

I stared at him openmouthed, too astonished to do or say anything.

"Doyle!" Frost came to stand near us, his hand moving toward me, as if he would take me away from the Darkness. But he let his hand fall back, because Frost, like me, wasn't certain what Doyle would do if he tried to wrest me from him. He was behaving so unlike himself that I was afraid, and, I think, so was Frost.

Doyle threw his head back and screamed. It was a sound of such anguish, such utter loneliness. The sound ended on a howl that raised the hairs on my body. He released me abruptly, and half threw me against Frost. Frost caught me and turned me so that his broad shoulders were between me and his captain.

Doyle collapsed to the floor in a pool of black leather, his braid curling like a serpent around his legs.

It took me a moment to realize that he was sobbing. Frost and I looked at each other. Neither of us had a clue as to what was happening to our stoic Darkness.

I moved toward him, but Frost held me back, and shook his head. He was right. But it made my chest tight to hear such broken sounds coming from Doyle.

Frost knelt beside him and laid a white hand on Doyle's dark shoulder. "My captain, Doyle, what ails you?"

Doyle covered his face with his hands and hunched over until his hands were nearly flat to the ground. He curled in upon himself, and his voice came thick with tears, and thicker with anger. "I cannot do it." He raised up on hands and knees, his head hanging down. "I cannot bear it." He looked up, and grabbed Frost's arm, much as he'd grabbed mine, almost pleading. "I cannot go back to what I was here. I cannot stand at her side and watch another take her. I am not that strong, or that good."

Frost nodded, and drew the other man into his arms. He held him tight and fierce, and the face he showed to me was raw with sorrow.

I had missed something. Something important. Something had happened not just to Doyle but to Frost as well. This was not his typical moodiness; this was mourning. But what did they mourn?

"What has happened?" I asked.

Doyle shook his head, pressed into Frost's shoulder. "She doesn't understand. She doesn't know what it means."

"What?" Fear was beginning to tickle my stomach, march up my spine. My skin was cool with the beginnings of dread.

Frost looked at me, and I realized that there were unshed tears glittering in his eyes. "The ring has chosen your king, Meredith."

"What are you talking about?" I asked.

"Mistral," Doyle said, raising his head, so I could see his face. "The ring has chosen Mistral. And I cannot let him have you."

I stared at him. "What are you babbling about? There is only one way for my king to be chosen, and I am not with child."

"Are you certain of that?" Frost asked. His face was so calm, empty of the emotional turmoil I would have expected from him. It was almost as if with Doyle fallen to pieces, he had to hold himself together better than was his wont.

"Yes, I mean . . ." I thought about what he'd said. "It's too early to be certain."

Doyle shook his head hard enough that his heavy braid rustled against the leather. "The ring has never come to life for any of us. You have never had such sex with any of us. What else could it mean but that he is the ring's choice?"

"I don't know, but . . ." In the face of his pain, I didn't know what to say. I looked from one to the other of them. Their belief was plain on their faces. I looked at them huddled together, light and darkness entwined, and my chest was tight. It was suddenly hard to breathe. The room felt hot and close. If I was pregnant from Mistral, I would lose them, both of them. I would be bound to Mistral, and I would be monogamous to him and him alone. The sex had been good, maybe great, but it was just sex, and . . . "I don't love him." The moment I said it, I knew it was a child's plea. A child's wish.

"A queen does not marry for love." Doyle's deep voice held the edge of tears.

"But wait, I thought the ring found your true love, your perfect match."

"It does," Frost said.

"Nicca and Biddy are completely gone on each other," I said. "They look at each other as if there is no one else in the world."

They both nodded. Frost said, "It was always thus with the ones the ring chose."

"But Mistral and I are not looking at each other that way."

"You did not see his face afterwards," Doyle said. "I did."

"As did I," Frost said.

I waved it away. "I was the first sex he's had in centuries. And it was magical sex, power-driven sex. That is heady stuff. Any man would look at me that way, but it was lust, not love."

Frost frowned at me. Doyle just stared as if his emotions had emptied him.

"I certainly don't feel that way about Mistral."

Frost looked positively suspicious. "You do not, truly?"

I shook my head. "If the ring had chosen him, then I'd be in love with him, right?"

Frost nodded.

"I do not feel that way about Mistral."

"How can you not want what we saw in the hallway?" Doyle asked, in a voice that had gone almost empty of emotion, as if it had all been too much for him.

"It was great, but has it occurred to either of you that maybe the sex was that magical because it is the first time I have had sex inside faerie while wearing the ring?"

Doyle blinked and tried to focus. I watched him fighting off the despair that was trying to numb him. Frost spoke for them both. "You have had sex inside faerie with one of us, surely."

I shook my head. "I do not believe so, and if I have, I wasn't wearing the ring. Even in Los Angeles, I often didn't wear the ring during sex."

"Because the power was too unpredictable," Doyle said. He looked up at me. "Were we fools to lock it away?"

The ring on my finger pulsed once, as if squeezing my hand. I swallowed hard and nodded. "The ring thinks so."

Doyle rubbed at the tear tracks on his skin. "You truly do not love Mistral?"

"No."

"You could still be pregnant," he said.

"The ring does fertility, but it does more than that," Frost said. "If Meredith does not love Mistral, then perhaps he is not the match for her."

"Does he think he is?"

I watched Doyle collect himself, gathering all that dark reserve. "Most likely."

"I know that Rhys does, for he said so," Frost said.

"Does Galen?"

"He was much besotted with the ring's power. The men that were besotted will most likely not be thinking that clearly."

"Only you, Rhys, Doyle, and Mistral himself did not seem drunk with power."

"Mistral was a part of the magic. Rhys did not appear in time."

"But why the two of you?"

They looked at each other, and it was Frost who spoke, and Doyle who would not look at me. "The ring has no power over you if you are already in love."

"If it is true love," Doyle said, and then he did look at me, and I almost wished he had not. His eyes held the pain that he had let me glimpse. The pain that must have begun to grow when none of them had made me pregnant in Los Angeles.

I looked at the two of them, and for the first time I realized that if it was a choice between the throne or losing these two men, I wasn't certain what I would choose. I wasn't certain I was queen enough to sacrifice that much. But as long as Cel lived, he would see me dead. And I could not give the rest of faerie to him, even if he swore to leave me and the ones I loved alive. I could not give my people over to him. He made

Andais look sane, and kindhearted. I could not give us over to Cel's sadism. I was too much my father's daughter to do it. But I stood there and felt the world sink down to nothing at the thought of losing Doyle and Frost.

I thought of something, and said, "So the fact that Galen was besotted means that he is not in love, not true love?"

They looked startled, glanced at each other, then both nodded. "I think the youngling would argue," Frost said, "but yes, that is what it means."

I tried the thought that my sweet, gentle Galen would be in someone else's arms, and the thought did not fill me with regret. In fact, it filled me with a certain peace to know that somewhere out there the ring would find him someone so that he would not mourn me.

I smiled.

"Why do you smile?" Doyle asked.

"Because the thought does not hurt." I went to them, and touched fingertips to both their faces. "The thought of losing the two of you . . . that is like a wound through my heart." I cupped their cheeks but was careful not to touch Frost's face with the ring. I wanted to touch them without the magic interfering. Doyle's skin was actually warmer than normal for humans, had been since the night he'd rediscovered he could shapeshift into animal form. Frost's skin was a little cooler than normal for humans. It wasn't always so, but often he felt cool to the touch. I'd first noticed it in Los Angeles after he, too, had found some of his godhead through the chalice's power.

I held them, hot and cold, light and dark, and wondered if there truly was a man in faerie who would make me forget them, and turn love-blinded eyes to someone else. I valued this love that we had built slowly over weeks and months. It had taken effort and trust, and I knew that even if all the magic in the world died, I would still love them. And after what they had shown me tonight, I thought they would still love me as well.

I moved their faces until they touched, so I could lay a kiss half on one and half on the other. I bent over them with my face between theirs. I whispered the truth against the silk of

Frost's hair, and the warmth of Doyle's skin. "To have you in my bed for the rest of my life, I would give up faerie, the throne, all that I am, or all that I might be."

Doyle's arm found me first, but Frost followed, and they pulled me to my knees, enveloped me against their bodies, pressed me hard and safe against them. Doyle spoke with his face pressed to the top of my head. "If there were anyone else worthy of the throne, I would let you." He laid his cheek against my hair. His grip was almost painful in its fierceness. "For the scent of your hair on my pillow I would trade my life, but I have served this court too long to give it into the hands of Cel."

Frost's hands trailed down my body, idly tracing the edge of my hip under the pants I'd put on. "The stories the prince's guards have told . . ." He shivered, hands convulsing against my body.

I pushed away enough to see their faces. "I thought the guards were too terrified of Cel to tattle on him."

Doyle pulled me in against them again, but turned me so that I half sat and half lay against their laps. "Some of the prince's guard have access to human newspapers and magazines," Doyle said. "They have noticed that your guards seem to be having a much better time than either the Queen's Ravens or the Prince's Cranes."

"I still can't get used to hearing them called Cranes. That was my father's bird, his guard."

"Many of them belonged to Essus's guard," Frost said. He held my hand in his. "They were simply given to Cel after Essus's death."

"Were they given a choice?" I asked. At the time, the least of my worries had been my father's guard, for had they not failed him? Had they not allowed him to be killed? Now I wondered how many of them would have dropped their vows as royal guard if they'd been given a chance.

Doyle cupped the side of my face, brought my attention to his face. "It was your sending for the other men last night that has sent some of Cel's birds to speak to us about life under him."

"Why did that loosen their tongues?"

"It showed that you cared for all your guard, not just the ones you like. Such caring is not something the Cranes have seen in many a year."

I could feel Frost's body shudder against mine. "I thought what we endured by the queen's hand was bad enough . . ." He shook his head. "Such stories."

"We cannot give the court over to him, Meredith," Doyle said. "I believe him truly mad."

"Being imprisoned and tortured isn't going to improve that," I said.

"No," he said.

"Tell her the rest," Frost said.

Doyle sighed. "You remember that the queen allowed Cel's need to be slacked by one of his guards."

I nodded. "Yes, and that night there was an attempt on both my life and the queen's."

"Yes, but we are still not absolutely certain Cel ordered it. It could simply have been those loyal to him moving in desperation to rescue him before he goes so mad that everyone sees him for what he is."

"You think the nobles would refuse to follow him?"

"If he tried to do to the court what he has done to his guard, yes," Doyle said.

I settled back in the curves of their bodies, fur and leather. "What has he done?"

"No, Meredith," Doyle said, "perhaps later when we have the luxury of time and hours to go before we would sleep. None of it is comforting bedtime stories."

"We have a murder investigation; trust me, we won't see sleep for hours," I said.

"What you need to know," Doyle said, "is that he has fixated on you."

"Fixated how?" I asked.

They exchanged another look. Doyle shook his head. But Frost said, "She needs to know, Doyle."

"Then tell her. Why must I always be the bearer of such news?"

Frost blinked at him, and fought not to show on his face what he and I were thinking. We hadn't known that bringing bad news bothered Doyle. He had been the Queen's Darkness, and the Darkness could speak hideous truth and be unmoved, or so it had seemed. It was as if the one outburst had stripped Doyle of some part of himself.

Frost said, "As you will then." He looked down at me. "He called one of the women guards by your name and swore that if his mother is so determined to have you with child, it will be his seed in your body."

I looked into that handsome face, and wanted to ask if he were joking, but I knew he was not. It was my turn to shudder. "I would rather die."

"I'm not certain he would care," Doyle said softly.

"What do you mean by that?"

"One of the lesser fey died during one of Cel's rapes." Doyle sighed again, and a look came into his eyes I hadn't seen often—fear. "He liked that she died during the sex. He continued to rape her corpse until her body became quite decayed."

I felt the blood drain from my face.

"Or so his guard say," Frost said.

"You saw their eyes, do you truly believe they lied?"

Frost let his breath out in a long sigh, and shook his head. "No." He bent over me, hugging me, burying me beneath a spill of silver hair. "I am sorry, Meredith, but we felt you needed to know."

"I was afraid of Cel before," I said.

"Be more afraid now," Doyle said. "Someone like that cannot be handed the keys to the Unseelie Court, especially now that power seems to be returning to us. With power, we are more dangerous. Too dangerous to be given over to a madman."

"Power returns because of Meredith," Frost said.

"Yes, but once power is reborn in the sidhe, it will be like a gun. It will not care how it is used."

"The Goddess may abandon us forever if the power is misused," I said.

"I thought as much, but think of the damage we could do before she took back her new gifts."

We sat on the floor and contemplated new possibilities for even larger disasters. Doyle hugged me tight, then stood up, and shook himself like a dog. He settled the leather coat around his tall frame, and said, "I thought to keep the news of Cel and his new madness until after we had brought the police inside, but..." He slid the dark glasses over his eyes, so that he was the tall, dark, inscrutable Darkness. Only the silver shine of his earrings gave him color. "We will escort you to the police and the FBI. I am sorry for losing control as I did, Princess, and for delaying us further."

I let Frost help me to my feet. "One fit in over a thousand years, I think you're overdue."

Doyle shook his head. "It is my fault that Rhys and the police are waiting in the cold. Inexcusable."

I touched his arm, but it was hard muscle encased in leather, as if he could not allow himself any softness. "I don't think it's inexcusable."

"If she comforts us again, we will be even later," Frost said.

Doyle smiled, a quick flash of teeth. "It is nice to be comforted instead of punished." He held up the fur cloak. "Please, just for now. We will find something else more to your liking, but just for now."

I still didn't like the idea of wearing the cloak, but after what I'd just heard about Cel and his guard, it seemed a lesser evil. I allowed him to put the cloak around me. "How does it look?" I asked.

The wall quivered like a horse's skin when a fly lands. Doyle shoved me behind him. Frost already had his sword naked in his hand. Doyle aimed a gun at the rock wall.

A full length mirror surrounded by a gilt frame floated up through the stone, shining in the darkness of the room.

I peered at it around Doyle's body, my pulse in my throat. "Where did that come from?"

Doyle still had a gun pointed very steadily at the bright surface. "I do not know." Almost all the fey could use mirrors to make a sort of phone call. Doyle and some of the other sidhe could travel through mirrors. We stood waiting for a figure to appear, for something terrible to happen. But the mirror just hung on the wall, as if someone had put it there to be a mirror and nothing more.

The tip of Frost's sword lowered.

Doyle glanced at us. "Why did it appear? Who sent it?"

Frost stepped closer to the mirror. "Meredith, look at yourself in the mirror."

Doyle looked skeptical but he moved so I could see myself. The red and gold of the fur went well with my hair and skin, and brought out the gold in my eyes. With the hood up, I looked delicate and a little ethereal, like something between a Victorian Christmas card and a barbarian princess. Well, a small barbarian princess.

"Now, thank the sithen for the use of the mirror, and say you no longer need it."

I frowned at him, but did as he suggested. "Thank you for the mirror, sithen. I do not need it right now."

The mirror stayed on the wall, as if it had always been there.

"Please, sithen, a mirror could be used to harm her, please take it away," Frost said.

It felt as if the very air shrugged, then the wall quivered again, and the mirror began to sink back into the wall. When the wall was empty stone once more I let out a breath I hadn't realized I was holding.

"Are you saying the mirror appeared because I asked how I looked?"

"Hush," Frost said, then he nodded.

"Now that," Doyle said, "is interesting."

"The sithen hasn't answered to whims since—" Frost stopped as if trying to think how long.

"Long enough, my friend, that I, too, am not certain when the last time was."

"So is this good," I said, "or not?"

"Good," Doyle said.

"But dangerous," Frost added.

Doyle nodded. "I would be careful what I said aloud from now on, Meredith. An idle comment could have grave consequences, if the sithen has truly returned to that much life."

"What do you mean?"

"The sithen is a living thing, but it does not think like any living thing I have ever known. It will interpret what you say in its own way. You ask how you look, and it gives you a mirror. Who knows what it might offer you, depending on what you said."

"What if I yelled for help, would it do anything useful?" I asked.

"I do not know," Doyle said. "I have heard of it giving you objects you asked for, but never touching people. But there are enchanted items locked within its walls, things that simply vanished. Some theorize that they did not go back to the gods, but inside the very walls. There are things that I would not want appearing before you without more help than this."

"More help than you and Frost?"

He nodded.

I started to ask what object could possibly be so dangerous that the Killing Frost and the Queen's Darkness could not keep me safe, but I didn't. One disaster at a time. It was almost as if something wanted to keep us here tonight, distracted by one semi-important event after another. I shook my head. "Enough, we are leaving now. Rhys and the police are waiting."

When we stepped out the door we were in the main corridor just inside the outer doors. My room should have been three levels down, and nowhere near this area. The guards waiting to accompany us were staring at us as we walked out.

Galen said, "That door wasn't there before."

"No," Doyle said, and he got everyone in formation, with me in the center, hidden once again behind a phalanx of guards. I would have said men, but at least three of them were female, including Biddy. She and Nicca would probably be useless in a fight. They were still too magic befuddled, but we were afraid to leave them behind. I was almost certain that without someone to stop them, they would have sex, and until I cleared it with the queen that was an automatic death by torture for both of them. Doyle did make them stop holding hands. He thought the police might get the wrong idea.

Cathbodua and Dogmaela had joined our little band. I suddenly had three women in my personal entourage who might have owed more allegiance to Cel than to me. Doyle made some noises about me needing ladies-in-waiting, and wouldn't it be useful if they were also trained warriors. But I knew the real reason. We took them with us because the queen might at any moment change her mind and demand them back into Cel's service. We took them out into the snow to meet the police because they were safer with us than without us.

Chapter 13

I DIDN'T SEE THE POLICE BUT I HEARD THEM, A RUMBLE OF DEEP male voices. Sound carried so much better on those still, bitterly cold nights. My cheeks were stinging, and my breath had fogged and frozen in the fur of the hood. Barinthus had kept me warm on the walk to the faerie mounds after the assassination attempt, but I walked on my own power now. The snow was knee high for me, and my boots didn't quite keep it from soaking into the knees of my jeans. I tried to call the feel of the summer sun to put inside my shield and help keep back the cold, but it was as if I couldn't remember what summer felt like. The moonless night was clear with a thousand stars flung across the darkness like bits of glittering ice, diamond glints across black velvet. I focused on the fight to lift one foot, then the next, and struggle through drifts that the taller sidhe walked through effortlessly. It was undignified for a princess to fall on her face, but it took effort to keep from doing it. I suppose that struggling through the snow wasn't exactly dignified either, but that I could do nothing about.

But it was Biddy who stumbled. Nicca caught her before she hit the snow. I heard her apologize, "I don't know what's wrong. I'm so cold."

"Stop, all of you, stop," I said. Everyone obeyed, some of them looking out at the snow, fingers near weapons.

It was Galen who asked, "What's wrong, Merry?"

"Are Biddy and I the only ones here with human blood?"

"I think so."

"I tried to conjure the feel of summer sun, and I couldn't remember what it was like."

Doyle had worked his way back to me. "What is wrong?"

"Check Biddy and me for a spell, a spell that attacks only human blood."

He pulled off one of his black gloves and put his hand just above my face, not touching skin, but searching my aura, my shielding, my magic.

He growled low and soft, but the sound raised the hair on the back of my neck. "I take it you found something."

He nodded. Then he turned to Biddy, who was half fainting in Nicca's arms. "I am sorry, Doyle. I am truly better than this."

"It is a spell," he told her, and lifted off her helmet to lay his hand above her face. He handed the helmet to Nicca and turned to me, unable to hide the spark of angry color in his eyes. He was fighting down his power, raised by anger. Anger at himself most likely for letting yet another spell slip under his nose. We had some truly subtle spells being worked on us. One of us would have noticed something big, but such small spells were harder to guard against.

"It is tied to mortal blood. It simply sucks at your energy, and fills you with cold."

"Why is Biddy more affected than Merry?" Nicca asked. He was covered completely in a thick cloak, except for his wings. They were held tight together as if they would stay warmer that way, and maybe they did. He was warm-blooded; moth wings did not change that.

I answered him. "She's half-human, I'm less than a fourth human. If it is seeking human blood, she's got more than I have."

"Are the human police affected?" Hawthorne asked.

Doyle put his hand back over me, and this time I felt a warm pulse of magic shiver over my shields. "It is like a contagion. It was put on either Biddy or the princess, then jumped from one to the other. If we do not remove it, it will spread to the police."

I looked up at him, speaking with the warmth of his magic against my skin, like breath. "What would it do to full-blooded humans?"

"It made a warrior of the sidhe stumble in the snow. She is disoriented, and would be useless in a fight."

Frost was staring off into the darkness. He and another fringe of guards were all staring out into the cold night. His voice carried to me. "Is this the beginning of a more overt attack?"

"Who would be so bold as to attack the human guards?" Amatheon wondered aloud. He'd been eager to come out into the cold, anything to be farther away from the queen, I think. But I remembered again that he had been Cel's creature for centuries. Did a few acts of honor and kindness erase centuries of allegiance? And as close to Cel as he had been, he had to have witnessed some of the horrors the female guards spoke of, didn't he? I made a mental note to ask him later, with Doyle and Frost at my back. Onilwyn was inside the faerie mound, because he had not recovered from the beating Maggie May and I had given him. Cold iron forces even the sidhe to heal human slow. Him I did not trust at all. Amatheon I was beginning to trust; was I wrong to trust him? Of course, the question itself meant I didn't trust him, not really.

"Who indeed," I said, and fought not to look at him, not to let him know with body language that I wondered if it was him.

Either I betrayed myself, or he felt insecure, because he said, "I will make any oath that I did not know of this."

"You said you were a man without honor," Adair said. "A man without honor has no oath."

"Enough," Doyle said, "we will not squabble amongst ourselves, not this close to the humans."

"Doyle's right. We will discuss this later." I raised my face up to him, and said, "Can you remove it so that Biddy and I do not infect the police?"

"I can."

"Then do it, and let us get this done."

"You sound angry," Galen said.

"I am tired of whoever is doing all this. Tired of these games."

"It is a good sign, in a way," Doyle said.

I looked at him. "What do you mean?"

"It means our murderer fears the human police, fears they may find him where our magic has failed." He stuffed his gloves in the pocket of his coat and slid my hood off, so that the cold air spilled around my face. I shivered.

"I am afraid I will have to make you colder before I am done."

I nodded. "Get this off of me, and I will warm myself."

He pushed my cloak back. The cold rushed in, stealing the shell of warmth that the cloak had made. I fought not to shiver as he spread his hands over me, not touching even so much as my clothing, but caressing just above my body. His power shivered over my aura, and it felt as if he scooped something off of me, almost like flicking an insect off my skin.

He raised his hands upward, cupped as if he truly held something. He called that sickly green fire to his hands. It was the painful flame that I'd seen eat along a body. It could cause death if you were mortal, or excruciating pain and madness in the immortal. Now he used it to burn away the spell that had clung to me.

Rhys's voice came from behind us. "What's wrong?" He had a gun naked in his hand, but held along his body so the police probably wouldn't see it from a distance. He saw the green light, and said, "What is it?" with a new urgency in his voice. "What am I not sensing?"

Galen answered him. "Someone put a spell on Merry."

"On both the human bloods," Frost said.

"It would have been contagious to the human police," Doyle said. The green flame vanished, leaving the night a little darker. He turned to Biddy, where she half sagged in Nicca's arms. "Let her go, Nicca."

"She will fall."

"Only to her knees in the snow. It won't hurt her." Doyle's voice was surprisingly gentle.

Nicca still held her against him. His wings flared out once, then clamped tight again.

"It's all right, Nicca," Biddy said in a soft voice, a little breathy. "Doyle will help me."

It was Hawthorne who came to him, and began to gently draw him away from her. "Let the captain help your lady."

Nicca allowed himself to be drawn away, but when Biddy collapsed into the snow, he moved to catch her, and only Hawthorne and Adair on each side kept him from grabbing her before her knees hit the snow.

Rhys gave a soft whistle. "That would have done bad things to our nice policemen."

"Yes," Doyle said, as he knelt in the snow, his greatcoat spreading out like a pool of darkness against the white. He passed his hands above Biddy, much as he'd done me, but he hesitated close to her belly. "That someone could lay such a thing on her while she wore this much metal . . ." He shook his head. "It speaks of great power."

"Or mixed blood," I said. "Those of us with a little human or brownie or a few other things can handle metal and magic better than a pure-blooded sidhe."

His mouth twitched. "Thank you for reminding me, because you are exactly right."

"Can you trail it back to its owner?" I asked.

Doyle cocked his head to the side, the way a dog does when it is puzzled by something. "Yes." His hands tensed above Biddy's body. "I can remove it, but I can also add magic of my own, and force it to fly back to its owner."

"You mean not just track it, but make it run back home?" Rhys asked.

"Yes."

"You have not been able to do that in a very long time," Frost said.

"But I can do it now," Doyle said. "I can feel it in my hands, my stomach. All I have to do is remove it, and add my power at the moment of its release. It will be a chase to keep up with it, but it will work."

"Who will go with you?" Frost asked. "I must stay with the princess."

"Agreed."

"I will go," Usna said. "No dog can outrun a cat."

Doyle gave him one of those fierce smiles. "Done."

"I, too, will go." It was Cathbodua, once a goddess of battle, now a refugee from Cel's guard. Her cloak was formed of black feathers, so that it sometimes seemed as if her fine black hair was part of the cloak, and if you looked at her from the edges of your eyes, her hair looked as if it were made of feathers. She was Cathbodua, battle scald crow, and though diminished in power, she was still one of the few in the courts who had kept her original name. Rumor had it that she had not been as abused by Cel, for he feared her. Dogmaela, who stood in armor next to her, had been nicknamed Cel's dog because she was given every awful task he could find. She had publicly denied him sex, and he'd never forgiven her. Cathbodua had done the same thing, and not suffered overly much for it. There was something about her, standing there in the snow, all black and feathered, with some air of . . . power that would give a braver man than Cel pause.

"You think you can keep up, birdie?" Usna said.

She gave him a smile cold enough to freeze the smile from his face. "Don't worry for me, kitty-cat, I won't be the tail end of this race."

Usna made a catlike growl. "Remember who the predator is here, birdie."

Her smile widened, and filled her eyes with a fierce joy. "Me," she said.

"Us," Doyle said. "Keep her safe, Frost."

"I will."

"Oh, don't mind me," Rhys said. "I'm not fast enough to keep up, and apparently I can't be trusted with the safety of the princess."

"Help her with the humans, Rhys." Doyle glanced at Cathbodua and Usna. "Are you prepared?"

Cathbodua said, "I am ready."

Usna said, "Always."

Doyle turned back to Biddy. "This may hurt."

"Do it." She braced herself, hands in the snow.

Doyle flexed his hands, so that they looked like black claws against the silver of her armor. Biddy let out a sharp breath. His magic flared even through the shields that I held in place to keep me from being overwhelmed by the magic of faerie. Her aura, her metaphysical armor, flared like a flash of light that covered her body. Doyle plunged his hands into that flare of light and came out with a round ball of light, but the light wasn't the clean yellow-white light of Biddy's aura, it was a dark sickly yellow with an edge of orange flame to it. Doyle cupped his hands more closely around it until the flickering of the orange flames spilled out from between his fingers.

He stood carefully, as if he held a very full bowl of very hot soup. He stepped around Biddy, and the other guards spilled away so that there was nothing between him and the mounds but empty snow.

Usna and Cathbodua moved up on either side of him. Usna undid his long cloak and stood dressed mostly in leather, his breath fogging in the cold, his face eager, eyes shining with anticipation. Cathbodua's face was like pale marble, perfect, beautiful, and cold. Far from flinging her cloak off, she gathered it more tightly around her. I realized that her breath did not fog in the cold. I had a moment to wonder why, then Doyle flung his hands skyward, and the flame was now a bird, a falcon made of red and orange flame. It flashed shining wings once, twice, to gain altitude. Doyle undid his long black cloak and let it fall to the snow. He undid his weapons and flung them all to the snow. The falcon beat its wings twice more and stared down at us all with eyes made of fire, an arrogant look, as if to say, "You will never catch me." Then it was gone, streaking like some hand-sized comet, flaming into the night.

Doyle was simply gone. I know he ran, but it was like trying to watch darkness fall. You never really saw it happen. He was a tall dark shape, loping over the snow. Cathbodua was with him, though she didn't seem to be running. It was almost as if the long feathered cloak floated above the snow, and she with it. Usna trailed them both, but not by much. His multicolored hair shone in the starlight, sparkling like colored snow, as he ran graceful and full out behind them.

"He has his work cut out for him," Rhys said.

"Yes," Frost said, "you cannot outrun the Darkness."

"And anger travels on the very wind," Dogmaela said.

"Anger?" I made it a question.

"She is the scald crow. She is the dissatisfaction that drives men to quarrel."

"She starts the fight, then feeds on it," Biddy said, as Nicca helped her to her feet.

"She did once," Frost said, "but that is no more."

"You think not," Dogmaela said. "Cathbodua still enjoys a good quarrel, make no mistake about it, Killing Frost. She grows bored with so much peace."

"This is not peace," Frost said.

"Perhaps," she said, "but it is not battle, either."

"Let's hope not," Rhys said. "And now, children, let's go talk to the nice policemen before they freeze their badges off."

"Badges?" Dogmaela said. "Is that some new slang for balls?"

Rhys grinned at her. "And when we walk over there they will all get their badges out and flash them at the princess."

Frost and I both said "Rhys" at the same time.

Dogmaela said, "What an odd custom."

She was a literalist with almost no sense of humor. Rhys

was going to hurt himself with this one. I explained the truth to her as we all walked over to the parking lot. She gave him a dirty look. He smiled at her like a lascivious angel.

"Behave yourself," I told him under my breath.

"I have behaved myself," he said softly. "When you've talked to the head fed, you'll think I was a saint."

"Why?"

"Because he's not bleeding."

I looked at him and tried to decide if he was teasing me, too. His face said no. How bad could one FBI agent be? As the old saying goes, we were about to find out.

Chapter 14

THE POLICE, ALL FLAVORS, STOOD IN THE DECEMBER COLD. Maybe some of them had been in their vehicles trying to stay warm and only got out when they saw us coming, but somehow they had the feel of people who'd been standing around in the cold for a while. If it wasn't for us, then why weren't they in their cars, in vans with the heaters on? Because their chiefs were standing out in the cold. You didn't sit in a nice warm car while your officers stood ankle deep in snow. We'd had the parking area cleared off, but apparently snow had blown back across the surface.

I recognized Major Walters by the broad-shouldered square of him and his height. The man he was standing almost toe-to-toe with was shorter by at least five inches, and no one I knew. But I'd have bet good money he was FBI. And the way he was yelling at Walters, probably the head fed.

When I'd told Special Agent Raymond Gillett not to come,

I hadn't specified that he not send the feds. I would remember to be more specific if I ever spoke to him again.

Rhys tried to get their attention, but it was Frost's voice that cut across the squabbling. "Princess Meredith NicEssus," he announced, the words echoing over the cold, still air.

They stopped mid-argument, and turned to us in surprise, almost as if they'd forgotten I was coming. Then they both started trying to talk to me at the same time.

I held up my hands, letting them slip out of the cloak. "Gentlemen, gentlemen, please, one at a time."

They both tried to be the one at a time. I settled it for them. "Major Walters, why are you still here at the parking lot? Why haven't you come to the door?" I smiled as I said it, even with my eyes.

He jerked a thumb at the smaller man. "He won't let us step a foot off the parking lot. Says it's federal land, and that makes this case his."

I turned, still smiling to the fed in question. "And you are?"

"Special Agent John Marquez." And he actually bowed. "It's an honor to meet you, Princess Meredith."

I tried not to laugh. The bow was overdoing it. "I wish I could say the same, Special Agent Marquez."

He looked up, puzzlement on his darkly handsome face. "Have we done something to offend you, Your Majesty?"

I shook my head. "Majesty is only for the ruler, and I'm not it, yet. I called Major Walters and asked him to bring down his people, but I did not call the FBI, so I'm a little puzzled why you are here."

"Faerie land is federal land, Princess. That makes these crimes our jurisdiction, as I've pointed out to the major here."

"Ah, but technically it's faerie land, and neither of you has any jurisdiction here."

Marquez smiled condescendingly. "But you called for police help, and since the mounds are on federal land, that means us."

I shook my head. "Only if we ask for your help; until that moment it's our business."

He shook his head. "You did ask us, Princess. Special Agent Gillett got your call, and he referred it to our local office."

I'd figured as much, but it was still disappointing to know it for certain. "I made the call to Gillett out of courtesy and for old times' sake. I realize now I was wrong to have called him at all."

"But we are here now, and we have forensic facilities that the local St. Louis police can't match."

A woman broke away from the knot of locals. She had blond hair that was a little too perfectly yellow to be real and human. Dark glasses cut a pretty face so that it took you a moment to notice her eyes were large and long-lashed. "I'm Dr. Caroline Polaski, head medical examiner for St. Louis County, and I take exception to that."

"You can't compare your lab with ours," Marquez said.

"I did my internship with you, so yes, actually, I can."

"Internship, then you weren't good enough to make the grade."

She gave him a very unfriendly look. "Check your own records. I left because my husband got a better job here, and I got offered the run of the place. At your shop I'd have been someone's flunkie."

"Because you weren't good enough to be head of our shop," Marquez said.

This was getting us nowhere. "Stop it," I said.

They looked at me. "You want to know who is in charge here. That's what all the arguing is about, correct?"

Polaski and Marquez nodded. Walters just looked at me.

I smiled. "That's an easy question, ladies and gentlemen. I am."

Marquez gave me a look that, even in the dim light, said plainly that I was a little girl and shouldn't try to play with the big boys. "Now, Princess, your call for help indicates that you don't think you and your people are capable of handling a double homicide."

"I am in charge of this investigation, Agent Marquez. I am glad for your offer of assistance, and I will gladly accept, but let there be no confusion among any of us." I let my gaze take in Walters and the medical examiner. "I am in charge, and anyone who has a problem with that doesn't step one foot onto our land."

Marquez argued, as I'd expected him to. "You are not an officer of any kind, Princess. No offense, but this investigation needs more than just a private detective in charge of it."

"My private detective license isn't valid outside of California, Agent Marquez."

"Then you have no legal standing to take control."

I stepped into him so fast and unexpectedly, that he actually took a step back before he caught himself. I looked up at him, inches taller, and let him look into the delicate oval of my face framed by all that soft fur. "No legal standing, Marquez? I am Princess Meredith NicEssus. The only person who outranks me here on this land is the Queen of Air and Darkness herself. You and your people are here on my sufferance, and I think I've suffered enough."

"You can't mean that you're going to send us all away because I hurt your feelings." Goddess, he had an attitude.

"Not at all. I'm going to take Major Walters and his people with us, and let them do their jobs."

"And when they can't handle it, and you need our help, you may not get it, Princess."

And we might need their help. I hoped not, but we might. I had an idea. I turned to Walters. "Do you have a cell phone?"

He looked a little uncertain, but he held it out to me.

"Can I make a long-distance call on it?"

"Who are you going to call?"

"Washington, D.C."

Walters took in a deep breath. "Be my guest."

I dialed a number that I'd had the queen's secretary get for me before we came out here. I'd hoped not to use it, but I'd seen enough territorial disputes in L.A. to know that the feds and the locals could do more harm to an investigation than good, if they got into a serious pissing contest. Marquez was making this one serious.

After hearing my initial greeting and request, Marquez said, "You are not calling the president of the United States."

"No." I was on hold. "I'm not."

Marquez frowned harder at me.

A woman's voice came on the phone, and I said, "Mrs. President, how good to talk to you again."

Marquez's eyebrows went up.

I'd first met Joanne Billings when her husband was a senator. They'd come to my father's funeral, and their regrets had seemed the most sincere of the political people there that day. After that Senator Billings and his wife had made several visits to faerie, and I realized that Joanne Billings was a faeriephile. My father had not raised me to ignore a political advantage, and besides, I liked Joanne. She was open-minded about the Unseelie Court's unfavorable press, and made a point of talking us up in a positive light when she could. We exchanged holiday cards, and I made certain she was invited to my official engagement party, the one for public consumption. She had actually visited me at college once, without her husband, just to see how I was getting along, and by that time she and her husband were trying to get the young vote. Pictures of her with America's faerie princess didn't hurt. I understood that, and didn't think badly of her for it. I had even invited her to my graduation, and they had both come. We'd gotten photo ops together. One of the last things I'd done before vanishing from faerie and the public eye was to appear onstage with them at a couple of rallies.

We exchanged small talk, then she said, "I assume you didn't call at this hour for a social reason."

"No." I gave her the briefest sketch of the situation.

She was silent for a second or two. "What do you need from me?"

I explained some of what Marquez had said, and added, "And he threatened that if I didn't let him in now, he would make certain the FBI didn't help us later, if we needed their expertise to solve the crime. Could you talk to him for me?"

She laughed. "You could have called the diplomatic service, talked to your ambassador. You could have called a dozen people, but you called me first. You did call me first, didn't you?"

"Yes," I said.

She laughed again, and I knew she liked that I had called her first. I also knew she liked that I hadn't asked her to talk to her husband. "Put him on the line," she said, and her voice had already taken on that cultured, almost purring edge that it had on radio or television.

I handed the phone to Marquez. He looked a little pale around the edges. His end of the conversation was mostly "Yes, ma'am. No, ma'am. Of course not, ma'am." He handed the phone back to me, managing to look angry and sick at the same time.

"I think he'll behave himself now," she said.

"Thank you, very much, Joanne."

"When you've finally picked a husband, you better invite me to the engagement party." She was quiet for a second, then said, "I am sorry about what happened with Griffin. I saw the tabloid photos he gave to the reporters. I have no words to say how sorry I am that he turned out to be a such a bastard."

"I'm okay about it."

"Good for you."

"And you will get an invitation to the engagement party, and to the wedding."

She laughed again with honest delight. "All of faerie decked out for a wedding, I can hardly wait."

"Thank you, Joanne." We hung up, and I turned to Marquez. "Is there anything else you wanted to know, Special Agent Marquez?"

"No, I've had about all I can stand tonight, thank you very much, Princess Meredith," he said, and gave me a look that said I'd made an enemy. Gee, an enemy that wouldn't try to kill me. It was almost refreshing.

"You and your lab will be available if we need your expertise?" I asked, keeping my voice neutral.

"I promised Mrs. Billings we would be."

"Great," I said, then turned to Major Walters. He was trying not to look pleased and failing. He practically beamed at me. Local police spend a lot of time getting their hats handed to them by the feds; for once the shoe was on the other foot, and Walters was enjoying it. He waited until we'd walked out into the snow with a circle of my guards hiding us from the feds before he burst out laughing. A man of iron self-control.

Chapter 15

IT WAS FROST WHO PLACED HIS HAND AGAINST THE SNOW-covered hill and called the door. The opening appeared with a peal of music that made all the policemen smile, even Major Walters. It was the door to faerie, all humans go through smiling, but they don't always come out that way. Inside this hollow hill was a human who was going out in a body bag.

The door stretched wide and bright, though I knew the light was actually dim. It looked bright because we'd been walking in the snowy dark.

The police hit that dimly lit hallway and made exclamations of surprise. Cops do not show surprise, at least not those who have been on the job awhile. Cops are the best ever at jaded tiredness, boredom. Been there, done that, didn't want the T-shirt. One of the uniforms said, "Oh, my God, the colors are so beautiful."

The walls were grey and empty. There was no color.

Major Walters stared up at those bare walls, as if he saw something indescribably beautiful. All their faces showed delight, wonderment. Some *oo*hed and *aa*hed as if they were watching fireworks. The guards and I looked at empty grey walls.

"Rhys, did you forget to use the oil on the nice policemen?"

"The reporters didn't need it," he said. "How was I to

know that hard-boiled police and forensic scientists would be more susceptible to faerie magic?"

"They should not be," Frost said.

"What do you mean?" I asked.

"The queen gave vials of oil to the guard as a precaution in case the reporters became befuddled by the magic that is intrinsic to the sithen, but it was merely a precaution. The main hallways of the sithen have not affected humans in this way for more than fifty years."

"Well," I said, looking at the humans who were gazing around them as if the hallway were a carnival midway, "whatever is causing this, we need it to stop or they are useless to us. They can't do police work like this."

"Did a spell cause it?" Arzhel asked as he pushed the dark fur of his cloak back from a face framed by thick brown curls that spilled down to his knees. That thick mane of fur was held back from his face only by a silver circlet. He was dressed in hardened leather armor, sewn here and there with silver. His body under the armor was tattooed with fur, much as Nicca's had been with his wings. The tattoo was so real that it made you want to pet the fur that was not there. His face and most of the front of his body was bare and pale and as moonlight, like my own skin. It made the brown and gold of the fur look darker by contrast. With his armor and cloak, he could almost have passed for a human, except for the eyes. They were a reddish brown, a color that could have been human but wasn't. They weren't sidhe eyes either, but those of an animal of some kind. I'd found a picture in a book once, a two-page close-up of the eyes of a bear. Staring at the picture I knew I'd seen those eyes in Arzhel's face.

"It is not a spell," Frost said. "We would feel it."

Arzhel nodded. "Have you searched for it?"

"I have."

"As have I," said Crystall, his voice like chimes in the wind. He was still hidden behind his white cloak.

"Use the oil on them," I said. "Ears, eyes, mouth, hands, the works."

Arzhel asked, "The works?"

"The princess means to make certain they can function completely unaffected by the sithen," Rhys said, undoing his trench coat and taking a small stoppered bottle from the inner pocket of his suit jacket. He worked the stopper out of the dark clay bottle, then stood in front of Dr. Polaski. He asked her to take her glasses off, but it was as if she couldn't hear him, and maybe she couldn't. He took her glasses gently off her face. She blinked at him as he touched one eye just below the brow. "That you may see truly," he said. She jerked back from him, then stared around at the walls. She covered her eyes with her hands. "Oh, God, oh, God, what's happening to me?"

"Let me do the other eye, and you'll feel better," Rhys said. "Just keep them closed until I'm done."

He had to push her hands down from her face, but she kept her eyes closed. He touched the other eyelid, and said, "To see truly." He pushed her hair back from her ears, and traced the oil down the curve of one ear, and then the other, with the words "That you may hear truly."

"The music stopped," she said, and tears began to seep out from her closed lids.

He touched her lips. "So you may speak truly of what you find." He put her hands palm up. "So you may touch and be touched truly." He knelt and traced the tops of her snow-soaked boots. "So you may step truly and know what lies before you." He stood in front of her, and laid the last touch to her forehead. "So you may know and think truly." He did more than just touch there; there he laid a protective symbol. For a moment I saw the flare of magic trace the cool spiral and circle on her forehead, then it sank into her skin.

She blinked, and looked around her as if she didn't quite know where she was. "What the hell was that?"

"Welcome to faerie, Dr. Polaski," Rhys said, and handed her back her glasses.

Frost handed me a bottle. "Doyle gave me his, for he does not need it."

I took the offered bottle, and wondered where Doyle had

gone, and what he had found. "I would feel better if Doyle or the others would contact us."

"As would I," Frost said as he began to lay oil on Walters.

I turned to the only other woman in the group. She wasn't that much taller than myself, which was one of the reasons I chose her. When I took off the cloth cap, it revealed straight brown hair tied back in a ponytail, a little worse for the sock cap she'd been wearing. Her eyes were a solid medium brown. The face was a delicate triangle, pretty enough, but I'd been too much around the sidhe of late. She looked unfinished to me, as if her hair or eyes needed a different color to make her real.

I told her, "Close your eyes."

She didn't hear me, but it wasn't the walls she was staring at. She was watching Frost while he touched Major Walters's face. I finally touched her eyes just above her open lid, and she flinched away from me.

"Dr. Polaski, can you help her hold still?" I asked. She was one of the CSU, not the police. Polaski came to us, and said, "Carmichael, this will help. Close your eyes and let the princess touch you."

Carmichael seemed strangely reluctant, but she did what her boss said to do. She shivered under my fingers like a nervous horse, skin jumping. She got calmer by the time I'd done her hands, and she seemed calm as I touched the tops of her hiking boots, below the wet of her jeans. When I raised up to trace her forehead, her voice seemed normal. "I'd prefer a cross as the symbol," she said.

"A cross won't work," I said, tracing something much older on her forehead.

Those brown eyes opened to look at me, while I did it. "What do you mean, a cross won't work?"

"We aren't evil, Carmichael, just other. Contrary to popular myth, holy symbols won't stop our magic, any more than holding up a cross would stop a blizzard from harming you."

"Oh," she said, and looked a little embarrassed. "I didn't mean to offend you."

"It's all right, the church has tried to vilify us for centuries, but if you're ever in need of protection from faerie, I'd advise turning your jacket inside out instead of a prayer. A prayer can't hurt, but the coat turning will probably be more effective." I finished the last curve of the design and stepped back from her.

"Why does turning your jacket inside out help?"

"Most in faerie see only the surface; change your surface and the magic has trouble finding you."

"Why?" she asked.

"Well, it doesn't work if the person knows you really well and has never tried to deceive you."

"Never tried to deceive you—what do you mean?"

"Never tried to appear to be other than they are."

"Oh," she said again.

I watched delight vanish from the other humans' faces, as the oiling was completed. One policeman said, "I think I liked it better before. Now it's just grey stone."

"Where does the light come from?" Polaski asked.

"No one really knows," I told her.

"I thought this oil was supposed to make everything look ordinary," Carmichael said.

"It is," I said.

"Then why is he still so damned beautiful?" She pointed at Frost.

I smiled at his face going cold and arrogant. It didn't make him one bit less attractive. Goddess had made it impossible for him to be anything else.

"Maybe ordinary is the wrong word," I said. "The oil helps you see reality."

Carmichael shook her head. "He can't be real. His hair is metallic silver, not grey, not white, silver. Hair can't be silver."

"It's the natural color of his hair," I said.

"Should the rest of us be offended?" Rhys asked.

"Maybe you should be," Ivi said, "but she hasn't seen most of us out of armor and cloaks." He pushed the hood of his cloak back, and drew off the muffler that had hidden most of his face. Ivi's face was a little thin for my tastes, and I knew his shoulders weren't wide enough for me, but the pale green of his hair was decorated with vines and ivy leaves, as if someone had painted his namesake on his hair. When the hair was free, it looked like leaves blowing in the wind as he walked. His eyes were the startling green of emeralds. I guess if you haven't been raised around people with multi-colored eyes, the vibrant green of his eyes was worth a stare or two. Carmichael seemed to think so because her gaze went to him as if she couldn't help but stare.

Crystall swept his own cloak back to reveal hair that caught the dim light of the hall and turned it into rainbows, as if his hair were a clear prism that shattered light into colors. His skin was whiter than mine, a white so pure it looked artificial. He flung the lesser white of his cloak back over one arm, and that arm was bare. I had a moment to wonder what he was wearing under the long cloak and above the boots that I could see. His arm shone in the light, like white metal, a gleam that no true flesh ever held.

The woman's gaze went to him again, as if she could not help herself.

"Stop it, all of you," I said. "Leave her alone."

"I am doing nothing to her," Frost said.

I looked at his arrogant face and knew he believed that. Knew that some part of him never understood how handsome he was, not really. The queen's centuries of rejection had left their scars on our Killing Frost.

I patted his arm and turned to Rhys. "Since she seems less impressed with you and Arzhel, one of you gets to shepherd her through faerie."

"Me, too," Galen said.

I looked at him.

He gave a wry smile. "She isn't drooling over me either."

"Which one of us do you want to assign to her?" Rhys was shaking his head watching Carmichael look from one to the other of the men. The look on her face was somewhere between a kid overwhelmed in a candy store, or a small animal surrounded by predators; half eager yet half afraid.

"You choose, Rhys. You're in charge of guarding the police while they're inside."

"Not Frost?"

"He's in charge of guarding me until Doyle gets back." The words made me wonder again where my Darkness was, and where his spell had led him.

It was as if Frost read my mind, because he said, "I will send someone to see where he is."

I nodded.

"Galen," he said. "Find out where Doyle is, and what he has discovered."

I almost protested. If Doyle, Usna, and Cathbodua were all outgunned, then Galen was not enough to tip the balance, or so I feared.

I actually took a breath to say something, but Galen turned to me with a smile that wasn't entirely happy. "It's okay, Merry, I'll do whatever needs doing to bring him back safe to you."

I opened my mouth, and he touched his fingers to my lips. "Shhh," he said, and leaned in to lay a kiss where his fingers had laid their warmth. "You showed the world how you feel about me. That's enough. I don't have to own your whole heart." He left us at a jog, hand on his sword hilt, the thin braid of his hair bouncing against his back.

"Galen!" I said. But he didn't look back, and then the hallway turned, and he was gone. A feeling of foreboding came over me. Prophecy had never been my gift, but now I was suddenly so afraid I couldn't draw a good breath.

I grabbed Frost's arm. "He shouldn't be alone. Something bad. Something bad is coming."

Frost didn't argue. "Adair, Crystall, go with him."

The moment the other two men vanished around the corner the panic eased. I could breathe again. And something heavy dropped into my other hand, the one that was still hidden under the furred cloak. I grasped the heavy metal stem of the chalice. I let go of Frost, and put both my hands under the cloak to help hold the heavy cup. I'd never realized how heavy it was until that moment. Power is a burden.

"Are you all right?" Rhys asked.

I nodded. "Yes, yes." I did not want everyone in the hallway to see what I held, but I also knew that if my panic was true, it was because the chalice had warned me. I had meant to tell the queen that the chalice had come to me, but the time never seemed right to tell her. All right, she never seemed sane long enough to have a metaphysical and political discussion. Now the chalice had materialized in my hand, and that usually meant it had an agenda. Something it wanted, at this moment. Something I needed to do. If it had just wanted to help Galen, it wouldn't have been heavy in my hand. The chalice was quite capable of helping out magically without materializing. So why was it here now? What was about to happen? The tightness between my shoulder blades said, something bad.

I took a deep breath, and used my cloak and Frost's coat to give him and Rhys a flash of gold metal under my cloak. Rhys's eye went wide, and Frost's face went even more arrogant, more angry. Rhys turned surprise to that joking half smile that he wore when he wanted to hide what he was thinking. It had taken me months to realize what that smile meant.

It was Ivi's voice, full of laughter and with an edge of that joking that hid so much. "Oh, my," Ivi said, and I knew that he'd seen it, too. I half expected him to tell the rest of the hallway what he'd glimpsed, but he didn't. He just looked at me with that surprised laughter all over his face, as if he had beheld some wonderful private joke.

Hawthorne and Amatheon stood to either side of him, and they said nothing. Amatheon's pale face had gone bloodless inside the hood that he had kept in place to hide his beauty from the woman. His flower-petal eyes went wide, but I doubted anyone but myself and Frost could see his face past the hood. Hawthorne's reaction, or even if he had seen, was hidden behind his helmet.

"What is wrong?" Arzhel asked.

Amatheon said, "Nothing. I simply was not aware the princess was gifted with prophecy, that is all." His voice sounded a little breathy, but otherwise normal, maybe even a little bored. You do not survive in the high courts of faerie by giving things away. We are the hidden people, and most of us earn that name.

Arzhel put his head to one side, as if he wasn't entirely certain he believed Amatheon, but he said nothing. I did not know Arzhel that well, but I was certain he'd never guess that I held the chalice under my cloak.

Carmichael approached Ivi the way you'd sneak up on a statue in an art museum, afraid to touch it, compelled to run your hands down the smooth, hard curve of it. Afraid someone will tell you to stop.

"Carmichael," Dr. Polaski said. "Carmichael." She touched the other woman's arm, but she might as well have been touching the wall for all the good it did her.

"Rhys, choose someone other than Ivi to watch her," I said.

Rhys grinned, and moved himself between the woman's hesitating hand and Ivi's body. "Andais would have ordered me. I like a queen who delegates."

"She's not queen yet," Ivi said. The bright green of his eyes still held that flash of humor that had covered his surprise.

"What's wrong with her?" Walters asked. He'd gone to help Polaski, taking Carmichael's other arm. She didn't fight them, but she didn't look away from the men either.

"She's elf-struck," Rhys said.

"Elf-struck," Walters said, "but that takes sex with one of you, right?"

"Normally," I said, "but our history is littered with people who caught a glimpse of us in the woods and spent the rest of their lives fascinated with the fey." I sighed at the looks on most of the faces that were suddenly turned to me. "My oath, that it never occurred to me that any of you would be that susceptible to faerie."

"The princess is right," Amatheon said. "It has been centuries since I've seen any human so overwhelmed by merely entering the land." He spoke for them, but his face was all for me and Frost, who was standing behind me. Amatheon's face tried to ask a dozen questions that his words only hinted at. If he hadn't seen this reaction in centuries, what had changed? I'd known that power was returning to the sidhe, but I hadn't understood what that would mean for the humans I had so blithely invited inside. What had I done? And was it fixable?

"She has to leave," I said, "now."

Polaski looked at me. "What did you people do to Jeanine?"

"Nothing, absolutely nothing, I swear it."

"Some humans are more affected by faerie than others," Rhys said, "but it's usually not police, or anyone that's seen too much of the harsher side of things. If you're too jaded, you just don't believe in faeries anymore." He said it with a smile, but he was having trouble not showing how worried he was. I could tell, or maybe I was simply projecting.

"Carmichael is new," Polaski said. "She's good, but she's mostly a lab monkey." A look of anguish and guilt came over her face. "I didn't know not to bring her."

"We didn't know either," I said. "It's not your fault. It just never occurred to any of us that anyone would be this affected by just coming through our door."

"Is this permanent?" Walters asked.

I looked at the men. "I've only heard stories of this kind of thing. So, honestly, I don't know." I looked at the men. "Gentlemen, can you answer Major Walters's question, truthfully?"

"Absolutely truthfully?" Ivi asked.

I nodded.

He answered with a mocking smile, but I knew that the mockery was more for himself than anyone else. "Then I am not certain."

"What is so damned funny?"

"Nothing," Ivi said, "absolutely nothing. I admit to enjoying the lady's fascination because I never thought to see such instant obsession on a woman's face again." The humor leaked away to show some of the sadness that underlay most of Ivi's humor—a sorrow like some deep wound that cut through whatever he had once been, so that all that was left of Ivi was that biting humor and that sorrow.

"That is sick," Polaski said.

His face showed that he had one other emotion left to him,

arrogance. "And how would you feel, Doctor, if once upon a time you were so beautiful that men wept as you walked down a summer's lane, and then, one day, they no longer seemed to see you at all? A flower may be beautiful all on its own, but a person is never truly beautiful unless someone else's eyes show him that he is beautiful."

Walters called over one of his uniformed officers. "Take her back to the lab, get her away from the beautiful people."

"Miller, go with them. Take Jeanine home," Polaski said, "but don't leave her alone. Stay with her all night. When the sun comes up, she may be okay."

I raised eyebrows at Polaski.

"I read up on some of the things that can go wrong when dealing with your people. Nothing I read cautioned against bringing in new people, or I would have left her at the lab."

"The innocent have always been more susceptible to us," Hawthorne said.

"She's never been in love," I said, and was surprised to hear myself say it. "But she wants to be."

Polaski gave me a funny look. "How did you know that?"

I shrugged, using my fingers to keep the cloak closed over the chalice.

Ivi bent close to her face. "Be careful what you wish for, little one, you may get it, and not know what to do when you unwrap the bow." Again the words were laced with sorrow.

Jeanine Carmichael began to cry.

"Leave her alone," Polaski said.

"I am leaving her with sorrow, Doctor, not lust, not happiness, not beauty. I am making as certain as I can, that when she wakes tomorrow she will remember sorrow, like a bad dream. I wish that she remembers nothing that will send her seeking us again."

"You're disturbing, did you know that?" Polaski asked.

Ivi gave that mocking smile. "You are not the first to say it, though I believe the last woman phrased it differently. She said I was disturbed."

Polaski looked at him as if she couldn't decide if he was joking or telling another bitter truth.

Chapter 16

WE WAITED FOR THE POLICE TO RETURN TO US AFTER ESCORTING their befuddled colleague away. The hallway should have been a short trip, but that long expanse of grey stone had grown longer, and now there was a curve that hid the door from view. The entrance to the sithen never changed.

"I believe the sithen wishes us to have some privacy," Frost said.

The chalice under my cloak grew warm against my skin. I let my breath out in a sigh, and simply nodded. I did not like the chalice appearing like this. It amplified magic, and we'd had some very strange and powerful things happen between the guards and myself when the cup was present. It was almost as if the chalice didn't want to leave me alone to solve the murders. The cup pulsed so hard that it made me gasp.

Hawthorne reached to steady me, but Frost caught his hand and gave a small shake of his head. Too dangerous in the open with the humans coming back so soon. Some things we did not want to explain to the police. Some things we couldn't explain to anyone.

If everyone in the hallway had glimpsed the chalice, it would have been a quicker conversation, but we had guards with us who had been standing where they could not see, so we talked around it.

Ivi began, "I'm all for solving the murders. But I also think that we should be trying to make the princess queen instead of playing copper."

A pulse of power shot from the chalice along my skin. It

raised the hair on my body, and collapsed me to my knees. Frost and Hawthorne kept everyone else from touching me.

"What is wrong with the princess?" Dogmaela said.

"And why do you not want us touching her?" This from Aisling, who was still hiding behind his hood and muffler so that only the spirals of his eyes showed. He'd been one of the queen's men, and never mine before or even now. His eyes were not the three rings of color common among the sidhe, but a spiral painted in lines of color, with his pupil at the heart of the design. As a child I'd once asked him how he could see out of them, and he had smiled and replied that he did not know.

Frost, Hawthorne, and I exchanged glances. All the other guards looked at me where I knelt and waited. Waited for me to make up my mind.

The sweet scent of apple blossoms filled the air, and that sense of peace that could come when you worshipped filled me. I wasn't certain it was a good idea but I got to my feet and flung my cloak back, revealing the chalice in my hands.

"That isn't . . ." Dogmaela began.

"It cannot be," Aisling said.

"But it is." Ivi looked at me with a seriousness that the laughter did not touch. He shook his head. "You've had it since you arrived back at the courts, haven't you?"

I nodded.

"How?" Dogmaela asked. "How?"

"It came to me in a dream, and when I woke it was real."

Several of them were shaking their heads.

Ivi grinned suddenly. "You fell to your knees when I said we should be trying to make you queen, instead of playing copper."

The chalice pulsed between my hands, and my body reacted to it. For an instant my skin glowed white, my hair was a crimson halo around me, and my eyes glowed green and gold, so that for a heartbeat I saw the color out of the edges of my vision. The power vanished as instantly as it had come, leaving my pulse thudding in my throat.

"Hmm, that was fun," Ivi said.

"You just want to fuck her," Dogmaela said, and she made it sound like a dirty thing. An unusual attitude among any fey.

"Yes," Ivi said, "but that doesn't make me wrong."

"The police will return soon," I said, my voice still a little breathy from the power rush.

"And once they return, the investigation will take all your attention," Frost said. "Whatever we are to discuss, it must be now."

I looked up at his face, so carefully arrogant. "Are you saying I should take time out of solving a double homicide to have sex?"

Hawthorne's quiet voice came. "I am sorry that Beatrice and the reporter are dead, but Ivi is correct in one way. My life and the lives of my fellow guards will not change if these murders go unsolved. Prince Cel becoming king will change a great many things." He removed his helmet, exposing his wavy hair, held back by braids, and the green, pink, and red of his eyes. He was lovely, but all the sidhe were lovely. I'd never really thought of how he compared to the other men. It was as if I'd never really seen him before, never noticed that he was fair of face, broad of shoulder, even by sidhe standards.

Frost made a motion that caught my eye. "Meredith, are you well?" His hand hovered just over my shoulder, as if he wanted to touch me but was afraid to.

I dragged my gaze from Hawthorne, and I was suddenly dizzy. "Is it the chalice?"

"Hawthorne," Frost said, and the one word was enough.

"I did not try to bespell her, I merely thought about how much I desire to have what Mistral had in the hallway. Not just the taste I had."

"I cannot blame you," Frost said, with a sigh. "But the fact that your desire turned into magic so easily means you gained more from the hallway than just a taste of pleasure."

"As much as I desire an end to my celibacy," Aisling said, "the chalice sits before us. How can you talk of anything else?"

"Your needs must be paler things than mine," Hawthorne said.

Amatheon finally spoke as if to himself. "The chalice returned to Meredith's hand. How can this be?"

I looked up at him, watched the struggle in his flower-petal eyes. "You mean that the chalice would never return to the hand of some mongrel half-breed like me."

He swallowed so hard it looked as if he were choking on years of prejudice. "Yes," he said in a voice that was a harsh whisper. He fell to his knees as if some great force had knocked him down, or he had lost the strength in his legs.

He gazed up at me, and the many colors of his eyes glittered in the light, not with magic, but with tears. "Forgive me," he said in that same harsh whisper, as if the words were being torn from his throat, "forgive me." I didn't think it was me he was begging forgiveness of.

The chalice moved toward him, my hands held it, but it was not my will that moved it.

He buried his face in his hands. "I cannot." His broad shoulders began to shake, and I knew he was crying. I let go of the chalice with one hand, so I could touch his shoulder. He sobbed, and threw his arms around my waist, clutching me so hard and sudden that I half collapsed against him. The chalice touched the back of his hair, and that was all it took.

I stood in the middle of a huge, barren plain. Amatheon was still pressed to my waist, his head buried against my body. I wasn't certain that he knew anything had changed.

I smelled apple blossoms again, and I turned toward the scent. The hill that I had seen over and over again in vision stood in the distance. I could see the tree on top of it. The tree that Mistral and I had stood beside while lightning struck the ground. I had seen the plain, but never stood upon it.

Amatheon raised his head from my body so that he could look up at me. The movement of his head brushed the lip of the cup along his bound hair. When he felt the hard metal of it, he pressed himself against it, the way you would lean into the caress of a hand. Only then did he seem to see the plain.

He was very careful not to move from between my body and the touch of the chalice, but he reached down with one hand to touch the earth. His hand came up with grey dirt so dry that it trickled from between his fingers like sand.

He looked up at me again, eyes glittering with the tears he either refused to shed, or could not shed. "It was not like this once." He pressed his head back against the metal of the chalice, as if seeking solace from the touch. "Nothing will grow in this." He opened his hand wide and let the wind take the dirt. "There is no life here."

He raised the hand that was coated in the dry, dead earth up to me like a child that has a boo-boo, as if I could fix it.

I opened my lips to say something soothing, but what came out wasn't my voice and wasn't soothing at all. "Amatheon, you kept your name, though you have forgotten who you are, what you are," the voice said, deeper than my normal voice, rounder vowels.

"The land has died," he said, and the tears finally flowed.

"Do I look dead?"

He frowned, then shook his head. Again the chalice rubbed against his hair, but this time I felt the silken caress of his hair across my skin, down my body. It made me shiver.

"Goddess?"

I touched his cheek. "Has it been so long, Amatheon, that you do not know me?"

He nodded, and the first tear fell from the edge of his jaw. That single drop of moisture fell onto the grey earth, leaving a tiny black print. But it was as if the earth underneath us sighed.

"We need you, Amatheon," and I agreed with the Goddess. The land needed him, I needed him, we needed him.

"I am yours," he whispered. He drew the sword at his belt, and held it up in his hands like an offering. Then he put his head back, so that his throat stretched tight. His eyes were closed, as if for a kiss, but it wasn't a kiss he was waiting for. I understood then that if one tear felt so good to the land, then other body fluids would feel even better.

I understood then what he was offering, and with the Goddess riding me, I knew that his blood would return life to the land. He was Amatheon, a god of agriculture, but he was more than that. He was the spark, the quickening, that let the seed grow in the earth. He was that magic bridge between dormant seed, dark earth, and life. His "death" would bring that back to the land.

I shook my head. "I just saved his life, I will not take it now."

Her voice came from my lips again. "He will not die as men die, but as the corn dies. To rise again, and feed his people."

"I do not doubt that," I said, "and if that is your will, so be it, but not by my hand. I work too hard to keep my people alive to start slaughtering them."

"But this is not real death. This is vision and dream. It is not real flesh and blood that Amatheon offers you."

Amatheon had opened his eyes and lowered his head and his sword. "The Goddess is right, Princess. This is not a real place, nor are we truly here. My death here would not be true death."

"You have not seen the visions that I have seen, Amatheon. I dreamt of the chalice and woke with it solid and very real in my bed. I would not slay you here, and find your bleeding corpse in the hallway."

"Will you leave the land barren?" the voice said, out of my mouth. Having both sides of the conversation coming out of my mouth was a little too psychotic for comfort. And this energy, this Goddess, felt heavier, not just a comforting presence. "Why are you not happy with me?"

"I am very happy with you, Meredith, happier than I have been with anyone in a very long time."

"I hear your words, but I feel your . . . impatience. You are impatient with me, and not about this."

She thought her response, but I was mortal, and female, and I had to say it out loud. "You think I waste your gifts by trying to solve the murders."

"You have your human police. Even now Cromm Cruach has them using their science for you."

It took me a second to realize she was referring to Rhys, his original name.

"Not his real name," she said with my mouth, "but the last true name he owned."

"Rhys had a name older even than Cromm Cruach?"

"Once, though few remember."

I started to ask the name, but I could feel her smile, and she said, "You are distracted by trivialities, Meredith."

"Forgive me," I said.

"I do not mean Cromm Cruach's true name, I mean these deaths. They will be reborn, Child. Why do you mourn them so? Even true death is not an ending. Others can find your murderers and clues, but there are duties that only you can perform, Meredith, only you.."

"And what exactly would those duties be?"

She motioned at Amatheon. "Make my land live."

Amatheon offered his sword up to me again, and closed his eyes. He put his neck back at an angle where I could have a clean strike.

"You've done this before," I said.

He opened his eyes just enough to look at me. "In vision, and for truth."

"Doesn't it hurt?"

"Yes." Then he closed his eyes, and lifted the sword up higher, as if that would make me take it sooner.

"He is a willing sacrifice, Meredith. There is no evil here."

I shook my head. "How is it that you, who have all eternity, are so impatient, and I, who have only a few decades, want to take the longer road?"

In that moment I felt her sigh, and her happiness at the same time. It had been a test of sorts, not of good versus evil, but of the direction this revival of power would take. She had offered me a quicker, more violent way to bring faerie back to its power. I knew with a knowledge as solid as the foundations of the world that Amatheon would die. It would be true death. The fact that he would rise from that grave, and be reborn to his "life," did not change the fact that it would be my hand that slit his throat. *My* hand that spilled his blood hot across the earth, across my skin. I gazed down at him as he knelt, eyes closed, face peaceful.

I took the sword by the hilt, and lifted it from his hands. Those hands went to his sides, limp, only a slight tension in the fingers letting me know that he was fighting the impulse to guard himself from the blow.

He had gone from hating me for my mongrel blood to offering me up his pure sidhe flesh, and letting me spill that same pure blood in a hot wash across the ground.

I leaned over him and pressed my mouth to his. His eyes opened, wide and startled. I think the kiss surprised him more than any blow could have. I smiled down at him. "There are other ways to make the grass grow, Amatheon."

He stared up at me, uncomprehending for a moment. Then the shadow of a smile caressed his lips. "You would refuse the call of the Goddess?"

I shook my head. "Never, but the Goddess comes in many guises. Why choose pain and death when you can have pleasure and life?"

The smile widened just a bit. He unbent his neck from its almost painful offering position, then looked from the sword in one hand to the chalice in the other. "What would you have of me, Princess, Goddess?"

"Oh, no," she said, and this time it wasn't my lips. There was a hooded figure not far from us, her feet not touching the bare soil. In fact she was misty, and try as I might, I could not see her clearly. The hand that held the hood close was neither old nor young nor in between. She was all women and no woman. She was the Goddess. "Oh, no, Amatheon, she has made her choice. I will leave her to that decision. She does not need me to finish this task." She gave a small chuckle that held something of the dryness of an old woman's voice, the rich melodious sound of a woman in her prime, and the lightness of a girl. "I do not often agree with Andais, but in this I might. Bloody fertility goddesses." But she laughed again.

"I did not know that Andais still spoke with you, Goddess."

"I did not stop speaking to my people, they stopped listening to me, and after a time, they could no longer hear my voice. But I never stopped speaking to them. In dreams, or that moment between waking and sleep, there is my voice. In a song, the touch of another's hand in theirs, I am there. I am Goddess, I am everywhere, and in everything. I cannot leave, nor can you lose me. But you can leave me, and you can turn your back on me."

"We did not mean to leave you alone, Mother," Amatheon said.

"I was not alone, Child. I cannot be truly alone, but I can be lonely."

"What can I do, Mother, to repent?"

"Repentance is an alien concept to us, Amatheon. But if you wish to make it up to me . . ."

"Yes, Goddess, with all my heart."

"Make the earth live again, Amatheon. Spread your seed over that which is barren, and make it live again." She began to fade like mist in the sun.

"Goddess," he said.

Her voice floated to us. "Yes, Child."

"Will I see you again?"

Just her voice now, young and old at the same time. "In the face of every woman you meet." And she was gone.

He gazed at the spot where she had been, and only when I let the sword fall to the ground did he turn to me.

"What would you have of me, Princess? I am yours in any way you want me. Whether by my life, my blood, or my strong right arm, I will serve you."

"You sound as if you're about to pledge me your sacred honor like some knight of old."

"I am a knight of old, Meredith, and if it is my honor you want, you may have it."

"You told Adair you had no honor, that the queen had taken it with your hair."

"I have touched the chalice and seen the face of the Goddess. Such blessings are not given to the unworthy."

"Are you saying your honor is intact because the Goddess treated you as one who is honorable?"

A quick puzzled look flashed through his multicolored eyes, then he said, "Yes, I suppose I am."

"Say what you are thinking."

He smiled, a quick flash of real humor, that made his face less perfectly handsome, but more real, more precious to my sight. "My honor was never gone, because no one can take your honor from you, not without your letting it go. I was going to say that you have given me back my honor, but I understand now."

I smiled at him. "No one can take your honor, but you can give it away."

The smile wilted around the edges. "Yes. I let fear take my honor from me."

I shook my head.

He smiled again, almost embarrassed. "I mean that my fear became more important than my honor."

I stopped his words with a kiss. I wrapped my hands across his back, the chalice still held in my right hand. His arms came up tentatively, as if he wasn't certain how to begin. I think the sex would have been slow and gentle, but I held the symbol of the Goddess, and I was the living symbol of the Goddess. An impatient Goddess. The chalice pulled us backwards as if there was some huge magnet underneath the ground. When the chalice met the earth, it went into the ground, and I was left holding nothing. Amatheon's back hit the spot where the chalice had vanished, and his spine bowed, eyes fluttering closed, his fingers convulsing against my back, his body pushing against mine. The strength of his hands, the solidness of his body, and the raw need in his face, all of it pulled me down to him, put my mouth against his, my hands eager on his body. When my hand slid between our bodies so I could cup the hard, thick length of him, he shuddered and cried out. His eyes were wild when he looked up at me again.

"Please, Princess." His voice was so hoarse it didn't sound like him.

"Please what?" I whispered against his mouth.

"I cannot promise how long I will last."

"What do you want, Amatheon?"

"To serve you."

I shook my head, so close above him that my hair brushed his face when I did it. "Say what it is you want, Amatheon."

He closed his eyes, and swallowed so hard it sounded

painful. When he opened his eyes again, he was calmer, but there was something in those flower-petal eyes that was still cautious. His voice was a whisper, as if he didn't want to speak his wish too loudly, as if someone might overhear him. "I want you to ride me, to press my naked body into the dirt. I want to watch your breasts dance above me. I want to feel your body slipped over mine like a sheath to a sword. I want to watch your skin shine, your eyes and hair dance with power while I shove myself into you as far and as often as I can. I want to hear you cry out my name in that voice that women use only at the height of their passion. I want to pour my seed inside your body until it spills down the sides of you, and trails down my own hips. That is what I want."

"Sounds wonderful to me," I said.

He gave a small frown.

I smiled, and touched the lines between his eyes that would have been frown lines by now, if he'd been able to wrinkle. "What I mean, Amatheon, is yes. Let's do all that."

"You mean I get my wish," he said.

"Isn't that what we used to do, grant people's wishes," I whispered, smiling.

"No," he said, "we, none of us, ever granted wishes."

"It was a joke," I said.

"Oh, I'm . . ."

I put my finger on his lips and stopped him. "Let's make the grass grow."

He frowned.

"Fuck me," I said, and removed my finger from his lips.

He smiled that bright smile that made him seem younger and more . . . human. "If that is what you wish."

"Now who's offering to grant wishes?"

"I will grant anything that is within my power to give you."

I sat up and pressed my most intimate parts against his most intimate parts, and even through all our clothes, the sensation was amazing. He was so hard, so very hard, that it must have been a pleasure that was nearly pain.

"Give me this," I said, and it was my voice that was hoarse now.

"Willingly. Let us get out of our clothes, and it will be done."

I stared down at his face with that eager hardness pressing up through my jeans. It sounded like a plan to me.

Chapter 17

OUR CLOTHES FELL TO THE EARTH LIKE THE RAIN THAT HAD forgotten this land.

He lay back against that dry, parched earth, like a jewel laid upon a rough grey cloth. He had begun to glow before all his clothes had come off. When I brushed my hand over his bare arm, his skin glowed behind my fingers as if lightning flared underneath his skin, as if the lightest touch of my fingertips on even the most neutral parts of his body was almost too much. I wondered what he would do if I touched less neutral places.

I laid the very tips of two fingers against the swell of his upper chest. Light blossomed at my touch. His whole body glowed bright white, but around my fingers the light glowed orange and red like true flame. Where I touched him, his body ran hotter, and that red, hot heat followed my fingers down his body. I traced down his stomach, and just the touch sped his breathing, made him writhe against the dry earth. His eyes fluttered shut and his hands scrabbled at the bare earth, and all I had done was trail fingers across his stomach. I lost patience then, I wanted to see what he would do when I wrapped my hands around that most intimate part of him.

I think he expected me to at most trail my fingers across the long swollen bit of him, to give him some warning, but I didn't.

I wrapped my hand around him and squeezed. He cried out. His upper body came up off the ground, and the feel of him in my hand closed my eyes, bowed my back, because he was so much harder than I'd imagined. So hard, so terribly hard, that he felt more like smooth, hard marble, except he was so very warm.

"Oh, don't, don't do that, Merry-girl, or I won't last."

"So hard," I said, and my voice sounded breathy and hoarse.

"I know," he whispered, "too hard. I will not last."

"Then don't last," I said.

He frowned at me, eyes still wild. "What?"

"Then don't last, for this first time, meet your need. You can prove your stamina next time."

"Next time," and he laughed. "I don't believe in next times. All that's real to me is you, here, now."

He sat up and leaned in toward me. We weren't touching now, just close.

"If I am not good enough, you won't want me again."

I leaned in toward him, putting our faces very close together. "Did she judge you all on just one night?"

His eyes widened. "Yes," he whispered.

"I don't."

He smiled. "Are you saying that Frost and Doyle were less than spectacular the first time?"

I had to smile. "No."

"Then who?"

I shook my head. "Everyone was wonderful, some just got spectacular with practice."

He drew back far enough to see my face clearly. "You mean that?"

"Yes."

"They can't all have been amazing."

"If they weren't, I'll never tell."

"You won't tell," he whispered.

I started to touch his face, but he pulled back just enough to be out of reach.

"Tell what?" I asked.

He gave me a look, a look eloquent with meaning.

"Oh," I said, and smiled again, but it was a gentler smile. "No, Amatheon, I won't tell."

He wrapped his arms around me, pulling me in against him. His back was covered in the dry, powdery dirt. I expected it to be rough, but it wasn't. It was smooth and fine like the softest talcum powder. It did not distract from the warm smoothness of his skin but seemed to add texture like icing spread over warm, rich cake.

I pulled back enough to show him my hands covered in the soft, dry powder.

"So soft." I looked up at him.

"Does it feel as soft against other places as it does on my hands?"

He drew me close, and just before his lips touched me, he whispered, "Let's find out."

Chapter 18

WE ROLLED OURSELVES IN IT UNTIL WE LOOKED LIKE GREY ghosts. The shine of our magic was dimmed by it like Christmas lights shining through snow.

He pressed his hardness against the front of my body and the back of me. He was almost painfully hard, pressed between our bodies. He thrust against my stomach, my ass, but he would not enter me. He rubbed his body over me as if his manhood were another way to caress my skin. Even his balls were high and tight, and the few times he let me touch him there, he quivered, shivering with his need. My hand found that a second pulse lay in his groin, beating against the palm of my hand. He moved my hand away from him. He pressed and teased against me, doing a parody of position after position, but he would not enter me. He would not give himself to my hand or my mouth.

When he had covered us, nearly head to foot, in the soft, powdery dust and shown me the promise of his body, the strength of it, he pushed himself against and across my body, and I begged him to enter me.

"Please, Amatheon, please, no more teasing. Enter me, take me."

"I thought you were going to be on top." His voice was teasing and full of pleasure.

"Lie down for me and I'll be on top." I tried to push him to the ground, but he stayed on his knees and would not be forced to the ground.

His hair lay in rich coppery waves around his face, caressing his broad shoulders. Even the greyish-white of the dust could not dim the rich color of that hair. The multilayered colors of his eyes glowed like individual jewels, sapphire, emerald, ruby, amber, and amethyst. Even the black pupil seemed polished and shining with power.

When his hair had first broken free of the French braid, Amatheon had tried to stop, tried to pull away, as if his shoulder-length hair were something shameful. I had shown him with my gaze, with my hands, that he was beautiful, all of him.

By the time he knelt shimmering with power through his coating of dust, there was nothing left of that hurt. But still he denied me.

"Please, Amatheon, please, lie down for me, or take me." If he'd had a shirt, I would have grabbed him by it, but what I tried to grab to help persuade him, he would not let me touch. He trapped my hands between his and said, "It has been forever since a woman, any woman, has begged for my touch."

He pressed our hands against his chest and closed his eyes. His breath went out in a long sigh. "The land has been too long untended, Meredith, too long unloved. It fears it is too late and there is no life to awaken."

"You are the land, Amatheon," I said, "and you live. Yield to me and I will love you. Please, please, Amatheon, please let me love you."

"You speak of love so easily, do you mean sex?"

I closed my eyes and laid my forehead against his hands where they still trapped mine.

"I am no longer certain what I mean. I think I would say almost anything, do almost anything, in this moment, if it would make you say yes."

"Yes to what?" but his voice held that teasing note again.

"Fuck me," I said, still with my eyes closed, my head pressed against his hands.

He used his grip on my wrists to swing me around. He flung me to the ground. I barely caught myself with my hands in the dirt, barely kept my face above the ground. I drew breath to protest, but his weight was suddenly on top of me, pressing me to the ground. He jerked me up on my knees, so that I was on all fours. He shoved himself against my body, I think he meant to shove inside me, but the angle wasn't quite right. and he had to use his hands to move my hips ever so slightly. Again I started to say something, but he had his angle, and he shoved himself inside me, as hard and fast as he could. He shoved himself in until his balls smacked against my ass. I screamed, because he was too hard, and the angle was sharp, and I knew that as much as I'd begged, if he kept this position, I would be begging him to go before many thrusts. I'd felt men be hard and eager before, but never this hard. So hard, I wondered if it hurt him, too?

"Do you feel that?"

"Yes," I gasped.

"Is this really what you want?"

"A different position, then, yes."

"What position?"

"Me on top."

"Why?"

"So I can control how deep you go. I've never felt anyone so hard."

He drew out of me as abruptly as he'd entered. He turned me around, keeping only one hand in his as he lay down on the ground. He drew me down on top of him, but it took both of us to slide me over him, to put that quivering hardness inside me.

The feel of him sliding inside me flung my head back, closed my eyes. I fought my own body to stay high on my knees and not slam him into my cervix until I was ready for it.

His hands touched my hips, brought my attention to more than just the part of him that was inside me. "I want to see your face while you ride me."

I looked down into his face and saw at last that look. That look that is dark and eager and all lust, but something else as well. Possession. In that moment, in a man's eyes is the sure knowledge that you won't say no. That you are, for that moment, his.

I gazed into the heat of his eyes, not the heat of magic, of faerie, but the eternal magic of male and female, of that eternal dance that truly did make the grass grow, the flowers bloom, the crops ripen. It was all in his face, that spark that keeps it all going.

"Amatheon," I said, voice heavy with sighs.

He frowned up at me. "What is wrong?"

I smiled. "Nothing, absolutely nothing," and I rolled my hips forward and began to ride him.

I rode him until his hips began to rise and fall with mine. I rode him until his hands convulsed around my breasts and I cried out. I rode him until his body began to lose rhythm, and the earth underneath my knees began to change. I was using the hard surface for my leverage, and suddenly I didn't have the leverage needed to keep the rhythm I wanted. That was my first hint that the ground was growing soft, and Amatheon was beginning to sink into it.

I hesitated above him, and his hands gripped my waist.

"Don't stop, Goddess, don't stop."

I stopped fighting to use my knees and used my hips instead. I used hips and stomach muscles to move me over and around him as the ground began to sink beneath us. I could no longer keep the tip of him from the end of me, but it didn't hurt now. Now it was wet and open and ready.

I rode my body over him now, as fast and hard as I could, back and forth, grinding myself against him, over him, around him, over and over and over until his hands convulsed at my waist and he yelled, "Merry, look at me!"

I looked down into his eyes gone wild a second before his body bucked underneath mine, body straining a breath before orgasm caught me. I fought my body, fought not to look away, not to throw my head back, or close my eyes, as the pleasure took me, rolled me, climbed my skin in waves of warmth, convulsed my body around his, until we both cried out while I fought to keep eye contact. Fought to let him watch my frantic eyes, the near pain-filled look in a woman's face. I gave him all I could for as long as I could, but finally the orgasm was too much and I screamed, full throated, head back, eyes closed. I screamed as he pressed himself inside me, and the earth sank under us like black water.

I felt his body leave me before I opened my eyes and found myself kneeling on the rich black earth. I touched the ground where he had been, and it crumbled, black and moist in my hand.

I gazed off across the plain, and it was all black and rich. I knelt in the soft, moist earth and wondered, "Amatheon, where are you?" I was left alone.

Then I was kneeling on rough stone, in the half-light of the sithen hallway. One moment in the heart of vision and the next back in faerie. If I hadn't been on my knees already, I would have fallen. But I was saved from pitching face-forward onto the floor by my own hand and Frost's hand on my arm.

"Consort save us," he muttered, and that was my first hint that something had gone wrong. Before I could even look around, I was suddenly flat to the floor with him on top of me, shielding me. It was entirely too much like the assassination attempt at the press conference. My pulse was suddenly in my throat, and I fought two disparate urges—to look around and to make myself as small a target as possible.

Frost gave me no choice. With his body on top of mine, his chest pressing my face into the stone, I couldn't move.

He raised up just enough to draw the gun that was under his right arm with his left hand. I watched his arm extend to point farther down the hall. I could see enough to know that this wasn't the entrance hallway. As I lay there, his body pressing me painfully into the stone floor, I felt his body react to the shot, as the explosion of it echoed off the stones. He fired again, the shot jerking his body above me. A man cried out, but I did not know the voice.

"I'm getting you out of here." He said it as if I was going to argue, which I wasn't. Getting out of there sounded just fine. Where was everyone else? Why was Frost the only person with me?

He fired twice more in quick succession, his free hand already on my arm. He stood, pulling me with him, already moving us down the larger hallway, putting a wall between us and our enemies, but I could see what lay in the smaller hallway now. I stumbled, and might have struggled against Frost's hand if he'd given me the chance. But I think he knew that, and he moved with all the speed and strength that being pure sidhe gave him. He had me up against the wall, and around the corner, out of the sight and aim of the attackers I still hadn't seen. What I had seen was Crystall with his hands covered in white light, and Adair wading into men, sword already bloody. But that hadn't been what made me push against Frost's pinning arm, as he held me against the wall. Galen, lying on the floor, a pool of blood spilling out underneath him. He hadn't been moving.

"Let me go," I said to Frost.

He shook his head, his eyes anguished. "No. Your safety takes precedence over anything else."

I screamed at him, and fought against him, but it was like struggling against steel with muscle around it. I could not move him unless he let me. He had pressed his body along the line of mine, pinning me completely to the wall; I had no room to try to hurt him enough to make him let me go. He'd known I would fight him.

I screamed the only word that mattered to me in that moment. "Galen!" I screamed his name until my throat went raw, but there was no answer.

Chapter 19

THERE WAS THE SOUND OF RUNNING FEET. FROST KEPT ME pinned to the wall with only his chest, drawing a gun from behind his back, and pointing both guns in opposite directions down the hallway. To draw the other gun, he'd been forced to move his body enough off of me so that I was able to reach the gun at the small of my back. He'd been right to trap me, for my first instinct had been to run to Galen. No thought, no logic, just truth. Frost had given me those few moments to think. I aimed away from the corner where Galen lay, at the sound of running feet. They would be upon us in seconds.

I wasn't scared anymore. I was calm, that breathless, icy calm that is part anger, part terror, part things there are no words for. Galen was hurt, I would hurt them back. Somewhere in the back of my head was a thought that didn't say hurt but said another word. I pushed it back and aimed.

My finger had actually started to squeeze down when I realized it was Nicca and Biddy, and the rest of the guards who had been with Frost in the hallway before Amatheon and I took our little trip. I let my breath out and raised the gun carefully toward the ceiling. I started to shake almost immediately, realizing how close I had come to putting a bullet through Nicca's chest. If the gun had had a shorter pull . . . A bullet through an arm or shoulder could be healed, but one in the heart, well, sometimes yes and sometimes no.

Nicca and Biddy stayed with us, gun in his hand, sword in hers. They were both among the gentlest of the sidhe, but now they looked grim, and tall, and muscular, and dangerous, like tigers and lions. Dangerous simply because of what they are. I had never seen resolve such as this on Nicca's face.

Frost stayed with me, his body still shielding me. The thought of another man I loved getting hurt because of me seemed more than I could bear. If I hadn't been clinging to the gun with both hands to make sure it pointed only at stone, I would have pushed Frost away. Stupid, but until I knew how badly Galen was hurt, I didn't want to risk anyone else. Especially stupid since the rest of the guards had just run around the corner. Magic filled the air, crawling over my skin. The sound of metal on metal. A man cried out, and then a woman's cry, not of pain, but of rage. I wanted no one else to risk themselves for me today. I could do nothing but endanger them all.

My eyes were hot and tight with things I did not want to cry away. Someone was moaning softly. All else was small sounds; the brush of metal against stone, footfalls, movement, but not fighting. The fight was over. The question was, Who had won? If Doyle or Frost had been with them, I wouldn't have doubted the outcome, but Frost was still standing, tense and ready in front of me. His grey eyes were still searching down both directions of the hallway, as if he didn't trust anyone else to keep watch. Without Doyle here, neither did I.

The two men trusted no one else as much as they trusted each other. When had I begun to believe that only these two could keep me safe? When had I begun to put my faith in these two men and lose it in the others?

Hawthorne came around the corner, his crimson armor spattered lightly with blood, as if someone had taken a red ink pen and shaken it at him. He was cleaning his blade with a piece of cloth that looked as if it had been jerked off someone's body. "It is over."

Adair was at his back, helmet tucked under one arm. Without his hair to cushion his helmet, there were marks on his forehead and against his neck, where it had rubbed. "They are subdued or as dead as we can make them, Frost, Princess."

I started forward, gun still held carefully in my hand. Frost stopped me. "Put up the gun, Princess."

I looked at his arrogant face, but saw the pain in his eyes. "Why?" I asked.

"Because I do not trust what you will do with it, if he is as gravely injured as he appeared to be."

My heart was suddenly hammering painfully in my chest, as if I couldn't quite breathe around it. I opened my mouth to say something, but finally closed it. I swallowed and it hurt, as if I were trying not to choke. I just nodded, and put the gun back where it belonged. I settled my cloak over it, as a matter of habit. Don't want to ruin the line of the clothes if you can help it. Habit is what we have when the inside of our head is screaming, and we're so scared that it sits like dry metal on our tongues.

Frost stepped away from me and started to put up his guns, but I didn't stay to watch him finish the smooth, two-handed movement. I was already heading for the corner. One word kept going through my head over and over, Galen, Galen, Galen. Too scared to finish the thought. Too scared to do anything but run for him. I should have been praying to the Goddess harder than I'd ever prayed before. I'd just been in her presence, so she would have listened. But I didn't pray to her or any deity I knew. If it was a prayer, it was a prayer to Galen. I cleared the corner, and saw him. Lying on his back, eyes closed, arms outspread, one leg bent under his body, and blood everywhere. A sea of blood, across the stone floor, spilling out and around him. So much blood, too much blood. The thought finished in my head, the only prayer I had to offer . . . Galen, don't be dead, don't be dead, Galen, please, don't be dead.

Chapter 20

I FELL TO MY KNEES BESIDE HIM. THE BRIGHT RED OF THE BLOOD framed him, so that his hair was greener than I knew it to be. A moment before I had wanted to hold him more than anything in all of faerie. Now I hesitated, my hand hovering over his face. I wanted to touch him, have him open his eyes and smile up at me. I was afraid to touch him, afraid he would be cold to the touch, afraid to know.

I made myself touch the side of his face. His skin was cool but not cold. A tightness in my chest eased minutely. I touched the side of his neck, pushed my fingers against his skin, searching. Nothing, nothing, then a faint flutter. The relief made me slump, my hand sliding down the side of his neck into the curls at the back of his head, but they were heavy with blood. I raised my hand up, and the fingers were bright with blood. "Where is it all coming from?" I didn't realize I'd said it aloud until Adair answered me. "We have not had time to check for his wounds, Princess."

I nodded to let him know I'd heard him. "We have to get the bleeding stopped."

Adair knelt at Galen's shoulders. "I have sent for a healer."

I shook my head. "His skin is cool. We need to stop this blood loss now, not wait for a healer."

"A sidhe who can die from blood loss is no sidhe at all." I glanced up to find Kieran, Lord of Knives, kneeling with his hands bound behind his back. But Ivi still kept the lord at sword point. Kieran had only one hand of power, and it was the only magic left to him, which made many among the sidhe consider him weak. But that one hand was a deadly one. He could use his magic like a blade to stab deep into the body, even from a distance. I knew now how Galen had fallen without even drawing a blade or a gun. But why ambush Galen?

My gaze traveled to the other three kneeling there. The rest were all women of Cel's guard. That did not surprise me. There was another richly dressed lord, lying on his side, moaning. His hands were tied behind his back, but there was a smaller pool of blood beginning to seep out from him. His face was turned away from me, and it didn't matter who it was. Later it might, but now, unless he could heal Galen, I didn't care who he was.

Adair helped me turn Galen onto his side. He was limp as the dead. I was having trouble breathing again, past the taste of panic. There were two wounds in his back, deep and clean. Somehow, miraculously, they had missed the heart. They were still fearfully deep, but bleeding out this quickly wasn't from a wound in his back, especially if it missed the heart.

We eased him onto his back, and when his body settled against the blood-slick floor, there was a fresh gush of blood from his leg. I crawled to his legs, and found the third wound, high up on the thigh. They'd cut his femoral artery. A human could bleed out in twenty minutes. The blood should have been spurting out. The fact that it was only seeping meant that he had lost most of the blood in his body. Which meant that even if someone could close the wounds immediately, he might not recover. The sidhe can take a lot of wounds, a lot of blood loss, but there has to be enough blood left to keep the body running, the heart pumping.

Frost had remained standing in front of me during all of it, guarding me. I couldn't argue with his division of labor, not with Galen lying limp and pale on the floor. I was a great deal easier to kill than Galen.

But Frost had watched as we found the wounds. "Where is the healer that you sent for?"

Adair shook his head. "I do not know."

"We're running out of time," I said. "We have to close the wounds and keep what little blood he has left inside him."

"I can close his wounds," a woman's voice said. We looked to find one of the kneeling prisoners smiling at us. Her hair was the color of yellow corn silk, her eyes triple colors of blue, silver, with an inner circle of light, if light had a single color. I'd never known what to call the final color of Hafwyn's eyes.

The other women said, "No... You cannot help them. You betray our master..." and other less complimentary things.

Hafwyn shrugged with her hands still bound behind her. "We are captured, and our master is still imprisoned. I think it would not be a mistake to have some favor on other shores."

She raised one of her dark eyebrows. With her very blond hair, in a human I would have thought dye, but in a race where your eyes could be three different colors, what was black eyebrows and blond hair?

"You are a traitor to your oath if you do this," Melangell said. There was blood running down her face from a wound that had split the side of her helmet. If she'd been human, her brains would have spilled out, but she was barely bleeding.

"I never made an oath to Prince Cel," Hafwyn said. "It was Prince Essus I vowed to serve. When he died, no one asked if we would serve Cel, we were simply given to him. No one living has my oath of loyalty." She looked at me as she said it, and there was something in her face, some need, some message.

"Can she really heal him?" I asked.

"She can close his wounds," Adair said, "but that's all."

"It is more than any of the rest of us can do for him," said Hawthorne. "Though, in truth, it never occurred to me to ask Galen's assassins if they could help heal him." I searched his face for the irony that should have gone with those words, but he simply looked as if he were stating a fact.

"Do we trust her?" Nicca asked.

I laid a hand against Galen's cooling skin. "No," I said, "but untie her anyway." Earlier that day I had been ready to give Galen up to an unknown lover. But that was different from losing him to death. I could live with his smile being for someone else if I knew he was happy. But to never see that smile again, to never feel his hand warm in mine again . . . I couldn't stand that.

Frost touched my shoulder, made me look up at him. "You must move away before I will allow Hafwyn to touch him."

I started to protest, but he touched my face and shook his head. "This could be a ruse to get close to you. I will not risk you to save him." His hand went around my arm, and I had little choice but to go with him, though I was still reluctant to stop touching Galen. If we couldn't save him, these would be my last moments to touch him while he felt . . . alive.

Hafwyn knelt in the drying blood in her leather armor. She took off the leather gauntlets and tucked them into her sword belt. She settled her short sword more solidly at her hip, and I fought the urge to scream for her to hurry. She was entirely too calm, but then she had helped kill him. Why should she truly want to save him? Was this just a play effort on her part? She would do us a favor, but it would not work, so she could curry favor with us yet lose no favor with Cel and his people. Goddess help me, there were moments when I wished I did not see so many motives for the people around me. It was not a comforting way of looking at the world.

I cuddled in against Frost's body, my arms clinging around his waist, my cheek pressed so hard against him that I heard his heartbeat. He wrapped his arms around me, though it meant he would have to move me to draw almost any of his weapons. As a bodyguard he should have moved me to the side, left himself some room to maneuver, but as my lover, my friend, and Galen's friend, I knew that he wasn't clinging to me just for my comfort. It was impossible not to like Galen. It was his gift to make people like him. The tension in Frost's body as he held me told me more clearly than any words that I wasn't the only one who would miss Galen. It said something about our Galen that he had melted the Killing Frost.

Hafwyn pressed her hands over the wound in his thigh.

She was at least starting with the more life-threatening wound. Her skin had looked white, but it was gold the way that Galen's was green, so pale that something had to make you see that other color. Her magic turned her skin a pale solid gold, as she glowed. Strands of her hair struggled to escape the knot that she had it in, her hair moving in the wind of her own magic.

"She's a healer," Hawthorne said. "Why is she being wasted behind a sword?"

We had expected Hafwyn to have some small healing ability, but what was glowing and dancing along our skin was not small. All the healers with this much magic were not allowed to be warriors, not in the front lines anyway. Their talents were too valuable, and too rare among us now, to risk them.

Watching her shining hands rise from his body, I began to hope. Her voice echoed with magic as she asked, "Can someone turn him over so that I do not waste the healing on smaller things? It has been so long since I have been allowed to use my powers to their full benefit, I am a little out of practice."

Hawthorne and Adair rolled Galen over for her, Hawthorne cradling his head and shoulders so Galen's face did not touch the blood. I would remember that little extra care he took with Galen, and it would earn Hawthorne something.

Hafwyn laid her hands on Galen's back, and my skin prickled with the effort she put into him. She could have closed his wounds, but simply from the sensations her healing chased across my skin, I thought she was doing more.

"NO!" shouted one of the other female guards, still kneeling, still bound. "You are saving him." Aisling placed his sword tip at her throat. She had to stop talking or risk piercing her own skin against Aisling's sword point.

"Siobhan will see you dead for this," said Melangell.

Siobhan had been Cel's captain of the guard. She and a handful of others had also attacked me overtly. I had killed two of the attackers, more by accident than on purpose, and she had surrendered. I had assumed she was dead. She'd tried to kill a royal heir. She should have been dead. When we weren't in front of so many hostile ears, I would ask someone.

Hafwyn leaned back from Galen, a smile on her face. "Siobhan is still locked in a cell in the Hallway of Mortality. She won't be killing anyone for a while yet."

Galen shuddered in Hawthorne's arms. The first breath he took was loud and gasping, and he thrust himself up off the floor, eyes wild. He collapsed almost immediately, and only Hawthorne's arms kept him from falling flat to the floor.

"You are safe," Hawthorne said. "You are safe."

Frost let me go to him. I don't know if he trusted Hafwyn now, or if he knew he couldn't have stopped me without a fight. I did have enough sense left to go on the far side of Galen's body, closer to the wall than to Hafwyn.

Hawthorne spilled Galen's upper body into my lap. I cradled him against me, looking into those green eyes, that face, that smile. Tears streamed down my face, though I was laughing. I had so many emotions that I felt drunk.

"I have not been allowed to heal anyone in decades. It felt so good."

I looked up at the woman who was still kneeling in all that blood. She was crying, too, and I didn't know why.

"Why would anyone forbid you to use your powers?" I asked.

"It is a secret, and I would not go back to Ezekiel's tender care for anything or anyone, but I can say this: I tried to heal someone that Prince Cel did not want healed. I went against his express orders. He told me I would be a bringer of death until he told me I could heal again."

"That is a waste of power," Hawthorne said.

She glanced at him, but her attention was all for me. "But today, for you, I have gone against that order."

"He will see you raped and skinned for it," said one of her fellow guards.

Neither Hafwyn nor I even bothered looking at the other woman. "Why would you risk that for me?" I asked. "You just tried to kill Galen, why heal him?"

"Because I am a healer, it is what I am, and I do not want to be this anymore." She touched her sword. "Does saving him buy me anything from you?"

I nodded. "I would not promise until I hear what you want, not even for Galen, but yes, it buys you something."

She gave a small smile. "Good." She took a deep breath and let it out as if she were steeling herself for some great effort. "Queen Andais announced to the court today that you needed more guards. She said that any who wished to could offer their services to you, but that only the ones who bedded you could stay with you."

"I knew about the first part, but not the second," I said.

"She said all guards."

"What are you asking me, Hafwyn?"

She leaned in toward me, hands at her sides. I fought the urge to lean away from her. I saw Hawthorne look to Frost, as if asking what to do. I couldn't see what Frost told him, because Hafwyn's face was all I could see. She kissed me gently, eyes open. There was no passion to the kiss, no promise of anything, just a touch of lips.

"Take me," she whispered, "take me to your bed, take me here, take me anywhere, but please, Goddess, please, don't leave me here for Cel. I owe him no vow, so I break no vow by asking this of you. I served Prince Essus as his healer for centuries. When he went into exile when you were six, if I had known she would give me to Cel, I would have gone into exile with you. But I thought that exile from faerie was the worst of fates. I ask you, as his daughter, do not leave me here. Now that the queen has opened the way for me to ask, I ask, I beg." Her eyes glittered with tears and when she could not keep them from falling, she bent her head down so I would not see.

It was Galen who reached for her first, but I was only moments behind. She collapsed into us both. Her shoulders shook with the emotion of her sobs, but she was absolutely silent. How many years had it taken for her to learn to cry silently? To hide away this much pain.

I stroked her yellow hair, and said the only thing I could say, "Yes."

Chapter 21

ADAIR STUMBLED AS HE ROSE FROM BESIDE US, CATCHING HIMself against the wall. Blood was seeping out from underneath his breastplate. "You are hurt," I said.

"Innis's warriors are as skilled as ever," he said, in a voice that was a little tight with pain.

I felt a little spurt of surprise. Innis had always been among the most neutral of nobles. He hadn't seemed to care one way or the other who ruled, as long as he and his clan were left alone. They specialized in necromancy of one kind or another. Once upon a time, some of them could raise true armies of the dead. Innis's skill had always been to raise phantom armies that could bleed you, kill you. You could cut them, but they could not die. I understood now why he was the one on the ground. They had had to hurt him badly enough to stop him doing magic.

Hafwyn raised her head from Galen's chest. Tears still traced the pale gold of her skin. "I have some healing left to me tonight. I could not bring another back from so close to the veil, but I can look at your wound." She looked at me. "I can be of use to you, Princess Meredith, I swear that I can."

"I believe you, Hafwyn. Attend to Adair's wounds, unless someone else is hurt worse." I looked at Crystall, who was still standing with a weapon pointed at Kieran. After Adair's show of bravado, I thought I'd better simply ask. "Is anyone else wounded?"

Kanna, the only one of the prisoners without a sword at her throat, spoke up, "Lord Innis, Conjuror of Phantoms, is badly injured." Her voice was very neutral as she said it. Her long brown hair was coming loose from its ponytail, beginning to show the heavy fall of it around her pale face. Her eyes were wide, as if she might be in shock, but her voice gave none of that away.

"Why should I care if he is injured?" I asked.

"He is a free lord of the court you seek to rule," she said.

"He is merely one lord among many, Kanna. I see no extra value in him, merely because he had enough power and political savvy to stay out of the guards."

"Others see the free lords as more valuable than we of the guard."

"That is because they have forgotten that once it was considered an honor to be asked to join the royal guard. Once it was not a punishment, but a reward."

"You speak of things too old to bear remembering," Kanna said. "You were not there. You cannot know."

"I listen to our stories, Kanna. I remember our history. Many of our best and most accomplished warriors were not forced into the guard, but invited. It only became a burden and a punishment . . . later."

"You would leave a free lord to bleed to death, then?"

"If it is a choice between a man who risked his life on my order to save one that I love, and a man who tried to take the life of the one I love, then yes, let him die if he can. Wasn't it you, Lord Kieran, who said a sidhe who can die from blood loss is no sidhe at all?"

Crystall had to move his sword back a little to give him breath and space to talk. "Innis is of the purest blood, not some pixie half-breed."

"Funny how all blood looks the same when it is spilled upon the ground," I said. "Are any of my people hurt besides Adair?" I looked at Kieran when I spoke, watched his face. I was rewarded because he looked puzzled.

"You truly would let Innis die."

"Give me a reason not to let him die," I said.

"He is not important enough to me to bargain for," Kieran said.

"Then he will lie there and bleed until I decide otherwise."

"Innis's clan is powerful, Princess. You do not want them as your enemies."

I laughed at that. "He has already proven himself my enemy."

"We did not attack you," Kieran said.

Adair was still leaning against the wall, bleeding. "Look at his wound, see how bad it is, and I ask for the last time, are any of the rest of you hurt?"

Aisling spoke still wrapped in his cloak, so that most of him was hidden. "I let this one get past me." He emphasized his words by driving the edge of his sword a little tighter against Melangell's throat. Enough that a thin edge of crimson began to flow.

"Was it you that nearly cleaved her helmet to her skull?" I asked.

"Yes, but only after she bloodied me." He sounded disgusted with himself.

"Frost, choose someone to take Aisling's place, so we can see to his wounds."

"Hawthorne," Frost said, and one word was enough. He put his helmet back on, and went to take Aisling's place.

Dogmaela was standing there between the two groups, as if she didn't quite know what to do. Melangell was her captain of the guard. Unless she was willing to make the same offer that Hafwyn had made, she would have to go back under Melangell's rule. In the middle of such a power struggle was a tricky place to be. Dogmaela was like Galen; you could see her struggle with the problem on her face, in the posture of her body. She had fought with the others, but now she didn't know where her loyalties lay. The fact that she was so divided made me put her in the untrustworthy category.

Hafwyn and the other wounded moved to one side, leaving me with Galen cradled in my lap. I slid my hands down the front of his shirt. "You need to start wearing armor."

"Unless it was enchanted armor, it would not have helped," Adair said. Hafwyn and Aisling were helping him remove his armor in pieces. The padding underneath was soaked crimson with blood. The wide, clean cut was plain in the padding, low on his side. "He was able to do this to me, even with the armor."

"Your armor is still worthy of its maker," Kieran said. "I could not pierce it. I had to find a seam."

"No true sword could have found the opening you used," Adair said. The padding peeled off in layers. The linen shirt next to his skin was a ruined red mass.

"That is why magic will always win against weaponry," Kieran said.

"It was not magic that stopped Innis," Crystall said.

"It was human magic," Kieran said.

"Guns are not magic," Crystall argued, "they are weapons."

Kieran shook his head. "What is human science but another name for magic? Even now, the princess has brought human spell casters into our sithen. She allows human magic free range inside the only refuge we have left."

"That's a reason to attack me," I said, "but not a reason to attack Galen. Why him?"

"Perhaps we are attacking all your guards, if we find them alone," Kieran said.

"No," Galen said with his head still in my lap, "when I came around the corner Melangell said, 'We've been waiting for you, green man,' then you hit me in the back. Where were you hiding? I must have passed right by you."

"Innis can hide in plain sight," Frost said, "and he can hide one or two with him, if none of them moves." Frost was still very much on alert, guarding me. He hadn't looked at a wound, or participated in the conversation. He was working and it showed.

"So Kieran, why Galen?" I asked.

"Lord Kieran," he corrected me.

I shook my head, my hand sliding a little farther down Galen's chest, so I could feel his heart beating against my palm. "Fine, Lord Kieran Knife-Hand, answer my question."

He looked at me, his face arrogant and handsome in the way that most of the sidhe were. But his was a cold beauty, or maybe I was just projecting. "You have captured me, but you cannot make me answer your questions. Take me to Queen Andais so I may get on with my night."

I stared at him, with Galen's heartbeat under my hand. Was Kieran being that brave, or did he believe that the queen would do nothing to him? "You have attacked a royal guard. You will not be getting on with your night, Lord Kieran."

"Siobhan nearly killed a royal heir, and yet she lives. Imprisoned, but she lives. The queen's pet torturer fears the touch of Siobhan's skin, so she has not even been tortured. She will sit in her cage until Prince Cel is released, then she will be his right hand again. If that is all the queen does to a would-be assassin of royalty, then what more can she do to us? Nerys's house still lives, even though all of them turned traitor. They tried to kill both you and the queen herself, and they have lost nothing." He sneered at me, all that beauty turning ugly.

"That is why you and Innis agreed to this," I said. "You saw Nerys's people go free, and you think you will go free, too."

"The queen needs her allies, Princess."

"How can you be her ally if you toadie for Cel?"

"I toadie to no one, but I admit to preferring him to you. There are many who feel the same."

"Of that I have no doubt." I looked at him, so sure of himself, and I needed him not to be. I needed whatever information he possessed, and I needed the court to fear me. To fear harming my people. If the queen would not put that fear into them, then I had to figure out a way to do it myself.

There was a sound like a great hollow gong being struck.

"What is that?" I asked.

It sounded again before the first echoes had died.

Frost reached for a knife at his belt. "I have a call." It was Rhys.

"What are you doing, Merry? It was all I could do to keep Walters and the police from running to check out your screams. Is Galen all right? You were screaming his name."

Galen spoke from my lap. "I'm touched that you care."

Rhys chuckled. "He's fine."

"He was attacked, though," I said.

"Who?"

"Nobles and guess whose guards?"

"Let me think . . . Cel?"

"Who else?"

"But why does he keep picking on Galen?"

"I'm about to try to find out. How is the evidence collection going?"

"Okay. I put a guard on each of the humans, as per your order. We figured out how the reporter strayed outside the magical boundaries we set up."

"How?" I asked.

"He had small iron nails in the soles of his shoes."

"Cold iron," I said. "He'd done his research."

Rhys's reflection wavered as he nodded. "And he came here planning to try to see something we didn't want him to see."

"I guess it is part of the job description for a reporter."

"I guess so." He sighed, and it was heavy.

"What's wrong, Rhys?"

"Major Walters insists on seeing you in person. He says that the reflection could be an illusion."

"I'm a little busy here." I glanced at our prisoners.

"I figured that, but if you don't put in an appearance soon, he's going to want to come looking for you. Just a heads-up."

"I'll be there as soon as I can."

"I'll try to keep him pacified." The sword was suddenly empty, only my own distorted reflection showing.

I handed Frost's blade back to him and looked at the prisoners. If I had been certain how the queen would take it, I would do something drastic to at least one of the nobles. But Kieran was right, the queen did need her allies. I didn't think Kieran qualified, but Andais might, and I didn't want her angry with me if I could avoid it. Still, Kieran's reasoning meant that Andais was losing her hold on the court nobles. That was bad, because I didn't have enough political clout on my own to compete for the throne, even though I was still of the ruling bloodline. If Andais failed as queen, they would see me as a threat, no matter who took the throne after her.

Hafwyn's voice came with a thread of anger to it. "Let me see the wound, Aisling."

"I dare not let you see more of my body."

"I am a healer. We are immune to most of the contact enchantments. If it were otherwise we could not heal the sidhe."

Aisling was holding his white cloak close around the bloody front of his tunic.

"Take off your tunic so I may see your wound."

He shook his head, spilling his hood back, and revealing a veil like some of the Arabic countries make their women wear. It was a thin, gauzy, golden cloth, so you saw his head and face through the haze of it. Only his odd eyes were free of the cloth, showing pale skin, and a lace of pale eyelashes.

"I'd forgotten that you covered your face," I said, and hadn't really meant to say it out loud.

"Much is forgotten," he said, hands still holding his cloak around his bloody side.

"I said I forgot that you covered your face, not why."

"Yes, yes," Hafwyn said, "the most beautiful man in the world. So beautiful that if a woman, or even some men, look upon your face they will be instantly besotted with you and unable to deny you anything." She grabbed his cloak and tried to wrench it from his hands, and finished the rest through gritted teeth. "But I am not asking you to take off your veil, just your tunic."

"I fear what effect it would have upon a mortal."

Hafwyn stopped struggling with him, and leaned back on her heels, I think too surprised to know what to do. I realized then that he meant me. How could I ever truly rule here if they still thought of me as a human?

Kieran spoke my thoughts out loud. "Even the guard itself thinks of you as only mortal, and not sidhe."

I would have argued with him, if I could have. "Are you saying, Aisling, that your bare chest is enough to bespell me?"

"I have seen it happen before to humans."

I gazed up at him, Galen still in my lap. "Aisling, do you think of me as human?"

He lowered his eyes and would not look at me, which was answer enough. "I guess that's a yes."

"I mean no disrespect, Princess Meredith. If you are sidhe enough to look upon me, that would be a fine thing, but what if I did bespell you? There is only one remedy for the enchantment."

"And that would be?"

"True love. You must be in love with someone else before you can look upon me."

"Not entirely true," Hawthorne said from his place at Melangell's side. "Aisling's magic can overcome even true love if he wishes it and tries hard enough. Once he could make anyone fall hopelessly in love with him."

"Lust, not love," Adair said. "There is a difference, you know, Hawthorne."

"It has been so long since I had either that I'm not sure I do remember the difference," Hawthorne said.

Adair leaned against the wall in the torn remnants of his padding and undershirt. He smiled, tiredly, with an edge of pain to it. "Aye, I hear you."

I had this horrible urge to kiss Adair, to take that edge of sorrow from his smile and see if I could get a real one.

"Can you sit up?" I asked Galen.

"Yes, but I'm enjoying the attention." He grinned up at me.

I bent over him, hugging him with all my body while he lay in my lap. I whispered against his skin, "I'm so glad you're alive."

He rubbed his face against my breasts, since they were so conveniently placed. "Me, too."

Galen sat up and I waited to make certain he was steady. Just seeing the blood painted on the back of his body tightened my chest all over again. I had to swallow past something hard and crushing in my throat.

I turned to Adair, still bleeding, still hurting, because I gave an order. I didn't strike the blow, but I'd put him in harm's way. I knelt in front of him, reached out to touch his face. He actually flinched, as if he wasn't sure he wanted to be touched, or wasn't sure if it would hurt. Knowing my aunt, I could understand that.

"You look sad," I said. "I don't want you to be sad."

"I'm too hurt to do much, Princess." His eyes were wide, showing too much white.

I shook my head. "Would she really offer you intercourse when you were this injured?"

He understood who "she" was. "She has before, not to me, but . . . others."

Offer them sex after years of nothing, when they were too hurt to enjoy it, or too hurt to perform. Auntie Andais was a true sadist.

"A kiss, Adair, nothing more. Just a kiss, because you seem to need it."

He gave me a puzzled look out of his triple yellow eyes. "Just because I need it. I don't understand."

"Are you lesser fey now, to give a kiss because someone needed it," Kieran said. "It is not a sidhe custom."

"No, it isn't, because we've forgotten who we are," I said, "what we are."

"And what are we?" Kieran asked, his voice sneering.

I leaned in toward Adair. His eyes were still too wide. "The amount of power we raised earlier would hurt me now, Princess." His voice was breathy, but he was against the wall, and there was nowhere else for him to go.

"No power, just touch." I laid a soft, chaste press of lips against Adair's mouth. He stopped breathing for a moment, and I tasted more fear than desire in him. I drew back from him to watch his face and saw the fear turn to puzzled wonderment.

"I don't understand you, Princess."

"Because she is not sidhe."

"You asked what we are, Kieran." I turned and looked at the kneeling man. "We are deities of nature. We are, in a way, nature personified. We are not humans, no matter how our form may ape them. We are something else, and too many of us have forgotten that."

"How dare you lecture us on what the sidhe are, when you stand as the most human of us all, the most lesser of us all."

I stood up, stretching my legs, which were a little stiff from holding the weight of Galen's upper body. "When I was a child I would have given anything to be one of the tall slender sidhe, but as I have grown into adulthood I value more and more my mixed heritage. I value my brownie blood, my human blood, not just the sidhe blood that runs in my veins.

"Aisling, take off your shirt. If I am too mortal to look upon your chest, then I am too mortal to be your queen. Let Hafwyn see which of you is the more injured so one of you may be healed."

He began to argue.

"I am Princess of Flesh and Blood, daughter of Essus, and I will be queen. You will do as I order. Adair loses blood while you act like some bashful maiden."

Even through the veil I could tell that I'd pricked his pride, and all males are alike when it comes to that. He threw his cloak to the ground and jerked his tunic over his head in one quick motion. He didn't wait for me to tell him to take off his underthings. He simply stripped them over his head, hesitating only at his face, so he could be sure of keeping his veil in place. I didn't argue the veil; his face had once bespelled goddesses and sidhe alike.

It wasn't his chest that made me stare, though it was a very nice chest, with wide shoulders and a lovely stomach except for the cut that traced blood from his waist to his ribs. What made me stare was his skin, which looked as if it had been sprinkled with gold dust, shining and sparkling in the light. In sunlight he would dazzle the eye. I'd seen his nude back in the midst of all the other guards when the queen had been driven mad by a magical poisoning. She had ordered them all to strip and they'd done it for fear of her.

"It is as I have feared," he said.

I shook my head. "I have seen you nude, Aisling, unless there is someone else with gold dust on their skin."

"When she saved us," Adair said, "you were on the floor."

Aisling shivered, though whether from Hafwyn's hands on his wound or the memory of what the queen had almost done I wasn't sure. "I had forgotten."

"Not so mortal, after all," Galen said from where he'd moved to sit against the wall.

"Or perhaps the great Aisling has lost his power," Melangell said, "and he hides behind his veil not because he can bespell us all, but because he cannot."

He stiffened, and this time I was almost certain it wasn't from anything Hafwyn was doing. "His wound is shallow. Adair needs the healing more."

"Then do it. I'm needed with the police."

Aisling hugged his bare upper body, as if something hurt him. Melangell laughed.

Hawthorne put his blade a little closer to her skin, and the laughter quieted, but still chuckled out from between her lips.

"Why did you attack Galen? Why him?"

Hafwyn answered, "He was chosen because he is the only one of your guards who is a green man."

Melangell hissed, "You don't know enough to help them."

"She's right," Hafwyn said as she had Adair lift the cloth around his wound. "I know why they chose him, but not why him being a green man marked him."

"Does Melangell know?"

Hafwyn nodded. "She knows almost everything that the guard plans. Perhaps not everything that the prince did before he was imprisoned, but most."

I nodded. "Good." I went to her, staying well out of reach because even with her hands bound I did not want to risk her touching me. She'd once been able to love a man to death. It wasn't the sex, but the touch of her skin. She had lost the power, or so I'd been told, but caution was better.

"I give you one last chance, Melangell. Tell us why you targeted Galen, not once but twice, for we know that Cel paid the demi-fey to try to ruin him. Why is it so important to Cel that I not bed Galen?" I motioned Hawthorne back enough so she could talk if she wanted to.

"I will not betray my master, for I did take oath to Cel. I never served your weak-willed father."

I smiled at her sweetly. "My father is great enough to withstand petty insults. You refuse to answer my questions."

"No magic or torture you can devise will make me forget my loyalties." She shot a spiteful look at Hafwyn, who was busy healing Adair.

"Aisling, are you well enough to come here for a moment?"

"It is a scratch, nothing more." If he'd been human he would have needed at least ten stitches, maybe more. I would not have called it a scratch, but it wasn't my body. He came to me, his sword naked in his hand.

"Put up the sword, Aisling."

He did, hesitating only a moment. "What would you have of me, Princess, if not my sword?"

"If you show your face to a sidhe woman will she tell you anything you ask her?"

"You mean to make her besotted, so we may question her?"

"Yes."

Melangell's eyes had gone a little wide.

"I have never used my powers in that way."

"Would it work?"

He thought about it. "Yes."

"Then let us see if she will tell us for lust what she will not tell for loyalty."

I motioned for the guard on Kanna, the other of Cel's guard, to turn her to face the far wall. Dogmaela had already gone to the other end of the hallway. She may have had divided loyalties, but not enough to join her kneeling comrades. Or enough to protect them. Interesting that Melangell and Kanna had spoken only to Hafwyn, as if Dogmaela was not even there.

Aisling's hands rose to his golden veil. "You should look away, as well, Princess."

I nodded and moved back. Though I could admit to myself that there was an almost unbearable urge to look at his face. To look on someone so beautiful that one glimpse would make you fall instantly in lust with them. A beauty so great that one glimpse and you would betray all you held most dear. I did wonder.

Frost knew me too well, took my arm to move me just a little more to Aisling's back. He gave me a look, and I shrugged. What could I say?

Aisling removed his veil, and all I could see was that his hair was yellow and gold, like streaks of honey, and, like the gold in his skin, shining together. It was braided in complicated knots so that it looked much shorter than the hair actually was. If no one could look upon his face, who did his hair?

"She has closed her eyes," he said.

"Hawthorne, cut her eyelids off. They'll grow back."

She did what I'd hoped she'd do; at the first touch of the knife tip, she opened her eyes. Her eyes blinked, and Hawthorne moved the knife back. Her gaze moved up Aisling's body, as if drawn against her will. I knew when she reached his face because I saw it in her eyes. Saw the shock of it over her face. It was a frightened look, as if she looked not upon great beauty, but great ugliness.

Hawthorne turned his face away. Lord Kieran did, too. Only Crystall looked upon Aisling's naked face without flinching. He smiled, as if he saw something wonderful. His clear, white skin filled with radiance, as if the sight had kindled his magic. Only when his hair was shot through with color like prisms in the light did he turn away, as if he could not bear the sight any longer.

Melangell screamed, and it was a sound of irretrievable loss. The echo of it died on the stones, and her eyes filled with . . . love. It wasn't lust, no matter what Adair had said. Her eyes filled with the mindless devotion of teenagers in their first crush, or newlyweds on a perfect honeymoon. She looked at Aisling as if he were her entire world.

Melangell had never liked Aisling, never had much use for him. Now she looked at him the way a flower gazes at the sun, and it made me sick to see it. I didn't like Melangell, but this was . . . wrong. If there was no cure for it, then I had done something far worse to her than any torture I could have devised. To be hopelessly, completely in love with someone who hated you. There isn't even a level in Dante's hell for that.

Frost seemed to understand because he said, "Aisling, ask her the question."

"Why did you attack Galen?"

"To kill him." Maybe she wasn't as totally besotted as she appeared.

"Why did you want to kill him?"

"Because Prince Cel wants him out of Meredith's bed."

"Why does he want that?"

Melangell shook her head hard, as if trying to clear her thoughts.

Aisling knelt in front of her, putting his face and upper body close to her. "Why does Cel want Galen out of Princess Meredith's bed?"

She'd closed her eyes again. "No," she said, "no."

"You cannot close me out of your mind, Melangell. You have seen me. You cannot unsee me now." His voice was a whisper, but it seemed to trail down my skin. It made me shiver and it wasn't directed at me.

Frost whispered against my ear, "Her power was once similar to his; it may mean she can escape him."

"She could kill with her touch."

"But how do you get a man to touch you, Meredith? By making them want you."

It made sense, though frankly Melangell was beautiful enough without the extra lure.

He leaned in and I thought he would kiss her, but she pushed backwards as far as Hawthorne would let her go. "Don't touch me," she said.

"You said my power had faded, Melangell. Why fear my touch if I am but a ghost of what I was? Why does Cel want Galen out of Meredith's bed?" He grabbed her face between his hands, and she screamed, though not in pain. "I am willing to test my magic against yours, Melangell." He kissed her, long and lingering.

Frost had tensed beside me. Which meant that once even a

kiss from Melangell had been a dangerous thing. That I had not known. Dangerous indeed.

Aisling drew back, and her face was raw with need. "My sweet, tell me, why does Prince Cel want Galen out of Meredith's bed?"

She swallowed hard enough that I heard it across the room, but she answered, "The prophecy said the green man would bring life back to the court."

"What prophecy?" Aisling asked.

"Cel paid a prophet to tell him if Meredith would be a true threat. She would bring life back to the court with the help of the green man and the chalice. Galen was the only green man that she took with her. When we saw what she did at the press conference, we knew that he was her green knight."

"Has it occurred to any of you that green man is a metaphor for vegetative deities, or even another name for the consort?" I asked.

Melangell ignored me, but when Aisling asked the same question, she answered, "Prince Cel said the prophecy meant Galen."

"And do you believe everything Cel tells you?" I asked. When Aisling repeated the question, she answered, "Yes."

"Fool," Hafwyn said from behind us.

"What else did the prophecy say?" Aisling asked.

"That if someone of flesh and blood sat on the throne, Cel would die."

"What did he think 'flesh and blood' meant?"

"Mortal."

"You all must have been frantic when the princess returned with flesh and blood as her hands of power."

"Yes," Melangell said.

"Is there anything else Cel has done that we should know about?" Aisling asked, and I made a mental note that he was a thorough man.

She bent forward as if in pain. Hawthorne had moved back, as if he wasn't comfortable touching her. His power was not similar to either of theirs, so maybe he was in danger of being bespelled by Melangell. Whatever the reason, when her hands moved, the cloth that tied them unwound, and since Hawthorne was turned away, he did not see it. Aisling went for his sword, but he was kneeling and at a bad angle. Her hands came up, and she clawed her eyes out while we watched. Only when blood and wet liquid ran down her face did she stop.

"You cannot force more secrets from me now," she said, and her voice was full of her usual rage.

Aisling let his half-drawn sword go back into its sheath. "Melangell, you cannot unsee me. I told you that."

I couldn't tell if she was crying or if it was just pieces of her eyes. "The sight of your shining face will be the last thing I will ever see. I hate you for this, but I cannot regret it."

"Oh, Melangell," he said, and he touched her face.

She laid her bloody, drenched cheek against his hand the way a lover would. She let him cup her face for an instant, then she drew away from him, and said, "Take me to the queen, take me to a cell, I care not. But take me away from him."

Hawthorne drew her to her feet and rebound her hands, checking the knots. "What do you want me to do with her, Princess?"

"It is my right to be taken before the queen," Kieran said.

"Yes, it is, but it is not her right. If Cel were free, then we would take her to him, but . . ." I shook my head, and looked away from her ravaged face. "Frost." I buried my face against his chest. "Frost, I don't know what to do with her."

"Take her to a cell. Tell Ezekiel she is not to be touched until he hears further from the princess."

"What of Kanna?"

"Take her, as well."

"The lords?"

"Take them to the queen, see what she does with them."

He assigned different guards to the duty. He sent Dogmaela along with the lords. She spoke to me as she pushed Kieran past me. "I am not a lover of women."

It was such an odd comment that I just answered it, "Neither am I."

"But Hafwyn . . ."

I realized then that while we'd been trying to solve the mystery of Galen's assassination attempt, and Cel's treachery, that she had been worrying about her virtue. She wanted to be free of Cel, but not badly enough to lie with a woman. To be free of Cel, I would have slept with things that had never even been human, and never would be. I knew a lesser evil when I saw it. Looking into Dogmaela's face, I didn't know whether to laugh or cry. I still had visions of Melangell's eyes dancing inside my head. I'd probably have nightmares about it.

"I will bed Hafwyn and anyone else who wishes to come with me, not because I am a lover of women, but because I would not leave anyone in Cel's power if I could save them. Now take Kieran before the queen and report truthfully and fully about his crimes."

She went, and the others went with her, two of the guard carrying the still unconscious Lord Innis between them. He left a trail of fresh blood as they vanished around the corner.

Aisling had his golden veil wrapped around his face and hair again. The bloody cut on his side was almost healed.

"You gained from using your power," I said, my face still half-hidden against Frost's chest.

"I gained from besting her at her own game, yes. Once she was almost a match for me."

"She has lost much of who she was," Frost said.

"Once she was Sweet Poison."

I wanted to ask him if he was upset about what Melangell had done. Didn't it bother him that a woman had torn her own eyes out rather than look upon his face? But I didn't say it out loud, any of it. I had asked him to do it. It was my responsibility. To say that I hadn't understood was no defense. You did not use magic that you did not understand because of shit like this happening. I buried my face against Frost's chest, so I could not see Aisling, even in his veil.

He laughed, a deep, rich masculine sound. "I was called Terrible Beauty." But his voice said he was pleased with himself.

I wanted to say I didn't understand, but I didn't. It wasn't a good enough excuse anyway.

Chapter 22

MAJOR WALTERS, THE POLICE, THE CSU TECHS, AND DR. POLASKI, the medical examiner, had nothing but complaints. Their laptop computer wouldn't work. Their cell phones didn't work. Nothing they had with them that used electricity, or even batteries, worked. Was that me screaming earlier, and why had I been screaming Galen's name? Glamour hides a multitude of sins, and both Galen and I were good enough to hide the blood. As long as no one touched us, and found that the cloth felt tacky with blood, we were fine.

"We weren't certain what would happen to your modern tech down here. I'm sorry it's not working," I said. I wanted to avoid the screaming issue altogether, but I didn't want him angry at me. Police do not like to be fucked with, especially if they've just, maybe, pissed off all the local feds on your behalf. No matter how much Walters had enjoyed my handing Marquez his hat, it still might make life difficult for him.

"There are things inside the sithen that are frightening. One of them almost attacked Galen. It scared me, that's all." I turned, hoping to get away from Walters and his questions. I just wasn't up to word games at that moment. Melangell's face kept coming back to me. Frost's assurance that her eyes would grow back if she were allowed to be in faerie and not in the Hallway of Mortality was small comfort if she couldn't be cured of a hopeless obsession with Aisling. We had stolen something from Melangell if she couldn't cure herself of the love.

Walters grabbed my arm. I hadn't expected him to touch me. "Princess Meredith, what aren't you..." His voice trailed off because the arm he grabbed was tacky with the blood that covered it. He jerked me nearly off my feet, and my concentration was simply not good enough. Frost moved in to protect me, but the glamour slipped. Walters got a flickering look at what I was hiding.

He looked past me at the others, and they were all busy trying to do their jobs, collecting evidence with none of their gadgets working. He didn't let go of my arm. "We need to talk," he said, his voice surprisingly calm.

"In private," I added.

He nodded.

Frost said, "Let go of the princess."

"It's all right, Frost." I led the way around the corner and a little way down the hall. Shiny white marble with veins of gold and silver was replacing the grey stone where Mistral and I had made love. It was as if something that we had done was changing the very nature of the sithen. The queen would not be pleased, but one problem at a time.

When we were alone except for my ring of guards, he said, "Show me what I'm feeling, Princess, because it's not the same thing I'm seeing."

Should I have tried to trick him? Maybe, but I was tired of games. We still didn't know where Amatheon had disappeared to. The chalice had gone AWOL, and who knew when and where it would reappear. The only reason I had had Frost with me when I suddenly materialized in the other hallway was that he had grabbed me when I started to fade. But for that, I would have appeared alone, unguarded, in the middle of the fight.

I dropped the glamour, and had the small satisfaction of watching Major Walters's eyes go wide before he found his cop face. But I'd seen the moment, and knew I must be even messier than I thought.

"What the hell happened to you?" He had let me go and now had some of the drying blood on his hand.

"There was another assassination attempt," I said, leaving out that it wasn't aimed at me. "Galen was injured in the fighting." Truth, as far as it went.

Walters looked at Galen. I nodded, and Galen dropped the glamour. He even turned around so Walters could see the worst of the blood.

"How is he up walking around?"

"The sidhe heal faster than mere mortals," I said.

"He lost that much blood and he's healed?"

"I'm a little light-headed," Galen said, "but give me an hour or two, and I'll be good as new."

"Jesus, I wish we could heal like that."

"So do I," I said.

He looked at me. "I forgot, you're mortal, like us."

I shrugged. "That's the rumor."

"You don't heal as fast as the rest of them."

"No."

"Your arm isn't in a sling anymore," he said, and motioned to it.

"No, it got healed in a ritual." The sex with Mistral had healed it, but I didn't need to overshare that much.

He shook his head. "Is any of this blood yours?"

I shook my head. "No."

"His last time," he pointed at Frost, "now his," he pointed to Galen. "You're going to get one of them killed."

"I hope not." I let my voice show how tired I was, how unhappy I was at the thought.

"Go back to L.A., Princess. Take your men and go."

"Why?"

"Because there have been two assassination attempts in two days, plus a double homicide. Someone wants you dead, and doesn't care who gets hurt. If they want you dead bad enough, they'll succeed. Maybe not tonight, or tomorrow, but if you stay, they will kill you."

"Are you trying to scare me, Major Walters?"

"I'm trying to have you not die on my watch. I agreed to come into your murder scene partly to help my career, I admit that. But if you die with me inside your faerie land, I will never live it down. I'll always be the one who let you die."

"If they kill me, Major Walters, the only thing you could

do to stop them would be to die before me. I don't think that's very helpful."

"Are you making a joke?"

I sighed, and rubbed my forehead, fighting off an urge to scream. "No, Major, I am not joking. What hunts me here is nothing you can stop or protect me from. I need your help to solve these murders, but truthfully, if I'd known it was this dangerous in faerie right now, I wouldn't have brought you in."

"We're police, Princess Meredith. We're used to taking our chances."

I shook my head. "Do you have enough evidence? Do you have what you need?"

"Dr. Polaski wanted to know what would happen if we gave you evidence that pointed to someone."

"Did she find something?"

"She wanted to know what—" He paused over his words. "—use you would make of any evidence we gathered."

"We'd use it to hunt down and punish the murderer," I said.

He shook his head, wiping his big hand on the side of his jacket. "What about a trial?"

I smiled, and knew it wasn't pleasant. "There are no trials inside faerie, Major Walters."

"So you'll use our evidence to kill someone?"

"The punishment for murder among us is usually death, so execute them, yes."

"Then we'll have to go back to the lab and contact you later."

"You did find something," I said.

He nodded. "If this was going to trial we'd want to run it through a computer. If what we've found is going to be used to execute someone without a trial, we want to be even more cautious."

"What did you find?" I asked.

He shook his head. "Not yet."

"You do realize that the murderer could be the one behind the attempts on my life. By not telling me what you suspect, or who you suspect, you could be signing my death warrant. By the time you've analyzed your data, it could be too late for me."

His hands made fists, and he closed his eyes. "I told the doctor that in so many words. She won't budge."

"So you don't know either," I said.

"I know it's a print of someone we took samples from, and the only ones we had access to were the ones in the hallway."

"The guards," I said.

"And the kitchen staff," he said.

I looked at him. "One of the royal guards, that's what you think, isn't it?"

"It's who I'd be afraid of, if I were you."

"I could compel her to tell me what she knows, or have one of my guards do it."

"Using magic on anyone connected with the police is a felony, Princess."

"I'm immune to prosecution."

"You'd never again get help out of my office, or anyone else on our side of the river. You might never get help from anyone. No other human law enforcement agency would trust you. Bringing us in here and mind-raping us." He shook his head. "I may not agree with Polaski, but I'll fight to keep her free will and choice."

I looked into his pale eyes, and knew he meant it. I could maybe get something useful out of Polaski and never be able to trust or be trusted by the police again, or I could let them go and hope that the doctor knew what she was doing. If I hadn't wanted their expertise, then why had I brought them into the sithen in the first place?

"I trust Dr. Polaski's judgment, and your stubbornness. I'll abide by the rules."

Frost moved beside me, as if he would have disagreed. "We will all abide by the rules of my agreement, is that clear?"

Some nodded. Ivi was smiling as if he couldn't quite believe me. Or maybe he was just amused at some private joke of his own. You never knew with Ivi.

"I understand," Frost said. "I do not agree, but I will abide by it."

Walters nodded. "I'll try to hurry the doctor and her techs and get it to you as soon as I can, but a print out of place isn't proof of murder. It isn't proof enough to execute someone."

"Not in a human court," I said.

"See, talk like that will make Polaski sit on her evidence. You'll never get it."

"But I'm not saying it to her, am I."

"You think I'd give it to you, if I had it."

"I think you understand, more than she does, how dangerous things are right now for me and my guards."

He looked at me for a long moment. "Maybe, but I agree with Polaski on one thing: I wouldn't want to be the person who gave you just enough evidence to get the wrong person killed. Once someone's dead, Princess Meredith, there's no fixing it. No going back. I'd want to be dead certain that I had the right person before anyone got the ax."

"So would I, Major, and I'll push to see that we get more proof."

"You said they'd use the evidence to simply execute."

"I said they could and probably will, but I, like you, want to be sure. Fairplay and all, but more than that, Major Walters, once someone is executed for the crime the investigation stops. If we execute the wrong person, then the murderer is still free to kill again. I don't want that."

"So it's not about executing the wrong person for you but about letting the guilty go free."

"A guilty murderer that gets away with it once may try again."

He nodded. "If they get away with it once, most of them seem to get a taste for it." He looked at me. "If everyone but you is supposed to be immortal down here, then how did this Beatrice die?"

"That is another problem, isn't it?"

"Perhaps . . ." Aisling said.

I didn't want to look at him. I realized I was angry with him. Angry about what he'd done to Melangell. Angry that he didn't seem to feel bad about it. His tone of voice had sounded almost as if he had enjoyed it.

Mistral suddenly joined our group. "Excuse me, Princess. Queen Andais longs greatly to speak with you." His face was utterly neutral as he said it. Too neutral. Something was wrong.

"Princess Meredith, why not appeal directly to this doctor?" Aisling said.

I took in a lot of air and let it out slow, then I turned very deliberately and looked at Aisling. "It's not a bad idea," I said, my voice sounding more matter-of-fact than my face felt.

Aisling smiled. I could see just enough of his face through the gauze to know that.

I looked away from him. I tried to make it casual, but I don't think he, or any of the other men, was fooled. Maybe Mistral wouldn't understand why I didn't want to see that ghostly smile, but then he didn't know that I'd unleashed Aisling's smile on someone else.

"No," Walters said.

We all looked at him. "Why not?" I asked.

"I shouldn't have told you."

"You're in charge here, right? Of the human side, at least."

"Technically, but she's the chief medical examiner, and she's in charge of her people. If I were the chief of police, yeah, but I'm not."

"So you cannot make her cooperate," Frost said.

Walters shook his head. "She'll be pissed if she knows I told you as much as I did. If she gets pissed, she'll be even less likely to share."

"Then why did you tell us?" Aisling asked.

I kept my gaze on Walters this time as he said, "Because it's got to be one of the people who were here in the hallway with us. Because they're the only ones we took prints from. I won't give you a name just because their print was where it shouldn't be, not if you're just going to kill them. But I don't want you getting killed either."

"Why, Major Walters, I'm touched." I didn't smile when I said it.

"Give me your word that the suspect won't be harmed in any way, and I'll help you talk to Polaski."

"I give you my word that I will do everything within my power to keep whoever it is safe from harm."

"Doing everything in your power isn't the same thing as promising that they won't be harmed," Walters said.

"No, it isn't, but I'm Princess Meredith, not queen. I am not absolute ruler here. You can promise me things, but if the chief of police overrides you, then where does that leave me?"

He shook his head. "Fine, talk to Polaski, but she's not going to be happy with either of us."

"Why should she be any different?"

"What?" he asked.

I shook my head. "Just ignore me, Walters, I'm not feeling my best."

"If I'd had two assassination attempts on me in two days, I'd be pissed."

I thought about that. It wasn't getting myself killed that bothered me; it was getting everyone else killed. There's a reason why the president and his family aren't supposed to date the secret service agents who guard them.

There was still blood on Galen's hand, his blood, dried, a little tacky still. Too much blood. Too much was happening in too small a space of time. Holding Galen's hand made me start to tremble. I realized in that moment that I was going to break down.

"Can you give us a few minutes, Major, please?" My voice was only a little shaky.

He started to argue, but something in my face made him simply nod and walk back down the hallway. I fought it off until he was almost out of sight, then the first sob came. I clung to Galen, felt the glamour slip away, and lost it. I cried and sobbed until I started to hyperventilate. I couldn't breathe, and my knees started to buckle. Galen took me to the ground, put his back against the wall, and let me wrap my legs around his waist, let me hold him as close as I could short of sex.

Galen stroked my hair, and said, "It's all right, it's all right."

"Long, deep breaths, Meredith," Frost said, kneeling beside us. "Slow your breathing or you will pass out."

I fought the wordless, screaming panic. I fought to breathe, and couldn't do it.

Galen stroked my hair and lied to me. "It's okay, we're safe, I'm safe." Lies, all lies. My body was screaming, "Can't breathe, can't breathe, can't breathe."

Frost grabbed my face between his hands, held me so tight it hurt. He made me look at him. "Meredith, Meredith!" He kissed me. Maybe simply to stop the noises, or because he couldn't think of anything else to do. The Queen's Ravens are trained in weapons, hand-to-hand combat, battle strategy, even politics. Hysterical women are not on the list.

His mouth closed over mine, and I struggled against it. There was no air. I fought free of Galen's arms and clawed at Frost. He breathed a cold wind into my mouth. The moment the cold touched me, I stilled, as if my body just stopped. I think even the blood in my veins stopped. A moment of nothingness, silent, still, cold. It was like being thrown into freezing water; the shock of it stopped the hysteria, stopped everything for a moment.

Frost drew away from the kiss, and my breath rushed back in a huge, chest-hurting gasp. I took several deep, painful breaths in a row, while he held my face, and stared into my eyes, as if searching for me. His grey eyes held that tiny snowscape in them again, and I felt as if I were falling forward, falling forward into Frost's eyes. He blinked, and the sensation stopped, but some night I was going to have to see what would happen if I kept looking into those snowy eyes. But not tonight. Not tonight.

"Princess Meredith," a woman's voice said, "I'm sorry to intrude."

I wiped at the tearstains on my face, which didn't help, since all I succeeded in doing was putting more of Galen's blood on my face. I must have looked a horror when I turned around to face Dr. Polaski.

Her breath came out in a gasp, which let me know just how bad I looked. You don't get people who work in forensics gasping much. "Major Walters filled me in on some of what's been happening here today." She shook her head and took her glasses off, wiping her forehead with the back of her hand.

"We do not want the general public to know what is happening inside faerie," Frost said.

"I can keep my mouth shut." She looked at me, and I saw something in her face that was almost pity. "Are you able to talk to me, Princess Meredith?"

I took a deep breath, and it shook a little. My voice sounded hoarse, and I had to clear it, but I finally managed, "Talk to me, Dr. Polaski, I'll listen."

The guards parted for her to come closer to us. I was still sitting in Galen's lap, my legs wrapped around his waist. If the intimate position made her uncomfortable, she didn't show it. I stayed where I was because I still wanted to hold Galen as close as I could. It was a way of clinging to him without looking like I was clinging to him. Galen's hands rested at the small of my back.

Polaski knelt down beside us so we were eye level. "I need to know a few things, and you are the only one I can ask, but by asking, I will give away the suspect I'm most interested in."

"Understood," I said.

She put her glasses back on and shook her head. "I don't think you do. Walters told me that you won't put whoever I find on trial. You'll torture them or just kill them. Is this true?"

"Yes," I said.

She waited, as if she expected me to say more. Then she smiled, and said, "No human I know would have just said yes to that. They would have felt they had to justify taking another life. They would have felt so many things." She looked at me with those long-lashed eyes. "But you don't feel what we would feel."

"It isn't fey versus human, Doctor, it's cultural. I was raised in a world where torture is the norm for crimes, and execution is used when necessary, though it's rare. We do not keep someone on death row for twenty years while they search for legal loopholes."

"I've seen some awful things in my job, Princess Meredith, and there are a handful of people who I would sleep easier knowing they were dead." She sighed. "I need your word that you will not execute the person I'm about to reveal."

"I can't promise that, not without lying."

"Your word that they won't be executed until I have processed the evidence we've collected."

I looked at Frost, and Mistral beside him. "Do you think I can promise that and not be forsworn?"

"I think the queen would put weight to your word of honor, and not offend the human police," Frost said.

"That wasn't a yes," I said.

"A simple yes might not be true," he said; his face was its arrogant best, empty, careful. I thought it was more for the doctor's benefit than mine.

"Mistral?" I asked.

"She is very interested of late in courting good public relations. The reporter's death is bad enough. She won't want it bandied about that we executed someone without proof."

"So that's a yes," I said.

He looked at Frost, they both looked back at me. Mistral said, "She's Andais, Queen of Air and Darkness." He shrugged.

"Your word that you won't let them execute anyone until I have processed the evidence," Polaski said.

I thought about what I could promise Polaski, and finally said, "My word that I will do everything in my power to see that no one is harmed irretrievably before you have contacted us again."

"Harmed irretrievably." She almost smiled. "I've never heard anyone say it like that before."

I just looked at her, willing my face to show nothing.

"All right, I'll take your word. Don't disappoint me."

"I'll try not to," I said.

"Can the little faeries change shape?"

"Many of the fey have more than one form."

"Can the little ones be big, like human size?"

"When you say 'little,' do you mean the small, winged fey, the demi-fey?"

She nodded.

"Some of them can change form to be almost human in size. But it's rare among them."

Galen started to massage my back. I wasn't sure who he was trying to comfort, himself or me.

"How rare?"

"Rare enough that until recently we thought they'd lost the ability."

"We know of only one demi-fey who can do it now," Frost said.

Polaski glanced up at him. "Here's the other question. Could some spell or bit of faerie magic interfere with what I'm seeing?"

Frost, Galen, and I exchanged glances. Frost said, "I trust Rhys to have done everything possible to protect you from overt spells."

"But could someone have magically imposed one hand-print on another?" she asked.

"They would have to understand how prints work," I said, "so that leaves out anyone who hasn't watched television, which is most of the guard. But if they understood how prints worked, they might be able to make one print appear to look like another."

"Would they be able to switch prints?"

"I don't believe so, but I cannot be certain," Frost said.

Mistral said, "I do not know how these prints work, exactly, but they seem to be like tracks of an animal."

"Not a bad analogy," Polaski said.

"Then I agree with Frost, it would be hard to change them in reality."

"So they're more likely to mess with what I think I'm seeing than with what I'm actually seeing?"

We all agreed on that.

"Then I need to get out of here and check my findings with a working computer outside faerie."

"Your early questions point at one of the demi-fey on the kitchen staff," I said.

She nodded. "But only if they can change shape so that they are as big as you. The handprint is about the size of my own hands, but matches one of the demi-fey."

"Which one?" I asked.

She shook her head. "I won't tell you that."

"If you don't tell us, we'll simply imprison all of them."

"All of them?" she asked.

I nodded. "Careful for you is not falsely imprisoning someone. Careful for us is imprisoning too many to make sure we get the guilty one behind bars."

She sighed, then nodded again. "All right, Peasblossom."

The surprise showed on my face before I could stop it.

"Why the surprise?"

"Because she and Beatrice were very close. I've known her a long time by human standards. I can't imagine Peasblossom hurting Beatrice."

"Then someone's messing with me because I got a handprint on Beatrice's back." She looked up at the men. "Can I use someone as an example?"

Aisling started to step forward but I said, "Ivi." He stepped forward with a teasing look in his eyes that I didn't like.

Aisling stepped back with a smile.

"If you could turn around, please?" Polaski said to Ivi. The man turned without a word, giving her his back. "Could you remove the cloak, please?"

"With pleasure," he purred suggestively. He undid the neck of his cloak, and let it fall to the floor to lie across Dr. Polaski's feet. She was now looking at the full fall of his hair, medium and dark green with its pattern of white vines and leaves like his namesake.

She reached to move his hair back, but the moment she touched it, she froze.

"Stop it, Ivi," I said.

"I have done nothing," he said, but the smile was satisfied now, as if he was happy with the effect he was having on her.

"Step away from her," Frost said.

"I obey the princess, not you."

"Step away from her," I said.

He put on his mocking smile, but his green eyes held some fierce knowledge that I did not understand. But he obeyed. The moment Polaski wasn't touching his hair, she seemed to blink awake. "Sorry, what were we saying?"

"What's happening?" I asked Frost.

"He has regained some of his old powers."

"And that would be?"

"To say someone was like Ivi's hair was to say that they were compelling, whether you willed it or not. To be caught in ivy meant to be entrapped. To be ivy climbed meant that your lover was destroying you in some way," Frost said.

"I don't remember any of these sayings," I said.

"You would have no reason to know them," Hawthorne said. "It has been centuries since we spoke of Ivi in this manner."

"No wonder you look so terribly satisfied," I said.

"I have gained much simply by being in the hallway with you while you . . ."

"Enough," Frost said, "we are not alone."

Ivi dropped to his knees in front of me. "I would do anything to be in your bed for a night, for an hour." His eyes weren't mocking now. His face was as serious as he ever got.

"Get up," I said.

"The queen likes us on our knees."

"Well, I don't."

I looked at Frost. "Who can she touch without a problem, just in case?"

"Hawthorne will do as he is told, and his enchantment is more active magic," Frost said.

I nodded. "Hawthorne, go help the doctor demonstrate."

He went to her, having to walk around the pool of hair that had spread around Ivi's kneeling body.

"You must choose two of the green men; let me be one of them," Ivi said.

"Don't make the princess ask you twice. Get up," Mistral said.

Hawthorne gave his armored back to the doctor. "I guess

the armor doesn't make a difference for this." She touched the smooth crimson armor tentatively, then with more assurance, as if she'd expected something to happen. "Beatrice was stabbed here." She pointed to a place on his back where you'd be almost certain to get the heart. "The knife went in deep." She left two fingers at the spot where the knife went in, then placed her other hand flat alongside it. "I have an almost perfect handprint right here, where someone braced to take out a deeply embedded blade. I have almost the same print pattern on the second victim. But I also have partial fingerprints where the knife was wiped clean of blood. They may or may not be Peasblossom's."

"If we are sure it is her print, then she would be our murderer," I said.

"Yes, but if she is, then where's the blade? Rhys traced it to your bottomless pit. The other kitchen help say that once Peasblossom found the bodies, she didn't leave the area. She didn't have time to go all the way to your pit to dispose of the knife."

"Someone else did it for her," Mistral said.

"We found one good, clear handprint on the wall near the reporter's body. It doesn't match any of the guards in the hallway, but the hand is of a similar size."

"Sidhe," Adair said.

"Probably," she said.

"So either Peasblossom is a ruthless killer and had an accomplice, or the killer is imposing her print over his to hide his guilt."

She nodded.

"Can't we check her for spells?" Galen said.

Frost shook his head. "We have no one with us who is good enough at subtle magic. Humans tend to reek of magic once they've been in the underground for an hour or more. To differentiate between the things that might simply cling and those that are deliberate we would need Doyle, or Crystall, or Barinthus."

"I could do it," Aisling said.

"No," I said.

"Don't you trust me?" he asked, with that ghostly smile.

"Not around Dr. Polaski and her people, no."

"You were able to gaze upon my naked body and not be bespelled. Perhaps I have lost some of my allure for mortals."

"Or perhaps Meredith is a sidhe princess," Mistral said, "and not mortal."

"Using your powers has made your tongue bold, Aisling," Hawthorne said.

Nobody seemed to like him much. Had everyone been as shaken as I had been by his little show?

Aisling looked at Hawthorne. "You gazed upon me without anything between my face and your eyes. That is a hero's task, or was it harder to resist my beauty than you let on?" He sighed, and the teasing left his voice, replaced by sorrow. "After going so long with our needs unmet, there is no shame in being attracted to what you once would not have been. We all crave the touch of another sidhe. Sometimes I think I will go mad without the touch of another being."

Hawthorne did a brave thing then, clasping Aisling's shoulder in a brotherly way. I wondered if he would have risked it if the man had still been shirtless. "We have a chance to break our long fast."

"With the princess," Aisling said.

Hawthorne nodded.

Aisling stepped away from Hawthorne's hand and moved to me. It took a great deal for me not to flinch away from him. He knelt beside Galen and me.

"There will be no princess for me," Aisling said. "She will not risk it now." He looked down at me. "Will you, Princess?"

I didn't know what to say because he was right. I did not want him touching me. I said the only thing I could think of: "I will not rule it out, but I fear you now, Aisling, where I didn't before."

"I'm missing something," Polaski said.

"Be happy you missed it," I said.

She walked toward me. "No, you're hiding too many things from me, Princess. I need to know what is happening here, or you get nothing from me and my people."

As she came to stand over us, she brushed against Aisling

and started to fall. Galen and I reacted, knowing that Aisling must not touch her with his bare skin. I stood between them, pushing Aisling backwards. Galen came to his knees and caught Dr. Polaski before she could hit the floor.

The doctor was safe with Galen, but I was in Aisling's arms, and I wasn't safe at all.

Chapter 23

HE CAUGHT HIS BALANCE, AND ME, WITH HIS ARMS AND HIS body. Perhaps he stumbled more than he needed to, so he would be able to hold me tighter, but it wasn't him that made my hand slip underneath his tunic to glide along bare skin. Fear choked me, ran along my skin so that it was like small electric shocks, tingling out to my fingertips. I saw Melangell's face, her empty, bloody eyes, and waited for his magic to take me. I stared up into those odd eyes, with their inner knot, bound in four empty loops. There was no sign of the blue of his eyes. Something was missing.

I traced my hand up the curve of his spine, so warm, so firm, so real. He leaned over me, as if to kiss me through the gauze of his veil. I leaned back, his hands tightened around my body, holding me against him. If I had not seen him with Melangell I would have simply let him kiss me, but some things once known can never be unknown.

I smelled roses. I was suddenly drowning in the sweet, almost cloying scent of roses.

Aisling hesitated. "Do you smell that?"

"Yes," I whispered.

A voice whispered through my head. "With Amatheon I

bid you hurry, and you turned from haste, and chose the longer road. You risked losing that which you cherished."

I whispered, "Galen."

Aisling's arms loosened around me, but I grabbed for him, because I was suddenly dizzy.

"Now I tell you that this must wait, or you will lose again."

"Doyle."

"Darkness cannot be lost for it is always with us, but there are other more fragile powers. Hurry."

"Who?" I asked.

"Who are you talking to?" Aisling asked.

"Hurry," the voice in my head said, and with a last whiff of roses she was gone again.

"Where?" I asked.

It wasn't words. It was more like the feeling that had come over me when I told Frost that Galen could not search alone for Doyle. But this wasn't panic, it was just a knowing. I simply knew where I needed to go. No doubts, no logic, just knowledge.

"Who are you talking to?" Aisling said again, his voice shaky, almost afraid.

"I am not afraid to touch you," I said, "but there is no time. We must get to the throne room, now."

"Why?" Galen stood with an arm still around Dr. Polaski, casually, the way he would have touched another sidhe. She was looking at me as if she'd never seen me before.

"Why did everything smell like flowers?" she asked.

I shook my head, and yelled for Rhys as I started down the hallway. He came to the head of the hallway, leaving behind the scientists, police, and bodies.

"Peasblossom's print is where it shouldn't be, but it may be a sidhe using magic to implicate her. Put her gently in a cage until we can figure it out."

"But..."

"No arguments. Just do it, Rhys."

His face did a rare show of arrogance, going cold. "As the princess orders."

"I don't have time for ego-stroking, Rhys." I started to run.

I couldn't explain why, but I ran down the hallway with its patches of glittering marble like some brilliant jewel peeking out of the grey matrix of the stone.

Frost and Galen ran on either side. Mistral came behind, and the others trailed after. We were down to less than ten guards, but it wouldn't be a matter of numbers. Something bad was happening, and we could prevent it just by arriving in time. I thought about the mirror that had appeared in my room, simply because I wished to see myself in the fur cloak. As I broke into a full-out run, I whispered under my breath, "We need to get to the throne now!"

Nothing happened for a handful of heartbeats, then the stones shifted beneath my feet. I didn't hesitate. I didn't pause. I didn't stumble. I trusted that the sithen would get me where I wanted to go. I ran, as the world streamed around me, grey stone flowing into white marble, as if the walls had turned to liquid. Then we were running on dried, dead ground. I had a second to recognize the pool and fountain that stood before the great double doors that led to the entry chamber for the throne room, but the fountain was now in the center of a huge formal garden spreading on either side. The fountain had always stood in the center of a bare hallway.

Crystall and the guards I'd sent with the lords to the queen were standing in the middle of that garden. They turned frightened eyes to me. I had no idea what about the garden made Crystall look so shaken, and I didn't ask. Panic filled me, adrenaline like fine champagne screamed through me. The double doors opened without a hand to touch them. My pulse was choking off my air. I fought the pain in my side to keep upright and running.

The climbing roses of the entry chamber, filling the darkness with crimson blossoms, writhed and slithered like great thorned serpents overhead. I ran, and the vines did not try to hinder us. The last set of double doors was just ahead. The court lay just inside them.

I whispered, "Open," and the doors swung inward. I raced from the dimness of the roses to the brightness of the court, and staggered, almost blinded by the difference in light. I could see nothing but light and shadow and half shapes. Exhaustion danced across my vision in starbursts of grey and white. Through the thundering of the blood in my ears, I heard Queen Andais yelling.

I yelled, "Stop . . . this!" It took the last of my air, and Galen caught my elbow or I would have fallen. My vision came back in pieces. The court was dressed for a party, or an expensive funeral. A lot of black, a lot of silver, a lot of jewels.

Andais was on the steps leading up to her throne, staring at me, at us. Barinthus stood at the bottom of those steps. He stood so he could keep both the queen and us in his sight. I knew in that second what was happening, though not why. Why didn't matter to me.

"By what right do you stop me from issuing challenge to anyone, niece?" Her voice held a rage that made the air itself heavier on my tongue. She was the Queen of Air and Darkness. She could make the air so thick my mortal lungs couldn't breathe it. She'd nearly killed me that way. Was it just last night, or the night before?

"I beg a private audience with you, Aunt Andais." My voice was breathy, and if Galen hadn't had a death grip on my elbow, I'm not sure my legs would have held me. Supernatural strength and magic were fine, but I wasn't used to running like that.

She smiled. "Begging is not done on your feet, Meredith." She walked back up to her throne, the long black skirts trailing behind her like a cloak of darkness. She settled the skirts with a practiced gesture, fanning them out around her. The color framed all that pale skin and black hair, the tri-grey eyes with the dramatic eye makeup. Diamonds and midnight-dark sapphires graced her throat and gloved wrist.

I dropped to one knee. Galen helped make it graceful, and knelt with me. Everyone with me knelt when I did. "I beg a private audience with you, Aunt Andais, Queen of Air and Darkness."

"Why are you and Galen covered in blood?"

"I have much to share with you, my queen, but some of it might better be served to your ears alone."

"Has there been another attempt on your life?"

"Not on mine, no."

She shook her head, as if she had a fly buzzing around her, and she was ridding herself of it. "You speak in riddles."

"I would speak clearly with you in private."

"Let us handle our public business first," she said, and pointed to Barinthus, who was still standing between the throne and our group. "The ring acknowledges him, and you have helped him break his vow to me."

"The ring knows Lord Barinthus. You said that I was to fuck as many of the guards as often as possible. Wasn't that your order to me?"

Her face narrowed down to angry lines. "Perhaps my words were hasty, or perhaps you do not know that Barinthus made a vow to me before I allowed him to join this court. One that only he made, and now he has broken it."

"He has done nothing that will set him as king to my queen."

"Have a care, Meredith, I know that he had sex with you."

"Sex that was more magical than real, nothing that would get me with child."

"He had release in your body."

"No, he had release, but our clothes were in place, and he has never entered my body with so much as a fingertip."

"You swear this?" she asked.

"I do."

"I was told that Barinthus had moved from kingmaker to would-be king."

"I tell you that he has not broken the vow he made to this court. The ring recognizes who it will, and bestows its gifts where it will, but he has broken no vow."

"Why did you not say this, Barinthus?" she asked.

"You would not believe me, Queen Andais."

She seemed to think about that for a second or two, then gave a very small nod. "Perhaps not." She looked at me. It was the kind of look that a hawk gives to grass when it's almost certain there's a tasty morsel down there.

"I have heard many stories about your activities. Now I

wonder how much is true, and how much is exaggeration designed to set me against my allies and you."

"Until I know what you have been told, I cannot say, Aunt Andais."

"We are in the throne room, Meredith, use my title."

"My queen." I bowed my head, so she would not see my face. This wasn't good. This wasn't good at all.

Chapter 24

"DID THE RING CHOOSE A COUPLE AMONG THE GUARDS?" HER voice was very neutral when she asked.

I was glad I was staring at the floor because so much had happened that I'd almost forgotten about Nicca and Biddy. Murders, metaphysics, the Goddess, the chalice, Amatheon vanishing, the attack on Galen, Cel's prophecy about the green men, the lords who waited just outside, so much, and this was what she began with. Why?

"Yes, Queen Andais, the ring did choose a couple."

There were murmurings from the nobles in their seats on either side of the floor. "Describe what happened."

I did as she ordered. I talked of the phantom child, and what I had seen and felt.

Someone said, "The ring lives again."

Andais looked at the man who had spoken. "Do you have something to add to this discussion, Lord Leri?"

"Only that this is surely good news, my queen."

"I will decide what is good news, Leri."

He bowed. "As my queen wills."

She turned her attention back to me. "The ring lives again

after centuries. It chooses a possibly fertile pair, and you don't think this is important enough to tell me."

"Much has happened since the ring chose them, Queen Andais. I thought finding the murderer, or murderers, took precedence."

"I decide what takes precedence here, not you." She stood. "I am still queen."

I lowered myself to both knees, and Galen moved with me. "I have never questioned that."

"Liar," she hissed, and the room echoed with that one word.

Okay, this was bad, really bad. "What have I done to anger you, Queen Andais? Tell me and I will do my best to remedy it." I kept my face down so that I was staring at the well-worn stone floor. I did not trust my expression. Fear might excite her, and puzzlement might anger her. I had no expression that I could give her.

"Mistral. Come to me, captain of my guard." He got up off his knees and answered her command.

I watched him as he mounted the steps to her. He made a sound of startlement more than pain, as she grabbed a handful of his rich, deep grey hair and used it to jerk him to his knees before her. "Did you fuck him?"

I tried to see the trap in the question but failed. I answered truthfully, "Yes, my queen."

She let him go so abruptly that he nearly fell down the steps, catching himself with one hand. He stayed kneeling awkwardly, most of his face hidden by the glory of his hair. He lowered his eyes, but not before a rumble of thunder echoed through the throne room.

The nobles moved restlessly, looking up and around. Andais's voice purred as she knelt beside Mistral, stroking his hair. He shivered like a skittish horse when she touched him. "Was that you, Mistral?"

"Forgive me, my queen, I have not had such power in years. My control is not what it was, my apologies, my queen."

"Two 'my queens' in one sentence—you must feel guilty indeed."

"I have done nothing to feel guilty over, my queen."

She kept stroking his hair, but she looked out at me. "Have you not?"

He kept his face carefully down. Mistral had never been that good at hiding his emotions. "What have I done to anger you, my queen?" His voice was almost neutral, the distant rumble of thunder was not. His powers were newly reborn, and he was struggling.

"Did the princess bring you back into your power?" She kept petting him idly like a dog. I'd seen her do that with a guard now and then. She'd stroke and pet them all night in front of everyone, then leave them with only those caresses, and nothing more. I'd seen her reduce some of our greatest warriors to silent tears. She petted Mistral, but the anger in her face was all for me. Why was she angry that I'd had sex with Mistral? What had we done wrong?

She walked down the steps, her black dress slithering behind her. "Could you bring any of us, all of us, back to our power? Is one good fuck from you all it takes?" Anger was making her skin pale, starting that first hint of moonlight glow. Her triple-grey eyes were beginning to shine, as if darkness had light in it.

I put my hands on the floor and lowered my face on top of them. I abased myself before her, because I had no idea why she was this angry with me. I had no idea what someone had been whispering in her ear.

She stood so close that the trailing edge of her skirt brushed along my body as she moved past me. "Answer me, Meredith."

I thought of several answers, discarded them all, and finally said, "I move as the Goddess wills it."

She came fast, her heels clicking on the stones. She knelt, put her gloved hand under my chin, and raised me up to meet her eyes. "That is not an answer."

My voice was breathy around my pulse. "I have no other answer." If I even hinted that I might be able to bring others back with sex, she might order one of her sex shows, and I wasn't sure that I would survive it. And there were nobles here with whom I could barely have a casual conversation, let alone share my body. There were those who were my enemies, and I wasn't certain having them come back into their full powers was a good idea.

She slid her other hand into my hair, grabbed a handful of it, and jerked me to my feet. I fought not to let the anger show in my eyes, and knew that I failed.

"It is not just my powers that are returning," Mistral said from the steps.

She turned to look at him, and I knew that he had deliberately distracted her from me, offering himself to her anger.

She kept her painful grip on my hair, her other hand stroking along the side of my face, much as she had touched his hair. "What are you babbling about, Mistral?"

"Most of the guards that experienced the magic of the ring have regained at least some small magic that had been lost."

Her grip tightened in my hair until I fought not to make a sound of pain. Andais liked that, and I did not want to encourage her. "Are you saying that she has brought others of my guard back to their power?"

"Yes, my queen."

She turned back to me, and I didn't like anything I saw in her eyes. She loosened her hold on my hair just a little as the silk of her gloved hand stroked my cheek and continued down along my neck. Under other circumstances it might have been exciting. Now it just scared me more.

"How many of my guards have you had sex with, Meredith?" She moved her face in close to me, as if she meant to kiss me. "How many of my guard have you given release?" She spoke the last word above my lips, and I knew she was going to kiss me before her lips touched mine.

I felt movement all around me, and knew that the guards were standing. Everyone with me had been in the hallway when Mistral and I had sex, so they all stood to answer her question. They stood to draw her attention from me to them. My bodyguards, my men and women. Some of them had spent centuries like well-armed mice. Quiet, hiding, trying to be invisible. Now they stood and purposefully made a spectacle of themselves.

She had moved back from me when they stood, leaving the taste of her lipstick on my mouth. "She fucked all of you?" She sounded as if she didn't believe it.

"You asked only who has had release," Frost said. "When the power filled the hallway, it touched all who stood there."

"You mean the power when Mistral and Meredith came together made all the guard in the hallway orgasm?"

"Yes," Frost said.

She laughed and let me go. "How many fertility deities are in your lineage?"

"Five," I said.

"Five," she repeated, as she paced away from us. "Now you don't even have to touch them to bring them power, is that what you're telling me?"

"I thought you would be pleased that magic returns to the sidhe," I said carefully.

Afagdu, one of the nobles, spoke from his chair, his eyes the only color in the white of his face and the black of his hair and beard. "Our magic returns; is that not what we have all wished for, Queen Andais?" His voice was mild, careful. Afagdu and his entire house belonged to no one. They were one of the four or five truly neutral houses.

Dylis stood in a gown of yellow that complemented her hair and brought out the tri-blue of her eyes. She was head of one of the sixteen houses, and had never been my friend. "You know that I have never liked Essus's daughter. I agreed with you, my queen, when you tried to drown her in childhood. But if the ring lives on her hand, and can bring children back to the sidhe, then I will follow her."

A sort of mixed endorsement but I took it.

"You follow me, Dylis, until I say otherwise."

The woman gave a curtsy. "You are our queen. I misspoke myself. I meant only that if Meredith can give us back our children, then I would rethink my objections to her."

"Politely and politically spoken, Dylis. But if you mean Nicca and Biddy, they are both guards sworn to me and mine, and no one else. The guards serve me and my blood." She smacked her hand against her chest to emphasize her words.

"Do you forbid a couple the ring has chosen to bed?" Afagdu asked.

"Royal guards serve royalty, this is their function," Andais said.

"They will still serve you," he said, and his voice was careful again.

She shook her head. "Not if there is a child."

"But a child would be a great blessing." This from one of Nerys's ladies.

"The head of your house tried to kill Meredith just last night, or had you forgotten that, Elen?"

She gave a curtsy so low that she almost disappeared behind the table. "If the ring truly lives on her finger, then Nerys was wrong, very wrong. If the Goddess blesses Meredith with her gifts, then we were all wrong."

"Would you have us all childless because your bloodline is?" asked Maelgwn, the wolf lord. He was naked from the waist up except for a hood and cloak of wolf skin, complete with most of the animal's face sitting above his own. All his people had been shape-shifters until they lost the ability.

"I am queen and my blood inherits this throne."

"You have your brother's blood standing in front of you," Maelgwn said, his mocking smile and his happy, peaceful eyes taking me in. "There she stands, your blood. If your niece can bring blood back to all of us, then your line is indeed powerful magic."

"I have held the guards in abstinence for more than a thousand years. They wait at my pleasure, and the pleasure of my son."

"And at your niece's pleasure," Afagdu said. He seemed to be helping me, but I didn't trust it. He helped no one but himself and his clan.

Andais waved that away as if it was unimportant. "Yes, yes, on Meredith's pleasure." She looked at me then. "Though I did not intend the pleasure to be so . . . pleasurable." She came down the steps again, gliding toward me in her heels and silk. "The guards are for our pleasure, Meredith, not us for theirs. I'm not certain you understand that, niece." She walked past me, and I knew where she was going.

She stopped by Nicca and Biddy where they knelt. I glanced back and found that they were holding hands. They were also staring very hard at the floor, as if she wouldn't hurt them if they didn't look up. If only it were that easy.

She ran her fingers through the heaviness of Nicca's chestnut hair. He went very still under her touch. "I like him in my bed, but not for sex. He frightens so easily. He doesn't like pain, do you, Nicca?"

If I hadn't been kneeling within a yard of him I might not have heard his answer. "No, Queen Andais."

"I taught him that in a night, did you know that, Meredith?"

"Taught him what, my queen?"

"To answer any question I asked him with yes or no, and never, ever to leave off the Queen Andais." She ran her hand down the side of his face until she cupped his chin. She raised him to look at her. "Would you like another lesson, Nicca? It has been long since I made love to a man with wings. It might be interesting."

"Queen Andais," I said.

She didn't even look at me.

"My queen, you said that the guards who came to my bed were mine to keep." I made my voice as neutral as I could, but I knew it was a bad idea to say it.

"Would you not share him with me?"

I thought about that. "Perhaps, but after he and Biddy have had their night."

She touched Biddy, turned her face upward, so she gazed down at both of them. "But if she gets with child then they will be married and monogamous, and even the Queen of Air and Darkness will not be able to force him to forsake his marriage vows."

"My queen, Aunt Andais, if Nicca and Biddy could make a baby, then it might mean that others of the sidhe could as well. That is a good thing."

She let go of their faces and walked between them, forcing

them to let go of each other's hands. She traced the upper edge of Nicca's wings. "But he is mine, Meredith, my pretty toy, and I do not share my toys."

"You said that any guard who went to the bed of the princess was hers," Afagdu said. "Nicca is her pretty toy now."

She turned abruptly and started walking toward Afagdu and his table of lords. "What the queen gives, the queen can take away."

"Even the queen must honor her word," Afagdu said, "and you gave your word before the court that the guards who went to Meredith's bed were hers." The fact that he would say such bald truth to an angry Andais showed how confident he was that he could survive an attack by her. There were few magicians among us who thought they were her equal in magic; Afagdu was one of them.

"Few would dare make me eat my own words in open court, Afagdu. Do not let your magic make you bold beyond your abilities."

"Is it bold to speak the truth, my queen?"

But, of course, two could play at that particular game. "Very well, Nicca is Meredith's now, but Biddy is not. Meredith can do as she will with Nicca, but Biddy is not hers to give to another man. Biddy belongs to my son, to Prince Cel." She looked at me. "Would you steal even the women from his bed?"

"You cannot steal that which is offered," I said.

"And what does that mean, Meredith, with your Seelie eyes?"

I swallowed hard, and promised myself I'd think better before I spoke next time. "The ring gave Biddy to Nicca."

"So you say, but I say that the guards serve only my bloodline. So how do you propose to satisfy both the ring on your finger and your queen?"

"You said any guard who comes to my bed is mine to keep, correct?"

"Yes, so Afagdu has reminded me."

"Then I will take Biddy and Nicca to my bed. Nicca will

still be my lover, but he will also be Biddy's. Will that satisfy you, Aunt Andais?"

"I have never found Nicca able to serve more than one person in a night."

"I can bring him back to readiness with a touch," I said.

"Can you really?" Her voice was thick with scorn. Her eyes had gone back to being angry.

I didn't like the look or the tone, but I answered her, because not answering was probably worse. "Yes, my queen, I can."

"Is this some new ability that you have gained?"

"No, Aunt Andais, it has always been my gift."

"I keep forgetting that you're a fertility goddess."

"Descended from, yes."

"I did not think you liked women, Meredith."

My neck was beginning to feel strained looking up at her six-foot height from my knees. "I do not, as a rule, but if this is the only way to satisfy both the ring and my queen, then I will do it."

She walked closer to me, forcing me to move my neck even farther back, as if she knew how awkward it was. "Would you do anything to see them make this potential child a reality?"

I saw the trap in her words and tried to avoid it. "Not anything, no."

"But much," she said, looming over me, "you would do much to have them fuck?"

I fought the urge to sit back on my heels, anything to get my neck out of the odd position. I did not want to answer this question, nothing good would come of it.

"Answer me, Meredith."

"Yes, Aunt Andais, I would do much so they could make the child the ring promised."

"Why do you care if they are with child?"

"Life quickens inside them. I saw it, felt it. It is a gift of the Goddess. How can I do anything but honor that gift? You wore the ring once when it was in its full power. You must remember how it felt."

She grabbed me by the hair, jerked my head even farther back, as if she meant to snap my neck. She growled low and close to my face. "I am not a fertility goddess. I took the ring off my enemy's finger. It was a spoil of war, and it worked for me, but its magic and mine are not complementary. I never saw a phantom child. I saw sex, obsession, love, but children . . ." She lifted me off my knees, by my hair. I put a hand back to try to keep it from hurting so much. "I never saw any children."

Our faces were almost touching now. It felt as if she was going to tear my hair out by the roots. "Why is it so important to you that Nicca and Biddy fuck?"

I spoke through gritted teeth, trying not to cry out. "Because I am a princess of this court and I have a chance to give the sidhe their first child in a century. It is my duty, my honor, to bring this child into being."

She let me go so abruptly that I fell, and only Galen's arm kept me from smacking my face against the floor. She touched his face, made him look at her. "Oh, he is angry. He doesn't like that I've hurt you. I never tried him out. I always thought he would be like Nicca, too gentle in bed, but he doesn't frighten as easily as Nicca. A disaster politically, but brave in that 'hero destined to die for a cause' sort of way." She cupped his chin in her hand. "Is he any good as a lover?"

If I said yes, she might want to borrow him. If I said no, it would be a lie. He was too gentle for me, too, but when I was in the mood for gentle lovemaking, Galen was just about perfect. "I think he is too gentle for your tastes, Aunt Andais."

"But not for yours?" She knelt down, making a pool of black silk in front of my downcast eyes.

"I have wider interests in the bedroom than you do, Auntie dearest."

"Why is it that any tender endearment from you always sounds like you're telling me to go fuck myself?"

"I meant no disrespect."

"I have heard that you like it rough, Meredith." She bent down, whispering, "Not as rough as me, or Cel, but rough enough."

"Not every night, Aunt Andais." I did not raise my face beyond her silk lap. I was in pain and tired of her insane games. It had never occurred to me that she would see all the new magic as a threat to her. So much had happened, there hadn't been time to keep her informed. But she was our queen, and I had made her look weak. Because she got her reports from others, the entire court knew I did not respect her enough to keep her informed or ask her opinion. If she was going this crazy about smaller things, what would she do when she found out that the chalice had returned and I had not told her that either? But that was something I would not reveal before the entire court. It was too dangerous.

"If you are not with child, you will never be queen." She spoke into my hair.

"Keeping Nicca and Biddy from their child will not gain me one," I said.

"Giving children to every couple in our court will not gain you my throne."

"If I could bring hundreds of children to the Unseelie Court, I would not need to rule it."

"Cel will kill you."

"I know that."

"Do you want to rule?" She said it as if it had never occurred to her to ask.

"I have no choice but to rule or die."

She grabbed me by the shoulders, and Galen tried to hold me from her, a mistake that cost me bruises as she jerked me away from him. "Do you want to rule?"

"If it is a choice between giving the court to Cel or me, I choose me."

"What if there were a third choice?" she asked.

"I know of no other choice," I said.

"Don't you, Meredith? Don't you know exactly who would rule here if he could?"

I must have looked as puzzled as I felt because she yelled at me, "Barinthus would rule here if I allowed it. He was always after Essus to kill me and take the throne, because that was as close to the throne as his vows could get him." She pointed to Barinthus, standing near the side of the steps.

"I told you that he and I have done nothing that could make him king to my queen. I will take whatever oath you wish. Who has whispered these lies to you?"

"Are they lies, Meredith, all of them?"

"I don't know what you have been told, but Barinthus making himself my king is a lie."

"Then tell me what else is a lie, Meredith. The ring has chosen a couple, but I had to hear it from others, not from your mouth. You have imprisoned my son's guards without consulting me. You have a suspect in the murders, but you have not told me who. You have fucked my new captain of the guard and divided his loyalties from me. Darkness and others ran into the night, and I don't know why." She stalked back to me, grabbed my arm, and screamed in my face, "I am queen here! Not you!"

I spoke quietly, too scared to be angry, too scared to worry about the bruising grip on my arm. "I came to tell you of all this and more, my queen, but you have given me no chance. You would not meet with me in private."

"And what is it that you are ashamed of, that you need whisper in private?"

"I am ashamed of nothing, but there are traitors among us that do not need to know all our secrets."

She jerked me up on tiptoe. "We have punished the traitors."

"May I show you more traitors, my queen? The ones who attacked my men and me."

"You said it was not another assassination attempt." She pulled me in against her body.

"I said not on me. They tried to kill Galen." I was close enough to watch her eyes, and see the flicker. She knew about the prophecy. That was why she'd insisted I bed vegetative deities when I entered faerie this time. It was all there in her eyes, and I saw something else there, before she could stop it. Fear. I saw it, and I think she knew I'd seen too much.

She threw me from her so hard that if my guards hadn't

been there to catch me, I would have fallen. Frost held me for a moment, then passed me to Galen, and put both of us out of reach of the queen. She'd have to wade through some of my guard, her guard, to get to me now. I wasn't sure being so obvious was a good idea, but I didn't want her to keep hurting me either.

"May we bring the traitors before the queen?" Frost asked.

She nodded, and started back to her throne, not looking back. I think she spent that walk working on her face and eyes, so that no matter who we dragged in, she wouldn't let the surprise show. It made me wonder who the queen was expecting us to bring before her. Did she know something that we didn't know, and needed to? What had that tiny flash of fear in her eyes been?

Crystall came to my order. The guards with him helped Lord Kieran walk in, but they had to drag Lord Innis. They dumped him at the queen's feet.

Her face was empty, cold, and arrogant. It gave nothing away as she stood on the steps. Mistral was still kneeling behind her where she had left him. Barinthus was still standing where she'd left him. I think he feared drawing her attention back to him.

"Kieran Knife-Hand, your wife has been telling me evil things. Telling me that Barinthus means to take my throne and that I should kill him before he comes back into his full power. I admit the thought occurred to me when I realized he had been with Meredith. Barinthus is many things, but dishonorable is not one of them. He gave his word; I believe he will keep it. In fact, I allowed him into our court on that belief." She moved down the steps until she stood just above him. "So why did I give such weight to your wife's evil words?"

After a moment she said, "Mistral."

"My queen."

"Rise, and come to me."

He did as she asked, but kept his hair over his face, as if he didn't trust his expression. I couldn't blame him.

"Bring Kieran's wife before me."

Kieran's house was led by Blodewedd, who was created from the spring flowers of oak, broom, and meadowsweet by Gwydion and Math to be a bride for Lleu Llaw Gyffes. Why would the Unseelie Court take in a woman who had betrayed her husband and her marital vows, and only failed to be a murderer because her husband was able to kill her lover? Because marriage by force is not recognized among us. She was created, then given as a sort of gift, like you'd buy a dog or a horse. Even in a day and time when women didn't always have the right to choose their partners, it was a little high-handed.

The one thing you always needed to remember with Blodewedd is if you're fair with her, she'll be fair with you, but don't betray her. Don't ever do anything she could take badly. She learned from her earlier mistakes. She does her own killing now.

Blodewedd stood as Mistral came for her table, and one of her people. Her hair was the startling yellow of the flowers that had formed her. Her skin was a soft, pale color that was somewhere between white and gold. She was almost doll-like in her beauty. The kind of woman men would create if they could, with high proud breasts a little bigger than was usual for the sidhe. Her eyes were huge and liquid dark, drowning and lustrous, owl eyes in that delicate face. Supposedly, she'd been cursed with them, cursed to be in the shape of an owl. If that were true, then she'd managed to cure herself of everything but the eyes.

"Madenn is mine to protect, Queen Andais. I would speak with her before you take her."

"Is your house traitor to me as Nerys's was, Blodewedd?"

"I would never betray a fellow sister of the dark." Blodewedd would go for years without uttering a word in court, then she'd come out with lines like that. "Nor would I tolerate such betrayal among my household."

"You may speak with her," Andais said, "but it must be publicly done. There will be no more secrets this night."

Blodewedd gave a small bow, then turned to the woman in question. Madenn was a small woman by sidhe standards, barely five-eight. But sitting there in her black dress with her dark hair and eyes, she seemed smaller, as if she had shrunk in upon herself. Her normally pale skin was pasty. Her hands were very still on the arms of her chair. She sat there immobile, her face frozen.

"Madenn," Blodewedd said, in a voice that carried through the hall, "your husband has been named traitor. What say you to that?"

Madenn licked her pale lips. "I do not know what to say." Her voice was breathy but more in control than her face and body.

"You must say something, for the Queen's Ravens come for you. You must give me some reason to protect you. If you swear to me that you are innocent of wrongdoing I will fight for you even against the queen herself. But I must know now, Madenn. I must know how much I am to risk for you, and if you are worth that risk."

I could not see Kieran's face, but even with his hands bound behind his back, he stood easier and more naturally than his wife sat in her carved chair. I watched what little blood was left in Madenn's face drain away.

"Fainting will not aid you," Blodewedd said, and her voice held an edge of that purring darkness that Andais's could hold. "Can you give me a reason for defying our queen about this? Give me a word of defense for you, Madenn, and I will use it."

Madenn looked up at her liege lord, and tears glittered in her eyes, but no words came. As admissions of guilt went, it was good enough.

Blodewedd bowed her head, and turned back to Mistral. "I cannot save her from her own actions."

"Take her, Mistral," the queen said.

Madenn did not move or speak until Mistral grabbed her arm. Then she held on to the arms of the chair like a child. She may have been delicate by sidhe standards, but she was still strong enough that making her leave her chair without hurting her wasn't really possible. She was saying one word, over and over again—"No, no, no, no"—in a high, thin voice.

"Hawthorne," I said.

"Yes, Princess."

"Help Mistral bring her out."

Hawthorne bowed to me, then moved toward them in his crimson armor, putting his helmet back on so he had his hands free. He went to stand on the other side of the woman's chair. Mistral shook his unbound hair back behind his shoulders, then nodded to Hawthorne, as if they'd discussed it. They both bent their knees, and raised the chair up with Madenn still plastered to it. They carried her and the heavy wooden chair, threading their way through Blodewedd's people, and out to the main floor. They carried it all easily, gracefully. If Madenn hadn't looked terrified, it would have appeared as if they were honoring her, carrying her like the May queen, to be worshipped by her subjects. The look on her face said that she was expecting to be the sacrifice, not the belle of the ball.

They put her chair down beside her husband. Her shoulders rounded, and I thought she was probably crying. "Meredith," the queen said, "come join me."

She didn't have to ask me twice.

She had taken her throne, leaving what had once been Prince Cel's throne empty for me. It had been my chair for only twenty-four hours. She motioned Eamon, her consort, from behind her throne to take his smaller throne that was a little lower on the dais. There was another throne lower down on my side, too. It wasn't for my consort of years but for the flavor of the day. Consort of the moment, perhaps.

The last time I'd sat here, the consort's chair had been occupied by Sholto, Lord of That Which Passes Between. It was only as I took my throne that I realized that Sholto and his sluagh weren't at their table near the door. Nor were they at the queen's back as guards. The sluagh were not here. He was king of his own court. The goblins were not here either, but they were often absent unless it was a planned event or a major holiday. This was neither, but Sholto never missed an occasion at court. He wanted too desperately to be accepted as sidhe to miss one.

Tyler, the Queen's pet human, curled at her feet. She asked, "Where is your little goblin?"

She meant Kitto. "He is helping Rhys watch over the police while they are inside faerie."

"Has there been some problem?" She was letting Kieran sweat, or seeing whether he would. Madenn was openly weeping, and if she hadn't been part of a plot to kill Galen, I might have felt sorry for her.

I told her briefly of the effect the entrance to faerie had had on Walters and his people. She seemed most interested.

"I wouldn't think that your little goblin would be a good choice to protect the police."

"He's almost guaranteed not to bespell anyone by accident."

"Not sidhe enough for that," she said.

I controlled the spurt of anger that followed her comment. "He became fully sidhe during an earthquake in California."

"The earth moved for you, how charming." She was being both terribly urbane and slyly insulting. I wasn't sure my nerves were good enough to keep up the small talk for much longer.

"Have you fucked anyone else today besides Mistral?" she asked.

"Actual intercourse, no."

"Then, Mistral, take your place on the dais, for Goddess knows it will probably be your last chance to sit here." I didn't like the implied threat in her words, but I couldn't argue that Mistral deserved the chair.

Frost had led the other men to fan out around me like good guards—that is, those who weren't guarding our prisoners. Barinthus was left standing on the floor. She looked at him, and it was not friendly. "Take your place with her guards, Barinthus. For it is where you have chosen to stand."

He hesitated a moment, then bowed and went wide around her, to stand on the far side of my guards. I think he was going to try to be as invisible as he could manage until we could figure out what had angered her. He had too many enemies to have any illusions. If he slew the queen, then most of the rest of the nobles would unite and kill him. Of course, Andais might not need the help.

Only one guard, Whisper, remained at the queen's back. When she'd offered the guards a chance to help me, I had not expected her to empty her stables, as it were. Perhaps she hadn't either. She had given them the choice of working for someone else, and they had leaped at the chance. Offer a man a chance to break a thousand years of celibacy, and he'll do a lot for you.

Of course, being mine meant they would be leaving faerie behind in a few days. Exile from faerie, if they followed me. Did they understand that? Did they care? And if they didn't, then how puzzled Andais must be to find that her greatest threat, exile from faerie, was not so great a threat after all.

Mistral took his seat on the consort's throne. He swept his grey hair to one side so that it caressed the edge of the chair like a cloak. I'd have given a great deal to see his face in that moment. To see him survey the court from the royal dais for the first time. If the queen's words were true and not just her anger talking, she planned on seeing that he did not get a second chance at the chair, which meant no second chance with me. Was it personal to Mistral, or had she finally realized that she could lose all her guard to the ring and my body?

Frost stood on one side of me, and Galen the other. I missed Doyle. Where was he? Where were Usna and Cathbodua? I clung to Galen's hand, because I couldn't seem to get enough of touching him. I'd held his death in my hands, now I wanted to wrap myself in the life of him. But I did not trust him to fight here among the lords of the sidhe and survive.

I think Andais thought we were giving Kieran and Madenn the silent treatment to wear them down. I was waiting for my queen to take the lead. I'd angered her enough for one night; I would do everything I could to avoid pissing her off again.

"Kieran, you have tried to slay one of our royal guards. Not in fair challenge, but in an ambush."

"If you think to trick me into challenging the young one, it will not work. If I challenge, then he chooses the method of the duel. He would choose weapons, and I cannot best him without magic."

"You admit that one of the lesser among my guard is a better warrior than you, Kieran?"

"Of course. The Queen's Ravens are the best warriors the sidhe have ever had. I would not be so bold as to think I could best him with metal." Kieran looked at me. His pale beard framed the smile that had not left his face. "Of course, if the young lordling thinks I have insulted him and wishes to challenge me..." He left it open.

I squeezed Galen's hand, and he laughed. Kieran's smile faltered.

"Was I ever that stupid," Galen said. "Goddess, I hope not." He raised my hand and laid a kiss against my fingers. I saw a hardness in his face then that had never been there before. "I am at Merry's side and in her bed, and I won't give that up because you hurt my ego." His usual grin flashed bright and clear, as if the shadow I'd seen on his face hadn't been there at all. "Besides, I'm flattered. You ambushed me with two magicians and three warriors. I didn't know you were that scared of me."

"I am not frightened of some jumped-up pixie." Kieran's face had begun to flush in anger.

Galen laughed, and pressed his lips to my hand again. "If you're not afraid of me, then why did you need so much help to kill me?"

"Oh, I agree," Andais said. "Only fear would make Kieran take so much help to slay one guard. If it were Frost or my Darkness, I might understand. Even Mistral, our lord of storms, but I did not know you feared Galen."

"I do not fear him," Kieran said again, but there was something in his voice that made me want to quote Shakespeare. The lady doth protest too much. What was it about Galen, even if he were the green man who would bring life back to the court, that would make Kieran pack so much firepower, as it were, to kill him? It was a very good question. I'd been too caught up in nearly losing Galen to really think about it.

"If you don't fear Galen, then what do you fear, Kieran?" I asked.

"Lord Kieran," he said.

"No, Kieran," Andais said. "She is heir to my throne, and will one day be your queen if you live that long. I think she can address you as I do, Kieran." There was that purring edge to her voice that either meant sex, or that you were about to be hurt, really badly. Sometimes it meant both.

"What do I fear?" Kieran said. "I fear the death of the sidhe, as a race."

"Do you fear that my niece's mixed blood will condemn us all to mortality?"

"Yes, as do many of us. They are afraid to speak of it, but they would act as I do, if they had the courage."

Andais looked past him. "I do not know, Kieran. I think your wife's courage is fast fading."

He looked at her, and there was something in his face, some question, or pleading. "If she would but speak with courage, this might end well."

Madenn gave a great hiccupping sob. She had once been a goddess of youth, which had left her permanently looking about fifteen, a young fifteen. The face she turned up at us now looked younger, as if her fear were stripping years from her.

"You have said many times that you would cleanse this court of the half-breeds." Her voice was breathy, and thick with tears. "We mean only to help you do what you always wished to do before she returned from the Western Lands and turned you from us."

Andais was leaning forward, and the anger was falling away from her. Kieran's face was beginning to regain its smugness.

"Crystall, search her for a spell, some trinket aimed at the queen."

Andais frowned at me. "What are you talking about, Meredith?"

"Please, Your Majesty, please," Madenn said, "help us."

I watched Andais's face soften.

"Hawthorne," I said, "if she speaks again before I give her leave, slit her throat. She'll heal."

He didn't argue with me, he simply unsheathed a knife, and put it against her throat, even as she tried to protest.

Andais looked away from her, shielding her eyes. "What is it?"

Crystall searched Madenn, and he was thorough enough that Kieran protested. "He is laying hands on my wife."

"If she is a widow then there will be no marriage vows to break," Andais said.

Kieran's mouth hung open for a moment, then he closed it, and I saw the first hint of fear in his eyes.

Madenn made a small sound, and Hawthorne pushed the tip of his blade in enough to draw a pinprick of bright crimson blood. She whimpered, but did not try to speak.

Crystall had to get very up close and personal with Madenn before he drew a little cloth bag from under her breasts. It was two pieces of cloth sewn together, almost a tiny pillow, the size of a fifty-cent piece.

I lowered my shields enough to see the little pillow glow, and there was a thin red line from it to the queen.

Crystall cut the threads that bound it, and spilled out a few dried herbs and seven strands of black hair. He held up the hair between his fingers, and the rest in his opposite hand. "A charm for you, and only you, Your Majesty," he said. "A charm of eloquence, so that her words be sweet to your ears."

Andais looked to Barinthus on the far side of the dais. "I may give you what I seldom give anyone, Lord Barinthus."

He bowed. "And what would that be, Queen Andais?"

"An apology." She looked at Madenn and Kieran. "Why would you risk death to kill Galen?"

"He doesn't think he risks death," I said.

She looked at me. "He has used magic to try and work wiles upon me. That is cause for me to challenge one or both of them personally."

"He told me that Siobhan tried to kill a royal princess and

she lives still, and is not being tortured because Ezekiel fears her too much. He said if you would not punish someone for that, then there would be no punishment for trying to kill a half-pixie guard."

She looked at him, and there was something in that look that made him take a step back, only to bump into the guards. "Did you say that, Kieran?"

"Not those words, no."

"Did you say the gist of it?"

He swallowed hard enough to be heard and nodded. "Nerys's entire house turned traitor, tried to kill you, my queen, and they live. Why is the life of one half-breed guard worth more than the life of the queen herself?"

"See, Meredith, you show mercy and they will use it against you."

"Nerys gave her life so that her house could survive," I said. "She paid the price for your mercy."

"Perhaps." Andais looked past them all to another house of nobles. "Dormath."

The man who stood was tall and almost impossibly thin. His skin was the whitest that our court could boast, the bloodless pale of a corpse. The black hood of his cloak was pushed back to reveal hair that was as white as his skin, so that he looked almost like an albino, except his eyes were large and luxurious and black. He looked very close to the modern idea of "death." I was told that once he was as handsome and muscular as any of the sidhe, but that centuries of people's beliefs had changed him. There were those who debated whether being the representative of death to that degree made him a weak-magicked fool who couldn't protect himself from mortal thought, or proved that he was one of the most powerful among us, and still worshipped by humans, in a way. His voice was deeper than expected.

"Yes, my queen," he said.

"Innis is one of yours, as is Siobhan. Are you traitors as Nerys's house were traitors?"

"No, my queen, I swear that I did not know of Siobhan's plan, nor of Innis's. This I swear."

"You interceded for Siobhan. You begged my mercy. I gave it because my son also valued her, and asked for her life to be spared. I listened to my son and one whom I thought was my ally."

"I am your ally, Your Majesty. My house is still your house."

"Two traitors, Dormath, two in one house. How can I trust that there are not more?" She was making idle circles with one finger on the arm of her throne.

"Is not the same thing true of Blodewedd's house?" he asked.

"Do not drag me into this, Dormath," Blodewedd said. "You who bear the name of your own dog, for you have shamed your true name."

"I have shamed nothing."

"Children," Andais said, her voice light, almost playful. The sound made the hair on the back of my neck stand up. "You see what mercy gets you as a ruler, Meredith. Do you understand now? Mercy is for the weak, and the dying."

"I know how Kieran has interpreted your actions."

She looked at me, and I really didn't want that much of her attention in this mood, but I had it. "And how is that?"

"That if you would not kill someone for trying to kill me, then you would do even less to someone who tried to kill Galen."

"Do you think he had the right of that? Do you think he has no punishment coming?"

"I think Siobhan should be executed and Kieran be made an example of."

"An example how, if not executed?" she asked.

I licked my suddenly dry lips. "I had not thought that far, Aunt Andais."

"Ah, but I have, and that is the difference between being queen and being princess." She opened those red, red lips to say something awful, but the big double doors crashed open, and Doyle appeared.

Chapter 25

USNA AND CATHBODUA CAME BEHIND DOYLE, DRAGGING SOMEone between them. Someone wearing a white fur cloak that was decorated with bright spots of crimson.

"Darkness," Andais said, "how good of you to join us. Who are you bringing so unceremoniously before us?" Her voice still purred with a satisfied tone, promising pain to someone. Doyle had just given her another choice of victims.

"Gwennin, the white lord, a little worse for wear."

Gwennin, I knew, was no friend of Cel's. He was no friend of anyone he considered pure Unseelie. He had been one of the last cast out of the Seelie Court, and he still acted as if he might someday go back there. The Seelie might welcome back an exile from among the humans, but once you became Unseelie, you were unclean and unforgivable.

I watched Doyle stalk toward me. He was the tall, dark hunter, the grim figure who had frightened me as a child, but I had to fight an urge to tell him to come to me. I wanted his arms around me. I wanted to be held, to feel safe. Sitting here in open court I didn't feel safe. What had driven me from faerie three years ago was happening all over again. There was too much death, too many attempts. Eventually, if enough people want you dead, they will succeed. It's simple mathematics. We had to survive every assassination attempt. They had to succeed just once.

Gwennin was not an ally to any of the lords we had "arrested." I couldn't imagine a plot that could hold all those before me. Was there more than one plot against me? And what did any of it have to do with the murders?

"Gwennin," Andais said, sounding puzzled, "you are no friend to those here." She said aloud what I'd been thinking. I wondered if that was a good sign or a bad one. Was I getting better at the politics, or was she getting worse?

"He says he acted alone. That he resented the princess inviting in the human police. That it was beneath our court to take their help. So he set a spell that would have rendered them useless, or even killed them, if we had carried it to them."

"Carried it?"

"He put it on Biddy, for she is half-human, and everyone of human blood she touched was contaminated."

Gwennin found his voice, even flat on the floor between Usna and Cathbodua. "That the spell was able to work on the princess proves she is human."

Cathbodua gave him a backhanded slap. "Speak when you are spoken to, traitor."

"Yes," Andais said, "they are all traitors. So many traitors. But none of them tried to take Meredith's life. They tried to take Galen's, they tried to stop the humans from entering our sithen, but they have not tried to kill Meredith. Interesting, that."

I thought about it, and realized she was right. I looked at Doyle, and he met my look with one of his own. It was interesting, and puzzling.

"Why would Cel's guard be more interested in killing your green knight than in killing you?" Andais said conversationally.

I tried to keep my voice as casual, and almost succeeded. "If any of his people try to kill me, Cel's life is forfeit, but killing my allies is not an automatic death sentence for their prince."

"But why Galen, Meredith? If I were going to strip you of your allies it would be Darkness or the Killing Frost."

"Or Barinthus," I said.

She nodded. "Yes, that was well done." She looked at Kieran and his wife, who still had Hawthorne's knife at her throat. "If I kill Barinthus, then one of my most powerful guards is dead. If he kills me, then you are rid of me, and can be the first to suggest that he needs to die for his actions." She moved in her chair as if settling her skirts more comfortably. "Oh yes, Kieran, good plan. You made only one mistake."

He looked up at her. "And what was that?"

"You underestimated the princess, and her men."

"I will not make the same mistake again," he said, and gave me an unfriendly look.

"Kieran, that sounded like a threat to the princess." Andais looked at me. "Did that not sound like a threat to you, Meredith?"

"Yes, Aunt Andais, it did."

"Frost, did Kieran just threaten the princess?"

"Yes," Frost said.

"Darkness," she said.

"Yes, he threatened the princess, or threatened to plan better the next time he plots to kill you, your majesty."

"Yes, that is what I heard, as well." She looked out at the nobles. "Blodewedd, did you hear him threaten me and mine?"

Blodewedd took in a deep sighing breath, then gave a small nod.

"I need to hear it aloud for all the court," Andais said.

"Kieran has been foolish this day. More foolish than I or my house can support or salvage."

Kieran looked at her, frightened for the first time. "My lady, you are my liege lord, you cannot mean . . ."

"Do not involve me in your stupidity, Kieran. Madenn is your wife and has always been your shadow. But if you could have persuaded more of your own house to take your part, I do not believe you would have enlisted Innis's help."

"An interesting point." Andais gazed down at the unconscious form of Innis. "Dormath, I offer you a choice. One of your people must die. Innis or Siobhan, choose."

"My queen," Doyle said, "I would ask that Innis be spared, and Siobhan . . ."

"I know who you would kill, Darkness." She looked at me. "I even know who you would have me slay, Meredith, but you are not their liege. I want Dormath to choose, so that the rest of his house will understand that he will not protect them."

"My queen, do not make me choose among my lords and ladies."

"Would you take their place, Dormath? Would you offer yourself to save Innis and Siobhan both? I am willing to entertain such a bargain, if you are willing to offer it."

Dormath's face got even whiter, something I didn't think possible. He blinked his large, dark eyes slowly. Were we about to see Dormath, the door of death, faint?

"Come, Dormath, it is a simple question," Andais said. "You are either willing to pay for the crimes of your house, or you are not. Nerys was willing to give her life for her house."

Dormath's voice came thin and reedy, as if he was struggling to keep it even. "Her entire house had joined her in her treachery. My house is innocent of wrongdoing, save for these two."

"Then choose, Dormath. I cannot deny the princess her call for a death. She is within her rights."

"A death, yes," Dormath said, "but not an execution. She is within her rights to challenge them to combat, and take their life if she can."

"That might be true, Lord Dormath," I said, "if Siobhan had attacked me one-on-one, but she did not. She attacked with the aid of two others. She ambushed me. This was no one-on-one combat. This was an assassination attempt, pure and simple."

"Innis did not even attack you," Dormath argued, "he attacked the green knight. Surely it should be he who demands the life debt."

"Do you think he will show more mercy than the princess?" Andais asked.

"I think Galen has always been a fair man," Dormath said.

Galen pressed my hand tight in his and sighed. It was not a happy sound. "I tried to be fair, and just, and good, whatever that means. Siobhan told me once that I belong in the Seelie

Court, where they try to pretend they are something they're not. I asked her what they try to pretend to be. Human, she said, and made it sound like a curse." I watched his face grow solemn, and very unlike my Galen. "Do you really expect me to help you save the lives of the people who tried to kill me?"

The two sidhe looked at each other, and it was Dormath who looked away first. He spoke with his eyes lowered, so that he met no one's gaze. "One tries to know their opposition and use their strengths and weaknesses against them."

"Why am I your opposition?" Galen asked.

Dormath spoke to the queen as if he hadn't heard Galen. "My queen, I would ask that you do not make me choose between my people. One has done, perhaps, the lesser crime, but I have more affection for the other."

"Answer Galen's question," Andais said.

Dormath blinked those deep, shining eyes and looked at her. His thin face showed nothing. "And what question would that be, my queen?"

"I tire of word games quickly, Dormath," she said. "I suggest you bear that in mind. I will tell you once more. Answer Galen's question."

Dormath shivered, and the long black cloak gave the illusion of feathers settling around his body. "I do not think your son would want this question answered in open court."

I looked at Andais then, my aunt, my queen. I did not know what Dormath was referring to, but she might. She had helped hide her son's secrets for centuries. Her face was cold beauty, arrogant and perfect, every line of her like some statue carved to be the beauty that drives men not to love but to despair.

"Answer as much or as little of the question as you will, Dormath. Know that if you answer as fully as you might you will forfeit all of Prince Cel's allies. For they will feel you betrayed them. Know also that there are those among us now who will condemn you as the blackest of traitors for going along with his plan."

Dormath put out a long pale hand to steady himself against the table. "My queen . . ."

"Dormath, if you do not answer the question I will consider it a direct challenge to me, personally."

"You would slay me to keep from revealing what he has done," Dormath said.

"Is that what I said? I don't believe that is what I said." She looked at me then. "Is that what I said, Meredith?"

I wasn't entirely certain how to answer that question. "I do not believe that you threatened Dormath with death if he revealed what Prince Cel, my cousin, has done. Nor do I believe that you have encouraged him to reveal all that he knows."

"Go on," she said, and she seemed pleased with me, though I wasn't sure why.

"But you have stated clearly that if he does not answer Galen's question, you will challenge him to single combat, and kill him."

She nodded and smiled, as if I'd said a smart thing. "Exactly."

I looked from her to Dormath, and I had a moment of pity for him. She had set him a riddle that might not have an answer, not one that would keep him alive anyway.

He was still propping himself up on the tabletop. His face showed clearly that he did not see a way out of the maze of words she had thrown up around him. "I do not believe that there is a way to answer the green knight's question without revealing much that I do not believe you want known."

"I do not believe that you know what I want, Dormath. But if you remain mute, I will kill you, and there will be no argument that it is unfair, for it will be one-on-one against me."

He swallowed, and his throat looked almost too thin to hold the bobbing of his Adam's apple. "Why are you doing this, my queen?"

"Doing what?" she asked.

"Do you want the court to know? Is that what you want?"

"I want a child who values his people and their welfare before his own."

The silence in the room was profound. It was as if all of us took a breath and held it. It was as if the very blood in our veins ceased to move for just that instant. Andais had admitted that Cel valued nothing but himself, something I had known for years. She had raised him to believe that faerie and the sidhe and the lesser fey owed him. He had been the apple of her eye, the song in her heart, the most precious thing in her world for longer than this country had existed, and now she wanted a child that valued others above themselves. What had Cel done to so disillusion his mother?

Dormath spoke into that silence. "My queen, I do not know how to give you what you desire."

"I can give you what you want." Maelgwn's voice had lost its usual amused smoothness. He sounded serious and gentle at the same time, a tone I'd never heard from him.

Andais looked at him, and with only her profile I could tell it wasn't a friendly look.

"Can you, wolf lord, can you truly?" Her voice held that edge of warning, like the pressure in the air before you even know the storm is coming.

"Yes," he said softly, but the word carried through the hall.

She settled herself against the back of her throne, her hands very still on the carved arms. "Illuminate me, wolf."

"There are two children of your line who have come of age, my queen. One child has reawakened the queen's own ring, and now offers almost anything to be allowed to enjoy the ring's magic. A child who says bringing children to all the sidhe is more important to her than gaining the throne, or protecting her own life, or filling her own belly with life. These are all things that most of the nobles in this room, perhaps everyone in this room, would give anything to have. Is that not a child who puts her people's welfare above her own?"

I sat very still. I did not want to draw her attention to me. Maybe what Maelgwn said was true, but the queen didn't always like or reward the truth. Sometimes a lie got you further. Andais's most beloved lie was that Cel was fit to rule here. She herself had opened the door to the nobles finally speaking the truth. That Cel would have been almost no one's choice, if they'd had any other choice that didn't include a half-breed mortal. Only my father had ever had the courage to tell Andais that there was something wrong with Cel. Something that went beyond just being spoiled or privileged.

Andais spoke as if she'd heard my last thought. "When my brother got his new bride pregnant so quickly, there were those who urged me to step down. I refused." She turned and looked at me. "Do you want to know why I called you home, Meredith?"

It was so unexpected that I gaped at her for a moment, then managed, "Yes."

"I'm infertile, Meredith. All those human doctors have done everything they can for me. That is why you must prove yourself fertile. Whoever rules after me must be able to bring life back to the courts. Maelgwn accused me of condemning all of you to be childless because my line is. I can only give you my word that I did not believe it until recently. If I could go back . . ." She sighed and slumped as much as her tight bodice would allow. "I wonder what we would be now, we Unseelie, if I had allowed Essus to take this throne these thirty years and more." Her eyes held a pain that she'd never let me see before. That one look answered a question that I had wondered about. I knew that my father loved his sister, but until that moment I had not been sure that she loved him back. It was there in her eyes, in the lines of her face, even underneath the makeup. She looked tired.

"Aunt Andais—" I started but she shushed me.

"I have heard whispers in the dark, niece of mine, whispers that I did not believe. But if the ring truly lives for you, if it has begun to choose fertile couples for you, then perhaps the rumors are true. Is Maeve Reed, once Conchenn among the Seelie, with child?"

I opened my mouth, then closed it. There had to be some among us who were spies for the Seelie Court. It would endanger Maeve to say yes, but Taranis had already tried to kill her. She was in another country now, as safe as we could make her. It was more dangerous not to answer, because we had told no one that Maeve Reed had been exiled from faerie because she had refused the king's bed on the grounds that he was sterile. Which meant that, unlike Andais, Taranis had known a hundred years ago that he was infertile. He had kept his throne and condemned his people to diminish and die rather than step down. The Seelie were within their rights to demand his death as a true sacrifice to the land for that oversight.

I'd thought too long, and Andais said, "Meredith, what is wrong?"

Frost squeezed my shoulder, Galen was very still beside me. I looked at Doyle, and he gave a small nod. Truth was the lesser evil. I whispered it. "Yes, she is with child."

Andais was looking from me to Doyle, as if she longed to ask why I had hesitated so long, but she was a better politician than to ask. You did not ask a question in public to which you did not know the answer. "Answer so that everyone can hear you, niece."

I had to clear my throat to make my voice carry through the hall. "Yes, she is with child."

A sigh of murmurs ran through the assembled nobles.

Andais smiled, as if she was satisfied with the reaction. "Did you work a spell for her, a fertility spell?"

"Yes," I said.

The murmur grew, swelling like the sea as it sweeps toward the shore.

"I heard her husband was dying even then, is that true?"

I nodded. "Yes."

"Treatments for cancer can leave a man sterile or unable to perform."

"Sometimes," I said.

"But you managed a spell that got a dying man to perform one last time for her?"

"Yes."

"Who played the part of the consort to your goddess? Who was god to your goddess for this spell?"

"Galen." I pressed his hand against my chest, as I said it.

The ocean of murmurs burst upon us in a confused babble. Cries, almost shouts. Some did not believe it. I heard at least one male voice that I could not quite place say, "That explains it." I would ask Doyle or Frost if they recognized the voice later.

Andais looked at Kieran still standing bound at the foot of the steps. "I slew Galen's father before I, or the noble lady who brought complaint of magical seduction, knew she was pregnant. You almost slew a warrior who had helped work magic to create life in the womb of a sidhe woman and a dying human."

Kieran looked confused, as if he was thinking very hard. "I would say I do not believe it, but you have spoken too much truth today, my queen, for me to doubt this. And you do not like Galen enough to lie to save him."

"We never lie, Kieran."

He bowed. "I meant . . ."

"I know what you meant." She leaned back against her chair, almost cozily, like a cat settling in. "What did Cel's people tell you that made you agree to do this traitorous thing?"

I expected Kieran to argue, or fight her, but he simply answered. "That the green man would bring life to her." He nodded at me, since he could not point.

Andais looked at Dormath. "And what did Siobhan tell you?"

"That the green man would return life to the land of faerie."

Kieran's face showed his panic. He tried to fall to his knees, I think to bow lower, but hands caught him, kept him on his feet. "That is not what I was told, my queen, I swear it. I would never destroy a chance for our court to be brought back to what we were, never."

"Dormath," she said, "explain to Kieran the wording of the prophecy that Prince Cel paid the human psychic for."

Dormath bowed to her, then said, "The green man will bring life back to the land of faerie. The ruler is the land, and the land is the ruler. Their health, their fertility, their happiness, is the health, the fertility, and the joy of the land itself."

"Well put, Dormath, and very true. If you killed Meredith's green knight, and he was destined to be the king who brought back children to the sidhe, then what would you have done to us, Kieran, Madenn?" She didn't wait for them to answer. "By killing him you would have destroyed all our hopes and dreams."

"But it is Mistral and Meredith who have begun to awaken the dead gardens, and the magic of the guard. He was with her when the ring chose Nicca and Biddy," Kieran said. "It is Mistral who sits in the consort's throne, not the green knight."

"True enough, and perhaps the ring has chosen the storm lord to be her king. I myself interpreted the term 'green man' to mean any of our green gods, but perhaps I have been too literal. Green man can be another name for god, or consort." She shook her head. "I do not know for certain. I do not know if it is irritating or reassuring that prophets still speak in riddles even in this very modern America." She turned to me. "Go help Nicca and Biddy make the child you saw. But abide by my rules; if I find you have given him first to Biddy, I will be cross. But take Galen and one other green man to your body this night, as well."

"What of the traitors, Aunt Andais?" I asked.

"You go try and make babies; I will tend to them. I will give you a united court, Meredith. It will be my first and last gift to you." She put a hand in front of her face and said, "Leave me, take the guards who are green men with you, but leave me the ones who are not."

Frost's hand tensed on my shoulder, and I must have made some small sound of protest, because she looked up at me. She glanced at Frost and Doyle, and anger filled her eyes. "Take your Darkness and the Killing Frost. They are yours, but I will need some of the guards to help me punish the traitors."

"And Biddy and Nicca," I said quietly.

She waved her hand impatiently. "Yes, yes, now go."

Frost's hand eased up on my shoulder. He gave a small nod. I got up, bowed to the queen, and we moved toward the doors, leaving her to punish the traitors. She probably wouldn't kill them, but she'd make sure they regretted their actions. Of that, I had no doubt. I shouldn't have looked back, but I did. I saw Crystall, Hafwyn, Dogmaela, and others try to control their faces. Mistral and Barinthus were among the unreadable.

I stopped. Frost grabbed my shoulder, and Galen still had my hand. They tried to get me moving again, but I balked. I couldn't save everyone, I knew that, but . . .

Doyle didn't try to stop me, he simply looked at me with his impassive face. He would give me room to rule. I spoke with Frost and Galen's hands tight against me. The tension in Frost's hand was almost painfully tight.

"May I take a healer with me, my queen, just in case there are any more emergencies? We sent for a healer when Galen was injured but the healer never arrived."

She nodded, but her attention was already fixed on her victims. She stood above Kieran, one hand idly stroking the blond hair that he had so carefully braided back behind his head. "Yes, take any but my own healer."

"Hafwyn," I said.

She couldn't keep the relief off her face as she started across the floor.

The queen called after her. "Meredith, if you wish a healer you must take one who still has their powers." She actually put her hands on her hips as if she was impatient with me.

"Hafwyn healed Galen and Adair."

She was looking at me now, paying attention. "Healed them how? She lost her ability to heal years ago." She managed to look both irritated and relieved. "She is one you brought back into her powers tonight."

"No, my queen, Hafwyn has always been able to heal with the laying on of hands."

"I was told that she had lost her ability to heal," the queen said.

"Hafwyn," I said, "did you ever lose your ability to heal?"

She shook her head without turning around to face the queen, as if she was afraid to look away from me, or afraid to look back.

"Then why is she a guard?" the queen asked. She came down the steps, and I felt everyone around me tense. We could have left, gotten away, and I was putting us all at risk. But for the first time ever Andais seemed willing to hear awful truths about Cel. I wasn't sure how long this new mood would last, and there were things that would happen only when she was willing to believe Cel was a monster.

"She healed someone Prince Cel had forbidden her to heal. He told her that from that day forward she would bring death only, and no longer be allowed to heal."

Andais glided across the floor toward us, her dress making a hissing sound. Hafwyn paled. "Is this true, Hafwyn?"

The guard swallowed hard and turned around to face the queen. She dropped to one knee without being asked or told. "Yes, Queen Andais, it is true."

"You had the ability to heal grievous wounds by touch and he forbade you to use your gift?"

Hafwyn kept her face down, but answered, "Yes."

Andais looked at me. "She is yours, but I cannot allow you to strip Cel of all his guards. Even a queen cannot help another sidhe break their vows of loyalty and service."

"Hafwyn breaks no vow coming to me, for she made no vow to Prince Cel. I am told that many of the prince's guard made no new vows to Cel."

Something passed through Doyle's eyes that let me know he at least understood why this was worth the risk.

Andais frowned at me. "This cannot be true. Cel offered my brother's guards a chance to join his service after Essus's death. They made vows to serve Cel."

Hafwyn abased herself lower on the floor, but said, "My queen, Cel told us you gave us to him. He did not ask our permission or if we wished to serve him. He told all of us that our vows had been made to a prince, and he was a prince."

"He said you all chose to serve him," Andais said in a voice gone hollow with surprise.

Hafwyn kept her face pressed to her hands on the floor, but she answered. "No, my queen."

Andais looked at Biddy. "Did you give your vow to Cel?"

Biddy shook her head. "No, and he never asked for it."

Andais turned back toward the throne. "Dogmaela, did you give oath to Prince Cel?"

"No, my queen," she said, eyes wide, and face a little frightened.

Andais screamed, a loud, sharp, inarticulate scream that seemed to hold all her frustration. "I would never have given my brother's guard to anyone, not even my own son. All those who did not make oath to Cel are free to choose to leave his service."

"Are we free to offer our service where we wish?" Hafwyn asked, her head raised just enough to look up at the queen.

"Yes, but if you wish to go to the princess's service my order stands. To serve her, you must truly serve her in the way that the guard has always served my blood and my house."

It was Biddy who said, "Prince Essus did not force us to serve him and only him."

Andais looked at her, and shook her head, then looked at me. "What would you do with your guards if I allowed it?"

"I would free the women of the celibacy since, as you pointed out, they cannot get me pregnant. After I am with child and know who the father of my child would be, I would free the men from their celibacy, as well."

"And if you never get with child?"

"Then I would keep those I preferred in my bed, and let the others find lovers. A half-dozen men, give or take a few, is enough for me, I think."

"And what if I said that any you did not keep must come back to me?"

"You told me once that you made the celibacy rule because you wanted their seed for yourself, but if you cannot be pregnant, then why not let them see if there are other women in the court they could get with child?"

"So fair, so evenhanded, so like Essus." She gave us her back and began to walk toward her throne. "Take the guards you have around you and go. And know this, your ill truths will make our traitors' punishments all the more fulsome. For my anger will need flesh and blood to be stilled."

To that there was only one thing to say. "I will go and do as you have bid, Aunt Andais." I bowed to her back, and we got Hafwyn to her feet and left. I did not need anyone's urging to know that I had pushed her about as far as she'd be pushed this night. We left her caressing Kieran. The last sound we heard before the doors closed behind us was Madenn's scream. I started to look back but Frost and Galen had too firm a grip on my arms. There would be no more looking back tonight.

Chapter 26

THERE WAS A STORM OF BUTTERFLIES OUTSIDE THE DOOR TO MY room, as if someone had broken a kaleidoscope and thrown the colors into the air, and those colors had stayed, floating, whirling. For a moment I didn't see the tiny hands and feet, the gauzy dresses and loincloths. I saw only what their glamour tried to show me. A cloud of insects, rising like beauty itself into the air. I had to blink hard and concentrate to see them for what they truly were. Galen pulled back against my hand, stopping all of us just short of that rainbow cloud.

Galen's reaction made me remember another time when I'd seen such a cloud of the demi-fey. Galen had been chained to the rock outside the throne room. His body was almost lost to sight under the slowly fanning wings of the demi-fey. They looked like butterflies on the edge of a puddle, sipping liquid, wings moving slowly to the rhythm of their feeding. But they weren't sipping water, they were drinking his blood. Galen had shrieked long and loud, his body arching against the chains. The movement dislodged some of the demi-fey, and I glimpsed why he was screaming. His groin was a bloody mess. They were taking flesh as well as blood.

Galen's hand tightened painfully around mine. I looked up at him now, and found his eyes a little too wide, his lips half-parted. I knew now why Cel had bargained with the demi-fey to try to ruin Galen's manhood. At the time it had simply seemed like another of his cruelties.

The kaleidoscope of butterflies and moths parted curtain-like, and Queen Niceven hovered in midair on large pale wings like some ghostly luna moth. Her dress sparkled silver; the diamonds in her crown were so bright in the light that the dazzle of it obscured her narrow features. I knew what she looked like because I'd seen her thin, near skeletal beauty before. Though only the size of a Barbie doll, she was thin enough for Hollywood. Looking at her all asparkle and pale white, I understood why people had thought the fey were spirits of the dead or angels. She looked like both and neither. Too solid to be a ghost, too insectlike to be an angel.

If Galen hadn't been clinging to my hand I would have moved forward to speak with her, one royal to another, but I couldn't ask him to go closer to that pretty, bloodthirsty cloud. Doyle saw my dilemma, and went forward, to bow before her. "Queen Niceven, to what do we owe this honor?"

"Pretty words, Darkness," she said, and her voice was like evil, tinkling bells, "but a little late, don't you think?"

"A little late for what, Queen Niceven?" he asked in his polite, empty court voice. The voice that he used when he didn't know what political storm he had fallen into.

"For courtesy, Darkness, for courtesy." She flew a little higher so she could see me better over Doyle's tall form. "Now I am not even good enough for the princess to address me directly."

I called to her, as Galen's hand convulsed around mine. "You know full well why Galen doesn't want to come closer to you and your kin."

"And are you attached to your green knight? Are you one with him in flesh, so that you cannot come closer without him coming, as well?" She'd moved her head to one side, and I could see her pale eyes now. She wasn't even trying to hide how angry she was. I'd seen her crown a thousand times, and never seen the jewels catch the light so brilliantly. Only then did I realize that the light in the hallway was brighter than normal, closer to the brightness of electric lights.

"See, she pays no attention to us. The roof of the hall holds more interest for her than my court."

I blinked and looked back to the flying queen. "My apologies, Queen Niceven, the brilliance of your crown quite dazzled me. I have seen your beauty many times, but it has never been so eye-catching as tonight. It made me realize that the light in this hallway is finally bright enough to do you and your finery the justice it deserves."

"Pretty words, Princess Meredith, but empty ones. Flattery will not wipe away the insult you have laid against me and my court."

I had no idea what she was talking about. Was I so tired that I had forgotten something important? For I *was* tired, an aching tiredness that comes after being up too long, or after too many things happen in too short a space of time. I had no idea what time it was. There were no clocks in faerie. Once it had been because time moved differently here than outside. Now there were no clocks allowed because they would work. Just another reminder that faerie wasn't what it used to be.

"What insult has been done to your court?" Doyle asked.

"No, Darkness, she did the insulting, let her do the asking." Her wings looked like some great moth, but they did not move like moth wings, not when she was angry. They blurred and buzzed as she flew past Doyle to hover in front of me.

Galen pulled back so hard, I stumbled against him. He caught me automatically, but that put him closer to the tiny hovering fey. He seemed to freeze against me, his arms pinning mine.

Niceven hissed, flashing tiny needlelike teeth, and darted in. I think she only meant to land on my shoulder, but Frost put his arm in her way. He didn't try to hit her, but her guard reacted, flying toward their queen. They descended on us like a swirl of rainbow leaves, with tiny pinching hands, and sharp biting teeth.

Galen yelled and threw up a hand, turning so that he used his own body as a shield against them. He started to run, but he tripped and fell, landing on the ground with me underneath him. He caught himself with one arm so that I didn't take his full weight. My face ended up buried in the rich green smell of crushed leaves. I opened my eyes and found myself nearly buried in greenery. I thought for a moment that Galen and I had been transported, but my fingers found the bareness of the hallway stone underneath. I looked at the far wall, and saw the other guards still standing around us. Plants had sprung from the naked rock.

Galen had curled himself over me, shielding me with his body. He was still tense and waiting for the first blow. A blow that did not come. I turned enough to see his face, his eyes screwed tight. He had given himself over to one of his greatest fears to protect me. He hadn't seen the flowers yet, but the others had.

Niceven's voice hissed, "Evil sidhe, evil, evil sidhe. You have bespelled them."

"Interesting," Doyle said, "very interesting."

"Most impressive," Hawthorne said, "but whose work is it?"

"Galen's," Nicca said.

Galen's body had begun to relax above me. He opened his eyes, and I watched his puzzlement as he looked at the plants that had filled the hallway. "I did not do this."

"Yes," Nicca said again, in a voice that was very certain, "yes, you did."

Galen raised up on one arm, so that he was half sitting above me. He turned and looked behind us, and whatever he saw covered his face in astonishment. I sat up and looked, too.

Flowers filled a small space of hallway. The winged demifey were cuddled into those flowers, rolling in the petals, covering themselves with pollen. They were reacting like cats to catnip.

Queen Niceven hovered above them, untouched by the call of the flowers. Less than a handful of her winged warriors were at her side. All the others had fallen to Galen's flowers.

It was an enchantment, that much I understood, but beyond that I was as lost as the look on Galen's face.

"He's the only one who has not had new power manifest." Frost poked at one of the nodding blossoms with the tip of his sword.

"Well," Doyle said, gazing at the flowers and the drugged demi-fey, "this is certainly manifested." He grinned, a quick flash of teeth in his dark face. "If his power continues to grow he could do this to human, or even other sidhe, armies. I had almost forgotten that we ever had such nice ways to win battles."

"Well," a voice said from behind us, "I leave for a few minutes and you've planted a garden." It was Rhys, back from escorting the police outside the sithen. Nicca told him what had happened. Rhys grinned at Galen. "What is this, the hand of flowers?"

"It's not a hand of power," Nicca said. "It's a skill, a magical skill."

"You mean like baking or doing needlepoint?" Rhys asked.

"No," Nicca said, not rising to the joke, "I mean it is like Mistral's manifesting a storm. It is a manifestation, a bringing into being."

Rhys gave a low whistle. "Creating something out of nothing. The Unseelie haven't been able to do that in a very long time."

Galen touched one of the largest cupped blossoms, and it spilled a tiny demi-fey out into his hand. He jerked as if he'd been bitten, but he didn't drop the delicate figure. A female dressed in a short brown dress, with her brown and red and cream wings fanned out on either side of her as she lay on her back in his hand. She was tiny even by demi-fey standards. Her entire body did not fill Galen's palm. She lay almost completely limp, a smile on her face, her eyes rolled back into her head. Her body was covered in the black pollen of the flower she'd crawled into. She wasn't just drunk, she was passed out, happy-drunk.

Galen looked more and more puzzled. He gazed up at Doyle, half holding the little fey up to him. "For those of us under a century, what in the name of Danu is going on? I didn't do this on purpose, because I didn't know it was possible. If I didn't know it was possible, then how could I have done it at all? Magic takes will and intent."

"Not always," Doyle said.

"Not if it is simply part of what you are," Frost said.

Galen shook his head. "What does that mean?"

"Maybe we should save the magic lessons for later," Rhys said, "when we're more alone." He was looking at the tiny queen who was still hovering above us, gazing at her fallen army.

"Yes, white knight, keep your secrets from me," she said, "for the princess has broken the bargain she made with me. My people are her eyes and ears no longer. We serve Prince Cel once more."

I got to my feet, careful not to step on the demi-fey who were passed out in and among the flowers. That would be bad on so many levels. "I did not break our bargain, Queen Niceven; you took Sage away. He could not take blood if he was not allowed near me."

She buzzed to hover in front of my face, her white wings moving in a blur of speed that would have shredded true moth wings. I knew from Sage that that blur meant she was angry.

"I bargained for a little blood, a little sexual energy to come to my proxy, and thus to me. I did not bargain for him to be made sidhe. I did not bargain for him to lose the use of his wings. I did not bargain for him to . . ."

"Be too big for your bed," I said.

"I am married," she said, and that last word sounded like a curse. "I have no lover save my king."

"No, and because you cannot have your favorite lover, you forbid him the pleasure of anyone else."

The wind from her wings played along my hair, buffeted my face. The air was cool, though her anger was not. "What I do with my court is my business, Princess."

"It is, but you accused me of breaking our bargain, and I did not. I am still willing to offer a taste of royal blood to you." I held my hand out slowly, gently, offering her my upturned wrist. I did not want another misunderstanding. "Do you wish to take the blood personally? You sent Sage as your proxy because the Western Lands are far from faerie, but now I am here."

She hissed at me like a startled cat and buzzed high into the air above me. "I would not taste your sidhe flesh for all the power in the world. You will not steal my wings from me."

"But Sage was always able to change to a human size. You are not, so you can't get stuck in a larger size."

She hissed again, shaking her head, sending rainbow dazzles to dance around the walls, on us, and the flowers. "Never!"

"Then choose another proxy," I said.

"Who would take such a risk?" she said.

A small voice came. "Someone who has no wings to lose."

I looked down until I saw a cluster of demi-fey against the far wall. None of them had wings, but they had other means of transport. Carts pulled by sleek, cream-colored rats, and one dainty chariot that had more than a dozen white mice tied to it. There were two ferrets with multiple tiny riders, one the standard black mask, the other an albino with white fur and reddish eyes. A Nile monitor that was nearly four feet long had two of the larger riders. The monitor was not only harnessed but muzzled like a dog that you're afraid will bite. Nile monitors could be vicious and ate anything small enough to catch and kill. If I'd been the size of a Barbie doll, I wouldn't have wanted one anywhere near me.

Movement on the wall brought my attention to the fact that there were tiny many-legged demi-fey clinging there. Some looked like tiny spider centaurs, eight legs combined with a rounded fey body hidden under a sway of gauzy cloth. One looked like a black beetle, so like that only staring showed the pale moon of a face under the insect camouflage.

"I spoke," said one of the men in a rat-drawn cart. There was a woman in the cart with him. She was pulling on his arm, trying to stop him from waving. "No, Royal, no," she said, "don't do it. There are worse things than not having wings."

He let go of the reins that led to a lovely rat, and grabbed the woman's arms. "I will do this, Penny. I will do this."

Penny shook her head. "I don't want to lose you."

"You won't lose me."

"I will if she makes you sidhe."

"I have no other size, Penny. She can't trap me in human size the way she did Sage, because it's not one of my abilities." He hugged her to him, petting her short dark hair, and looked up at me. His hair was short and black, and just under his bangs were two long graceful antennae, as black as his hair. His eyes were large and almond-shaped, and a perfect blackness like Doyle's, or Sage's, come to that. His skin was very white in contrast to all that darkness. The woman turned her head to gaze up at me, and she, too, had long graceful antennae. It was rare for any of the demi-fey to have antennae, but for those without wings it was doubly surprising.

The two pale oval faces stared up at me. There was a little more squareness to his jaw, a somewhat daintier curve to hers. He was a little taller than she, a little more broad of shoulder, narrow of hip, but beyond the basic differences that made them male and female, they looked identical.

"You're twins," I said, "Pennyroyal, Penny and Royal." It was a custom among the demi-fey to divide a name up among twins.

He nodded. She just stared at me. They were even dressed alike in gauzy tunics of deep purple. They were both dressed in more clothing than the majority of the demi-fey. Her dress covered her from neck to knees. His tunic covered him from neck to knees, as well. I realized as I looked at the wingless ones that they were all dressed in a similar fashion. The winged fey men went for what amounted to kilts or loincloths of gauze. The women were in mini-dresses or less. Only Queen Niceven wore a gown that swept to her ankles. She was their queen, she got more clothes, but I'd never noticed the marked difference in clothing between those who had wings and those who did not.

"I have not agreed to this," Niceven said, and came to hover at my shoulder.

"Please, Your Majesty, let me try. You do not know what it is like to be without wings, doomed to walk or ride forever."

She crossed her arms over her thin chest. "I feel for your plight, Royal, and all of you who are so cursed, but you might get a great deal more than just wings from touching this one." She motioned at me. "Look what has happened with the green knight."

"Would having one of your people able to conjure such enchantments be a bad thing, Your Majesty?" he asked.

She came to hover near my face. "How can I trust you, Princess, when you have insulted me and my court so severely?"

Doyle said, "You spoke of an insult when you first arrived. You said the princess had done it. What has she done?"

Niceven turned in the air so she could see him, then moved backwards so she could see us both as she spoke. "You arrested one of my people without asking my permission. Beatrice was not sidhe, she was mine. Though trapped in her human-sized form, she was demi-fey. Beatrice was cursed but she was not Andais's or yours. The murderer is one of mine, the victim is one of mine, and you did not give me even the courtesy of a message. No other court would have been so ignored." She moved close enough that the air from her wings brushed my hair against my face. "You would have at the very least contacted Kurag, Goblin King. He would not have had to learn of such a thing from rumor and gossip as I did. Sholto, King of the Sluagh, sat in the consort's throne for you last night. You would not have arrested his people without asking him first." She flew to the ceiling, and stayed there fluttering like an angry butterfly back and forth above us.

I watched her, all white and glittering, all hurt pride and wounded arrogance, and fear. Fear that her court had become so little among us that she truly was queen in name only. She was right.

"I should have sent you a messenger when we arrested Peasblossom. I should have sent you a message when we discovered that one of the murdered was a demi-fey. You are right, I would have notified Kurag, Goblin King. I would have contacted Sholto. I would not have done to them what I have done to you."

"You are a princess of the sidhe," Frost said. "You explain yourself to no one."

I shook my head and patted his arm. "Frost, I spend a great deal of time explaining myself to everyone."

"Not to demi-fey," he said, and his face was arrogant, cold, and heartbreakingly handsome.

"Frost, either the demi-fey are a court unto themselves, worthy of respect, or they are not. Queen Niceven is within her rights to be angry about this."

His hand gripped the hilt of his sword, but he didn't say anything. To insult them beyond a certain point was to break them as a court, as a people. He wasn't willing to do that.

"Merry's right." Galen stood slowly, being as careful where he put his feet as I had been. He still held the tiny brown winged fey asleep in his hand. "I may not like Queen Niceven and the demi-fey, but she is a queen and they are a court. We should have sent someone to tell her what was happening." He gazed up at the tiny queen. "I don't know if you care what I think, but I'm sorry."

She came slowly down from the ceiling. Her wings had slowed, fanning gently, so that the illusion of some graceful moth was back. "After what we did to you, it is you who offers us an apology." She looked at him, as if she had never truly seen him before. "You fear us, hate us. Why would you show us courtesy?"

He frowned, and I watched him try to put into words what was simply him. It had been the right thing to do, and for once it had even been the politically smart thing to do, but that hadn't been why he'd done it.

"We owed you an apology," he said at last. "Merry explained it. I wasn't sure that anyone else would agree with her, so I did."

Niceven floated over to face me. "He apologized to us because it was the right thing to do."

"Yes," I said.

She looked back at him, then at me. "Oh, Princess, you must keep this one close, for he is too dangerous to be left alone among the sidhe."

"Too dangerous," Galen said, "dangerous to whom?"

"To yourself, for one," Niceven said, fluttering over to him. She put thin, pale hands on the hips of her white dress. "I see goodness in your face, goodness and gentleness. You are in the wrong court, green knight."

"My father was a pixie, and my mother an Unseelie sidhe." He shook his head, vigorously enough that Niceven moved a little back from him. "No, the glittering throng wouldn't touch me."

Niceven gazed down at the flowers and her besotted people. "They might now."

"No," Hawthorne said, "Taranis doesn't forgive a sidhe who joins the darkling court. If you take your exile to the humans and wander lost for a few centuries, maybe he'll forgive you, but," he lifted his helmet off, "once you've been accepted here, there is no going back."

"Perhaps," Niceven said, "or perhaps not."

"Queen Niceven," I said.

She turned to me, her face carefully passive, her thin hands folded in front of her.

"What do you mean 'perhaps not'?"

She shrugged. "Oh, someone who can be a fly upon the wall hears things."

"What sort of things?" I asked.

"Things that I might share with someone who was my ally, and honored their bargains."

"If you will not take blood directly from me, then I will need a new magical proxy," I said.

She turned in the air, and looked at Royal and his sister in their rat-drawn cart. "Royal," she said.

He stood straighter, almost to attention, though without wings he could not be in Niceven's guard. "Yes, my queen."

"Would you taste the blood of the princess and share the essence with me?"

"Gladly, my queen."

Penny clung to him. "Don't, Royal, don't do it."

He drew her away from him, and looked down into her face. "How long have we dreamed of wings?"

She let her arms fall limp to her sides. "Forever," she said.

"I didn't give Sage wings," I said.

"No," Royal said, "you gave him wings." He pointed at Nicca.

"But Nicca wasn't tasting my blood when it happened."

Royal nodded, and stepped from the cart. He gazed up at me. "It was during sex."

I looked at him. He was about ten inches tall, a little shorter than a Barbie doll, but not by much. I tried to think of a polite way to say it, and finally settled for, "I think the size difference is a little much."

He flashed me a grin. "Sage has given a very full report to the court. I am willing to take blood while you have sex with others, in hopes that it will bring my wings."

I shook my head. "Nicca may have been a special case."

Royal gripped the hem of his tunic and lifted it off in one smooth movement, letting it drop to the floor. He was naked before me, miniature and perfect. He turned around, displaying a perfect tattoo of wings covering his back down to his upper thighs. The wings were almost black, with lines of charcoal running through them. The edges curled over his shoulders like the draping edge of a shawl. Bright scarlet and black graced his lower back and buttocks in soft curving stripes, like the ruffled edge of a petticoat.

He turned so that I could see that the black and scarlet was edged by a thin stripe of the dark, almost spots, cut with white, and a thin line of gold. That edging strip curved over the side of his hip, so that the sides of his hips were striped with color, too.

Nicca's wings belonged to some long-lost moth. Something that had flown the skies of Europe more than a thousand years before. But I knew what had painted itself upon Royal's skin.

"You're an underwing moth, an Ilia Underwing."

He looked back over his shoulder at me, smiling. "That's one of the names humans use." He seemed pleased that I'd known what his wings belonged to. His small face suddenly became very serious. "Do you know the other name for the Ilia?"

My pulse sped just a bit, which was silly. He was the size of a child's toy. The heat in his eyes shouldn't have had that strong an effect, but my mouth was dry and my voice just a little whispery. "The beloved underwing."

"Yes," he said. He started toward me, and if it hadn't been silly, I would have backed up. A man that is shorter than my forearm couldn't possibly have been intimidating, but he was.

Galen said softly at my shoulder, "He does know he's not getting sex, right?"

"So it's not just me who wants to back up a step."

"No," Galen said.

"You are very good," Doyle said.

I looked at Doyle, but all his attention was on the little man. "What do you mean?" I asked.

"Glamour," Doyle said.

"Are all the demi-fey as good at glamour as Sage and this one?" Rhys asked.

"Not all of them, but a great many, yes," Doyle said.

Rhys shivered. "I am not sharing the bed with this one. Sage taught me my lesson, I don't need another one."

"You're not on the menu for tonight, Rhys."

"For once, I'm glad," he said.

"Then who do I get to share you with?" Royal asked. As I looked down at him, the feeling of sex and intimidation became more intense.

"It's stronger when I look at you."

Royal nodded. "Because looking is all you're doing. Now, who am I sharing you with tonight?"

Galen answered, "Me, but, truthfully, I'm not sure I can do

it. I may have apologized for us, but I still don't want them touching me."

"You touch one of us right now," Niceven said.

Galen glanced down at the still sleeping fey in his hand. "But that's different," he said.

"In what way is it different?" she asked.

"This one's not scary." He motioned his hand up toward Niceven.

Royal laughed, and it was like chimes in a happy wind. "And am I scary, green knight?"

I was close enough to see Galen's pulse beating against the side of his throat. "Yes," he said, and his voice sounded as dry as mine felt.

Royal's laughter trailed away to something darker. "Such talk will turn a man's head, green knight." The look on his face showed just how pleased he was that Galen was afraid of him.

"Some glamour grows stronger with physical touch," Adair said. He'd kept his helmet on.

"Are you asking if mine grows stronger, oak lord?" Royal asked.

"Speculating, not asking," Adair said, as if to ask a question of a demi-fey was beneath him.

Well, Adair could be high-handed if he wished, but he wasn't stripping down for the demi-fey. "Does your glamour grow stronger with physical touch?" I asked.

He grinned up at me. "It does."

Galen whispered against my hair, "Can Nicca and you have this one? I'll take the next one."

I glanced back at him. "If you wish, yes."

He sighed, and leaned his forehead against the top of my head. "Damn it, Merry."

"What?" I asked.

"I can't pass on the scary parts if you still have to do them. Are you sure you have to do this?"

"Don't you want to know why Queen Niceven said that the Seelie Court might take you in if you offered them more power?"

"Yes," he said, "yes, damn it." He looked up at Niceven. "And she knew we'd want to know."

"A spy is only as good as his information, green knight."

"My name is Galen, please use it."

"Why?"

"Because the only people who ever call me green knight tend to try to hurt me."

She looked at him a moment, then gave a small bob in the air. "Very well, Galen. You have been truthful with me, so I will be truthful with you, but you will not find it comforting."

"Truth seldom is," he said. The tone in his voice made me hug his free arm around me.

"We feed not just on blood and magic."

"You feed on fear," Doyle said, and there was something about the flat way he said it that told me there was a story behind those few words.

"Yes, Darkness," Niceven said, "as do many things here at the Unseelie Court." She turned back to Galen and me. "I think the green . . . Galen will be a feast fit for a queen."

"Then let's begin the bargaining," I said.

"We have struck our bargain, Princess."

I shook my head. "No, the bargain about what Royal can do, and can't do, in my bed and on my body."

"Are we really such a fearsome thing that you have to bargain as closely with us as you would with the goblins?"

"You chastised me for treating you as less than the goblins, Queen Niceven. If I do not negotiate with you as I would the goblins, isn't that just another kind of insult?"

She folded her arms under her small breasts. "You are not like the other sidhe, Meredith, you are always difficult, tricksy."

"You would try and bat your tiny eyes at me, and have me think Royal and the rest of you are harmless? That you are the children's storybook characters you ape? Oh no, Queen Niceven, you can't have it both ways, not with me. You're either dangerous or you're not."

She gave me a perfect child's pout. "Do I look dangerous

to you, Princess?" Her voice was wheedling, and for just a moment I felt like saying, "No, of course not."

Galen gripped my arm tight, squeezing. It helped me think.

"I've seen your true face, Queen Niceven," he said. "Your glamour won't work on me now, not even with it pushing at me like some sort of wall."

"Yes," Nicca said, "I've never felt any of the demi-fey this strongly before."

"The demi-fey are the essence of faerie," Doyle said. "As faerie grows in power, so will they, apparently." He didn't sound entirely happy about it.

Niceven turned to him. "Why, Darkness, if I didn't know better, I'd say you were afraid of us, too."

"My memory is as long as yours, Niceven." The cryptic statement seemed to please her.

"You're afraid to bring us back into our full power, and here the princess has bargained to help us do just that. Irony is sweet when it is on the right foot."

"Be careful how much irony you enjoy, Niceven, too much irony can be bad for you."

"Darkness, is that a threat?" Her voice didn't sound gentle at all now.

"A warning," he said.

"Am I important enough for the Queen's Darkness to threaten? My, we have moved up at court."

"You'll know when Doyle threatens you, little queen," Frost said.

She bobbed in the air, and again because of Sage, I knew it was their version of a stumble. "I am not afraid of Darkness."

Frost leaned into her, the way you'd intimidate someone by invading their personal space. Some of the effect was ruined by her wings and her size, but not all of it.

"I am not afraid of the Killing Frost either," she said.

"You will be," he said.

And that was how the negotiations began. They ended with a crowd of wingless demi-fey inside my room, and none of the sidhe happy about it. Niceven's idea was that perhaps it had been Sage's continuing to feed from sidhe blood that had done the damage. I couldn't argue her logic. If I didn't like Royal after tonight, I could choose one of the others, but all of them got to be in the room. We compromised, but she wouldn't tell us what she knew of the Seelie Court until after we had fed Royal. Tomorrow, she promised, if she had fed off him and scoured out our magic from his flesh. Tomorrow, we might learn some of the secrets of the Seelie Court. Tonight, we had to pay for those secrets in blood, and flesh, and magic. And, as usual, someone would be tasting my blood, taking a bit of my flesh. Where was a stunt double when you needed one?

Chapter 27

RHYS PACED BY THE BATHTUB, THOUGH THERE WAS PRECIOUS little room for pacing. The bathroom was bigger than most standard modern bathrooms, but once you squeezed in Frost, Doyle, Galen, Nicca and his wings, Kitto, and me, no bathroom short of Queen Andais's personal bathroom would have been big enough. Kitto was running the bath, playing servant, which he'd started doing more and more. Andais had offered me servants, but Doyle had refused on the grounds of my safety. We couldn't trust anyone as we trusted each other. That was part of the reason. The other part was that the servant would spy for Andais, and we had too many secrets for that. We didn't share that part with Andais.

"When I escorted Major Walters and the good doctor to their cars, the FBI was still there."

"Persistent bastard," I said.

Rhys shook his head, and stopped beside me. "No, Merry,

not persistent. Carmichael, who thought our Killing Frost was so pretty, had just gotten to the cars, too."

"What are you saying, Rhys?" Doyle was leaning to one side of the door.

"That according to the FBI and the people who escorted Carmichael out, only a few minutes had passed since I put Carmichael outside of the mound."

"It's been hours since then," I said. I was sitting on the corner of the wide marble edge of the tub, trying to make myself small, so we weren't too crowded.

"Not according to the humans outside," Rhys said.

"What does that mean?" I asked.

"It means that the sithen is playing with time," Doyle said.

"Time always runs funny inside faerie," I said.

"But only in pockets," Rhys said, "and only by a few minutes, maybe an hour. Faerie has been on the same time schedule as the mortal world since before we came to America." He leaned against the double sinks, fitting himself beside Galen.

Nicca had most of the far corner of the room for himself and the sweep of his wings. "What does it mean?"

Frost spoke from the wall on the other side of the door. "It means that it isn't only the sidhe and the demi-fey who are regaining some of their old powers."

"You told me that the humans reacted to the entrance to faerie as if the hallway had its old glamour," Doyle said. "Why should we be surprised that the sithen is gaining back other abilities as well."

I hugged my knees, trying to ignore the scratchy dried blood on my jeans. Kitto was testing the nearly full tub. I said, "Sometimes you talk about the sithen as if it's just a building, sometimes you talk as if it's a being in its own right, sometimes you speak of the sithen as if it is faerie. I asked my father once if the sithen was alive, and he said yes. I asked if it was a person, and he said no. I asked if it was faerie, and he said yes. I asked if it was the totality of faerie, and he said no. Does anyone alive today actually know what the sithen are?"

"You do ask the most difficult questions sometimes." Rhys crossed his arms, the white of his trench coat framing his pale suit. A wet line on his trousers showed where the snow had stained the cloth. He'd made two more trips outside that night than most of the rest of us.

"Does that mean you can't answer the question, or you won't?"

"You're Princess Meredith NicEssus, our future queen; if you order it, we have to answer," he said.

I frowned at him. "I did not order you to tell me, Rhys, I asked."

He rubbed the heel of his hand against his good eye, and when he lowered it, he looked tired. He might be boyishly handsome forever, but his face could still hold lines of weariness now and then. "I'm sorry, Merry. But if the sithen is messing with time, then we're going to have to post a guard outside of faerie, so that we can figure out the difference between the two places chronologically. That will tell us how bad it is right now, but . . ."

"But not how big the difference will grow," Nicca said.

Rhys nodded. "This could get really bad."

"I'm losing something here," I said. "Why do you all look so worried?"

"Don't look at me," Galen said. "I don't know why they all look gloomy about it either. I mean the sithen does a lot of weird stuff; it always has."

"And what if the sithen decides to make the difference between inside faerie and outside faerie not just hours to minutes, but years to days?" Rhys said.

Galen and I exchanged a look. He said, "Can it do that?"

I said, "Oh."

"It has in the past," Rhys said.

"I thought that the queen or king of the court controlled the time difference," I said.

"Once," Doyle said, "but that ability went away long ago."

"Wait," Galen said, "did you say the queen could control how big the time difference was?"

Several of us nodded.

"Didn't the old stories say that only hours would pass inside faerie, but centuries would pass outside in the human world?"

"Yes," Doyle said, looking at Galen as if he had said something smart.

"We accomplished a lot in the last few hours, but the rest of the world has used up only a few minutes. In effect, our sithen is moving faster than everybody else. Isn't that opposite of the way it used to work? Didn't mortal time move faster than ours?"

I watched the rest of them exchange glances, except for Kitto, who seemed totally absorbed in running the bath. "By the looks on everyone's faces, I've missed something."

"We had a lot to do tonight," Galen said. "We still have a lot to do tonight, and while we get all of it done, the outside world moves at a crawl. The question is, are we the only sithen experiencing the time shift?"

Rhys hugged him one-armed. "You know, you're smarter than you look."

"Don't compliment me too much, Rhys, it'll go to my head." But he was smiling.

"Am I slow tonight, or is everyone else just faster than I am?" I asked.

"Exactly," Doyle said.

I frowned at him. "Exactly what?"

"Did you at any time tonight say out loud that you needed more time?" Doyle asked.

"I might have said something like, we don't have enough time to investigate the murder and play court with the queen. Not those words, but . . ." I looked at Doyle. "Are you saying that I might have wished this into happening?"

"You did make a mirror appear in your room," Doyle said, "simply by wanting to see what the cloak looked like."

I was suddenly so scared that cold tingled down to my fingertips. "But Doyle, that could mean that anything I say could be taken literally by the sithen."

He nodded.

"We must find out how time is running in another sithen,"

Frost said. "If the goblins or the sluagh are gaining hours on the mortal world, then faerie itself has decided to change. Sometimes it does that."

"And if it is only our sithen?" Nicca asked.

"Then Meredith must be very, very careful what she says." He was looking at me, and I could almost watch some idea coming to life in his mind.

"What are you thinking?" I asked him.

"Not just him," Rhys said.

"No, not just him," Galen said. He shivered, rubbing his arms as if he was cold, too. "For once I know what the bad news is before anyone says it."

"Then fill me in," I said.

"If only the queen can make time change inside the sithen, and Merry was able to do it . . ." Galen said, and left it unfinished.

"Once upon a time," Doyle said, his voice seeming deeper, as if the low-growling echoes needed to fill all the small room, "even if you fought your way to the throne, or were elected by all the other rulers as high king, or high queen, you still could not rule a faerie mound. You could not sit on the throne of a specific sithen unless the sithen itself accepted your right to rule."

"I haven't heard that story," I said.

"It is a forbidden story," Frost said, looking at Doyle.

"Why would it be forbidden?" Galen asked.

I made the logical leap this time. "Andais wasn't chosen by the sithen," I said.

"She was in Europe," Doyle said, "but when we arrived in America, the new faerie mound did not."

"What do you mean 'new'?" I asked.

"Faerie is not just a physical location. The moment Andais stepped into the new mound here, it should have been the same, but it wasn't."

"We all assumed it was because of the third weirding, the one that the American government forced on us before they would allow us to move here," Rhys said. "So many of us lost so much power that we—" he shrugged—"sort of looked the other way about the sithen not cuddling up to Andais."

"She did allow the nobles to enter the sithen and have us watch them one by one," Frost said. "If the sithen had reacted to any of them more than to her, she had agreed to step aside."

"My aunt agreed to let the throne go to any noble the sithen chose?" I said.

"Hard to believe, I know," Rhys said, "but she did. We all assumed that the last weirding had taken too much of her power for her to rule us. Then the worst happened."

"The sithen knew none of them," Doyle said.

"Okay, I understand how that would be bad, but why is it forbidden to talk about it?" I asked.

"Did Prince Essus ever explain to you how the various faerie courts came into being?" Doyle asked.

I started to say yes, of course he had, but he hadn't. "I know that once the sidhe were not simply two courts, Seelie and Unseelie, but dozens, with different kings and queens, like the goblin court and the sluagh, but more independent."

"So independent that we fought among ourselves, until we all agreed that we needed a high king," Rhys said. "Once there was only one sidhe high ruler, not two."

"I know this one," I said. "The first Unseelie sidhe ruler was cast out of the Seelie Court, but he refused to leave faerie. He went from court to court and asked for entrance, but they feared the sidhe, and so finally the only fey court left was the sluagh. The most frightening and least human of all the fey. They took him in, and from that time on any sidhe who was cast out of other courts could petition to join the sluagh."

"Very good," Rhys said, "but do you know when the Unseelie became a sidhe court, separate from the sluagh?"

"When there were enough sidhe who didn't want to be called sluagh," I said.

"Almost," Doyle said.

"Why almost?" I asked.

"At one time, a fey of a certain kind would simply become

powerful enough, magical enough, for the very stuff of faerie to acknowledge them, and create a kingdom for them. One of the sidhe who had joined the sluagh was our first king. Faerie created a place for him to rule, and the sidhe left the sluagh's court and made one of our own."

"Okay," I said.

"We're all afraid to say it," Rhys said, "because we've all managed not to say the part that is most likely to get us in trouble."

"What part?" I asked.

"A court without a ruler begins to fade," Nicca said.

They all looked at him as if surprised he'd had the courage to say it. It took me a moment to understand the implications.

It was Galen who had said it out loud. "Goddess save us, that's what's been happening to our court. We had no true ruler, so the sithen was dying. Our slice of faerie has been dying."

"Not just ours," Doyle said.

"Who else?" I asked.

"Our bright cousins follow a king whose sithen did not know him."

"Their sithen didn't know any of their nobles either?" I asked.

"Rumor has it, and it's only rumor, that instead of welcoming sidhe who the sithen recognized, he exiled them," Rhys said.

"It's not rumor," Doyle said.

We all looked at him. "Who?" I asked.

"Aisling," he said.

Something on Frost's face told me that he had known. The rest looked as shocked as I felt. "They had a true king and Taranis exiled him?"

Doyle and Frost nodded.

"But that is monstrous," Nicca said. "Even Andais was willing to give up her throne if a true queen could have been found."

"Does his court know?" I asked Doyle.

"Most, no."

"But some?" I asked.

"Some," he said.

"How can they support him? The Unseelie had no choice but to fade, but he had a new king to sit on the Seelie throne. They didn't have to fade."

"Did our sithen recognize Aisling when he came here?" Galen asked.

"No," Doyle said.

"Why not?" he asked.

Doyle shrugged, and I guess that was answer enough, or the only answer he had.

"The bath is ready," Kitto said, his voice as neutral and empty as a servant's.

I touched his shoulder, and he gave me a small smile. Something occurred to me. "Did the goblin mound know Kurag when you came to this country?"

"I am not important enough to know such things. I do not know."

"The goblins are less faded than the sidhe. They are still what we left them."

"But wait," Galen said, "the Seelie sidhe are less faded in power than we are. Why is that? Shouldn't both courts be fading at about the same rate?"

"They should be," Doyle said.

"But they aren't," I said.

"They don't seem to be," Rhys said.

"You've thought of something," Doyle said.

"What made Taranis desperate enough to help release the Nameless, one of our most dangerous magicks, into the human world to kill Maeve Reed? She'd been exiled from faerie for more than a century. It couldn't have just been Merry's visit to her. That could have gotten him to send someone to assassinate Maeve, but not to release the Nameless." Rhys shook his head. "I've been thinking about it, and I can't make it make sense."

"Like his inviting Merry to his ball," Galen said. "That makes no sense either. He's hated her all her life."

"Not hated, Galen, you have to think more of a person to

hate them, and my uncle doesn't think anything of me. I was more a nonentity at the Seelie Court than here at the Unseelie Court."

"So why is he so hot to see you? Why now?"

"None of us have liked this sudden invitation," Doyle said, "but we have had our discussions, and we are going to accept."

"I still think it's too dangerous for Merry," Galen said.

"We will be there to protect her," Doyle said.

"You know, it would be really interesting to take Aisling as one of my honor guard."

"I do not believe that Taranis would allow him to pass into his court," Doyle said.

"If he refuses any of my guard it is within my rights to take insult and refuse the invitation," I said.

They all looked at one another. "It has possibilities," Rhys said.

Galen nodded. "I like anything that keeps Merry from having to attend this ball."

"How can you say that?" Frost asked. "You saw what just the touch of Aisling's power did to Melangell. Taranis has negotiated that only the guards who have visited Meredith's bed may accompany her to the ball."

It wasn't the horror of Melangell's sightless eyes that I was remembering, it was the moment when Aisling held me and I'd noticed that his eyes were empty, as if pieces were missing. Aisling had been trying to gain a kiss through his veil. The Goddess had come to me, and there had been no warning in my mind. No caution about touching Aisling. Was I sidhe enough to bed Aisling, veiled or unveiled? Or was it more simple than that? True love was supposed to be proof against Aisling's magic. Was I in love enough to resist? And was the risk of Aisling's body worth the chance to avoid whatever scheme Taranis had in store for me?

"If you do not get into the bath soon it will begin to grow cool," Kitto said.

I hugged him, and he hugged me back. "Kitto is right. Galen and I need to get clean."

"Then have sex," Galen said.

I smiled back at him. "Yes, then have sex."

"And Nicca, as well," Doyle said, "so he will be free to go to Biddy."

I nodded. "I'll give them the bed. The first time you have sex with someone shouldn't be in a bathtub, it's too awkward."

"You're going to have sex in a bathtub with a six-foot-tall man with wings." Rhys grinned and shook his head. "I think I want to watch this."

"You must include Royal," Nicca said.

"I haven't forgotten him," I said. "We just didn't need him taking all our news back to his queen."

"He will spy for Niceven," Frost said.

"I'm aware that Royal's first duty will be to his own queen and court."

"Your bedroom is crawling with wingless demi-fey," Rhys said. "It's like an infestation."

"Queen Niceven doesn't want Meredith to feed any one demi-fey too many times in a row," Doyle said.

"I do not want to share her bed with the demi-fey," Frost said.

"Oh, Frost," I said.

He held up a hand. "I'm not saying I won't, but I don't think any of us want a demi-fey with us every time we make love."

"Your bath is going to get cold," Kitto said again.

I stood up, and started peeling off the bloody clothes. "Everybody who isn't getting in the tub, leave. The night isn't getting any younger."

Frost winced. "Will that make time speed, or slow?"

"I forgot," I said, with my shirt in my hands, and the bra still to go. "I just forgot, it's an expression."

"You cannot afford expressions," Doyle said.

"I'll do my best, but it's almost impossible to watch every word you say."

"You must try, Meredith, you must try."

"Let's find out first if the goblins and the sluagh are moving at human time or our time before we panic, Merry," Rhys said.

Doyle nodded. "Take some men of your choosing and go."

"Why am I the one who keeps having to go back and forth in the snow?"

"Death does not feel the cold," Doyle said.

"No, but neither does the dark, and you get to stay nice and warm." He went for the door. "I'll leave more men than I take. This is more spying than fighting."

"But you might need to fight," Doyle said.

"Take at least two others with you," I told him.

"Aye, aye, Cap'n." He did a mock salute, then walked out.

I looked at Frost and Doyle, still standing on either side of the door. "Unless you're staying to watch, it's time to thin the number of people in here," I said.

"Do you wish an audience?" Doyle asked.

The question caught me off guard. I actually thought about it, then shook my head. "No, not really." I looked at him, studied that dark face. "I didn't know you enjoyed watching."

"I don't. Very few among the guards enjoy voyeurism."

"The queen beat it out of us," Galen said.

Doyle nodded. "Almost literally."

"I, for one," Frost said, "do not wish to watch whether you will it, or no."

"I would never ask anything of you, Frost, that I thought would hurt you, not if I had a choice."

He started to get offended, or to pretend he didn't understand me, but then his face softened, and he even gave a little smile. "I know you would not. It is not Galen and Nicca with you tonight that bites at me. It is the demi-fey. I do not like him. I do not like a princess of the sidhe having to use her body as a bargaining chip."

"Frost," I said, going to him, "a royal woman's body has been a bargaining chip for thousands of years. At least I'm not bargaining myself away in marriage. That might be my fate if I were human."

"Married to that . . . thing." The look on his face was so shocked it was funny. I laughed, I could not help myself. He jerked as if I'd struck him.

I touched his arm, but he pulled away. I'd had enough. "First, the demi-fey are a part of this court. The way the sidhe treat them, the way everyone treats them, is a disgrace. They are either part of us or they are not." I watched his face close down, watched that sullen arrogance close around him, but I didn't stop just because his feelings were hurt. I couldn't afford to keep stopping every time he got his feelings hurt, it happened too often. "Second, I'm tired of your acting as if your blood and body are too precious to be bargained with. I put my flesh and blood up for grabs a lot for you, all of you. You won't feed anyone. You won't even let a single demi-fey watch. Rhys won't let goblins touch him, or the demi-fey either now."

"He fell to the power of Sage's glamour," Frost said. "He will not risk it again."

"Fine, but I'm risking it. Galen has more reason to be afraid of the demi-fey than either Rhys or you, and he's going to do this for me, for us, tonight." I moved closer to him, but didn't try to touch him. I didn't want to see him pull away. "I know you covered my body with yours, that you offered your life for mine today. But so did Galen. He nearly paid with his life tonight, yet here he stands ready to let a demi-fey touch him."

"What do you want of me?" Frost asked.

"I want you to stop pouting about me sharing myself with the lesser fey, when you won't let your so-white flesh be touched by them. I want you to stop making me feel as if I'm the whore and you're too good for it." I realized I was angry, really angry. But it wasn't Frost I was angry with, I was just angry. And I hadn't been able to be angry at the people I most wanted to be angry with, so suddenly this unreasoning anger flared. My skin ran hot with it, making me glow through the dried crust of blood and gore.

I stepped back from him. "I am tired, Frost, and there is still much for my body to do tonight. By our bargain I must be with Royal, in some way. By the queen's order I must be with Galen and Nicca tonight. And one other green man before dawn finds me." I thought about it. "I need to bed Sholto before we go to the goblin court tomorrow night so we can count on the sluagh as our allies." I shook my head. "I did it again, didn't I?"

"Before dawn finds you," Doyle said, "yes."

"But there is too much to do, and the clock starts ticking again at dawn."

He nodded. "I would offer my blood in your place if it would satisfy Niceven."

I smiled at him. "I know you would, but the demi-fey don't seem to like you. Later, when we have the time, I'd like to know the story behind that."

"No," Doyle said, "you will not like the story, and I will not like telling it."

He looked so solemn, almost sad, that I touched his arm, and said, "Unless I need to know it, you may keep your secret feud with Niceven's court a secret."

"Would you really let the little fey touch you?" Frost asked.

Doyle looked at his friend. "Yes, if it was necessary."

"How can you let those things touch you?"

"How can I ask of the princess what I would not give myself?" Doyle said.

Frost bent his head, eyes closed. He took in a lot of air, as if he were trying to get enough breath for some long, deep dive. His breath came out in a shaky rush. He opened his eyes, and they were raw with emotion, like grey wounds. "I would never ask of you a thing that I would not do myself, Meredith. I am sorry."

I touched his arm, and this time he didn't pull away. I leaned into him, and offered my face up for a kiss. There was enough height difference that if he didn't bend down to kiss me, I couldn't make him. Not without a chair to stand on. But I didn't have to get a chair.

Frost met me halfway, bending down, his hands on my arms, steadying me on my tiptoes. We kissed. I meant it to be a chaste kiss, a "good-bye for the night" kiss, but he had other ideas.

His lips pressed against mine, hard, fierce. His tongue pushed at my mouth, and I opened to him, let him slide inside my mouth. His breath shuddered inside my mouth, as if he were breathing me in, and he crushed me against him. He lifted me off my feet and wrapped me around him. He fed at my mouth with tongue and teeth and lips, until I made small sounds at the force of his mouth, the near painful grip of his arms and hands. I melted against him; when he drew back from the kiss, I was light-headed, and tried to keep the kiss going. I'd forgotten where we were, what I was supposed to be doing. I forgot myself as I had at the press conference. I forgot everything but the taste of his mouth, the feel of his body. I forgot everything but Frost's kiss.

He drew away from me while I fought to kiss him again. I was making small, protesting noises as he tried to slide me down his body and set me on the floor. I wrapped my legs around his waist, and refused to be set down.

"Meredith, Meredith." I think Doyle's deep voice had been talking to me for a while. I finally looked at him. He smiled and shook his head. "He has to go now, we both do."

I looked back to Frost, who had finally wrapped his arms back around me when I wouldn't let him drop me. He looked terribly pleased with himself. "Now I can leave you to others."

I shook my head, because what I wanted to say was don't leave, but I couldn't. It wasn't that I didn't want Galen, but . . . Frost seemed to always be able to make me want him.

"If you are leaving, then you need to put her down," Doyle said.

He let me slide down his body, and I let him do it, this time I did. My knees were a little unsteady, and he had to keep his hand on my arm for a moment, before I could stand on my own.

He laughed, a purely masculine laugh. "Goddess help me, but I do love you."

"Enough, Frost," Doyle said, "we have other work to do tonight." He motioned for the door, and this time Frost went where he was told. Doyle turned to me at the open door. "I will not try to compete with that." He said it with a smile.

I raised up on tiptoe, my hands on his chest, and said, "It isn't a competition."

He lowered his face to mine. "In the mortal words of the human world, the hell it isn't." He kissed me, firm and thorough but chaste compared to what Frost had done, then he drew back from me. "Do you wish me to send in the demi-fey?"

"Let us get the blood off of us first. I'll send Nicca or Kitto for Royal."

"As you wish." His eyes flicked behind me, then he touched my face, and closed the door behind him.

I turned around to find that two of the other men in my life had undressed while I was preoccupied. Galen's body was covered in patches of dried blood. It wasn't lust that made me go to him and wrap myself around his nude body, it was fear. Later there'd be time for lust, but in that moment I just wanted to hold him, wanted to feel him warm and alive in my arms. My hands couldn't seem to avoid feeling the dried scratchiness of blood. It was everywhere on the smooth perfection of his skin. My hands found the still-healing wound in his back. I shivered.

He hugged me. "Are you cold?"

"A little," I said aloud. To myself I acknowledged that it wasn't the kind of cold that a coat or a bath would help.

"Let's get in the water then." He smiled down at me as he said it, as if a little hot water would solve everything. If only life were that simple.

Something must have shown on my face, because he frowned at me. "Are you all right?"

I nodded and sighed. So much to do, so many alliances to forge and strengthen, so many enemies to find. I should have been hurrying, should have had my list of goals and been breaking my back to get through them. But in that moment I couldn't think of anything that seemed more important than holding as much of Galen against me as I could manage. Naked in a bathtub doesn't solve everything, but naked with someone you love doesn't hurt anything either.

Chapter 28

THE BATH WAS STILL HOT WHEN I FINALLY SLID INTO IT, WHICH meant that Kitto had drawn it hotter than I liked. He had known that we would talk too long and had planned for it. He'd begun to anticipate my needs, not in the way of a lover or a friend, but in the way of a good servant. Unobtrusive, quiet, just there when needed. No friend or lover I'd ever had had been unobtrusive. Messy, joyous, heartbreaking, wonderful, but never unobtrusive.

I looked at him as Galen slid into the bath. Kitto was one of the oldest of my men, and the oldest among us don't always like being thanked, so I didn't. "You drew the water too hot, so it would be just right by the time we got in the tub. You knew we'd talk too long."

He ducked his head, not meeting my eyes. "There was much to talk of."

I leaned against the edge of the marble tub, until I could touch his shoulder. "You always seem to know what I'm going to do before I do."

He raised eyes that were unsullied by white, only a bright clear blue. I saw uncertainty there before he lowered them again. "What's wrong, Kitto?" I asked, stroking my fingers up and down his bare shoulder. He'd stripped down to just a thong, as he often did when he did anything messy. To save his clothes, he said. I got the feeling that Kitto owned more clothes now, with me, than he'd ever owned in the goblin court.

He shook his head, sending the black curls of his newly grown hair brushing across his shoulders. A few inches longer and it would have been punishable by torture. Only the sidhe were allowed long hair. He was sidhe now, with his own hand of power. As with Nicca's wings and Mistral's reborn power, so Kitto's sidhe magic had come after sex. With the new power should have come a new confidence, but it had not.

Galen leaned over the tub edge to touch Kitto's other shoulder. "What's up, Kitto, you can tell us."

Kitto flashed him a rare smile. "You are both the kindest sidhe I've ever known." He glanced behind at Nicca. "All of you."

"You're sidhe now, too, Kitto," I said.

He shook his head. "I will never be truly sidhe, not to some."

Nicca knelt behind him, his wings sweeping out along the floor. "Who has been saying such things to you?"

Kitto shook his head again, and Nicca's arms came around from behind, hugging him. Kitto stiffened, as if afraid. I leaned up over the tub edge until I could lay a kiss upon his lips. When I drew back from the kiss, he raised frightened eyes to me.

"What did they say to you?" I asked. I was really worried now. I'd never seen him quite like this, and I didn't like it.

He dropped his gaze again, and wouldn't look at me as he said it. "They said that I would never be anything but a filthy goblin. That only a whore would share her bed with me." He looked up then, and his face was so hurt, so confused. "I didn't think any fey called another whore. It is not our way."

"Oh, Kitto," I said.

"I should not be here if it hurts your chances of being queen." He started to bend down, as if he would make himself smaller, but Nicca's arms wouldn't let him do it. Nicca held him tightly but gently against his body.

"They are jealous," Nicca said.

Kitto looked over his shoulder at the other man. "Jealous of what?"

"Of you," Galen said.

Kitto blinked at him, and shook his head. "No, not of me."

"You are the first non-sidhe to be brought into his power in centuries," Galen said. "No matter how common it used to be, it isn't now. They are jealous that Merry could do it, and you could become it. They're afraid of you and what it might mean if more of the sidhe-sided goblins could be made sidhe."

I looked at Galen.

"What?" he said. "It's true."

"Yes, but I . . ."

"Didn't think I'd noticed," he said.

I had the grace to look embarrassed. "Let's say, I didn't think you'd noticed so much, and so well."

He smiled, a little sadly. "I'm learning just how stupid everyone thought I was."

I touched his shoulder. "Not stupid, never that."

"Foolish then, or oblivious."

"Oblivious," Nicca said. "Can't truly argue that one."

I had to smile. "You did seem oblivious to most of the politics."

Galen nodded. "I was, maybe I still am, but we all have to keep our wits about us. We all have to see what there is to see, or we are going to die." He gripped my arms, sloshing the water against our bodies. "When it was just my life and there was no chance that I would ever be in your bed, I didn't care that much." He hugged me against him. "There's too much to lose now, and I don't want to lose any of it."

I wrapped my arms around him, held him as tight as I could. My hands traced the patches of dried blood, covering all of him that hadn't gone in the water. I trailed my hands down and found that even in the water, the blood still clung. So much blood, so terribly much.

"I'm sorry that I didn't pay attention before," he said, his cheek against my hair. "I didn't see a point to it, if I couldn't have you. I don't see everything, not the way Doyle does, or Frost, or even Rhys, but I do see some things, and I'm trying to see more."

There was a lump in my throat so big I couldn't swallow past it. My chest felt tight, and it was hard to breathe. My eyes were suddenly hot, and I knew I was about to cry only a second before it started. I didn't want to cry. He was safe. We were safe. But feeling the dried blood made me remember the moment I'd seen him lying on his back in a lake of his own blood. That heart-stopping moment when I'd thought he was gone. Thought I'd never hold him warm against me again. Thought his arms would never press our bodies together again. That I'd never see his smile or hear his voice or gaze into his living eyes.

Galen stroked my hair and raised my face up to his. "Merry, are you crying?"

I nodded, because I didn't trust my voice.

"Why?" he asked.

Nicca said it for me. "She thought she'd lost you today, Galen."

Galen stared down into my face. "Is that why you're crying?"

I nodded again, and buried my face against his chest. He leaned back into the water, cradling me against his body. He stroked my skin, petted my hair, and whispered, "It's all right. I'm all right."

"But what about next time?" I asked.

"The queen made it clear that I might be the key to bringing babies back to the sidhe. I don't think they'll want to hurt me now."

"Cel's people will," Kitto said.

We looked at him.

"I hear things because no one notices me."

I felt a twinge at that because I'd done it, too. He'd accused me once of talking over him like he was a dog or a chair. That was before he had become my lover, but even now it was easier not to notice him than the rest. He had survived in the goblin mound by being unobtrusive, as invisible as he could make himself. He still had the habit of it.

"I heard some sidhe saying that they did not believe that anyone of Andais's line would be able to bring life back to the Unseelie."

"Who said this?"

"They saw me, after they had spoken. I think they would have tried to hurt me, but King Sholto came down the hallway. He had some of his sluagh with him."

"Was this today?" I asked.

"Yes."

"If he was here, I wonder why he didn't come to the throne room."

"I do not know, but he was wounded," Kitto said.

"Wounded?" Galen said.

"How badly?" Nicca asked.

"He had an arm in a sling, and a bandage on the side of his face and head."

"Who could harm a warrior of the Unseelie, and the King of Sluagh, that badly?" Nicca said as if he was simply thinking aloud.

"Goblins could," Kitto said, "if they caught him unaware and unable to use his magic. There are warriors among my people who could best any you have, except for your sidhe magic."

"Or another sluagh," I said softly.

They all looked at me. "There are some among his people who think that by coming to my bed he will become full sidhe, and they will lose him as their king."

"I heard it was mostly his harem of night hags," Nicca said.

"Did everyone but me know that his hags were his harem?" I asked.

Nicca and Galen exchanged glances. "We envied him as the only guard who had an outlet for his desires," Nicca said.

"They're afraid that the touch of sidhe flesh will steal him away," Galen said.

"No one but Merry would sleep with him," Nicca said. "No other sidhe would risk bearing his child, for fear it would be a monster."

I shook my head. "Once the Unseelie welcomed any child.

It was the way of our court. When did we become an anthropomorphic club? When did two arms, two legs, and human beauty become the ideal?"

"Long before either of you were born," Kitto said.

Nicca nodded. He was cuddling Kitto now more than just holding him. Kitto's eyes still looked fragile, as if he believed whatever the sidhe had said to him. No name-calling truly bites deep unless, in some dark part of us, we believe it. If we are confident enough then it's just noise, but Kitto wasn't confident, not in the least.

He spoke in a small, low voice. "I looked almost sidhe as a baby. My mother must have kept me for a few months, then the scales appeared around my spine, and when the teeth came in, so did the fangs. That was enough for her to leave me by the goblin mound, to either be taken in or killed. She left me there knowing that the goblins liked to eat a bit of sidhe flesh." He huddled in on himself, wrapping Nicca's arms closer around him. I couldn't tell if it was on purpose or accidental that the movement wrapped the other's arm tighter. Most fey like to be touched, it comforts them, but the goblins are a different race than most. They like sex, but touch can as easily lead to violence as sex among them, and there is very little touching that is only comfort and not sex.

"But you're wrong, Meredith. The sidhe, even the Unseelie, never took in every child. Goblin-sided babies that looked less than pure sidhe were left to die outside the goblin mounds."

"The goblins took in their sidhe-sided children," I said.

Kitto shook his head, and only Nicca's arms kept him from curling into a little ball. Only Nicca's strength kept the smaller man upright. "Not always," Kitto whispered.

I reached out to touch his face. Galen, with his longer arms, could touch more of him. He found a hand to hold on to, and Kitto gripped the hand he offered. If I hadn't been almost touching his face with mine, I might not have heard what he whispered next. "Sometimes they raise them until they're big enough to eat. Not enough meat on a baby." He looked up at me, his eyes shining with unshed tears. "When I got big enough, the woman who wet-nursed me wouldn't let them have me. Because I was smaller than normal, it had taken me longer to get big enough, so long that I was talking, and she had grown fond of me. She fought for me. She bled for me. She saved me, but when she needed me, I was too small, too weak, to save her." A look of rage crossed his face, and he closed his eyes as if he didn't want me to see it. "One of the sidhe today said something, like he knew. He said I'd always been small, too small to be a real goblin, too small to be sidhe, too small to be anything but a burden and a danger to those around me." Kitto looked up at me. "I didn't think any sidhe visited the goblin mounds except for your father, and you. How did he know?"

I wanted to say that the sidhe in question had guessed. Had simply looked at Kitto's small size and used it to be cruel. That he hadn't known Kitto's background, but only made an educated guess. But would it be more cruel to tell Kitto that his past was so obvious that a stranger could see it written on his body, or to let him believe that his history was known for certain by sidhe who dealt with the goblins more than they should?

Galen decided for me. "They didn't know, Kitto, they just guessed. They were being mean. That's all. They didn't know that what they said would hit so close to the truth."

"Guess?" Kitto said, looking at him. "Guess? They guessed? How? How could they know? How?" He gripped Galen's hand with his smaller ones. "Is my shame written across my body? Is it that easy to see that I am weak? That I am a burden to those around me? I am a danger to you even." He reached out to me then, gripping my hand so tight it almost hurt. "If I got you with child, they would never accept me as king, or you as queen. The two sidhe lords said they'd see you dead before they'd let a goblin-sided sidhe sit on the Unseelie throne."

I wanted to ask who "they" were, but he might not know their names, and to ask it now seemed cruel. The two lords hadn't been talking of conspiracies. They had simply been giving voice to their prejudices. They had said the cruelest truths they could find. But if they had truly planned on killing him, and me, then they wouldn't have told him. They wouldn't have taunted him with it. Or they wouldn't have let him go unscathed after overhearing them. His clean, unbloodied flesh meant they didn't really mean it. They were bullies, nothing more. I could get him to describe them for me later. Tonight, I didn't want to make him dwell upon it. I wanted him to forget about it, at least for a little while.

I wanted to caress him, to hold him until that look left his eyes. But there was no room tonight on my dance card, not unless I could figure out a way to combine people again. Galen would sleep in big puppy piles, but he didn't like sharing sex. Nicca shared just fine, and I think he would have agreed to almost anything just so he could get to Biddy in the next room. I didn't mind being the one he rushed through. I enjoyed Nicca, but he did not speak to my heart and body the way Galen did, or Doyle, or Frost.

It was Galen who reached for Kitto. Galen who pulled him closer to the tub. "I'm sorry, Kitto, I'm so sorry, I didn't mean to say..." He didn't finish it, but he'd said enough to let me know that he knew he'd said too much. That he'd said aloud what I'd been thinking, and he understood that his comments had hurt Kitto. He understood it, and was willing to try to undo the hurt he'd inadvertently done.

Many humans watched the casual touching among us and mistook it for sex, but it isn't always. Sometimes you just need to be touched. Sometimes you see such hurt, such loneliness in another fey's eyes that you must do something, anything, to chase that look away. Sometimes sex isn't even about sex among us. Sometimes it's just the last resort for making someone smile.

Chapter 29

KITTO LAY BACK IN THE WATER, CRADLED AGAINST GALEN'S body. Galen trailed his hands over the smaller man's arms and shoulders, stroking strong hands through the now damp curls around his face. Kitto half floated, his eyes closed as he snuggled his shoulders and head against the curve of Galen's upper body.

I trailed my fingertips down the front of Kitto's leg, until I traced along the top of his foot. I knew he was ticklish there, and it earned me a smile, but his eyes stayed closed. I held his foot in my hands, and licked along the top of his foot where I had touched. It made him squirm and laugh. He opened his eyes, sinking his legs below the water and sitting up. Galen's arms spilled around his shoulders, holding him more securely against his own body.

I moved in against the front of Kitto's body, straddling his legs. I brushed myself over the loose thickness of his groin. It drew a sound of pleasure from him. But when he put his hands at my waist, it was to stop the movement of my hips.

Kitto's voice was a little strained, but his small hands were very firm at my waist, stopping me from pushing harder against his body. "It is Nicca who is meant to be with Galen and you this night."

"I am content to wait my turn," Nicca said from where he knelt beside the tub. His wings fanned gently at his back as he reached to trail his fingers in the water.

Kitto shook his head, water trickling down his face from his sodden hair, his black curls flattened against the white of his skin.

I moved my groin against his, and his hands on my waist could not stop it. His fingers tightened, and again he said, "No." But other parts of his body were already responding to even the light touch he was allowing me.

"Your body says otherwise," I said.

He swallowed hard and blinked those blue on blue eyes up at me. "I cannot be your king, Merry. Word has come from Kurag, Goblin King, that Holly and Ash have laid challenge on any goblin that takes their prize before they can."

I frowned at him. "And that means what?"

"Any goblin that does anything to become your king before Holly and Ash have had their chance will be challenged and killed by them."

"They have no right to dictate to you, Kitto," I said. "You are sidhe now. You have a hand of power. That is sidhe magic, not goblin."

He gave me a sad little smile. "You do not know them as I do. I would not anger them, not for anything in faerie." He touched the side of my face where the blood still clung. "Let me help you and Galen clean yourselves." He smiled, and it was a real smile, not so sad. "I am honored that Galen reached for me first. I know that that is not his way." He leaned in against the taller man's body and smiled up at him.

Galen smiled down at him and ran his hands down the other man's arm. "I wanted to see you smile."

Kitto smiled wider, amost a grin. "It means much to me that you care if I am happy or sad." He looked at me, and his face sobered. "But heed me on this, Merry, sidhe or no, princess or no, you should fear Holly and Ash."

"They will come to my body as the rest of you have. They will have their chance for kingmaking. I know to negotiate exactly what kind of sex they can have from me. Beyond that, why should I fear them?"

"We will be with Merry in the goblin court," Galen said. "We won't let anything bad happen to her."

"You make it sound so easy," Kitto said, gazing up at the other man.

"How dangerous are the twins?" Nicca asked.

"They are some of the most feared warriors of our court," Kitto said.

"They looked sort of puny standing next to the Red Caps," Galen said.

"I do not know what this 'puny' means," Kitto said.

"Small, weak," I said.

Kitto acknowledged it with a nod. "But size is not everything in combat. Holly and Ash have a reputation for viciousness among the goblins."

I stopped petting Kitto and went very still, because what he'd just said put things in perspective for me. For Holly and Ash to have earned such a fearsome reputation among the goblins spoke of terrible violence against a people who thrived on it.

"Goblins are stronger than we are," Galen said. "To be half-sidhe in their court must make life hard."

Kitto shivered, and he relaxed his hands on my waist enough for me to press the front of my body against the front of his. Galen and I held him between our bodies; he wrapped his arms around me, and clung to the feel of our bodies. "You have no idea, Galen, no idea how it marks you as victim. I was unlucky enough to be as weak as I look. Holly and Ash were beautiful children, blond and pale, and except for the eyes would have passed at either sidhe court. Even with the eyes they would have been accepted."

"Why didn't they petition to join our court?" I asked, my face resting on the top of Kitto's wet hair, and the warmth of Galen's shoulder.

"I do not know," Kitto said, "for they suffered when they were young males. Our females liked to make them perform, until they grew strong enough to fight them off."

Galen and I were frowning at him, but Nicca seemed to understand. "You mean the she-goblins raped them?"

Kitto nodded.

"It's not easy for a woman to rape a man," I said.

"It is possible," Nicca said, and he leaned his face against the one folded arm that graced the edge of the tub. His other arm was deeper in the water, as if he sought something below its surface. "The queen is fond of force."

I moved through the water to touch his shoulder. He started when I touched him, as if he had expected a far less pleasant touch. Nicca's brown eyes were a little too wide. Whatever memory he was thinking upon, it was a bad one. So many bad memories among the guard, thanks to Andais.

I laid a gentle kiss on his mouth, and drew back to stare into his face. "Let me clean up, and we will make love. Gentle love, and then you will have Biddy and that will be gentle, too."

He nodded, but it was a little too rapid, and his eyes still held that shadow of fear. I felt the water move before Kitto came beside me to add his hands to mine on Nicca's body. "Until I became a part of the princess's household, I did not understand that any sidhe could be forced to such horrors, not unless they had earned punishment." He touched Nicca's face. "I know now that there is pain in every court, and no one is truly safe." He kissed Nicca's cheek. "Let me help them rid themselves of the blood, and then the princess will take that sadness from your eyes."

Nicca smiled at him. "There are other things you can do with Merry besides intercourse. You, too, could have her do things to you that would take that sorrow from your eyes, Kitto."

He did that quick grin again, as if he was afraid to be seen smiling so broadly. "In the goblin court the one who gives oral pleasure is the lesser being. It shows that you are submissive to the one you are pleasuring."

"That's not how the sidhe see it," Galen said, moving to join us at the center of the tub.

Kitto flashed him another grin. "So I have seen whenever Merry could persuade one of us to let her but touch us."

"I like oral sex," I said.

"We know," the three of them said in unison, which made them all laugh.

"I don't like that Holly and Ash feel they can dictate to you, Kitto. But if you truly aren't comfortable with intercourse, then let me finish what I've only been able to start with all of you but Sage."

"With Sage you were forbidden to have intercourse," Nicca said. "Queen Andais doesn't want to risk a demi-fey on our throne."

I nodded. "So we did nothing that would risk Sage getting me pregnant." I looked at Kitto, and didn't fight the look that filled my eyes. "And now I'm supposed to do things with Kitto that won't let him get me with child either."

Kitto's breath shook on its way out, but not with fear. "If you were a goblin and looked at me so, I would be afraid, but I've learned what that light in your eyes means."

"What?" I asked, in a voice that was already grown lower with need.

"That you're about to do something to me that I'm going to like," he said. "Let me help you and Galen get clean."

"And then?" I asked.

He gave me a look that I've seen in men's eyes before, a look that says they know what we're about to do, and that there will be no going back, no stopping. "And then I will let you have your way with me."

"Other than the little you've allowed Merry to do to you, have you ever had anyone do oral sex on you?" Galen asked.

Kitto looked at him. "No."

I took in a long shaking breath and shivered when my breath ran out. I'd never gotten to be the first for anyone before. I was almost certain that the rest of the guard had had this particular pleasure performed by someone else once upon a time. I would be the first one to ever hold Kitto in their mouth, and suck, and lick, and bite, if he wished.

"Your face," Galen said, "like it's Winter Solstice and you've gotten every present you asked for."

"If you'd let me go down on you, you'd see this expression on my face more often," I said.

He gave me a look. "You're incorrigible."

I leaned around Kitto, closer to Galen. "If you'd only say yes, you'd find out just how incorrigible I can be."

I was rewarded with a look almost of pain, as if he wanted to say yes, but . . . intercourse had become everyone's goal, because we pursued a baby like some infertile couple.

"Me first," Kitto said.

"Me second," Nicca said, "though I think the queen will be upset if we do oral and not something that would gain you a child."

I nodded. "She was very specific about that, so yes. I don't want to disappoint Andais."

We all shivered in unison, and this time it had nothing to do with pleasure.

Chapter 30

THE TILE WAS TOO COLD TO LIE ON, BUT TOWELS TOOK CARE OF that. Kitto lay back on them, knees up, legs slightly spread so I could reach him better, an ivory dream against all that burgundy darkness. His sex was swollen and thick even before I got to kneel between his legs. Anticipation had done much of my work for me.

I slid my mouth over the swollen tip of him, like taking in a whole, ripe plum until my mouth was so full I couldn't bite down, and couldn't swallow. My mouth is full of the ripe, firm flesh, but with this plum, filling my mouth was only the beginning, so much left to swallow. The warm thick firmness of the fruit doesn't writhe in your mouth, as you move over it. It doesn't cry out as you lick along it inside your mouth.

Kitto's hands dug at the towels underneath him, bunching them in his hands, clutching the only thing he could find while he rode the pleasure.

Nicca's hands stroked along my ass, making me writhe and push myself against him, but he kept me from more of his body. He cupped my buttocks in both his hands, and the feel of him holding me like that made me suck at Kitto, hard and fast. Kitto cried out. I waited for Nicca to push himself against me, but nothing came, nothing but the promise of his hands on me.

Galen said what I was thinking. "Consort save us, Nicca, finish it." It made me roll my eyes past Kitto, to my green man as he knelt near Kitto's head on the edge of the towels.

Nicca's fingertips dug into my flesh, just a little, no nails, just the strength in his fingers that let me know that if he wished he could plunge his fingers inside my flesh. So strong, so very strong.

I writhed for him, and had to fight not to be too fierce on the tender flesh inside my mouth. I had to raise my mouth off of Kitto for a moment. Had to catch my breath, and fight off the urge to bite down. I kept one hand on the base of him, but changed the grip, so that my hand covered as much of him as I could. I came up off of his body with my hand already stroking his wet, quivering shaft.

I looked back at Nicca who was kneeling behind me, but no longer touching me. He looked brown and perfect kneeling there, with his hair still wet from the tub, clinging to his body in thick strands that tangled around his shoulders, arms, waist, and legs. His wings rose against all that chocolate-colored goodness like some spun sugar fantasy. I had a moment of regret about him going elsewhere, but only a moment. I wanted him happy more than I wanted him.

"Why were you waiting?"

"You are sending me to what amounts to my marriage bed, Merry. If this is to be my last time with you, I would like it to be exactly as I want it. You can say no."

I had to smile. "Ask, and I'll know the answer." Then I thought of something. "Are you unhappy about Biddy?"

"No," he said, but he frowned. "No, but there will be things I will miss."

"Such as?" I wasn't fishing for compliments. I truly wanted to know.

It was his turn to smile. "Such as watching you stretched underneath me, screaming your pleasure around another man's body, while I bring you, and pour my pleasure between your legs."

Just hearing him describe it with that look in his eyes tightened things low in my body. "I was offering that," I said.

"I want you on your back as you were with Sage. I want to see your breasts rise and fall with your breathing."

I went to him, touching his face, trying to see through this combination of passion and seriousness. It wasn't like him. "I want Biddy and you to be a happy time, not a sad one."

He smiled, but it held an edge of something that was not happy. "I remember a time when marriage was not the end of such joys but the beginnings of them. The sidhe never cheated on their partners, but if we agreed then others were brought into our beds."

He was speaking of a time before Andais was queen. A time before Christianity was anything but a heretic Jewish sect. Most of the sidhe didn't speak of it, for they didn't like talking about what they had lost. Who wants to talk of a time when the sidhe had not been outnumbered by the humans. A time when we married for love and not simply for children. A time when sex was about joy and sharing and not a relentless pursuit of pregnancy. A time when an unplanned baby didn't condemn you to a loveless marriage. I had felt such happiness when the ring chose Nicca and Biddy for each other. But was it a true love match? Yes, they were infatuated with each other, and yes there might be a child, but would there be happy-ever-after? Or would Nicca love her, bed her, share a child with her, yet regret. And would those regrets eventually destroy their love?

Suddenly I smelled roses. "Do you smell apple blossoms?" Galen asked.

"Yes," Nicca said, "like in the hallway with Mistral."

"Honeysuckle," Kitto said.

The scent was growing stronger. I had a moment of inspiration. It wasn't the same as channeling the Goddess, but . . . "When did the sidhe stop having children, Nicca?"

He blinked at me. "I can taste the perfume on the air."

"Answer my question."

"I don't know," he said, "long ago."

"Did we stop having children after we adopted the human ideal of one partner?"

"We adopted monogamy because the humans outbred us using it," Nicca said.

"Did they really?" I said. "Or did we begin to be outbred when we stopped being who and what we are?"

"What do you mean, Merry?" Galen asked.

I held up my hand to show the dull metal gleam of the queen's ring. "She said she took this off her enemy's body, but that she never saw babies with it. Lust, love, infatuation, but she could not see the babies. What if this is not the queen's ring, but a ring meant for a fertility deity? We were nature deities originally, before human need turned some of us more civilized. We are that which is primal, basic."

"The sidhe have not been that in a very long time," Kitto said.

I turned to find him still lying in the nest of towels, as if he hadn't moved. "What do you mean, Kitto?"

"The goblins were the last of faerie to embrace the idea of only one spouse at a time. Once, if the husband, the dominant partner, could protect, feed, and house more, then you were allowed more if they all agreed."

"I wouldn't think that the husband would care what the wife thought," Galen said.

"Technically, husband only means dominant partner, not the sex of a goblin, and he or she could bring anyone in without the wife's permission. But in reality, if you bring in someone your wife hates, then your home life becomes a battleground, and not even a goblin wants that."

"So you could be someone's wife?" I asked.

He nodded. "Yes."

"But not a husband," Galen said.

"I am not strong enough to be one." He writhed on the bed of towels. "Why do I smell honeysuckle as if summer has arrived and I am standing in the sun? It's so warm."

"You were in the hall when Merry and Mistral had their little fling," Galen said, his voice almost as light as his words. "Apple blossoms for me."

"Like standing in the orchard in spring," Nicca said.

The two men smiled at each other.

"Spring energy," Kitto said.

I looked at him. "What?"

"They're both spring energy," he said.

"And what are you?"

"Summer, when the land is hot and ripening." He writhed on the towels as he said it, his legs straining out as if he were close to orgasm. His body was thick and ripe again.

"And what am I?" I asked.

"Autumn," he said. "You are the land when the harvest comes. You are what the year works toward, Merry."

"And what is winter?"

"The long sleep," Kitto said.

I laid back against him, using his groin as a pillow. It brought a small sound from him. I gazed back at Nicca where he still knelt. "Tell me what you want, Nicca. Tell me exactly what you want."

"I want you on your back. I want to see another man push his way inside your mouth while I mount you. I want you to scream your pleasure around his body while I fuck you."

I nodded, rolling the back of my hair across Kitto's groin. He writhed for me. "We can do that," I said.

Nicca smiled.

Kitto's voice came shaky, but clear. "I do not know how to position myself for what you ask. Where do my legs go?"

"I'll show you," Galen said, and his voice was low with need.

I rolled my head back so I could see him still sitting behind us. The movement made Kitto writhe again. Two birds with one caress. "You've refused before," I said.

"I didn't say I would go that way, only that I'll help Kitto figure out where his legs go. A hundred words can't make as much sense as one good demonstration." His eyes were far more serious than his words, serious and dark with need.

"Well, as long as it's a good demonstration," I said, and my own voice was a little breathy.

"Oh, it will be," he said, and the look on his face was all male. I believed him.

Chapter 31

IT WAS MY TURN TO LIE BACK AGAINST THE TOWELS. TO LIE there and watch Galen crawl toward me. His body was already thick and hard, dark with the extra blood, darker than the rest of his body.

I wanted a lot of things from Galen, and had gotten most of them, but he like the rest of the men was so intent on making babies that he wouldn't chance going elsewhere. I watched him crawling closer and felt positively covetous.

He gave a laugh that was more nerves and anticipation than humor. "The look on your face, like I'm something good to eat."

"She did not look at me that way," Kitto said.

Which put me back to having to soothe his ego. I'd begun to notice the hardest thing about having this many men in my life wasn't figuring out what position for sex tonight but how to keep from hurting anyone's feelings or making anyone feel left out. It wasn't the number of bodies in the bed that made it complicated but the number of hearts and hands.

I reached out and touched Kitto's knee where he knelt so close. He was supposed to be watching, so he could learn where the legs went. "Galen was my first crush, Kitto, the first man that I ever lusted over. The first that I ever loved. I'd spent years fantasizing about him before he came to my bed.

You're new on the menu. I haven't had a chance to fantasize about you for so many unrequited years."

"Don't feel slighted," Nicca said. "She doesn't look at me that way either."

I looked down my body at him. "I didn't realize—"

He held up a hand to stop my words. "I do not feel slighted, Merry. All that had eyes knew how long you pined after Galen. You followed him around like a puppy when you were so young you didn't even realize why you found him so compelling."

I wasn't sure I liked the puppy remark, but I let it go, because when I was fourteen, it was probably embarrassingly accurate.

"Merry," Galen said, "you're blushing."

I covered my face with my hands, because I rarely if ever blushed. I wasn't blushing for me now, but for that long ago girl. The girl that I had been would have been mortified to know that her "secret" love was no secret at all.

Hands touched my wrists. "Merry." Galen's voice was as gentle as his hands, as he moved mine away from my face. "You blushed for me."

I actually couldn't look at him. "It's just the thought that everyone knew. I didn't know I was being that obvious when I was fourteen."

"We're all that obvious when we're fourteen," he said with a smile.

"It's been a few centuries since I was fourteen," Nicca said, "but if memory serves, Galen's right."

Kitto's comment was, "The goblins are not a subtle race."

"What does that mean, exactly?" Galen asked.

"It means that if a goblin lusts after another, everyone knows it. We do not see the point of hiding our admiration, unless we fear the goblin we lust after will take it as an insult. We are not subtle, but we can hide what we feel if we must."

I held my hand out to him, palm up. He took my hand, looking puzzled. "What would you have of me, Princess?"

"A smile," I said.

He looked even more puzzled.

Galen explained, "She wants to chase that shadow from your eyes."

Kitto rewarded us both with a shy smile, then shook his head. "I like being sidhe."

I squeezed his hand and would have said something comforting, but Nicca chose that moment to play his hand between my legs and suddenly I couldn't think of any words.

"You're not wet enough," Nicca said.

It took me two swallows to say with a suddenly dry throat, "Bath, always does that."

"Odd that such wetness makes a woman dry," he said, and his finger found my opening, slipped inside. It made me gasp, made my hand convulse around Kitto's. Nicca moved his finger inside me, gently, slowly. "I am not so large as some, but not small either. This dry it will hurt."

My voice came breathy. "Then make me wet."

"As my princess commands," he said, with a smile. He took his hand away from my body, and said to Galen, "Show Kitto where the legs go, so that when she is ready to be entered, I will have my view."

"Let me know when you're ready," Galen said.

"I won't have to tell you," Nicca said, "you'll know."

The scent of flowers had faded, like the dream of roses in a long-closed room. You open the door and get the hint of perfume, then it fades, and you wonder if you imagined it. Such is the passing of many spirits and powers in the human world. Many things that humans take for ghosts are the shadows of things that were never truly mortal.

Galen had faded a little, too, with all the talk, and I liked that better for oral sex. A little softness first, a little less size to begin with. He straddled my upper body, and as soon as he was close enough I tried to take him in my mouth.

He laughed, and held his hand in the way. "Let me get settled first; you'll pull a muscle in your neck doing it that way."

He moved his body closer to my mouth, settled his knees more firmly on either side of my shoulders. His groin filled my view, not just the head and shaft, but the tight firmness of his testicles, in their close-curled nest of darker green hair. My hands were trapped underneath his weight. I could touch his thighs, his ass, and the lowest edge of his back, but that was all my hands could reach. If I had known that I would have a chance to finally have Galen in my mouth, I might not have agreed to the change in positioning. With me on top I would have been able to guide more of what went into my mouth, and how. In this position I had to let the man direct it more. I wanted a hand to help angle him for my mouth. But I shouldn't have worried. Galen stared down at me, his eyes filling with that darkness that men get only in the most intimate of moments. He used his hand to move himself so that the angle was better. And once my mouth slid over the head of him, he adjusted his upper body so that when I sucked him down, I was able to suck all of him. He was soft, and silken inside my mouth, the foreskin rolling, something extra for my tongue to play with. I sucked eagerly to get all of him inside me. My lips rested solid against his body. I rolled him in my mouth, sucking, stroking, playing with him with tongue and mouth, while I still could. Even as I enjoyed the sensation of him soft, he grew in my mouth. I felt that bit of flesh go from soft and silken to hard and ripe. He filled my mouth and then my throat. I had to back off of him to draw a breath.

Galen drew himself out of my mouth. "This is supposed to be foreplay, Merry."

"You know what I want," I said.

He shook his head.

I trailed my hands along his ass. "Nicca will go between my legs, then with a touch, I will bring him back again. He will service me and Biddy this night. Why can't you go twice tonight, too?"

"I usually do."

I pressed my body upward, gripping his ass with my hands. I raised up enough so I could lick lightly on his balls. "Go once in my mouth, and once between my legs. Please, Galen, please."

Nicca's hands slid down my thighs, and I felt him settling between my legs a second before his tongue touched me, a quick caress that made me writhe and dig my nails, just a little, into Galen's body.

It made him close his eyes, and count his breaths.

"I would give almost anything to have a woman beg me like that," Kitto said. "Do not refuse such a gift."

I didn't look at Kitto, because I only had eyes for Galen.

Nicca's tongue licked inside my opening, then up in a sure, firm stroke. I had to learn how to breathe again, and when I opened my eyes, Galen was still there, looking down at me. Nicca began to lick in circles around the edge of me, long sure strokes, for he had found that quick ones only worked later, not at the beginning. That sensation of fullness was already beginning to grow low in my body.

"Please," I said simply.

He settled his body over me again, wrapped his own hand around himself, and gave me the angle my mouth needed. "A princess shouldn't have to beg" was the last thing he said before he slid inside my mouth.

Chapter 32

THE WEIGHT GREW LOW IN MY BODY, AS NICCA'S TONGUE CAressed in long, heavy circles, and at the top of that circle he found that spot, the one that would eventually turn that growing warm weight into pleasure. But he had to work me wet first, otherwise it would hurt and rub, not pleasure.

Galen had gotten over his reluctance. He put his hands on the floor just past my head, so that he could move his hips as if he were making love to my mouth. And it was making love, not a pounding, but a caress of muscled velvet sliding between my lips, a sweet, hard weight that made me open my mouth wide to him, so he could glide every inch from the smooth head to the end of the shaft where it met his body. Except we never got that far. He never put that much of himself inside me. Nicca had stopped what he was doing. I knew he was still lying between my legs, because I could feel his hands wrapped around my thighs, but he was still, giving only an occasional lick, just enough to not lose ground, but not even close to making me come. Normally, it would have been irritating, but it freed me to concentrate on the sensation of Galen in my mouth in a way he had never allowed before. Except that he was holding back. Never once did the soft, hanging weight of his testicles touch my face. He wasn't giving me his all, not even close.

He spoke, and his voice showed the strain, the control he was wasting on his movements. "You stopped," he said in a strangled voice. "Nicca, why did you stop?"

"I thought to let you both enjoy it without me distracting her too much. Though from what I saw her do with Sage and Mistral, you are being overly careful."

"I don't want to hurt her."

That was it. I managed to get my hands free and pushed. He came up off of me, holding himself above me effortlessly, as if he could have held himself poised and perfect forever. Just gazing down the length of his body like that made me shiver.

"I want to feel all of you in my mouth, Galen, all of you."

"Won't that hurt you?"

Nicca laid his head against my thigh, and said, "You were in the hallway, right? You saw her with Mistral."

He nodded. "I saw." There was a hunching of his shoulders when he said it.

I ran my fingers down the front of his body, down his chest, his stomach, and only him rolling away kept me from wrapping my hand around him. "What is wrong?" I asked.

"I will never be comfortable being that rough with anyone."

"You don't have to be rough tonight, just give me the length of you. Let me feel you in my mouth all the way down to your balls. I want all of you in me in every conceivable way. If there's an opening that can hold you, I want it."

He gave me a look.

"Galen, Galen, we're running out of time, don't you understand that? Doyle and Frost already think the ring has chosen Mistral for me."

He looked stricken, as if I'd stabbed him low and hard with something made of cold iron.

"I don't believe they are right, but I do not know. None of us do. So while I have you, I want you. Don't you understand that?"

He looked down, and he was small again, his foreskin covering him. "If what you did with Mistral is what you want, then why do you want me?"

"I don't want rough every night, Galen. Some nights I like gentle. Some nights I like to make love, not fuck."

"But some nights you like to fuck," he said. "I pretty much always want to make love."

I smiled at him. "I could argue that."

He tried not to smile, but failed. "Not if what you did in the hallway was fucking."

"That was fucking with Mistral. Sex depends on the person you're with, Galen. Lovemaking rises and falls on the rhythms of the people involved." I held my hand out to him. "Come to me."

He shook his head. "If I come to you now, I won't be able to come to you when Nicca finally enters you."

"I can bring you back with a little bit of magic."

"Yeah, but if you do it immediately, it hurts a little."

"You never told me."

I looked down my body at Nicca, who had gone very quiet, his head resting on my thigh more for a pillow now than for sex. "Does it? Hurt, I mean?"

"Until recently I almost always shared my night with Rhys, so with two of us in the bed there was more waiting between times. So no, it did not hurt. But if I had to go straight back to it, it might," he said.

"Doyle and Frost never complained," I said.

"I think pain is more useful for them in the bedroom than it is for me or Galen."

I thought about that for a second. "Maybe."

Galen's voice came soft. "Is the reason you want me this way that you don't want me to be your king?"

I started to say no, then hesitated. It wasn't my motive for the oral sex, but the last part was true enough, or had been.

"I want you like this because I want you," I said.

Nicca spoke with his head still pillowed on my thigh. "I've seen her do this with more than just Mistral. She does seem to enjoy it."

"Sage, you mean," Galen said, but still didn't sound happy. His face did what it almost always did: it showed his every emotion.

"Yes," I said, and wasn't sure what to do to reassure him. It wasn't like Galen to pout this much. This was more Frost's speed.

"Sage," he said again, "another who won't ever be your king."

I sighed. "We have a night of ecstasy in front of us, and you're spoiling it with hard questions, it's not like you."

"No, it's more like Frost."

He'd spoken exactly what I'd just finished thinking. He'd done that several times tonight.

He continued with, "You complain about his moods, but you seem to like him better and better. Maybe you like your men a little more complicated."

I didn't know what to say to that. Why do you love one man and not another? Why is it that one person's touch fills you with shivery heat, and the same touch from another leaves you cold? It is a mystery. But I could answer truthfully and still be comforting.

"I love you, Galen."

He just looked at me.

"Maybe I had forgotten just how much, but today . . . when

I saw you lying there . . ." My voice failed me, and I had to close my eyes to keep from seeing him lying in a pool of his own blood.

Nicca stroked my thigh, not for sex but to comfort.

"When I saw you there, like that, I thought I would die from grief. To never see your smile again." My eyes felt hot, and I couldn't decide if crying would make me feel better or worse.

He touched my face, and without opening my eyes, I knew it was his hand. His warm, gentle hand. I laid my cheek into that hand. I was reminded sharply of doing the same thing to Doyle only a few hours ago. Galen had failed me then, had not understood why Gillette's failing me had made me cry. But giving Galen into the hands of another woman who could give him his nights of gentle love was one thing; giving him up to death was another. That I could not bear.

I opened my eyes and gazed up at him. I met those green, green eyes.

"You're crying," he said, and the look on his face was one of wonderment.

"Not quite," I said, but my voice sounded it. I had to swallow hard to say the next part. "Maybe I have been pulling back from you. I didn't mean to." I touched his hand with mine, kept it pressed against my face. "What terrified me about you being king was that our enemies would kill you. If I was picking men who could survive that kind of treachery, it wouldn't be you, my gentle love."

"Like Dormath thinking I would just forgive him for almost killing me."

"Yes."

"The last thing I thought, the very last thought, was you. I was afraid that it was the beginning of an assault on all of us." He lowered his gaze and wouldn't look at me. "I thought, Doyle and Frost will keep her safe. That if one of us had to die first, it was better that it was me." His smile was more sad than happy. "I guess my actual last, last thought was, why me? If I'd killed someone first, it would have been Doyle, not me. I prayed to the Goddess for your safety, and I died."

"Not quite," I whispered.

He looked at me then, and the smile was almost a real one. "How can I blame you for looking to them for your king, when as I lay dying, they were who I thought of, too? Damn it, being a good person is not enough here, not to help keep us alive. I'm sorry for that."

"I thought it would endanger you more to be my king, Galen, but now I understand that they're going to try to kill you anyway." I spoke to the look on his face. "I didn't know about the green man bringing life to the court until the queen said it, but they are still going to kill as many of my allies as they can. They will strip me of my help, if they dare. So if you're in danger either way, then you might as well be king."

"I'm dead either way," he said, and the smile was back to being more sad.

I sat up, trying to hug him, but he moved away just a little. My movement forced Nicca to move from my thigh to the mound between my legs for his pillow. Not for sex, but gently, as a pillow for his cheek.

"Come to me, Galen, please."

"I cannot be your king, Merry. It would be the death of us all." There was a hardness to his face that I had never seen before. In that moment I watched years be added, not in wrinkles, or lines, but in experience, in the depths of his eyes.

"Will you give up your place in her bed?" Nicca asked, and his voice held the lilt of surprise.

"No," Galen said, his voice as grim as the look in his eyes. "I'm not strong enough to give that up, not yet, not until I have to. But it does open things up." He smiled with that somber look still clinging to his eyes, still making him look not like my Galen at all. "But I could take Nicca's place, and kiss you with more than mouths."

"You've done that before."

"But never where you could return the favor," he said.

"You will have other nights," Nicca said. "Would you deny me my last moments with our Merry?"

"No, not if it's what you want. I know if it were my last night with her, I'd want it exactly the way I wanted it." He looked almost back to normal, but there was a glint in his eyes that didn't go away, and that I was both relieved and sad to see.

"I want to bring her with my lips and tongue, then I want to see another man in her mouth. I want us both to fuck her, until we go inside her. That's what I want."

Galen nodded. "Okay."

"I do not care which of you it is at her mouth, but if it is you, Galen, I have one request."

Galen said, "Ask."

"You are taller than Kitto. If you could come at her from the side, and not in front. You partially block my view of her breasts, and since it is my last night with the largest breasts in the entire court, I want to see them."

"From the side it is," Galen said.

"I'll need my head propped up if we're going to do it like that," I said.

"We can mound the towels up," Galen said.

"Let me be Merry's pillow," Kitto said. "Rest your head in my lap, Princess."

The rest of us exchanged a glance, and the glance was enough. "Okay," I said.

Kitto's smile was bright, and so very happy. Such a small thing to cause him such pleasure.

Nicca moved his head back down my body, his hands encircling my thighs again. "Now, where were we?"

My mouth suddenly dry, I asked, "Isn't Galen supposed to be up here?"

"I won't last in your mouth if you're screaming an orgasm around me. I just won't. Let him bring you, then Kitto and I will go where Nicca wants us."

I might have argued for Galen to come closer sooner, but Nicca's mouth found me again, and his tongue and lips stole my words, stole my breath, and finally stole the world away. For a few precious moments, I forgot that we were in danger, that there was a throne to win, or that there was anything but Nicca's mouth between my legs. His mouth and my body became pleasure, as if there were no skin, no bones, nothing solid, only the overwhelming shivering joy of orgasm.

Chapter 33

WHEN MY EYES STOPPED ROLLING BACK INTO MY HEAD SO THAT I could see again, Nicca was grinning up at me. "That was a good one."

I still couldn't talk, so I nodded.

"You're good," Galen said.

"I have never talked to Biddy about sex. You run into a few women, now and then, who won't let you do this."

My voice didn't sound like mine when I said, "They're mad."

"Perhaps, but just in case it's the last, I wanted it to be good."

I had a little trouble focusing, but finally managed it. "I don't want to send you to her bed with regrets."

He came to his knees, and then climbed over my body until he could lay his nakedness along my own. The feel of his testicles pressed tight against where his mouth had just been made me writhe underneath him.

He stared down at me, supporting his upper body on his arms, but keeping his lower body pressed tight against me. No matter how gentle a lover, the look in his eyes was the look of every man, eventually. That knowledge, that fierce joy, that they have given you pleasure, and now they get to take their own. I do not know why all men have that look somewhere in their eyes, waiting to come out, but I have seen it too often not to know that it is there.

"Kiss me, take the sweet taste of you from my mouth." He lowered his face to me, and I raised up to meet him. We kissed, and he was wet from me, and tasted of something clean and fresh, like the first breath of morning after a rain, when the world is wet and pure.

He kissed me until our tongues, our hands, our arms, found each other. He kissed me until I had licked him clean of that taste, and left the wetness of my mouth behind. He drew back breathless, and said, "Perfect."

I understood what he meant, not that I was perfect, but that the kiss had been exactly what he'd wanted in that moment.

He raised himself above me on arms and knees. He was stretched tight and hard against the front of his own body. "I am ready."

"I can see that," I said, and my voice was breathy.

Nicca looked at the other men, and said, "Places, gentlemen." There was a note of command in his voice that I'd seldom heard, even in the midst of sex. I realized that this was the first time I'd had sex with him since he'd been brought into his power. Not his wings, but his power. We weren't certain what magic he had gained from it, but he'd gained other things that had nothing to do with magic, and everything with being comfortable in his own skin.

Kitto hesitated at my head as if he wasn't sure what to do next.

"Raise up, Merry," Galen said, "let him know where he's supposed to be." His voice and face were gentle when he said it, as if he'd picked up on Kitto's nervousness. Galen and I had kept our nights in Los Angeles to ourselves, so I'd really never seen him interact in an intimate setting with any of the other men. You can learn a lot about a man in the bedroom when it's not just two, but more. Someone who refuses to share, well, that tells you something about a man, too.

I raised up on my elbows. "Come, Kitto, let me rest my head in your lap."

He moved behind me, still uncertain, as if he expected one of the other men to protest. He settled behind me with his legs folded tailor fashion. I did not lay my head in his lap immediately, but bowed my head backwards so I could sweep my hair across his groin. I trailed my hair back and forth until he made noises for me.

I laid my head in the cradle of his legs, and found his sex pressed against the top of my head. Interesting, but his knees were also higher than my face. I rubbed my head against him like a cat. His breathing sped for me, but it wasn't going to work as a prop for Galen.

"Um," Galen said.

Nicca said, "What if Kitto almost lies under Merry, with her head resting on his stomach?"

We tried it. It took some maneuvering, especially to find a comfortable way for Kitto's legs to be underneath me. Nicca suggested that Kitto turn over on his stomach, which probably would have been easier, but I vetoed it. I wanted the press of him against my head. I wanted not just Kitto's body, but a very specific part, to be my pillow. I wanted the sensation of it, and I wanted to give Kitto at least that much. He'd given up his place for intercourse, and for oral sex. He deserved at least to be touched.

So I lay back against the line of Kitto's body, and my head was cradled on a pillow that was so warm, so firm, so erotic. I rubbed my head against that firm pillow, and Kitto cried out.

"A little less body language, Merry, or he'll go before anyone else," Galen said, but he smiled when he said it, shaking his head.

I stopped rubbing, and just lay there with my head pressed against Kitto. "What?" I asked.

"Just watching how happy that made you."

"Do you have a problem with it?" I asked.

"No," he said, and grinned suddenly, "and I can prove it." He crawled to us, and arched his body above my face, knees on one side, hands on the other. I wrapped my hands around him, and squeezed gently. It brought his breath out in a shuddering laugh. "Stop that."

"Why?" I asked, and put my other hand at his balls, cupping them, while I stroked along the length of him. I'd touched Galen hundreds of times by now, but I never quite got over the marvel of being allowed to touch him. I think it was because I'd wanted him long before it had occurred to me to want any of the other guards. They had been untouchable, and almost invisible to me, as I'd been to them. But Galen, he had always been real to me.

He looked at Nicca and said, in a voice that couldn't quite control itself, "I'd hurry if I were you, Nicca. She is so not going to behave herself."

Nicca gave that uniquely masculine laugh. "I'm not finishing until she does, I'll warn you of that now."

I ran my thumb over the round tip of him, and rubbed my head against Kitto at the same time. Galen shuddered for me, and Kitto made another satisfying cry. "We'll do our best," Galen said. He gazed down at me, smiling, eyes a little wide. "Is this a test of how much control we have?"

"No," I said.

"You're mad because I've said no to this for so long, aren't you?"

I thought about that for a second or two, then frowned. "Maybe, I guess, yes. I'm sorry. I want this to be about joy, not pettiness." My hands started to fall away from him, but he caught my wrist with one hand.

"Do your best, or your worst, and so will we. I'm sorry I denied you any part of me. I promise it won't happen again."

"Good," I said, and I pulled him down toward me. He didn't fight me. He just readjusted his hands and knees, and finally his hips until I could guide him between my lips. He was so full, so thick, that I had to open my mouth wider than was comfortable to let him push his way deeper inside. He pushed until he found the back of my throat. I forced myself to relax as he eased himself past that point of comfort. I loved the feel of a man so deep, but it was an acquired talent. I was blessed with no gag reflex, but there were other problems with the well-endowed. Breathing for one, and just finding an angle so they could fuck you but not hurt your throat. Badly done deep-throating gave an entirely new meaning to having a little sore throat. I moved my head, just a little, my head rocking gently on Kitto's body, as I worked with Galen to find that special position. I knew from experience that once I got excited enough I would have less trouble, that nothing would hurt while I was doing it, so I worked to make sure things didn't hurt later either. Galen was above me, truly trying to mouth-fuck me. It wasn't the same as going down on a man from other positions, because they had more control than you did. And they could not feel your body, as you felt it. They could not know when you could draw breath, or swallow, or when you needed to do either. I was trusting Galen to be gentle. I was depending on it.

He began to use his hips more, so that at the end of the thrust he was down my throat. I timed my breathing for when he was higher in my mouth, and swallowed about every other stroke. I moved my hands up his body until I found his testicles, so I could play with them as he went in and out.

"I take that as a yes," he said, in a voice that still sounded like his own.

I gave a small nod with him still in my mouth. I didn't want to move too much because we'd worked so hard to find just the right angle to let him do this. Galen had more length than most men that I'd let into this position. Kitto would have been more comfortable for it. But once Galen offered, I wasn't going to say no. I trusted him not to get carried away and hurt me. I wasn't sure I'd have trusted any of my other guards, except, perhaps, Nicca.

But Nicca had other duties tonight. His hands touched my thighs, and that one small touch drew a small sound from me. I think Galen took the sound for his doing, because he began to use his whole body, thrusting himself completely into my mouth, so that his balls slapped against my face. I put my hands on his thighs, not to caress, but to hold on.

My head moved with every stroke, and that made me rub against Kitto. He was like muscled silk against the side of my face.

Nicca pushed himself against my opening. He slid himself in slowly, one inch at a time. His voice came hoarse. "So wet."

Galen hesitated with his body plunged deep inside my throat. "Nicca, hurry, Goddess, hurry." He drew himself upward, and I had to take an almost gasping breath at the farthest edge of his stroke.

Nicca plunged himself inside me all at once, using the wetness that he'd made.

"Consort, but I love it when she feels like this," he said.

"Like what?" Galen asked.

"Tight and wet."

"Oh, God, yes," Galen said. "Yes." His body took on a more urgent rhythm, and I had to simply open my mouth wide, and trust that he would not hurt me. I was having trouble finding enough time between thrusts to both swallow and breathe. Even without a gag reflex I was fast approaching a point where I would have to make him stop long enough for me to catch up.

Nicca had found a rhythm that was faster, harder than any I'd had from him before, but he stayed low on his knees, so that his legs were spread wider. His hands were on my legs, holding them at almost a forty-degree angle. I would have told him to let me put my legs down, because from here his angle would be shallow, but once he slid himself inside me, I didn't want to move. It was exquisite. He slid only the front part of himself inside me, but every shallow stroke took him over that spot, that infamous G-spot, and something about his position, or mine, was perfect.

I closed my mouth around Galen, forcing him to slow up enough for me to swallow and breathe, then I opened my mouth for him. If I could have spoken, I'd have said it was going to be soon.

Kitto began to move against me, rubbing himself through my hair, caressing my skin with the heat of his body. His hips were rising and falling underneath me.

I had never had so many men's attention at one time. I had had three men in the bedroom, but never this intimately, never actual sex from so many at once.

Nicca began to glow first, but it was not the sun inside his skin this time, it was a candle that painted his skin the color of rich, dark amber, with hints of orange and gold, like the inner spark of some jewel. I could not see Kitto, but I felt him, incredibly warm against my body, as if he were a fire, settled and banked for the long winter's night. What I could see of his body gleamed pearlescent, a soft, shining white.

When the light came to Galen, it chased all the colors from him but a soft glow, like a lamp left on in a dark house so you can find your way.

I kept expecting Nicca's rhythm to speed up, but he stayed careful, gentle, so that he never varied. He knew he'd found the spot he wanted, we wanted, and he simply kept it.

Galen was fighting his rhythm, fighting to keep from moving too fast, too hard, for my mouth, my throat. I could feel the tension in his hips, the slight tremor in his arms, as he fought what he wanted to do. He wanted to fuck me, to truly fuck me, and he was simply too big for it, and he knew that. But the feel of him fighting it, the knowledge that he wanted to do things to me that would hurt and damage, and that only his discipline, his will, kept him from it, that was more exciting than anything else. What Nicca was doing felt better because of what he was touching. It was that that was filling me up with that heavy, warm weight. It was that movement that would eventually spill me over, but Galen's fight for control was what made me writhe. What relaxed my mouth and throat, what helped me find my own rhythm for breath and swallowing, so that I could give him more room to push inside me. He had to feel the muscles of my throat relax, and it drew a sound from low in his throat. It drove a shudder through him, and stopped him in midthrust for a moment while he fought his body, fought himself.

Nicca's hands grabbed my hips, kept me from moving there. But the rest of me writhed around Galen and against Kitto, where he lay quiveringly hard in my hair. Kitto responded by thrusting harder, the edge of him caressing the outer curve of my ear. That warm hardness curved along that hollow where the neck meets the ear, that warm place where a breath can make you shiver, and he was thrusting all of his sex over and over it. The silk of his balls brushed against my throat, while the rest of him kept touching that certain place just behind the ear, and up into my hair. To feel so much more of an intimate caress there made me writhe harder for Galen, and fight my own body not to move against Nicca. He had made it clear that if I moved, he'd lose the spot that we were both enjoying so much.

Somewhere in all that, I realized the room was black. That only our glow chased back the edges of the dark. My skin was a pale white luminescence, the gentle play of moonlight to guide you home through the dark.

That warmth between my legs built to heaviness, and I knew that we were only a few more caresses away. If I'd been able to talk, I would have told them, but since I had no words, I used what I did have. I made small, hungry noises around Galen's body, as that tight, heavy weight between my legs grew and grew. Galen thrust harder into my mouth, as if the sensation of me calling around him was too much for his ragged self-control. I was about to reach up, to use hands to slow him, when Nicca's body drove that one last time, and the last drop hit that heavy, warm pool deep inside me. It spilled me over in a rush of heat that spread out over my skin, through my body, and I screamed around Galen as he thrust as hard into my throat as ever he had thrust between my legs. Kitto cried out underneath me, his body arching against me. Nicca drove himself one last time inside me, as Galen spilled himself down my throat, and Kitto spilled hot against my skin, and decorated my hair with his seed.

Our bodies seemed to breathe in, and as we did, our glows all went dark, so that for an instant the room was in utter darkness. Then it was as if the entire world let out a collective breath that was warm and heavy and full of pleasure. That breath spread outward from us, so that we all glowed as if our skin could not hold such light, such warmth. We all screamed that pleasure, and the light burst out from us so that our eyes were dazzled and blinded by it. A tremendous crashing filled that light, a thunderous sound that shook the floor beneath me, and thrummed along my bones like the very walls of the sithen had convulsed with us.

We were left in the dark, collapsed upon one another. Galen dragged himself out of my mouth. And I had to cough, and turn my head to the side. "Did I hurt you?"

I had to clear my throat sharply to say, "Yes, but I liked it."

My voice sounded rough, not like me at all. It hurt to swallow, and my throat felt rubbed raw.

"Why did the lights go out?" Kitto asked.

"Why does the air taste like broken stone?" Nicca asked.

The first light into that darkness was a wavering, sickly greenish yellow flame. Doyle came with the fire on one hand and a gun gleaming dark in the other. Frost was at his side like the reverse of body and shadow. He threw a glittering ball of light into the room, and was down on one knee sighting down the guns in his hands, searching the room for targets.

"Where are they?" he asked.

"Who?" I asked.

"Your attackers," Frost said.

All of us on the floor exchanged glances, as best we could. "We were not attacked," Nicca said.

"Then what did that?" Frost pointed with one gun, and the glittering silver and white light moved where he pointed. The light hovered over the far wall of the bathroom, and we saw why he had asked who attacked us. The far wall was no more. Broken stone and debris showed a black, gaping hole.

Other guards, including Biddy, were at their backs, all with weapons drawn. "Is the princess hurt?" someone asked.

"No," I said, but my voice was still rough, so I wasn't sure they heard me. I had to try twice before I could make myself clearly heard. "I am fine."

Doyle sent Hawthorne and Adair to approach the far wall cautiously, their own balls of colored light acting like pet lanterns hovering just above their shoulders. One of them called back, "It's a garden. A small garden with a dry pool in the ground."

"What surrounds the garden?" Doyle asked from where he stood near us.

"Stone," Adair answered. "It is a cave of stone."

Doyle and Frost were staring down at us. Frost's face was pale under the arrogant mask. I glanced past them and saw the heavy door to the outer room hanging twisted and broken in its frame.

"We thought you'd been attacked," Doyle said, and his

voice held that edge of relieved fear that Frost's face could not quite hide.

"We're safe," I said.

"Why does your voice sound so rough?" Frost asked.

Galen raised his hand. "My fault."

Doyle shook his head, and put up his gun. He still held the sickly flame in the other hand, as if his hand was the wick for the candle. It was the only light I'd ever seen him call in the dark.

"Well, at least this answers one question," he said. "Sex inside faerie is different."

"The ring has chosen no one for me yet."

He gave a quick smile, a flash of white in his dark face. "That is good to know."

"Yes," Frost said, still pale, "that is good." He was gazing at the destruction of the room. "But if the sex continues to grow more powerful, how are we to keep Merry safe, and make her queen?"

Doyle tapped a piece of stone with the toe of his boot. "There is a circle of debris around them as clean and neat as if it had been drawn. Merry and her lovers were safe enough. I think it is the furniture and walls we will have to worry over."

"And anyone not in the circle with her," Ivi said, and turned his face to the multicolored lights that bobbed in the room. His pale face glittered darkly on one side.

"Is that blood?" I asked.

"Yes," Ivi said, and grimaced as he touched his forehead. "When the door exploded it sent shards of wood through the bedroom. Your new healer is tending the wounded."

"The demi-fey?" I started to get up, but was still trapped beneath everyone's bodies. Galen and Nicca began to roll off me, so I could sit up. Frost offered me a hand, and helped me to my feet. He pulled too hard, or my legs still weren't working, because he had to catch me or I would have fallen. He caught me in against his body, and said, "What is that in your hair?"

"Oh, Kitto . . ."

"No, Merry," Kitto said, "it isn't my seed."

Frost had a gun in his other hand, so it was Doyle who reached out and touched my hair. "Goddess save us."

"What?" I asked, and I didn't like how everyone was acting. Doyle helped me, drawing a strand of my hair closer to my face. There were leaves in my hair.

Doyle extinguished the flame on his hand with a shake, like you blow out a match by fanning it sharp in the air. Frost's light came back to float above our heads, and in the white light I could see that it wasn't just leaves.

"Mistletoe's entwined in your hair." Doyle glanced down at Kitto. "Is this your doing?"

"It was my seed in her hair, but I do not think I caused it."

Brii came to stand beside us; his long yellow hair was decorated with bits of wood. "May I?" he asked me. His hand was raised toward my hair.

I nodded.

He touched the mistletoe tentatively, almost as if he were afraid it would hurt him, or it would vanish if he touched it too hard. "It was once considered the seed of the god." He caressed the hard stems and the solid, thick green leaves, his fingertips gentle against the white berries.

"The seed of the god," he whispered.

It was a good sign, a sign of great blessing, but... "How badly hurt are the demi-fey? If the splinters could do that to Ivi... how hurt are they?" I asked.

"We are not certain," Frost said. "The blast of power threw us all to the floor or walls. They are small, and were thrown harder."

I pushed away from his arms. I started for the far door. He picked me up, the drawn gun pressing cold against my bare legs. "There are splinters everywhere," he said, as I tried to protest. I couldn't argue his point.

"Then take me to them. Let me see what my pleasure has cost my people."

"Your people?" Brii asked, his eyes shining pale and gold in the magical lights.

"Yes," I said, "they are Unseelie fey, and that makes them mine, makes them ours."

"That is not how the queen sees it," Ivi said, and the blood on his face gleamed in the lights. He'd come to stand beside Brii. Their long pale hair seemed to intermingle like entwining vines.

I shook my head and the illusion, or the trick of the light, went away, and they were simply standing close together. I touched Frost's arm. "Take me into the other room, let us help them."

"Help them how?" Ivi asked.

"Hafwyn can heal them."

"You would waste sidhe healing on a demi-fey?"

Frost answered for me. "That you would ask that of her says that you do not know the princess."

Doyle added, "She will not see it as a waste." He nodded, and as if that was an order Frost carried me toward the splintered door. Thin high-pitched screaming came from the other room. I prayed, "Mother help us, help them, heal them. Don't let my power be their doom."

I caught the faint scent of roses, and a voice like a warm wind. "Grace can never be doom." With that cryptic bit of wisdom, she was gone, and we were in what was left of the bedroom.

Chapter 34

IT LOOKED LIKE A MINIATURE BATTLEFIELD. SMALL BODIES were scattered across the floor like a game of toy soldiers gone horribly wrong. Tiny bodies were collapsed against the walls as if some giant hand had swept them away. The four-foot-long Nile monitor lay on its back, and just the twisted look of the body let me know it had finished its death throes. A piece of wood the size of a small dagger had pierced its throat.

Frost carried me in, his feet crunching on bits of wood and metal from the door. I kept staring at the dead lizard, because I was afraid to look elsewhere. Afraid to look too closely at those smaller bodies, afraid I'd find them just as still, just as dead.

Hafwyn had made a triage line of tiny bodies. It had seemed like we had so many men to guard me, and too many in my bed, but now suddenly, we needed more hands. More bodies to help us save others. The queen had stripped me of too many. And Rhys had taken some with him, as well.

"Send word to the queen that we need more men, and more healers."

Hafwyn looked up at me, even as she tried to hold a piece of cloth on a wound. "More healers? Do you mean to use sidhe healing on the demi-fey?"

"Yes," I said.

"The queen does not waste such power on the lesser fey."

She was right. In fact, there were some sidhe healers who would not willingly touch a lesser fey. As if they thought it was contagious. "Can you heal them?"

She looked surprised. "You truly mean for me to do this?"

"You are a healer, Hafwyn, can you sit here and watch them die, and not be pained by it?"

She lowered her head, and I watched her shoulders begin to shake. There was no sound, but when she turned her face back to me, there were tears upon her face. "Yes, it causes me pain to see such suffering and not be allowed to heal it."

"Then heal what you can, and I will fetch more healers."

"Who would you send to fetch them?" Frost asked. He was still holding me effortlessly, as if he could have held me so all night long. Maybe he could have.

I understood what he meant. Andais was probably deep into the torturing of the betrayers. And my aunt did not like being interrupted in the middle of her "playtime." People who interrupted her had a tendency to be forced to join the show. Did I send the one I liked the least, or the one who had a better chance of making her see sense?

"Who do you recommend?"

"Doyle," he said.

I turned in Frost's arms and looked at him. "If she is deep in her bloodlust then only Doyle has a chance of making her see sense. Ivi or Brii would end up as victim."

"And you?"

"She has never listened to me as she listened to Doyle." He said it without a trace of hurt ego. He simply stated it, fact. I believed him.

Doyle glided through the broken door, as if he'd heard us say his name. I told him what I wanted.

"I might be able to help heal some of them," he said.

I had forgotten that he had limited healing ability himself. One of the first times he had ever touched me intimately had been for him to heal a wound on my thigh. He could not heal with his hands, but with his mouth, so it was not something he offered often. It was too intimate. And his ability to heal was not great, as the healers of faerie measured it.

"You can heal?" Hafwyn asked, pushing at her yellow hair with the back of her arm. Her hands were too bloody to be used for tucking a strand of hair back.

"A little, but not by hand."

"Nodens," she said simply.

"One of my names," he said, "at the end."

"How bad an injury can you heal?" she asked.

"Superficial wounds, deep but narrow."

"Can you set bone?"

He shook his head.

She looked around at her patients. "I think Frost is right. I think the queen will hear you best, and if anyone can bring us more healers, it is you. You will be most welcome when I have more healers. We can conserve our strength, and let you finish a wound after we have begun it."

"Gladly," he said, "if you are certain?"

She nodded. "Go to the queen as the princess bids. Killing Frost is right; it is our best chance to save them."

Doyle nodded, gave a small bow to me, and simply started for the door. I called him back, a hand in his. I drew him in for a kiss, while I was still held in Frost's arms. Doyle's lips were warm, and soft, and he drew back from the kiss before I was ready for him to.

"And Doyle goes alone?" Galen said. "You warned Rhys that he might be attacked."

"He is the Queen's Darkness," Brii said. "No one would dare."

Galen shook his head. "No one goes alone, anywhere, not until we're back in L.A."

"And do you rule here already, green knight?" Ivi asked.

"No, but we can't afford to lose Doyle because we got careless."

I knew by the look on Doyle's face that he meant to argue. Then he smiled and shook his head. "He's right. We cannot afford to be arrogant or careless." He looked at Frost, and I knew that was who he most wanted to take, but I also knew that he would not strip me of both of them at the same time.

"I will go," Hawthorne said, "if you will have me."

"I will go, if you wish, but I think my place is here guarding the princess," Adair said.

"I agree." Doyle looked at Galen with a small smile. "Are you content with Hawthorne?"

"Take Brii, too," he said.

The smile left him. "I do not think that is necessary."

"It would take me too long to dress or I'd go with you," Galen said.

"Why so serious about my safety, Galen?" Doyle asked.

I wondered if Galen would tell Doyle what he'd said in the bathroom. He did. "I thought I was dead, and one of my last thoughts was it's okay, because you and Frost were still alive. I knew you'd keep Merry safe. I knew you'd get her out of here and back home to L.A. I thought, why kill me first? If I were going to do a first strike, it would be you I'd kill. I can't be the only one who's thinking that."

We were all staring at him. “What?” he asked.

“We’re not used to you sounding this smart,” Ivi said, “that’s all.”

“Thanks a lot.”

“If you intend to save lives, go now,” Hafwyn said.

Doyle gave a small bow in my direction. Hawthorne and Brii fell in at his back, and they left us.

I looked at Hafwyn. “What can we do to keep them alive while we wait?” She told us. Ivi spread his cloak on the floor so that I could kneel in safety, while we did what little we could to hold their blood in their bodies, and their lives in our hands.

Chapter 35

I WAS LEFT STARING DOWN AT ROYAL’S BODY. HE WAS ALIVE, but only because a stomach wound takes longer to kill. The wood had gone so far into his stomach that a piece of it came out the other side, missing his spine by a hairsbreadth. I pressed the cloth on either side of that wound. Hafwyn cautioned me to be careful, and not move him. Not until they had someone with more healing than she had left in her hands.

Royal’s sister, Penny, was at his side, her dress covered in blood. Her hands were too small to compress the wound, but her words were plenty big enough to rub the guilt like sandpaper across my heart.

“We came to you for wings, and you have given us death.” She threw herself onto her brother, yelling at me, “Evil, you are all evil. You have never brought us anything but humiliation and destruction.”

I couldn't argue with her, not with Royal's body pressed against my hands, his life bleeding away.

She tried to grab him up onto her lap, and that made him cry out in pain. Hafwyn interfered. "Penny, Penny, if you move him you injure him further."

But Penny had let her grief and fear swallow her. There was no reasoning with her. It was one of the other uninjured demi-fey who came and dragged her away. She cried and struggled, and the crème-colored rat that had pulled their chariot followed her like a frightened dog. It had kept its distance from Royal, as if it didn't know quite what to do. But to her, it came, as if to help the other fey take her away.

Royal touched my hand with his, barely covering my knuckle with his entire hand. He was one of the tallest of the fey in the room, but tall is relative when your world is full of people who look like children's toys.

He gazed up at me with his black eyes, his face so pale he looked ghostlike. But his chest still rose and fell against my fingertips, his stomach still convulsed as he closed his eyes, face pinching tight, with a spasm of pain. I felt him struggle not to writhe as that pain lanced through him.

I said the only thing I had left to offer. "I'm sorry." I didn't mean for this to happen, but I would not make excuses. Regardless, he was dead unless a fresh healer arrived within minutes.

I said it again. "I am sorry, Royal, I am so sorry."

He actually smiled at me, and that made my heart hurt. "I have had a sidhe princess say sorry to me." His face showed that pain again, and his body fought against my fingers.

"Don't talk," I said. "Help is coming."

He gave me a look, and it was eloquent. "There will be no help for me." His voice fell to a whisper, so low that I had to lean in to catch his words. "Queen Niceven made me . . . surrogate. Let me taste your . . . lips and blood . . . just once. Before . . ." Another spasm took him, and this time he couldn't quite make himself hold still. He writhed with the pain, and that caused him more pain, until he screamed. Blood flowed faster around my fingers and the sodden rags. He was going to die in my hands, and I could do nothing to prevent it.

I tasted the salt of my tears before I knew I was crying.

His eyes fluttered open, but they had that glazed look to them, as if he was already seeing things that the living do not see.

His lips moved, but I could not hear him. I leaned into him again, and heard him sigh, "Kiss . . . me."

I did what he asked, though I had never kissed lips so delicate. It wasn't until his lips brushed mine, like the caress of a tightly curled flower, that I felt his glamour. I had let my pity blind me to possibilities. Pity, and the fact that he was dying. You don't think of the dying wasting energy on sex. It was the most chaste of kisses, but his magic made it more.

His mouth pressed to my lower lip, and in that moment his glamour poured over my skin like water from a warm bath. I could not breathe through it, could not think, could not do anything but feel.

It was like an hour of foreplay in one small kiss. His hand touched my bare breast, and he bit my lip. The touch was so much more than that tiny hand should have been able to deliver, as if he caressed the front of my body with a hand as large as any man's. That small, sharp shock of pain was like the last thrust, the last lick, the last caress, for it spilled me over the edge and made me scream my pleasure into him. But it was as if his mouth were bigger. He were bigger. In that instant I would have sworn that I lay atop a full-sized lover, that the hands that touched me were another human or sidhe. That the body that I was pressed against was not only full-sized, but well-sized.

I forgot everything but the feel of his body under mine. His hands exploring me. His mouth feeding at mine. His body searching between my legs, trying to find my opening. I think I would have let his last glamour undo me, but a sharp pain stabbed into my side, and broke his magic. I came to myself lying atop him, as much as our differences in size would allow. The pain did not stop with his broken glamour. I tried to raise my body and the pain sharpened. I stared down the line of our bodies and found the tip of the wood in his middle had pierced my side.

Galen and Frost were there, trying to lift me up. I was about to tell them to stop when the wood came out. The wound was shallow, thank the Goddess, but I'd have to talk to them about looking before they moved me. None of them were used to dealing with someone who injured as easily as I did.

Galen called, "Hafwyn, Merry is hurt."

"No," I said, "it looks worse than it is. There are others who need her more than I."

"You are the princess, and they are only demi-fey," Ivi said.

I shook my head, as Galen cradled me in his arms, laying me on Ivi's cloak. "Doyle can heal it when he gets back," I said.

"At least let Hafwyn look at it," Galen said.

I nodded. "If she has time."

Of course, she came immediately. She knelt and cleaned the blood away with the cloth and bowl of water that Kitto had fetched for her. She explored the wound, which hurt, and removed some splinters, which hurt more.

Galen let me squeeze his hand while she took the splinters out with her fingers. Where were sterile tweezers when you needed them? Galen smiled down at me, and said, "I didn't know you were this strong. What a grip."

It made me smile, which was what he'd intended.

I caught a glimpse of Royal behind Hafwyn and Galen. The demi-fey lay utterly still, eyes closed. The hands that had caressed my body were limp on either side of him. I chased Hafwyn's hands away. "See to Royal."

She looked puzzled. I realized she didn't remember his name. "Royal, the demi I was helping."

Hafwyn went to Royal's body as I'd ordered. She started to lay hands on him, and his spine bowed upward, as if drawn by some invisible string. His breath came into his body in a great gasping rush. It left his body in a shriek that reverberated through the room. His scream was echoed by the other wounded. It was as if they were all having a fit.

"What's happening?" Frost asked.

Hafwyn shook her head. I don't think she knew either. Not good.

The small knot of uninjured demi-fey started forward, as if to try to help. Then they all fell to their knees and began to scream and writhe on the ground.

"Is it poison?" Adair raised his voice to be heard over them.

Hafwyn said, "I do not know, Goddess help me, but I do not know."

The wounds spurted blood upward like a dozen crimson fountains. The demi-fey without wounds still writhed, and called out in pain, but they had no wounds for the blood to be called from. For that was what it looked like. It looked like some version of my own hand of blood. Except I was not doing it, and no one else had the power to do it.

Then blood burst out of all of them like some hand was punching through their wounds. The wood pieces were pushed out in a last burst of blood and screams. It was as if the flesh itself was rejecting the wood.

The piece that had nearly bisected Royal was one of the last to come out, for it was one of the largest and most deeply embedded.

"Is this healing them?" Frost asked, making his voice heard above the demi-fey's screams.

"I am not sure," Hafwyn said. "I think so."

Even knowing that, it was hard to watch. Then I discovered something else. Hafwyn had not found all the splinters in my own wound. Those tiny splinters that she had missed began to push their way out of my flesh.

Galen looked down at me. I think I squeezed his hand again. He looked a question at me, but I shook my head. If Hafwyn could do anything to help ease pain, it wasn't me who needed it.

Frost had a gun in one hand, and a sword in the other. Adair stood a little away from him, weapon out, as well. Ivi had moved to the other side of the room away from them, and he, too, stood with bared sword. He had a look so serious on him that it almost didn't look like him. They were covering the room. They were going on the idea that this might be an attack. I didn't think it was that kind of a problem, but they were the bodyguards and I was not. Besides, I was too busy gripping Galen's hand and trying not to scream.

Two tiny splinters had worked their way out, blood spurting out of the wound in my side. It felt as if a fist were trying to punch its way out. I fought not to scream, to simply hold on to Galen's hand, but I couldn't hold my body still while the magic tried to shove its way through my body.

Frost was there, kneeling. "Merry!"

Someone yelled for Hafwyn.

My other hand reached into the air, and Nicca grabbed it. I had a moment to cling to Galen and Nicca's hands, a moment when the pain pulled back, and it was as if the world drew a breath. The three of us knelt in a well of silence. Galen asked, "What is this?" Him, I could hear. "Magic," Nicca said. Frost stood above us, looking for an enemy to strike down. Biddy was at his side, looking down at Nicca, but her sword was in her hand, too. They would guard me, but the kind of guarding we needed had nothing to do with swords. We needed better magicians, not better swordsmen.

The silence that held us seemed to swell out like a bubble until it burst. Then came the pain. It was as if a thousand fists were trying to shove themselves out through my body. It was as if every muscle was fighting to tear itself free of my bones. I was being ripped apart. I screamed, and fell back onto the floor. Other screams echoed mine, and the hands that I gripped convulsed tightly around mine. Through pain-narrowed eyes I saw Galen and Nicca collapsing with me, their mouths wide with screams.

Other screams joined ours; the demi-fey rolled on the ground, their tiny bodies bursting into a rain of blood as I watched. Then my own pain made me writhe so that I could only look up.

Blood gushed from the wound in my stomach. Blood sprayed out of Galen's arm. Nicca's shoulder turned into a fountain of blood. Then everything stopped, and it was so sudden, I thought I'd gone deaf. But then I heard small sounds of pain, and someone yelling, "Mother help us."

Galen had collapsed on top of me, our hands still clasped. I still held Nicca's hand, but I couldn't see him past Galen's body.

Frost appeared above me. "Merry, can you hear me?"

It took me two tries to say yes, but the voice was someone else's, distant and dry.

Hands lifted Galen off me, but I wouldn't let them take his hand from mine. They didn't argue, but simply laid him down beside me, so that the three of us were on our backs, staring up at the ceiling. It was a woman's voice that said, "The little ones, look at the little ones." There was something in her voice that made me turn my head, even though I was so tired.

Royal was closest to us. He had rolled over onto his side, curled around his stomach, curled around his pain. But there was something on his back. I had to blink hard to understand what I was seeing. Tiny crumpled wings were unfurling on his back. They were wet with blood, but they grew larger as I watched, expanding with every beat of Royal's heart.

"They have wings," Hafwyn said, "they all have wings."

Ivi was kneeling at our feet. "Look at your stomach."

I was almost afraid to look, afraid of what I would find. But it was just a moth, exactly where the wound had been. A beloved underwing moth just like the wings that were tearing their way out of Royal's back. It was only when Ivi moved to touch it that I realized it wasn't on me, but in me. The moth was embedded in my skin.

I didn't have time to be afraid, or horrified, or anything. The world went away in a swirl of dimming vision, and finally darkness. There were no visions, no manifestations. There was nothing but blessed oblivion.

Chapter 36

I WOKE, BLINKING UP INTO A CANOPY AS BLACK AS THE DARKness that had sucked me under. Black material was held in graceful folds on dyed black wood. I thought, almost idly, that it looked like the queen's bed. Fear speared through me in a fine, breath-stealing rush. It was never good to wake up here.

I must have moved my hand more than I thought because I brushed someone's arm. It made me jump and look to the center of the bed.

Galen lay, eyes still closed, face peaceful. He was still nude, as were we all. For Nicca lay on the other side of Galen. That the three of us were naked in her bed did not make me feel one bit better.

I looked out at her room, and it was completely black except for a fire in a large metal brazier in the center of the room. Why were the walls without light? Where was the light of the sithen?

Something moved in that blackness, and I tensed, expecting it to be the queen, but there was no flash of her white skin. I knew who it was before he stepped into the amber glow of the firelight. Doyle in a cloak as black as the rest of him passed in the outer glow of the fire's light to glide toward the bed.

"Doyle." I didn't even try to keep the relief from my voice.

"How do you feel?" His deep voice rumbled and the very sound of it lessened the panic that still fluttered in my pulse.

"Fine. Why are we here?"

"Because the queen willed it," he said.

I did not like that answer. It sped my pulse again. Someone laughed in the dark. I choked on the panic of my own heartbeat. I felt Galen tense beside me, and knew he was awake, but he did not move. He very carefully did not let anyone else know he had woken. I did not give him away, but I knew that feigning sleep would not help him.

The laugh came again, and I knew it wasn't the queen. My pulse slowed enough that I could breathe around it. "Who else is here?"

There was movement in the farthest corner of the room. I caught a glimpse of pale hair, pale skin, a white cloak. The figure was so pale, the room so dark, that it was almost as if the figure materialized from that darkness like a ghost. Though I knew he was not.

The glint of firelight made me certain of who it was. "Ivi," I said, and was not happy. He had scared me.

"Why unhappy to see me, Princess? I did offer up my cloak to guard your body."

"Why sit in the corner? And what was funny?"

"To see the fear on your face at waking here. I sat in the dark, because I am too pale to hide closer to the fire." The smile was gone by the time he came to stand at the foot of the bed. He leaned a shoulder against the big carved bedpost, huddling the cloak around him as if he was cold. His pale hair with its decoration of vines and leaves was trapped inside the cloak, so that it made a sort of hood around his face of his own hair.

"Where is everyone else?" I asked.

"Recruiting," Ivi said.

Galen raised enough to look at them both. He was lying on his stomach. "Stop being so closemouthed and just tell us what has happened while we slept." He sounded angry where I had sounded afraid.

I heard the door to the queen's bathroom open, before I saw by the fire's glow that it was Rhys in the doorway. He, too, was wearing a cloak around his body so that only his face and hair were bare to the dim light. "You've missed lots," Rhys said. He looked tired.

He came to stand beside the bed a little ahead of Ivi at his corner.

"So much in fact," Doyle said, "that I am not certain where to begin."

"Why doesn't that make me feel better?" Galen asked.

"He didn't mean it to make us feel better," Nicca said. "He's being the Darkness, all dour and frightening."

I started to sit up, and something moved on my stomach. I jumped, and looked down, and found that I hadn't dreamed it. There was a moth on me, exactly where the wound had been. I stayed propped on one elbow, and reached cautiously to touch its upper wings, all charcoal grey and black. It flicked its wings at me, as if irritated by the touch, flashing the bright red and black underwings, like blood and darkness turned to glitter. Its wings brushed against my stomach, and I swore I felt something more solid inside me. I reached toward it again, for the head with its feathery antennae. It didn't react until I touched it, then it flicked its wings again, but it also struggled a little. I felt it move inside me because the lower half of the body was embedded in my flesh.

I drew my fingers back, and I had the color of its wings on my fingertips, as if I'd touched a real moth. "What in the name of Danu is that?"

"It will not last, Merry," Doyle said. "It will become like a drawing on your skin."

"You mean like a tattoo?" I asked.

"Something like that," he said.

"How long will it keep moving like that?" I asked.

"A few hours," he said.

"You say that like you've seen this happen before."

"He has." Nicca propped himself up on one elbow, turning his body to face me. He had a white flower in the hollow between his shoulder and chest, startling against his deep brown skin. The flower had a yellow center and five petals raised above his skin, but the stem was lost in his flesh. Like the moth in me, the flower was alive, but embedded in his skin.

Galen rolled over onto his side and let me see his right arm. Just below the shoulder was a butterfly so large it took up all the width of his arm. Its yellow-and-black-striped wings folded back around his arm as the butterfly flexed, gentle and unhurried, as if it were feeding from some sweet-nectared flower.

"It doesn't seem to be afraid that it's trapped," he said.

I stared down at the moth on my own body. "No, they should be panicking, trying to free themselves. Why aren't they?"

"They are not real," Doyle said.

"They are real," Nicca said.

Doyle frowned, but gave a quick nod. "Perhaps 'real' is not the correct word. They are not free animals that would mourn their captivity."

I touched the moth's wings again, and it flicked them at me. Leave me alone, it was saying as clearly as it could. The sensation of having something alive wriggling inside me made my stomach roll uneasily. The more I touched the wings, the more irritated the moth became. I lay back against the pillows, closing my eyes and breathing around the sensation of it.

"Can you feel its legs inside you?" Galen's voice didn't sound any happier than my stomach felt.

"Yes," I said.

"It's not a good feeling," he said.

I opened my eyes and looked into his face. He looked a little greener than usual.

"Stop trying to pet them and they won't struggle," Rhys said.

I stared at the black, red, grey, and even white that was smeared across my fingers. "What are these things?"

"They are the beginning of tattoos," Doyle said, "marks of power."

I stared up at him. "You mean the tattoos that the sidhe once had? They were more like birthmarks, weren't they?"

"Some are born with the marks upon them, but many are not."

"Most of us acquire the marks as we enter our power in adolescence, or even adulthood," Rhys said.

"I remember my father telling me that our tattoos were why our people painted themselves for battle. The mark of their deity to protect them."

"Once, long ago," Doyle said, "the marks on their bodies did protect our followers. Protected them better than any armor, for it was a conduit to the power of the sidhe they invoked."

I realized that Doyle was talking to me like he used to, distant and formal. Was it Ivi's presence that had made him distance himself, or had something else happened?

"We were their gods," Rhys said.

"We were not gods," Doyle said, and his voice went lower with anger. "We thought we were gods, but when the gods themselves departed, we learned otherwise." He stared out into the darkness, as if he saw things long ago and far away. "They stripped for battle, painted themselves with our symbols, and were slaughtered because we no longer had the power to save them."

"A stubborn lot, the Celts," Ivi said. "They kept painting themselves long after it stopped working." He sounded wistful.

"They thought they had done something to make themselves unworthy," Doyle said, "so they strove to become worthy again." He turned away, gave me only the braid that trailed down his dark cloak. "We were the ones who were unworthy."

"All right, that's it," I said. "Why is Doyle beating himself up like this? What did I miss?"

"He's pouting," Rhys said.

Doyle turned his head, just enough to give Rhys a look that would have made most people run screaming. "I am not pouting."

Rhys grinned at him. "Yes, you are. You're pouting because the marks of power are on Galen and Nicca's bodies, and not yours. Two of us who never had the tattoos to begin with, and now they have the first ones, and we don't." The grin had faded by the time he got to the end.

"I don't remember being told that it hurt to get the marks. I thought they just appeared."

"Some did," Rhys said, "but for the first few of us to gain them, it was bloody, and it hurt like hell."

The three of us agreed.

"You were one of the first to gain the marks?" Doyle asked, not angry now, but looking at him.

Rhys nodded. "Cromm Cruach is only the last of my names, not the first, Doyle."

Then Doyle asked something that was very unsidhe, very rude. "Who were you before Cromm Cruach?" The older sidhe never asked that of anyone. It was too painful a reminder of lost glories.

"Darkness, you know better than to ask that," Rhys said.

Doyle actually bowed. "I am sorry, forgive me. It's just..." He made a frustrated noise. "I see power given to everyone, but I remain as I have been."

"Are you jealous?" Rhys asked.

Doyle hunched inside his cloak, then gave a nod. "I believe I am. Not just of Merry, but of the magic, too." Saying it out loud seemed to make him feel better, or clear his head. For he shook himself like a dog coming out of water, and he turned a more peaceful face to me.

"Most of the tattoos were like my wings. They appeared at birth," Nicca said.

The comment made me turn to him, because I realized what I'd missed. "Where are your wings?"

He rolled over and let me see them. I expected them to be the tattoo I'd always known on his back, but they weren't. They were raised above his body like the flower, touchable and real, but lying flat now, as if they were but a step away from the tattoo they had once been.

"Are they going back to being a tattoo?" I asked.

"Maybe," Rhys said.

"They don't know," Nicca said.

"Have you both been awake longer than I have?" I asked.

"No," Galen said, "but we didn't pass out as soon."

I leaned up, very carefully, against the headboard. The

moth flicked its wings, giving me a sudden flash of color, then settled back to its black and grey upper wings. Underwing moths, when at rest, try to blend in with tree bark. It wasn't the moth's fault that, trapped against the whiteness of my skin, it was very visible. It felt unnerving enough for the moth to move just a little. One of my new goals in life was not to scare it. I did not want to feel it truly struggle. I was very afraid that if it did, I might be quite sick. If a princess is not allowed to show fear, then nausea is completely out. Too unseemly.

Doyle seemed to understand my difficulty, because he helped me prop pillows under my back and head, so I could sit up and see the room, but not bend too much at the stomach. "How are Royal and the rest?" I asked.

"Your demi-fey is fine, though he is the only one who would not leave even to clean off the blood. He insisted that he stay and see you were well."

I looked out into the darkened room. "Is he here?"

"Outside by the door with Adair and Hawthorne."

Ivi wrapped his arm around the bedpost, showing a pale line of flesh. I realized that he must have been nude after he gave me his cloak, but I hadn't truly noticed when the room was full of blood and bodies. "He called you his white and red goddess." Ivi managed both to make a joke of it, and make it not funny at all. A smile with serious eyes.

"I am no one's goddess," I said.

"I don't know," Ivi said, wrapping more of himself around the bedpost, so that only the wood kept me from seeing all of him. "We sidhe have been worshipped for less."

"Long ago," Doyle said, "and far from here."

Ivi shrugged. "We were in the land of faerie then, and we are in the land of faerie now. That is not so far, Darkness."

"Where is everyone else?" I asked.

"Kitto and Frost and a few others have gone to fetch food for you all," Doyle said.

"Galen's comment about no one going anywhere alone." Rhys shrugged. "It was smart, so the new rule is three of us together at all times."

"We don't have enough men for that," I said.

"We do now," Rhys said.

I frowned at him. "I don't understand."

"The queen agreed that we needed more than just the green men," he said.

"So why is the room so empty?" I asked.

"We aren't enough company?" Galen asked.

I smiled at him. "It's not that, it's just that if everyone's here, I know they're safe."

"Why did we get winged insects and Nicca got a flower?" Galen asked.

"He already has wings," Rhys said. He moved when he said it, and I got a glimpse of something under his cloak.

"Is that a sling?" I asked.

He let the cloak fall open, and his right arm was in a sling.

"What happened?"

"First, we discovered that time is only running odd for us. Outside of our faerie mound time is creeping so slowly that the police probably haven't even gotten back to their lab yet."

"Get to the part where you've got an injured arm," I said.

"We were on our way back when three of the Seelie called for us to halt, and talk to them."

"They didn't say that, not like that," Nicca said.

Galen agreed. "Way too polite for them." He lay on his side, propped on one elbow, his right arm held carefully, so his butterfly wasn't disturbed.

Rhys grinned at them. "Okay, they called for us to halt, and wanted specifically to speak to me." The grin faded around the edges. "I was in charge. It was my fault that they caught us off guard." He looked at Doyle. "I could have gotten the other men killed."

"Killed?" I asked.

"They were using cold iron."

"You're joking," Galen said.

Rhys leaned his back more comfortably against the footboard, and shook his head. He looked grim. "We didn't expect that."

"Do not blame yourself for that part, Rhys," Doyle said. "Neither court hunts the other with cold iron. That is reserved for war, and we are not at war."

"Not yet," he said.

"What do you mean, not yet?" Galen asked.

"Did cold iron do that to your arm?" I asked.

He answered my question first. "One of them attacked me. We were three for three, but we didn't realize we weren't just having a little fun until they got serious." He shook his head. "If I hadn't surprised him, it would have been worse."

"Surprised how?" I asked.

"I used the death touch on him, but he did something to protect himself. My entire arm went numb. It's good we had so many healers in the room, though. They healed the wounds of sword and ax, but my arm . . . They bound it in a sling and told me to wait. I can finally feel something, pins and needles mostly, but I'm happy to feel anything in it."

"What happened to the Seelie you bespelled?" Nicca asked.

"They dragged him away insensible. He'll be out of it for a day or two, at least."

"Why didn't it kill him?" I asked.

"Goblins have no magic of their own; the sidhe do," he said, as if that explained everything.

"Did they give a reason for trying to kill you?" Galen asked.

He sighed again. "One of their royal ladies accused me and two others of raping her."

"What?" I sat up too abruptly, then stopped in mid-motion, afraid I'd crush the moth.

"Had she gone mad?" Galen asked.

"Don't know," Rhys said, "but they were serious about it."

"Who else did she accuse?" I asked.

"Me, Galen, Abloec."

"Why?" I asked.

"That we do not know," Doyle said, "but I doubt that the lady came up with such a desperate accusation on her own."

"Taranis?" I asked.

"Keep his name to a minimum," Rhys said, "just in case. I'd rather not be overheard."

"I do not believe he can hear just because his name is invoked," Doyle said.

"Humor me," Rhys said.

Doyle nodded. "Very well. Yes, I believe he is somehow behind this new problem."

"But why? What does he hope to gain?" I asked.

"That we will know as soon as the three of you have eaten."

"What do you mean?" I asked.

"The queen has requested your presence at her side when she contacts Taranis about this latest outrage."

"Taranis's men seemed to think we'd just let them arrest us," Rhys said. "That we'd just give ourselves over to Seelie justice." He laughed, and it was a bitter sound. "Justice? For the Unseelie at the Seelie Court? Please."

"They still believe that to join this court is to be deformed and made monstrous," Doyle said.

"I've never understood that one," Galen said. "They can look at us and know that we look just as they do."

"They believe we hide our deformities with our clothes," Doyle said.

Galen raised an eyebrow. "The queen answers the mirrors covered in nude guards most of the time. Anyone with eyes can see that every inch of the guards is fine."

"Ah, but that is evil Unseelie illusion," Rhys said. "Understand, my young green friend, that one of the things that makes the Seelie sidhe prefer exile among the humans to joining our court is the belief, the absolute belief, that being in the dark corrupts us. Makes us twisted and perverse. Most of them believe we have tails, and hooves, and monstrous penises."

"Well, big," I said, but the look on Rhys's face made me swallow my joke.

"They don't mean big, Merry, they mean ugly and awful. They paint us as monsters, because if the Seelie ever truly believed that we were just like them"—he shrugged—"I think some of them would put up with less shit from him. They would then have someplace to go besides mortal land."

"They fear Andais, as well," Doyle said, "and she has fostered that fear with her bloody mirror calls and her orgies."

"I have spoken with the king in the mirror, Doyle," I said. "I know now that touching the flesh of the guard helps ground us and keep his power at bay. I think that torture may do the same for the queen that sex does."

Doyle nodded. "Yes, it is a way to keep his power from overwhelming one."

"I've never actually sat in on a call between the two monarchs," I said. "Is it as scary as it sounds?"

"Disturbing," Rhys said, "more than scary."

"Disturbing how?" I asked.

"The king will try and use his magic to bespell and persuade us, including our queen. She will use her beauty to make him lust after her. She will also use those around her to distract both herself from his power, and the king in general."

"We'll have to warn her not to expose your new friends," Rhys said.

"You mean the . . ." and I motioned at the moth.

He nodded. "He won't like that we have them and his people don't."

"Did the queen see them?"

"She has been here, and seen what there is to see," Doyle said.

"Why does that sound ominous?"

"She was thrilled," Rhys said, and his voice was very dry.

"What did we miss?"

"Be glad you missed it," he said.

Doyle nodded. "Do not be surprised if your aunt suggests that you come to her bed some night." He frowned. "Though strangely she has lifted her ban about Nicca and Biddy. They are free to have sex when he feels well enough. She was very pleased at all of it. The wall and door exploding. The bewinged demi-fey. The dry pool. All of it seemed to . . ."

"Excite her," Rhys said.

I shivered, and the moth fanned its wings, as if it felt my

nervousness. Which made its body pull on my skin again. It was as if I could feel its legs inside my body. I had to swallow hard, to keep my stomach from being very unhappy with me.

"Did it move again?" Galen asked.

I nodded.

"I do not like feeling its legs move inside my body."

I nodded again.

"Don't worry," Rhys said, "they won't stay this alive."

The door opened, and Adair stuck his helmeted head in to say, "The food has arrived, Doyle." He looked at me, and added, "Good to see you awake, Princess."

"Good to be awake." I frowned around at the room. "Though a little more light would be nice." The light that was everywhere and nowhere in most of the sithen began to seep through the room.

"My, my, my," Rhys said.

"What?" I asked.

"When the lights went out in your room, the entire sithen went dark," Doyle said.

"Nothing we did could get the lights back on," Rhys said.

I swallowed a sudden lump in my throat. "Until . . ."

"Until you requested a little more light," Rhys said. "Yeah, the queen is going to have mixed feelings about the sithen's new affection for you."

"Mixed how?" I asked.

"Happy you're so powerful, pissed that the sithen isn't listening to her anymore."

I licked my dry lips.

"Enough of this until after they've eaten." Doyle called for the food to be brought in. Kitto came with a tray, and others followed behind with drink. Frost came as the first of the guards that just carried weapons. He looked at me, and gave me a smile that seemed to be reserved just for me. If he had any of Doyle's qualms about the new "tattoos" of power, they did not show. Maybe he was simply too relieved to see me awake. Or perhaps he worried less about power than Doyle did. Or maybe I didn't understand my two men as much as I thought I did. Me, not understanding the men in my life? That I believed.

Chapter 37

THE STEW WAS THICK WITH BEEF, THE BROTH DARK AND HEAVY with a faint tang of some meaty ale to balance the sweetness of the onions. Maggie May knew my favorite dishes, and this one had been on the list since before my father and I left faerie for the human world, when I was six. My eyes got hot, and my throat tight. It was the same stew it had always been, and it was nice to have something that hadn't changed, something that was the same as it had always been.

"Merry," Galen said, "are you crying?"

I shook my head, then nodded.

He put his butterfly-free arm around my shoulders, hugging me close. I must have bent over too much, because the moth on my stomach fluttered frantically. The feel of it struggling in my skin made the good stew roll uneasily. I sat up very straight. I had good posture, but until the moth was truly a tattoo, no slumping.

"Do you hurt?" Doyle asked.

I shook my head.

"You flinched," he said.

"The moth didn't like me slumping," I said. My voice was much steadier than my eyes. My voice didn't sound like I was crying, not one little bit.

Kitto moved between the table he'd set up, and raised his finger to my face. He came away with a tear shining on the tip of his finger. He raised it to his lips, and licked my tear from his skin.

It made me smile, and the tears fell a little faster because of it, as if I'd been holding my eyes very still to keep the tears from falling. "The stew is one of my favorite dishes. It hasn't changed. Everything else is changing, and I'm no longer certain that all the changes will be good."

I leaned into the warmth of Galen's body, and gazed at the others. I suddenly knew what I wanted. "Kiss me," I said.

"Who are you speaking to?" Frost asked.

"All of you."

Galen bent down toward me, and I raised my face to him. His lips touched mine, and my body moved of its own volition. My arms swept up his body, and we embraced as we kissed. My hands explored the naked warmth of his body, not as foreplay, but because twice in less than a day I had thought the darkness would take one or both of us, and we would never again hold each other this side of the grave.

We kissed, and his hands were strong and gentle on my body, and the tears came faster.

Galen broke the kiss first, but hugged me tighter, and said, "Merry, Merry, don't cry."

"Let her cry," Rhys said. "To have a woman waste tears over you is not a bad thing." He stepped up to me, where I still sat on the edge of the bed. He wiped my face with his good hand. "Are any of these tears for me?"

I nodded wordlessly, and touched his arm in its sling. He wiggled the fingers a little. "It will heal."

I nodded again. "I sent you out into the snow, and didn't even say good-bye."

He frowned at me, his one good eye perplexed. "You don't love me enough to shed tears at the thought of missing our last good-bye." He wiped fresh tears away with his hand, still frowning.

I searched his face, the scars that had stolen his eye long before I was born. I traced the lines of those marks in his skin. I put a hand on either side of his shoulders, and drew him close to me, until I could lay a kiss upon the smoothness of the scar where his other eye should have been.

The thought that he was right, that I didn't love him that much, made me cry harder, though I wasn't sure why. It just seemed wrong. Wrong that I sent him out into the dark and the cold, and hadn't cared enough to say good-bye. If someone's willing to die for you, shouldn't you care? Shouldn't it matter more than that?

I moved my face back enough to kiss him gently on the lips. He came to that kiss still puzzled, hesitating, so that even as we kissed, his body was stiff and uneasy. I balled my hands into the cloth of his suit jacket, pulling him down to me, forcing him to catch himself on the bed with his one hand.

I kissed him as if I would climb inside him. He responded to the fierceness of my mouth with his own. He let me pull him down onto the bed, onto me, though he was awkward with the one arm in a sling. His body pressed against me, but it was as if his clothes offended me. I wanted bare flesh. I needed to feel his nakedness against me. To let me know he was real, and all right. That he was all right with being third in command. With not being my greatest love, and still having to risk his life as if he was. I wanted to hold him and tell him I was sorry that my heart didn't have room for everyone, and most of all that he could have died out there in the dark and the cold, and we would never have known. That *I* wouldn't have known. The Goddess had warned me to protect Galen and Barinthus. But it was as if Rhys wasn't important enough to her to waste such power.

I would never be able to send him away again without wondering if I sent him to his death. I pulled his shirt out of his pants. I had to touch more of him. I had to tell him with my hands and my body that he did mean something to me. That I did see him. That I never wanted him to die in the dark where I could not find him.

He propped himself up on his good arm, so that I could slide the shirt free. I meant to run my hands over that pale skin, but Rhys let himself fall back upon my body, pressing his mouth hungrily against mine. I'd forgotten the moth. I'd forgotten everything but the feel of his body pressed against mine.

Pain, sharp and immediate like tiny needles, pierced the skin of my stomach. Rhys cursed, and drew back from me, as if something had bitten him, and maybe it had.

He raised up on his knees, and showed his stomach. It looked like a bloody version of the moth on my stomach. He touched it, and it was flat, one-dimensional. The skin around the outline and colors was ridged and red, puffy and swollen, but I could see the image of the moth on his stomach.

The other men crowded round, and it was Galen who asked, "It's not the same thing we have, is it?"

"No." Doyle touched it ever so gently, and even that made Rhys flinch.

"Ow," Rhys said.

Doyle smiled. "Either the moth did not like being crushed or . . ."

"Yes," Frost said.

"It cannot be," Hawthorne said.

"It cannot be what?" Galen asked.

"A calling." Doyle was pulling his black T-shirt out of his pants. I was about to point out that he'd never get the shirt off without taking his shoulder holster off first, but he raised the neck of the shirt over his head so that it sat behind his shoulders, still covering his arms, but leaving his chest and stomach bare.

"What is a calling?" I asked.

"What were you thinking just before you kissed Rhys?" he asked.

"That I didn't want him to go into the dark alone, and not be able to find him."

Rhys slid off the bed, acting as if he hurt, but he was using both arms again. He noticed it, too, because he took his arm out of the sling, flexing his fingers. "Healed." He looked down at the wound on his stomach, then up at me. "It's always the doom of any relationship to get matching tattoos." He tried to make a joke of it, but his face didn't match the lightness of his words.

I touched the moth on me, and it still flicked its wings, irritated at the touch. "Mine's still alive."

Doyle crawled up on the bed, and for once I moved back from him. "Explain, Doyle." I put a hand up, not touching, but ready to keep him away from my body.

"It may be that your mark of power simply struck out in irritation. They can do such things." He was above me now, on all fours, so that his body straddled mine but did not quite touch me. "But if it is a calling, then it will enable you to do just what you wish. You will be able to find Rhys in the dark or the light. You will have only to think of him, and your mark will guide you to him. Some of them would alert the bearer of the mark if the one they had called was in danger or injured."

"A true calling could do many things," Frost said.

"There has not been a true calling among us for centuries," Hawthorne said.

"How can you doubt," Adair said, and he had removed his helmet, so I could see him smiling. He looked so sure of it all. "She is our ameraudur."

Doyle started to lie down on top of me, but I kept my hand in the way. I had more questions before we continued with our little experiment. The moment my hand touched his bare chest, the pain was sharp and immediate. But it wasn't my hand that hurt, it was my chest, exactly where I touched Doyle. Blood trickled down his chest, just below the silver nipple ring. Other than a tightness around his eyes, he didn't react to the pain at all.

"That answers one question." Nicca moved to the far side of the bed, lounging and seemingly perfectly at ease. "It isn't just the mark not wanting to be touched."

Doyle bent down to give me a quick kiss. Nothing hurt, and a tightness in my shoulders eased that I hadn't even realized was there.

He smiled down at me, a quick flash in his dark face. "You did say you wanted a kiss."

"Why does this please you so much? It bloody hurts."

The smile faded. "I am never happy to cause you pain, Meredith, but that you are marking us, that is a great thing."

"Why?" I asked.

"It means you are a power." Rhys did not look pleased. "Once I marked others, but when I joined the queen's service, she marked me. Then even that faded, and there were no more marks, not like this." He ran his fingers lightly over the raised and reddened skin.

Hafwyn spoke in a low voice. "Do you want me to bandage them?"

"Until they heal, yes," Doyle said, and slid off the bed.

"The queen will be pleased, but others will not be," Hawthorne said. "There are those who always believed the marks were a sign of servitude to one greater than themselves. A mark that said plainly, this person is my master."

I looked at him still covered in armor, helmet in place. "Is that how you feel about it?"

"I did once," he said.

Frost pushed up his jacket sleeve to bare his lower arm. "If the marks work as they should, it will be important to be able to see them. They will carry messages between us, warnings. As much as I would love to press my body against yours, I would rather the sign be on my arm where it is easily seen."

Doyle sighed. "Better strategy than the chest. I did not think."

"You were befuddled with her beauty and the promise of power."

Doyle sighed again. "Yes."

Frost held his arm out toward me. I sat up carefully, still not wanting the moth to struggle. "Why does it hurt me every time? There are no marks on my skin."

"You already bear the mark," Frost said. "As for the pain . . ." He smiled at me gently, his eyes full of some knowledge that I did not have. "Merry, you should know by now that no power comes without a price."

I would have liked to argue, but I couldn't. He was right. I stared at his pale, muscular arm, waiting. I took a deep breath, and let it out as I laid my hand on him. His breath hissed out between his teeth.

I made no sound for a moment, then my breath came back in a gasp. I looked at Galen and Nicca still on the bed. "If we all three have marks, then what happens if we touch each other?"

"Let us not find out, not tonight," Doyle said. "I do not

know if it would work as it should between the three of you, not with all of you so . . . fresh."

Kitto came to stand beside Frost. "I would gladly carry your symbol, Merry."

I had to smile at him. If the marks really could help us keep track of one another, I didn't want to leave Kitto out. "Your arm, then."

He held his arm out, so trusting. I braced for it, and laid my hand on his arm. He hissed, like an angry cat, but did not pull away. When I drew back the moth was bloody on his skin.

I touched my own arm where it hurt. "Let's change arms for the next one, okay?"

"And who will be next?" Ivi said. "Nothing personal, Princess, but I bargained for sex, not slavery."

I frowned at him. "What do you mean by 'slavery'?"

"The marks mean we are your men," Doyle said. "They are proof that the Goddess has chosen us for you."

"So this won't work with just anyone?" I asked.

He shook his head. "Only with those who are truly meant to be yours."

"Define 'mine'?" I asked.

Doyle frowned. "I am not sure how to define it, in truth. Sometimes a fighter would come just when you needed him, and he would take oath. Sometimes it was a seeress, but they would be exactly who and what you needed to succeed at whatever quest had begun."

"The marks only start collecting people when there's great need," Rhys said.

"But once marked, it cannot be undone," Hawthorne said.

"The queen's marks faded," I said.

"Best not say we told you that," Rhys said. "Not outside this room."

"I will gladly take oath to the princess," Adair said. He laid his helmet on the bedside table and began unfastening the armor at his hands and arms. Frost moved to help him. It was easier to get in and out of plate armor with help.

I pressed my hand to Adair's bare forearm, but nothing happened.

"Shit," Rhys said.

Doyle nodded. "To join Andais and prove worthy of her mark, we had to fight."

"I do not think fighting will win them Merry's mark," Frost said.

"How important is it to mark them tonight?" Galen asked.

"The queen will be coming to fetch her for the call," Frost said.

"I would feel better if we did at least one. If she lies with Adair and still his skin does not take the mark, then perhaps she has called all she needs to win." Doyle moved to Adair's other side to help hurry him out of his armor. Frost, after a moment, went back to working on the other side. They began dismantling Adair's armor, exposing bits of skin and the undergarments that kept the metal from rubbing.

He looked from one to the other of them, and said, "You are jesting with me?"

"We do not jest," Doyle said, as he and Frost undid the straps that held the cuirass. They lifted together and peeled him out of most of the ornate armor. There was still a bandage on his side where Hafwyn had conserved her magic and not healed him completely.

"I do not share Meredith lightly," Frost said. He got the last of the armor off the other man. He began to help strip away the cut and bloodstained padding. "But what if we lose our battle because we lack one strong warrior more?" He shook his head hard enough to make his silver hair sparkle in the dim light. "I will not have my jealousy risk her safety, or the safety of my brother guards." He gazed down at the still bloody wound on his arm. "Meredith is a fertility goddess, among other things, but primarily that is where her power lies. Fighting will not win you her mark."

He and Doyle both stepped back, leaving Adair to finish the last of the undergarments himself.

"If you can win the lady's favor, then do it," Frost said, and his voice was almost empty of resentment. He was truly trying.

Adair looked to Doyle one last time. "And if the mark still does not touch me?"

"Then you will have ended your long fast, and drunk deep of our lady. For she is our lady. Whether she is yours as well remains to be seen." Then he stepped away, as had Frost on the other side. Galen and Nicca slid off the bed. Nicca said, "It's a big bed, but the first time should either be with someone who's sharing with you, or just you and the lady."

I realized then that Biddy was not in the room. I started to ask where she was, then Adair was beside the bed. He was nude. He must have stripped while I was looking across the bed at Nicca.

I had seen him nude before, and recently. The queen had made certain he met me at the court naked except for his weapons. Andais was never subtle, and she had been determined that I make love with as many of the vegetative gods as possible. I don't know if she'd thought their being nude would make us quicker, or if she had believed the sight of them nude would inspire lust in me. He was as beautiful now as he had been then. I expected to see lust, or at least eagerness on his face, but his eyes were downcast, and if anything he seemed reluctant.

I reached out, and took his hand. He did not respond, neither closing his hand around mine nor pulling away. "Adair," I said, "what is wrong?"

"It has been a very long time since I was with a woman." He dropped his gaze again.

"She will be gentle if you need it," Nicca said, from the foot of the bed now.

"Or not gentle," Doyle said.

"She will be what you need," Frost said. "It is her magic."

"It is, in part, what she is," Doyle said.

Adair looked at the men. "What is she?"

"She is the fertility of the land," Doyle said.

"She carried the hand of blood and flesh," Hawthorne said. "Those are dark powers."

"Oh, come on, Whitethorne," Rhys said, "blood and flesh have been making the crops grow as long or longer than sex."

"Do not call me that," Hawthorne said.

Rhys shrugged. "Fine, but she combines the fertility of both courts."

"The Goddess saw fit to give each court dominion over different areas of fertility," Hawthorne said.

"What the Goddess saw fit to divide, she can also remake," Doyle said.

I squeezed Adair's hand. It made him turn and look at me, a frightening glimpse of eyes, then down at the floor again. "I won't hurt you, I promise."

He spoke with his eyes still downcast. "I am more afraid I will hurt you."

Frost laughed.

It made all of us look at him.

He shook his head. "Do you remember what I said to you that first night?" he asked.

I smiled, and nodded. "Yes, and I remember what we did."

"You will not hurt her, Adair. Did you not see what she and Mistral did in the hallway?"

Adair licked his lips, and darted another glance at me. "Did you have an audience the first time?"

"Ah," Frost said, and a look almost of gentleness came to him.

Doyle put it into words. "We have all been where you are now. So long without the touch of a woman. We all wondered if we had forgotten how to pleasure anyone, including ourselves." He clapped Adair on the shoulder. "I will not say that we did not improve with practice after so long a fast, but we managed, all of us, from the first time, and so will you."

"I think he wishes less audience," I said.

"Who would you have stay, and who go?" Doyle asked.

"Let you and Adair decide."

That earned me a startled look from Adair. "You would let me choose who stays and who goes?"

"Most of these men are my friends and lovers, but they are not so intimate with you. Tonight is for your pleasure."

"I want it to be your pleasure, as well."

I smiled at him. "As do I. What I mean to say is, I have had my pleasure as I wish it. I would have you, this night, have your pleasure as you would wish it." I sat up, away from the headboard. "How do you want me? What do you want to do with me? What dream or fantasy has tormented you the most? What have you missed the most?"

He looked at me then, not a darting glance, but a full-out stare. His eyes glittered, and it wasn't magic. "Everything." He looked away, so I would not see him cry.

"Everything is a tall order," I said, "when we will be soon to wait upon the queen's call."

His shoulders hunched, just a little, almost as if I had struck him.

I squeezed his hand, and pulled him gently toward the bed. "It is a tall order, but I will do my best."

He looked at me then, and his eyes held disbelief. He simply did not believe that I meant what I said. He did not trust that I would not hurt him, or cheat him, or starve that part of him that Andais had abused for so long.

I went to my knees, and closed the distance between us, with my hands on his shoulders. "Kiss me, please."

"Please," he said, and he raised eyes to me that glittered with tears, but held anger. "You say 'please.' What trick is this?"

"I say please, so you know that it is not an order. I ask for a kiss, because I want one, but only if you wish to give it."

He looked back at the men ranged around the room. "Does she understand what this means to us, to be asked?"

Most of them nodded. "She understands," Doyle said.

"That's why she does it," Nicca said, "because she feels our need."

Adair turned back to me. "What would you have of me?"

"Only what you are willing to give," I said.

He came to my mouth with a sob, but the moment our lips touched, it was as if all the uncertainty vanished. His mouth ate at mine, his fingers dug into my arms. He climbed onto the bed and forced me back against it. He laid his body on top of me, and found, as most of them did, that he was too tall for true missionary position. His body was heavy with need, but not as heavy as it would grow. He grew larger even as he hesitated above me, supporting himself on his arms.

He held himself above me, working very hard not to touch any part of me. I remembered that when I had met him in the hall yesterday his magic had recognized mine. That even being this close to him with my clothes on had made our magic shiver together. Tonight it was as if his body was cold. His hand had been warm in mine. He was alive as any man, but his magic seemed locked away.

I gazed down the length of his body, his skin the color of sunlight through leaves, that wonderful shade of gold that no human suntan can touch. Sun-kissed the sidhe called it, and sun-kissed it was. I brought my gaze back to his face, and the threefold color of his eyes. Their inner ring of molten gold, then a ring of pale yellow sunlight, and last, and thickest, was an orange-red, like the petals of a marigold. His brown hair had been shaved so short that his face seemed more naked than his body, as if something more important than mere hair had been taken from him when the queen took all that beautiful hair.

I gazed up at his face, and said, "You're shielding your magic from me, why?"

"Barely touching, and our magic caused the healing spring to appear and run with water again. What will happen if we do more?"

I studied his face, his eyes, and saw... fear. Not cowardice, but fear of the unknown, and something more. That fear that you feel at the top of the roller coaster, when you're afraid of it, but excited about it, too. You want to do it, want to give yourself to the experience, but the desire doesn't make it not frightening. Less frightening, maybe, but not without fear.

"Not to put too fine a point on things," Rhys said, "but the queen's summons could come at any time."

"Not until she's done torturing Lord Gwennin," Frost said.

We looked at him. "I met one of the queen's maids on the

way up from the kitchens. She and Ezekiel have taken a personal interest in Gwennin."

"Poor bastard," Rhys said.

Even knowing he'd put a spell on me and Biddy, using our human blood against us, I couldn't do anything but agree with Rhys. Torture was one thing, being at the queen's mercy was another; to have both her full attention and her pet torturer's attention, that was an entirely new level of pain. One I had no wish to contemplate.

"But there is a little more time," Frost said, "that is all I meant."

I gazed up at Adair. "Lower your shields for me, oak lord. Let your magic call to mine, and make light and shadow dance upon the walls."

A look of something close to pain filled his eyes. He whispered so low that I think none but me heard. "I am afraid."

I didn't ask him what he feared, for to do that would risk the other men realizing what he'd said, and he obviously didn't want that. "Kiss me, Adair, just a kiss."

"It will not be just a kiss with you," he whispered.

I smiled at him. "Do you want me to make this offer to Ivi or Hawthorne instead of you?"

He lowered his face, almost making the top of his head touch my body. "No," and that was almost a shout. He raised his face to me, and there was that look of determination, anger, pride—all the things you usually saw in his eyes. "No," he said again, and he let go his shields.

Chapter 38

HIS MAGIC TREMBLED ABOVE MINE, SHIVERING OVER MY NAKEDness. I writhed under just a touch of his power, and the power wasn't even manifesting. He had simply stopped shielding as hard as he could. My voice came breathy. "Why does your power feel so different to me?"

He was still just above my body, on hands and toes. He had to swallow twice to say, "Our magic is similar."

"Like calls to like," I whispered.

"I am the power that makes the seed break forth from its prison and reach toward the sun." He began to lower himself, as if doing some exquisitely slow push-up. It was as if he were pushing himself down through layers of power, and our auras began to flare between us, like two different kinds of flame. I could see it inside my head with that vision that has nothing to do with optic nerves and everything to do with dreams. He spoke through the power. "And you are the earth that receives the seed."

"No," I whispered, "Amatheon is the earth."

"He is the plow, not the earth," Adair said.

I shook my head, shivering as his power curled over mine. Our auras, the very skin of our magic, pushed against each other, two pieces of a half joining together.

"Amatheon is the magic of the earth that quickens the seed. You are the heat of the sun that calls that seed to the light. Amatheon is the lord of the shallow dark, who holds the seed in its dark cradle until you call it forth." The words were mine, the voice was mine, but I knew the echo of the Goddess by now.

Adair's power flared so bright we both closed our eyes, as if the vision fire were real, like shielding the eyes from the sun. My power blazed in turn, a white luminance to balance his golden heat.

When the light died down enough to see his face, his eyes were one solid yellow glow, as if his power had swallowed the other colors. It was as if there were some great, golden candle inside his skin, glowing in a long, thick line down the center of his body, but leaving the outer edges of him in a kind of darkness.

My skin glowed as if the full moon were rising up through it. But the moon's light is a reflection of the heat of the sun. Reflecting Adair's power made mine grow brighter. It was as if his power was meant to feed mine.

His mouth hovered over mine as he whispered, "If I am that which calls forth the seed, and Amatheon is the ground that holds the seed, then what are you, Meredith? What are you?"

"I am the life that springs from the seed, Adair. I grow, I feed my people, I die, but am reborn. I wax and I wane. I give light and hide in the dark. I am always, and always will be."

"Goddess," he whispered. "Danu."

Our lips met, and he breathed in a rush of warmth through my mouth. It was as if I could inhale the essence of him, his magic.

He drew back from that kiss and magic trailed between our lips like something warm and thick and sweet. He whispered through that sweet power, "Meredith." I felt his body settle against mine. "Meredith," he said again. He slid his legs between mine, and I spread my thighs for him. "Meredith." He whispered my name like heat against my skin, as the thick curve of his body began to push between my legs, seeking. He was so hard that just feeling him thrust against me made me writhe. Made my hips roll toward him, help him find what he sought. He slipped inside me, and I expected him to have to push his way in, for he was not small, but he did not. He entered me like a sword finding, at last, its perfect sheath. The magic seemed to draw back for a moment, like a giant taking a breath. We lay on the bed in that most intimate of embraces, as close as man and woman can be, and it was like coming home. It was as if I had waited lifetimes for this man to hold me, for this body to be inside mine. I saw the same wonder in his face.

I watched the glow at the center of his body begin to spread outward again. I felt the magic begin to swell, the giant was about to exhale, and with the sensation of that rising magic, Adair began to draw himself out of me. He pulled himself out until only the round head of him remained inside me. The magic blazed to life, and a heartbeat before the power took us, he slid himself home deep inside me. He brought my upper body off the bed, screaming, my nails digging into his flesh, trying to hold on to something, anything, while his body, his magic, thrust inside me again and again. Until I was no longer certain which was flesh and which was magic, pounding through my body.

Then the world shifted. Through the blaze of white and yellow light that was our magic, our bodies, I saw a great dark space rearing above us. We were no longer in the queen's chambers. Doyle, Rhys, and Frost climbed to their feet, and stood watch over us. Part of me wondered where the sithen had taken us, but most of me didn't care. I cared for nothing in that moment but the feel of Adair between my legs. Our magic shattered the dark into shadows and dancing light, and still Adair thrust between my legs. Still the power pulsed and grew until I thought my skin could no longer hold it. That I would melt away and become the light. I screamed my pleasure into the fire-shadows of our lovemaking, and still it was not done.

I felt my nails tear along his skin, watched his body bleed yellow and gold like sunlight.

The ground underneath my body began to move under the thrust and push of Adair's body, as if I would sink into the ground as Amatheon had done in vision. The ground boiled and for a moment the earth was water, pouring around my body in a thick, warm tide. The water spilled inside me, so that Adair pushed himself through it, and forced that blood-warm water deep inside me. Hands came out of that warm liquid. Hands and flesh pressed against me, following where the liquid ran. Muscles, skin, a body, whole and real, formed beneath me. I knew who it was before Amatheon raised his face up enough for me to meet his flower-petal eyes. His body was already inside me when it became solid. Inside me, as Adair thrust inside, so that their bodies shared me.

I was glad now that the magic and Adair's body had worked so long and hard inside me. Even with all they had done, it was a tight fit, with so much stretching, pushing, fighting against each other's bodies.

I screamed again, and this time it was a mixture of pleasure and pain. They were almost too big, almost too wide for me.

Adair propped up on his arms, and Amatheon's hands found my breasts.

They found a rhythm together, and it was like having one great member thrusting inside me, as if they had become one, as wide as a young tree. I opened my mouth to scream, to tell them it was too much, and the orgasm was suddenly there, turning pain to pleasure, too much to just right. My body convulsed around them, and I felt their bodies convulse together. Then I could feel them again, two men inside me. And they thrust inside one last time, and they came again. It brought me screaming, tearing at their bodies. Their screams echoed mine.

We lay for a moment exhausted in one another's arms as the light began to fade. Adair had collapsed on top of me, and I could feel Amatheon's heart thundering against my back. It was a wonderful thing to lie between them, but almost as soon as I thought it, my body let me know that once the endorphins had faded completely I was going to be hurting, because I was hurting just a little now. Not pain exactly, but aching, and it would only grow worse. They were both still erect, though not as hard as they had been, but I needed them out of me before the endorphins faded completely. Otherwise it was just going to hurt. I wasn't entirely sure it wasn't going to hurt anyway. The two of them together had been my limit, not beyond it, but definitely at it.

I drew breath to ask them to move, but another voice filled the silence first. "Oh, Meredith, brava." She clapped, and others clapped with her, because when the queen applauds so do you.

The endorphins left in a rush, tightening my body painfully around the two men, almost as if my body was squeezing them tighter. It brought a small moan of protest from my body. I was going to be sore.

Adair slowly, carefully, began to draw himself out of me, which brought another sound of half-pain from me.

"Meredith," she said, "I didn't know you had it in you." Then she laughed at her joke, and was still laughing when Adair had moved enough of his upper body to reveal her to me.

Andais's body glinted in the thin light, glinted with fresh, and not so fresh, blood. She was covered in it. Her long hair was plastered along her body with blood and thicker things.

Amatheon tried to move out from inside me, but he was at a bad angle for it. Rhys came to help me, cradling me in his arms, helping give Amatheon a little more room to maneuver.

But it was Rhys's lifting that got me free of him. He stood with me in his arms, and I was just as glad, for I doubted I could have stood. Frost and Doyle stood by us, not quite guarding me against the queen, but close.

"We were coming to find you, niece. It seems we didn't need your policemen after all."

"What do you mean?" I said in a hoarse voice.

"We have a confession to our murders, Meredith, and we did not need forensics to get it." She bent down near her feet and raised her hand upward; a thick rope trailed down to something on the ground. My eyes saw it before my mind would accept it. There was a body at her feet, curled on its side, so covered in blood and so destroyed that I could not tell if it was man or woman.

Andais pulled on the ropes in her hand and the figure screamed. She wasn't holding ropes. She was holding intestines, and they were still attached.

Chapter 39

"DID YOU HEAR ME, MEREDITH? TORTURE HAS SOLVED YOUR crimes before the police could even finish processing their so-called evidence." She gave another jerk with her hand, and tore a ragged scream from the man's throat. I was almost certain it was a man.

I cuddled in against Rhys's chest, and fought to keep my face as blank as I could. I know I did not keep all the horror off of it, because it was too awful. It was simply one of the worst things I'd ever seen, and I could not hide entirely how I felt about it. I fought to hide my feelings, knew I failed, and finally wasn't certain I cared. Sometimes Andais became angry if you didn't appreciate her work. I could never enjoy it, so all that was left me was to show her how frightening, how nightmarish I thought her talents could be.

She gave a low throaty laugh. "Such a look, Meredith. Do you find Gwennin's fate terrible?"

I nodded, huddling in tighter against Rhys. His arms tightened around me. "Yes, Aunt, I find it terrible."

"But you cannot argue with the results, aye?"

I could have, but I chose to be indirect about it. "If you tell me it's Gwennin, then I will believe you, but in truth I would not have known him."

"Oh, it is he." She looked down at the figure at her side, tightening her grip on his body. He moaned, and that did not make her happy enough. She jerked again, and that made him scream again. That pleased her.

"What reason did he give for killing Beatrice?" I asked the

question without implying that everyone standing there would have confessed to anything, from the Kennedy assassination to the rape and pillage of Rome, to make the pain stop. No one could have withstood what she had done to him.

"She had come to his bed, then suddenly she began to refuse him."

"He killed Beatrice because she refused to continue as his lover?" I fought to keep the incredulity out of my voice.

Andais pulled, sharp and sudden, tearing another shriek from his throat. "Tell her what you told me," she said.

He coughed to clear his throat, and the sound was wet. He spat blood, then finally managed to speak. His voice was as broken as his body, hoarse and raw from screaming. "I did not mean for her to die. She is fey, immortal. I did not use cold iron or steel. It should not have been a killing blow." He coughed again, and started to fall flatter to the ground, but Andais kept her grip on his intestines, so he struggled to prop himself up on one skinless arm.

When he had recovered a bit, I asked, "You stabbed her in the back because she refused to continue as your lover?"

"She was a distraction, not a lover."

"A distraction?" I said. "Because she was lesser fey, and they can't be lovers?"

"Yes," he said in that raw voice.

Strangely, I wasn't feeling as sorry for him as I had moments ago. It was still pitiable, and no one deserved such treatment, but . . . "If she meant nothing to you, then why did her refusal of your attentions drive you to murder her?"

"I did not mean her death." His voice broke, not from tears but from the abuse Andais had forced on him.

"But, Gwennin, if she truly was only a distraction, you could have found a dozen like her. Many lesser fey would have jumped at the chance to bed a sidhe lord."

His formless face, that held only the shadow of his bone structure to let me know it was indeed him, could give me no emotion. Andais had stripped that away with his skin and flesh. But his voice held something. "They would not have been Beatrice."

And there was the truth. He had loved her in his way, and she had scorned him. He hadn't meant to kill her, only to hurt her as she hurt him. He had stabbed her through the heart as she had wounded him. He had no way of knowing that faerie had become so fragile that a blade that was neither cold iron nor steel could kill her.

"And the human reporter?" I asked. "Why did he have to die?"

"He was witness," Gwennin said.

My breath came out, and I cuddled in against Rhys, and wanted nothing more than to hide my eyes from the waste of it all. But I didn't hide, I kept looking. If I'd been 100 percent certain I could have stood on my own, I would have had Rhys put me down, but falling into the mud would have ruined what little authority I still possessed.

"I would ask that we wait on the human police and their science, just to confirm. It will make the press conference go better if the police can be up there confirming it all."

"Press conference? He dies no later than tomorrow."

"Aunt Andais, he killed a human reporter. If we do not show him well and fairly whole to the press, it could undermine all the good publicity you have built up over these long decades."

She let out an audible breath. "There is wisdom in your words, Meredith. The press will need him whole, or more whole than this." She smiled down at him. "It does seem a shame to waste such healing on one who is dead already."

I couldn't argue that, but said, "We dare not let the humans see him like this."

"You think it would offend the humans?"

"I think it would confirm all that the Seelie Court says of us."

"Your covering of mud, mine of blood—they look very much the same," she said.

I looked at my hand on Rhys's white shirt, and realized she was right. I was covered in thick, dark mud. Amatheon was as black with earth as the queen was with blood. His hair was plastered down the length of his body. When he'd vanished his hair had been shorn above his shoulders; now it seemed to be at least to his calves.

Adair was less filthy, for he had been on top. But his hair, too, fell in brown waves around his face, no longer shorn stubble. It did not touch his broad shoulders, but it was a start.

I turned my head, and found that my hair, plastered to my back and shoulders, was longer as well. It fell below my shoulders now.

"You have made a mess of the entryway to my throne room, Meredith."

"My apologies, Aunt Andais, it was not on purpose." My voice sounded almost normal as I said it. I tried not to look at the ruin of the man she held, but it was both hard not to look at him and impossible to look for long. I looked because still my eyes could not make the proud, tall, arrogant, handsome Gwennin, out of that raw, fleshless figure at her feet. Even knowing who it was did not help my mind see it. She had destroyed him.

Anyone, absolutely anyone, would have confessed to anything to stop such pain. I did not trust her "confession," but I dared not say that out loud. She was entirely too pleased with herself. After a good, successful torture, she was as happy as I ever saw her. I guess everyone needed a hobby.

"There is now a spring where you had your little threesome," she said.

I looked down and Rhys moved so I could see that, indeed, the ground was bubbling, and a small seeping spring had come to be. The water was spreading out, finding a channel for a small stream, or perhaps making a pool. It would take time for the water to find its way, and decide what shape it wished the earth to take. Whether it wished to be a deep, still pool, or a stream. Of course, some rocks for the water to dance over would make a happy sound.

I should have known better than to think it. My only excuse was that I was trying to find something else to look at, to think of, than that pitiable wretch that had once been a sidhe lord.

The earth shivered like the flesh of a horse when a fly lands upon it. Rocks began to rise up through the mud, pushing their way along the seeping course of the water.

"It seems the sithen is alive once more," Andais said, but her voice wasn't as happy as I thought it should have been. "I think a deep, reflecting pool to complement the pool we already have would be lovely, don't you, Meredith?"

I didn't know what to say because a yes would be a lie, and a no would be impolitic.

She gave me narrowed eyes, and said, "Do you disagree, niece?"

"I do not know what to say, Aunt Andais."

"The truth would be nice," she said in a voice that made it clear she didn't really want the truth, she wanted agreement.

"Your words say one thing, but your tone another, which leaves me wondering whether to obey your words, or the anger in them."

She laughed then, and it seemed a genuine sound. "Oh, Meredith, you have not just gained a few inches of hair, but a more diplomatic tongue." Then her eyes narrowed again, and she said, "Speak the truth, niece, do you think a reflecting pool is what the spring should become."

I licked my lips and glanced at Doyle, trying to ask with my eyes what to say.

She yelled, "Do not look at him for an answer. If you are to be queen here, then be queen. Answer me!"

"No, I do not think it should be a pool."

"Then what should it become, niece of mine?"

Rhys's arms tightened around me in warning, though I didn't need it. I could feel her anger, but she was trapping me. If I lied, something deep inside told me, I would be betraying the very magic that had brought the earth and water together. I could not lie, but she did not want the truth, no matter what she said.

She began striding toward us, dragging Gwennin, so that he screamed and moaned and begged and scrambled at the ground with broken hands. "What would you have of this new spring, Meredith. Some happy, bubbling stream?"

"Yes," I said. "Yes, that would be good."

The earth shivered again, and this time it began to fold away to make a path for the water to fill. The ground was shaping banks and a streambed for the water. More rocks began to appear to break up the flow, so that it would bubble and sing.

She stood now beside the still pool and its fountain. With its rock set with permanent chains, waiting for victims. "I want a formal garden on either side of this stream you are making."

I started to agree, but she held up a bloody hand. "No, Meredith, do not simply agree. Say something else, but make certain that you want it here. Make certain it is the framework you wish your happy, little stream to wander through."

I looked at Adair and Amatheon. "You helped make it, what say the two of you?"

"Meredith, Meredith," she said, "you cannot share power and rule."

"It was not my power alone that brought the earth here, or the spring. It took all three of us to make it. Why should they not help form it?"

To that she had no answer, but merely frowned at me. Even through the blood and gore, I could see her puzzlement.

The two men glanced from one to the other of us. Rhys had gone very still against my body, as if he was afraid to breathe.

"Answer her, oak lord, earth man, answer her," Andais said.

"A meadow would be nice," Amatheon said. "A nice flat piece of ground with tall grass, and flowers. Good rich soil that could grow anything you wished."

Adair nodded. "A nice sunny meadow, yes, that would be good."

I smiled at them—I could not help myself. "Yes, a nice flower and grass meadow, where the sun can shine down, and the moon caress."

Small green shoots began to appear in the fresh earth. They did not grow into big plants instantly, but they were there, and the room was suddenly full of that rich green growing smell that is spring. The earth was simply studded with that first blush of green. After everything else it didn't even surprise me. Then the ceiling vanished and the room suddenly seemed roofed, not with rock, but with a misty, uncertain sky. In that haze was a warm golden ball. There was a sun in this new sky. I had heard rumors, legends, that once we had had suns and moons in the underground, but I had never seen one, or hoped to.

Andais gazed up at the new sun. "You are correct, so it seems. It took all three of you to make this place, and all three of your powers have manifested. But mark me, Meredith. Now that the sithen lives again, it will answer to other magicks besides your own. Be careful what you awaken in others, for not all of it will be to your Seelie taste."

"I am Unseelie sidhe, Aunt Andais."

"We shall see, Meredith, we shall see." She gazed at me, then down at herself. She seemed to have forgotten that she was holding the intestines of a man in one hand. "We need to clean up. We have a king to see, and a new mystery to solve."

"What mystery would that be, Aunt Andais?" I asked.

"Why would Taranis risk war between our courts over a lie? Why would his men attack my men, over the lie of some Seelie strumpet?"

"I do not know, Aunt Andais," I said.

"Nor I, but we will know, Meredith. We will know." She released her hold on Gwennin, and closed the space between us. She was taller than Rhys by at least six inches, and she seemed even taller covered in blood, or maybe just scarier.

"Give your aunt a kiss, Meredith."

I opened my mouth to ask why, then closed it. She was doing it to be cruel, in part, but everyone I had touched today seemed to have gained from my touch. Perhaps the fact that I did not want to touch her would make it all the sweeter for her.

"Of course, Aunt Andais," I said, and my voice was almost neutral.

"Does the thought of putting your white flesh against me right now sicken you?"

That was a dangerous question. "You frighten me, Auntie, to say anything else would be a lie."

"Then kiss me, niece, and let me taste your fear on those red, Seelie lips."

I tightened my grip on Rhys's arm, like a child holding tight in the night. She bent over us, and I raised my face to her, obedient, afraid not to be.

She pressed her lips to mine, but it wasn't enough. She grabbed the back of my hair, and forced her mouth inside mine. She kissed me so hard that I either had to open my mouth or tear my lips on my own teeth. I opened to her, and she gave me the taste of her mouth, her lips, and the salty, caked sweetness of Gwennin's blood. I knew from that kiss that she drank his blood, for it was everywhere inside her mouth.

Blood is one of the most precious fluids. It is life itself, and can be a great gift when shared, but this had not been a sharing. This had been a taking, a rape of everything that he had been.

I dug my nails into Rhys's body to keep from gagging. I dared not show that much displeasure. I fought to breathe, fought to swallow, fought not to throw up on the Queen of Air and Darkness.

She fell back from the kiss with her eyes sparkling, her face rapturous. "Oh, you didn't like that at all, did you?"

I took deep, even breaths. I would not throw up. I simply would not. I had no idea what she would do if I did, and Gwennin at her feet reminded me what she was capable of. I had the very taste of him in my mouth to remind me. I fought not to dwell upon that taste. I mastered my breathing and my stomach, but knew that it had shown on my face. Nothing I could do about it.

She laughed, a sharp, fierce, happy sound like the cry of a hawk. "I think, before I give my throne away, that I will have to demand one night with you, Meredith. You are entirely too human, too Seelie. You would not like what I would do to you."

"If I would like it, you wouldn't see the point in doing it," I said, more anger than fear in my voice. I could not stop it.

She shook her head, almost sadly. "There you go again, Meredith. Your words are fine, but your tone says fuck you and the horse you rode in on."

I looked at her, and for once I did not try to hide. She liked that I hated her. She would enjoy forcing me into her bed, in part because I hated her, and she hated me.

"Say what you're thinking, Meredith. Tell your auntie dearest the words that will match those angry Seelie eyes." She purred at me, a voice that was anger, seduction, and the promise of pain all rolled into one.

Rhys tightened his arms around me, his body tensing. I said, "We hate each other, auntie dearest, we always have."

"And the fact that I would force you into my bed, how does that make you feel?"

"That I would rather be queen sooner than later."

There were gasps. Andais laughed. "Are you threatening me?"

"No. When I held Galen's dying body in my arms, I thought it was too dear a price to be queen of any court. I still think it, but thank you, auntie dearest, for reminding me that I will be queen, or I will die."

"Coming to my bed is not death, Meredith."

"Some deaths, auntie dearest, are of the soul rather than the body."

"Are you saying that if I force you it will kill your soul?" She laughed again.

"I am saying that it will kill something inside me, and you will enjoy its death."

"Yes," she said, "I will."

I smelled roses then, a soft, gentle perfume.

Andais looked around her. "What is that smell?"

"Flowers," I said.

"There are no flowers here."

I looked into her gore-soaked face. "There will be." Those three simple words held a promise of weight and power.

"Roses are fragile things, Meredith. They do not grow outside of walls without the skill of gardeners."

"The wild rose needs no walls to protect it," Doyle said.

She turned and looked at him. "What are you babbling about, Darkness?"

"Can you not smell it, Queen Andais? It is the scent of the meadow rose, the bramble rose, and it needs no walls to protect it, nor gardener to tend it. In fact, it is almost impossible to dig out or destroy once it takes root."

"I did not know you had such an interest in gardening, Darkness."

"This is a rose that makes its own garden wherever it happens to grow."

She stared at him, studying his impassive face, as if she saw something there that I could not read. "Do not fall too far in love with the rose, Darkness, for it has thorns."

"Yes," he said, "we must all beware the thorns when we seek to pick the rose."

"And will you prick me with your thorn, Darkness?"

"What good is a thorn to the rose, if it does not draw blood."

"Is that a threat?" she asked.

"What if that piece of her soul that you steal away is the piece that calls to the sithen? What if the piece of her happiness that you destroy is the very piece the Goddess calls to? Would you destroy all that has been awakened for a dark whim?"

"I am queen here, Darkness."

"And your brother Essus loved you well," he said.

That seemed odd even to me, and the queen frowned. "Why do you speak of my brother?"

"Why was Essus not king?" he asked in that empty voice.

She frowned at him. "He refused the throne."

"Not true," he said.

She licked her lips. "He would not kill me to get the throne."

"Essus loved you too well," Doyle said.

She turned back to me. "And his daughter does not love me at all. Is that what you mean, Darkness?"

"Meredith, daughter of Essus, does not love you, Andais, Queen of Air and Darkness."

She narrowed her eyes at him. "You are threatening me."

"I am saying that those who would have seen Essus on your throne were stopped by his love of you, and now there is no love to stand between you and harm."

I wished that I could have read her face better, but the blood masked much of it. "I thought you served me out of duty, Darkness."

"No, my queen, not out of duty."

"But you do not love me now, Darkness."

"No," he said, "you killed that part of me long ago."

"And if I say Meredith will never have my throne, never be queen, what say you to that?"

"Then we will go, all of us who wish to, and we will take exile in the lands to the west."

"You cannot mean that."

"I mean everything I say, Andais, Queen of Air and Darkness. I have always meant everything I have ever said to you." And a soft sound escaped him. It was a sob, and a tear glittered down his cheek.

"I did not . . ." She stopped and tried again. "I did not know."

"You did not see me," he said, and his voice was steady now.

"But you were always by my side."

"But you did not see me."

"Does she see you, Darkness? Does she really see you?"

He nodded. "Yes, she sees me. She sees us all."

They stared at each other for a space of heartbeats, and it was she who turned away first. "Go, and take your rose and her new thorns with you. All of you, go."

She did not have to ask us twice. Rhys started carrying me toward the far door. I was pretty sure I could have walked, but being carried in his arms sounded just about right. I wrapped my arms around his neck, and gazed back over his broad shoulder at my aunt.

The people who had been with her were still hesitating, waiting, unsure if they'd had their orders. She screamed at them, "Go, go! All of you, go!" They went, hurrying off. Even Gwennin tried to crawl away from her. She put a foot on the long thick strings of his intestines, and her voice came in an evil whine, "Not you, Gwennin, not you."

We made the far doors, were through them, and had them closing behind us as the first ragged scream cut the air. If I could have taken him with us, I would have. For I would not have left anyone to the queen's mercy.

Doyle suddenly shoved me behind him. I heard it a second later: running. A group of people running this way. Adair and Amatheon had no weapons to draw, so they gave me their bodies as living shields. I could not see around all the broad backs and drawn weapons. I had to wait, surrounded by men whom I no longer wished to put between me and danger. I needed guards that I didn't like quite so much. I heard Galen's voice, "Where's Merry?" Amatheon and Adair almost slumped with relief on either side of me. I fought the urge to laugh, or cry, or just push everyone away so I could see. But we all waited for Doyle to tell us to move, or not.

The men farther from us parted like a curtain, and only then did Amatheon and Adair move to frame me instead of shield me. Galen and everyone that we had left in the room were in the hallway, coming toward us. Doyle was assuring them that I was fine.

Galen pushed his way through the other men and paused before hugging me. He laughed. "What have you guys been doing, playing in the mud?"

The three of us exchanged glances. "We were playing in the mud," Adair said. "Amatheon was the mud."

Galen frowned at him.

"Later," I said. I had noticed a newly healed face among the guard: Onilwyn. "When did he join you?"

Galen seemed to understand who I meant. "We were running out to find you when he showed up."

"Why didn't you tell us what was happening?" Ivi asked. "We'd have grabbed on before Merry left so abruptly."

"There was no time," Doyle said.

"We barely touched them in time ourselves," Frost said.

Rhys asked, "How did you know where we were?"

Kitto came out from behind the taller men. He had a short sword naked in his hand. He held up his arm with the moth tattoo on it. "I followed this."

"And we followed Kitto," Galen said, hugging me against his body, spreading the mud on more of himself.

"May I approach, Princess?" Onilwyn said.

I looked at his face and tried to see arrogance, or hatred, but he was trying for neutral and succeeding. "All right, yes."

The other men made a sort of impromptu corridor for him to walk down. Galen kept one arm around me, so that I was tight to his side. Amatheon and Adair took up posts on either side of me; even unarmed and muddy they looked like the guards they were. Once I'd thought Amatheon and Onilwyn were friends, but the message was clear from all the men. They were my guards, and they weren't entirely certain Onilwyn was one of them.

He dropped to his knees in front of me. "I have heard such rumors, Princess Meredith. If even half are true, then I can only beg forgiveness and offer myself to your service."

"And what of Prince Cel?" I asked. "What will you do when he is free once more and demands your loyalty back?"

"My oath was to the queen, never to him."

"You gave him your friendship, Onilwyn."

"Prince Cel has no friends, only toadies and bed partners."

I stared into his face, tried to read a lie there, but found none. "I don't trust this change of heart, Onilwyn."

"Tell me what I must do to prove that I am sincere."

I thought, and nothing came to mind. A high, mournful scream came from behind the doors at our backs. The men who hadn't known of Gwennin's fate jumped or looked toward the door. Onilwyn paled. "Who is that?" he whispered.

I told him.

"Gwennin was her ally."

"No longer," Doyle said. "Now he is only meat."

Onilwyn looked at the floor, and when he raised his face back up, there was something in his eyes. Something close to pain. "Cel spoke of the day he could take his mother's place. He means to take her place in every sense of the word, Princess. He craves to have the ladies of the court as his playthings. His fantasies are darker than you can imagine, Princess Meredith. He dreams of you, Princess. He says, if his mother would have you pregnant, then it will be his seed that fills your belly." He said that last in a voice hoarse with dread, perhaps worried how I would take the news.

"I know of my cousin's plans for me," I said.

Onilwyn looked surprised. "Who . . ."

"A friend," I said. I answered before Doyle could finish shaking his head, telling me not to reveal that Cel's own guard had betrayed him. I did not trust this new, more sincere Onilwyn any more than he did.

"I would be your friend, Princess."

"You just want sex," Galen said, and he sounded a little hostile about it.

"Yes, as all of us do, but I offer true loyalty to her now."

"What did you offer to her before?" Amatheon asked.

"I was Cel's spy, as you were."

"I supported his claim to the throne. I did not spy for him."

Onilwyn shrugged. "Have it your way, but I came for the promise of sex, and to be Cel's eyes and ears."

"And now?" I asked.

"I am whatever you need me to be."

"You should hit him in the face with frying pans more often," Rhys said, "he seems to like it."

Another shriek cut the air. Followed by a helpless sobbing.

"Let us be away from here," Doyle said, "before she tires of her new toy and seeks another."

We all began to follow him down the hallway. Onilwyn stayed on his knees, so that we left him alone like that, kneeling before doors. I wondered what the queen would do if she came out and found him like that. Something horrible, no doubt.

He watched me with a lost look on his face. It was as if he was someone else inside Onilwyn's skin.

"Come, Onilwyn, I would not leave you like a present before the doors."

He gave a small smile and got to his feet, hurrying to catch us up. I did not like his change of heart. It was too abrupt. Or, perhaps, he was simply the perfect toadie, and like all good bootlickers, he was following the power. If he had changed sides, it was because he thought it would gain him power at court. It was why all toadies toadied. How many others would Cel lose to me in the next few weeks? And how many would wait, neutral, to see who was left standing at the end?